# Victoria Hislop

The Thread

headline
review

First published in Great Britain in 2011
by HEADLINE REVIEW
An imprint of HEADLINE PUBLISHING GROUP

First published in paperback in Great Britain in 2012 by
HEADLINE REVIEW

2

Cataloguing in Publication Data is available from the British Library

ISBN 978 0 7553 7775 6 (B-format)
ISBN 978 0 7553 7776 3 (A-format)

Typeset in Bembo by Palimpsest Book Production Limited,
Falkirk, Stirlingshire

Printed and bound in Great Britain by
Clays Ltd, St Ives plc

Headline's policy is to use papers that are natural, renewable and recyclable products and
made from wood grown in sustainable forests. The logging and manufacturing processes are
expected to conform to the environmental regulations of the country of origin.

HEADLINE PUBLISHING GROUP
An Hachette UK Company
338 Euston Road
London NW1 3BH

www.headline.co.uk
www.hachette.co.uk

Victoria Hislop read English at Oxford, and worked in publishing, PR and as a journalist before becoming a novelist. She is married with two children. Her first novel, *The Island*, held the Number One slot in the *Sunday Times* paperback chart for eight consecutive weeks and has sold over two million copies worldwide. Victoria acted as script consultant on a 26-part TV adaptation in Greece, which achieved record ratings for Greek television. Victoria was the Newcomer of the Year at the Galaxy British Book Awards 2007, and her second novel, *The Return*, was also a Number One bestseller. *The Thread* spent nine weeks in the *Sunday Times* hardback chart, and was widely acclaimed. Her books have been translated into more than 25 languages.

Victoria also writes short stories and her first collection, *One Cretan Evening*, is available as an ebook.

Visit www.victoriahislop.com.

Praise for *The Thread*:

'A sweeping, magnificently detailed and ambitious saga that wrestles with the turbulence of the period Hislop covers . . . All those who loved *The Island*, her hugely successful first novel, will fall on it'
*The Sunday Times*

'Hislop does her research and is very good at interweaving the lives of individuals into the backcloth of great events, giving the reader a history lesson that doesn't feel like one . . . Recommended'      *Daily Mail*

'A gripping and expansive family saga that has war, lost love and family bonds at its heart . . . We are treated to [Hislop's] ability to meld historical fact with her take on the subtleties of family life, its secrets and disappointments'      *Sunday Express*

'Its oddly vehement political edge and fervent multicultural sympathies cut through the helpings of schmaltz and sentiment to generate Hislop's characteristic sour-sweet flavour. That taste can clearly tickle the palate of millions'      Boyd Tonkin, *Independent*

'Hislop's view of history in her novels is, just like the writer herself, a compassionate and generous one, and possibly this is also a huge part of their appeal. *The Thread* is a more ambitious novel than her previous

books, more expansive in its sweep of history, more controversial in its political stance. Her many, many fans will be delighted with what is her best novel yet'
*Scotsman*

'A history that readers might well feel grateful for a lesson in'
*Daily Telegraph*

'The novel's overarching power derives from the fluidity with which these rapidly changing times are treated. Time will show that heritage can be violated, rebelled against and ignored, but that in Thessaloniki, blood isn't always thicker than water'
*Spectator*

'A brilliant page turner and destined to become a reading group staple, *The Thread* is rich with drama and historical detail'
*Glamour*

'It's an evocative exploration of the past's hold on a family, with an exquisite love story at its centre'
*Good Housekeeping*

'Enthralling . . . A brilliantly put-together tale spanning the generations'
*Red*

## Praise for *The Return*:

'*The Return* aims to open the eyes, and tug the heartstrings, of readers who mostly won't have read Orwell, let alone Cercas . . . These days, the battle of historical memory against forgetting has to be fought on many fronts. Hislop deserves a medal for opening a breach into the holiday beach bag'
*Independent*

'Capture[s] the chaos and disintegration of Spain during the violence of the thirties and forties in a dramatic, immediate way . . . keeps you reading at breakneck speed right to the end'
*Sunday Express*

'Powerful stuff'
*Daily Mail*

'Hislop has followed her first book *The Island* with another sun-warmed novel, this time set in Spain . . . all told in a clear compelling narrative'
*Harper's Bazaar*

'Brilliantly recreates the passion that flows through the Andalusian dancers and the dark creative force of *duende*'
*Scotland on Sunday*

'What sets Hislop apart is her ability to put a human face on the shocking civil conflict . . . Stirring stuff'                    *Time Out*

'Hislop marries an epic family saga with meticulous historical research, and it's a captivating partnership'                    *Easy Living*

'A gripping read'                    *Woman & Home*

Praise for *The Island*:

'This is a vivid, moving and absorbing tale, with its sensitive, realistic engagement with all the consequences of, and stigma attached to, leprosy'                    *Observer*

'Passionately engaged with its subject . . . the author has meticulously researched her fascinating background and medical facts'
                    *The Sunday Times*

'Hislop's deep research, imagination and patent love of Crete creates a convincing portrait of times on the island . . . A moving and absorbing holiday read that pulls at the heart strings'                    *Evening Standard*

'A beautiful tale of enduring love and unthinking prejudice'
                    *Daily Express*

'War, tragedy and passion unfurl against a Mediterranean backdrop in this engrossing debut novel'                    *You* Magazine

'A page-turning tale that reminds us that love and life continue in even the most extraordinary of circumstances'                    *Sunday Express*

'Hislop carefully evokes the lives of Cretans between the wars and during German occupation, but most commendable is her compassionate portrayal of the outcasts'                    *Guardian*

'The story of life on Spinalonga, the lepers' island, is gripping and carries real emotional impact. Victoria Hislop . . . brings dignity and tenderness to her novel about lives blighted by leprosy'                    *Telegraph*

*By Victoria Hislop*

The Island
The Return
The Thread

One Cretan Evening and Other Stories (ebook)

For Thomas Vogiatzis, my friend and *daskalos*

With special thanks to:

My aunt, Margaret Thomas (1923–2011),
for her bountiful love and encouragement.
Ian, Emily and Will Hislop
David Miller
Flora Rees
Konstantinos Papadopoulos
Evripidis Konstantinidis
Minos Matsas for his inspiring music and for permission to quote from
*To Minore tis Avgis.*
The cast and crew of *To Nisi/The Island* for everything they taught me.
The Benaki Museum Photographic Archive, Athens.
The Hellenic Centre, London.
The London Library for providing the tranquil surroundings in which
to write this book and to all my silent companions therein.

This story is about Thessaloniki, Greece's second city. In 1917, the population comprised an even mixture of Christians, Muslims and Jews. Within three decades, only Christians remained.

*The Thread* is the tale of two people who lived through the most turbulent period of the city's history, when it was battered almost beyond recognition by a sequence of political and human catastrophes.

The characters and many of the streets and places they inhabit are entirely fictional, but the historical events all took place. Greece still carries their legacy today.

# Greece & Asia Minor

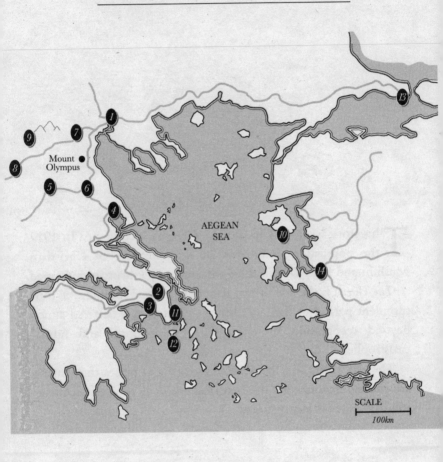

Mount Olympus

AEGEAN SEA

SCALE
100km

1. Thessaloniki

2. Athens

3. Piraeus

4. Volos

5. Trikala

6. Larissa

7. Veria

8. Ioannina

9. Grammos Mountains

10. Mytilini

11. Makronisos

12. Giaros

13. Constantinople (Istanbul)

14. Smyrna (Izmir)

# Thessaloniki

Like the characters themselves, the places where they live are entirely fictional.

1. Irini Street
2. Filipou Street
3. Sokratous Street
4. Komninos Showroom
5. Synagogue
6. Komninos Mansion
7. Komninos Warehouse

'What I would like you to do, my dear, is to imagine you are a child again. I hope it won't be difficult, but you need to get the style right. I want you to embroider one picture that says "Kalimera" in big letters – you know the sort of thing, with the sun rising and a bird or a butterfly or some such creature in the sky. And then, a second one with "Kalispera".'

'With the moon and the stars?'

'Yes! Exactly that. But don't make them look like the work of a clumsy-fingered child,' she said smilingly. 'I've got to live with them on my walls!'

Katerina had done very similar pictures many years ago, under her mother's instruction, and the memory came back sharply.

Her Kalimera was filled in with big loopy stitches, in a glossy, yellow thread, and Kalispera was in midnight blue. She enjoyed the simplicity of the task and smiled at the result. No one would be suspicious of something that was found on the wall of every Greek home. Even if they got stripped out of the frame, the precious pages they had to conceal would be encased inside a calico backing. It was normal to hide the untidy mess on the reverse side of the stitching.

Although there were a dozen people in this small house, there was uncanny silence. Their concentration was absolute, their clandestine activity urgent. They were saving the treasures that connected them with their past.

# Prologue

*May 2007*

I T WAS SEVEN thirty in the morning. The city was never more tranquil than at this hour. Over the bay hung a silvery mist and the water beneath it, as opaque as mercury, lapped quietly against the sea wall. There was no colour in the sky and the atmosphere was thick with salt. For some, it was the tail end of the night before, for others it was a new day. Bedraggled students were taking a last coffee and cigarette alongside neatly dressed, elderly couples who had come out for their early morning constitutional.

With the lifting haze, Mount Olympus gradually emerged far away across the Thermaic Gulf and the restful blues of sea and sky shrugged off their pale shroud. Idle tankers lay like basking sharks offshore, their dark shapes silhouetted against the sky. One or two smaller boats moved across the horizon.

Along the marble-paved promenade, which followed the huge curve of the bay, there was a constant stream of ladies with lap dogs, youths with mongrels, joggers, rollerbladers, cyclists and mothers with prams. Between the sea, the esplanade and the row of cafés, cars moved at a crawl to get into the city, and drivers, inscrutable behind their shades, mouthed the words of the latest hits.

Holding a slow but steady path along the water's edge after a late night of dancing and drinking, a slim, silky-haired boy in expensively frayed jeans ambled along. His tanned face was stubbled from two days without shaving, but his chocolate eyes were bright and youthful. His relaxed gait was of someone at ease with himself and the world, and he hummed quietly as he walked.

On the opposite side of the road, in the narrow space between the little table and the kerb, an elderly couple walked slowly to their usual café. The man set the pace with his careful steps, leaning heavily on his stick. Perhaps in their nineties, and both no more than five foot four, they were tidily dressed, he in a crisply ironed, short-sleeved shirt and pale slacks, she in a simple floral cotton frock with buttons from neck to hem, and a belt around her middle, a style of dress that she had worn for perhaps five decades.

All the seats in every café that lined the promenade on Niki Street faced out towards the sea so that customers could sit and watch the constantly animated landscape of people and cars and the ships that glided noiselessly in and out of the dockyard.

Dimitri and Katerina Komninos were greeted by the owner of the Assos café and they exchanged a few words concerning the day's general strike. With a huge percentage of the working population effectively having a day's holiday, the café would have more business so the owner was not complaining. Industrial action was something they were all used to.

There was no need for them to order. They always drank their coffee in the same way and sipped at the sweetened, muddy-textured liquid with a triangle of sweet pastry, *kataifi*, between them.

The old man was deep into his perusal of the day's newspaper headlines when his wife patted him urgently on the arm.

'Look – look, *agapi mou*! There's Dimitri!'

'Where, my sweet?'

'Mitsos! Mitsos!' she called out, using the diminutive of the name shared by her husband and their grandson, but the boy could not hear above the trumpeting horns of impatient cars and revving engines as they roared away from the traffic lights.

Mitsos chose that moment to look up from his reverie and glimpsed the frantic waves of his grandmother through the traffic. He darted between moving cars to reach her.

'*Yiayia!*' he said, throwing his arms around her, before taking his grandfather's extended hand and planting a kiss on his forehead. 'How are you? What a nice surprise . . . I was coming to see you today!'

His grandmother's face broke into a broad smile. Both she and her husband adored their only grandson with passion, and he in turn bathed in their affection.

'Let's order you something!' said his grandmother with excitement.

'Really, no, I'm fine. I don't need anything.'

'You must need something – have a coffee, an ice cream . . .'

'Katerina, I'm sure he doesn't want an ice cream!'

The waiter had reappeared.

'I'll just have a glass of water, please.'

'Is that all? Are you sure?' fussed his grandmother. 'What about breakfast?'

The waiter had already moved away. The old man leaned forward and touched his grandson's arm.

'So, no lectures again today, I suppose?' he said.

'Sadly not,' responded Mitsos. 'I'm used to that now.'

The young man was spending a year at Thessaloniki University, studying for an MA, but the lecturers were on strike that day, along with every other civil servant in the country, so for Mitsos it was a holiday of sorts. After a long night in the bars on Proxenou Koromila, he was making his way home to sleep.

He had grown up in London but every summer Mitsos had visited his paternal grandparents in Greece, and each Saturday, from the age of five, he had attended Greek school. His year in the university was almost at an end now and though strikes had often meant missed lectures, he was totally fluent in what he thought of as his 'father' tongue.

In spite of his grandparents' pressing invitation, Mitsos was living in student accommodation, but made regular weekend visits to their apartment close to the sea where they almost overwhelmed him with the fierce devotion that is the duty of the Greek grandparent.

'There's been more industrial action than ever this year,' said his grandfather. 'We just have to put up with it though, Mitsos. And hope that things get better.'

As well as the teachers and the doctors, the garbage men were striking and, as usual, there was no public transport. The holes in the roads and cracks in the pavement would remain unrepaired for many months more. Life at the best of times was tough for the old couple and Mitsos was suddenly aware of their frailty as he glimpsed his grandmother's badly scarred arm and his grandfather's twisted, arthritic hands.

At the same moment he noticed a man making his way along the pavement towards them, tapping a white stick in front of him. His route was an obstacle course: cars illegally parked half on the pavement, uneven verges, random bollards and café tables, all of which needed to be negotiated. Mitsos leaped to his feet as he saw the man hesitate, finally baffled by a café sign that had been planted right in the centre of the pavement.

'Let me help you,' he said. 'Where is it that you want to go?'

He looked into a face that was younger than his own and with almost translucent sightless eyes. The skin was pale, and across one eyelid zigzagged a clumsily sewn scar.

The blind man smiled in Mitsos' direction.

'I'm OK,' he replied. 'I come this way every day. But there's always something new to deal with . . .'

Cars thundered past on the brief stretch of road that took them to the next set of lights, almost drowning out Mitsos' next words.

'Well, let me take you across the road at least.'

He took the blind man's arm and they walked together to the other side, though Mitsos could feel his confidence and determination, and was almost embarrassed to have helped him.

As they stepped onto the pavement opposite, he loosened his hold on the man's arm. Now their eyes seemed to meet.

'Thank you.'

Mitsos realised there was a new danger for the blind man on this side of the road. Close by was a sheer drop into the sea.

'You know the sea is right there, don't you?'

'Of course I do. I walk here every day.'

Promenaders seemed lost inside their own worlds, or immersed in their privately pounding music, and were oblivious to the man's vulnerability. Several times his white stick caught their eye in the fraction of a second before a potential collision.

'Wouldn't it be safer, less crowded, to go elsewhere?' Mitsos asked him.

'It would, but then I'd be missing all of this . . .' he replied.

He indicated with a sweep of his arm the sea around him and the curving bay that stretched in a satisfying semicircle before them, and then pointed dead ahead, to the snow-capped mountains that lay a hundred kilometres away across the sea.

'Mount Olympus. This ever-changing sea. The tankers. The fishing vessels. I know you think I can't see them, but I could once. I know they are there, I still have them in my mind's eye, and I

7

always will have. And it's not just what you are looking at, is it? Just close your eyes.'

The young man took Mitsos' hand and held on to it. Mitsos was surprised by the smooth, marble coolness of his fine fingers and was grateful for the physical reassurance that he was not alone. He realised what it would be like to be standing there in the dark, a solitary, vulnerable figure on this busy esplanade.

And in that moment, as his world went black, Mitsos felt his senses heighten. Noises that were loud became a deafening roar, and the heat of the sun on his head almost made him swoon.

'Stay like this,' urged the blind man as Mitsos felt a momentary withdrawal from his grip. 'Just for a few minutes more.'

'Of course,' he replied, 'it's shocking how intense everything feels. I'm just trying to get used to it. I feel so exposed in this crowded place.'

Without opening his eyes, Mitsos could tell from the tone of the response that the man was smiling.

'Just another moment. And then you will feel so much more . . .'

He was right.

The strong smell of the sea, the dampness of the air on his skin, the rhythmic lap of the waves against the sea wall were all magnified.

'And you realise it's different every day? Every . . . single . . . day. In the summer the air is so still, and the water so flat – like oil, and I know the mountains disappear in the haze. The heat bounces off these stones and I feel it through the soles of my shoes.'

Both men stood facing out to sea. It could not be described as a typical Thessaloniki morning. As the man had said, no two days were ever the same, but there was one constant in the sweeping view laid out in front of them: a sense of both history and timelessness.

'I feel people around me. Not just people like you who are in the present, but others too. This place is crowded with the past, teeming with people – and they are as real as you. I can see them neither more nor less clearly. Does that make sense?'

'Yes, it does, of course it does.'

Mitsos did not want to turn his back and walk away, even though this young man would not see it. Just in those few moments with him, he felt his senses had been stirred. Philosophy classes had taught him that the things you see are not necessarily the most real, but this was a new experience of it.

'My name's Pavlos,' the blind man said.

'And mine is Dimitri or Mitsos.'

'I love this place,' Pavlos said. His words were heartfelt. 'There are probably easier places for a blind person to live, but I wouldn't want to be anywhere else.'

'No, I see . . . I mean, I can understand that. It's a beau—, I mean an amazing city.' Mitsos quickly corrected himself, annoyed by his own carelessness. 'Look . . . I'd better get back to my grandparents,' he said. 'But it's been great to meet you.'

'It was good to meet you too. And thanks for helping me across.'

Pavlos turned and walked away, resuming the rapid tapping of his spindly white stick. Mitsos stood and watched him for a while. He was quite sure that he could feel the warmth of his eyes on his back. He hoped so and suppressed the urge to rush towards him, to share his walk along the sea, to continue talking to him. Perhaps another day . . .

*I love this place* – the words seemed to echo around him.

He returned to the café table, visibly affected by this encounter.

'That was nice of you to give him a hand,' said his grandfather. 'We see him most days when we are out and he has had a few near misses on this road. People just don't care.'

'Are you all right, Mitsos?' asked his grandmother. 'You seem a bit quiet.'

'I'm fine. I'm just thinking about something he said . . .' he replied. 'He loves this city so much, even though it must be really hard for him.'

'We can sympathise with that, can't we, Katerina?' responded his grandfather. 'These uneven pavements are difficult for us and nobody seems to be doing anything about it, in spite of election promises.'

'So why do you stay?' asked Mitsos. 'You know that Mum and Dad really wish you would come and live with us in London. Life would be so much easier for you there.'

The nonagenarians had open invitations from their son, who lived in leafy Highgate, and also from their daughter who lived in the States, in a wealthy Boston suburb, but something kept them from choosing an easier life. Mitsos had often overheard his parents discussing this.

Katerina shot the briefest glance at her husband.

'Even if we were given as many diamonds as there are drops in that ocean, there is nothing that would induce us to leave!' she said, leaning close to her grandson and gripping his hand. 'We will stay in Thessaloniki until we *die*.'

The strength of the words took the boy completely by surprise. For a moment, her eyes blazed and then they welled up but not in the way that old eyes sometimes seem to water for no apparent reason. These were tears of passion that rolled down her cheeks.

They sat there for a while in silence, Mitsos absolutely still, aware only of his grandmother's firm grip on his hand. No one spoke or moved. He looked into his grandmother's eyes, seeking more explanation. He would never have guessed that she was capable of such an outburst, having never thought of her as anything other than a kind elderly lady with a gentle disposition. Like most Greek women of her age, she usually let her husband speak first.

Eventually his grandfather broke the silence.

'We encouraged our children to go elsewhere for their education,' he said. 'It was the right thing to do at the time, but we assumed that they would eventually return. Instead, they stayed away for good.'

'I didn't realise . . .' Mitsos said, squeezing his grandmother's hand. 'I didn't realise how you felt. Dad did once talk a bit about why you sent him and Aunt Olga away, but I don't know the full story. Something to do with a civil war?'

'Yes, that was part of it,' said his grandfather. 'Perhaps it's time we told you more. If you are interested, that is . . . ?'

'Of course I'm interested!' said Mitsos. 'I've spent my whole life half-knowing things about my father's background and not being given answers. I think I'm old enough now, aren't I?'

His grandparents looked at each other.

'What do you think, Katerina?' asked the old man.

'I think he should help us carry some vegetables back home, so that I can cook his favourite *gemista* for lunch,' said Katerina brightly. 'How about that, Mitsos?'

They took the street that led away from the sea, and found a shortcut through some of the narrow old streets towards the Kapani Market.

'Careful, *Yiayia*,' Mitsos said as they found themselves in front of the stalls, where the road was carpeted with pieces of rotten fruit and stray vegetables.

They shopped for shiny crimson peppers, ruby-coloured tomatoes as spherical as tennis balls, dense white onions and dark purple aubergines. On top of the shopping bag, the vendor laid a bunch of coriander, and its fragrance seemed to fill the street. All these ingredients looked good enough to eat raw, but Mitsos knew that his grandmother would transform them into the rich, savoury stuffed vegetables that had been his favourite dish as long as he could remember coming to Greece. His stomach began to rumble.

In the area where meat was sold, the floor was slimy with blood that had dripped from the cutting blocks. They were greeted like family by their usual butcher, and Katerina was quickly served with one of the sheep's heads that stared at them from a bucket.

'Why are you buying that, *Yiayia*?'

'For stock,' she replied.

'And a kilo of tripe, please.'

She would be making *patsas* later. For a few euros she could feed all of them for days. Nothing was wasted here.

'It's a guaranteed cure for hangovers, Mitsos!' said his grandfather, winking at his grandson. 'So your grandmother has your best interest at heart!'

A ten-minute walk through the dilapidated streets of old Thessaloniki brought them to where his grandparents lived. Just outside the entrance, on the corner, they stopped to greet Dimitri's best friend, his *koumbaros*, at the periptero. The two men had known each other for more than seventy years and no day went by without a heated discussion on the latest news. Sitting in his kiosk all day, surrounded by the papers, Lefteris was better informed about the city's politics than anyone else in Thessaloniki.

The apartment building was an ugly four-storey block built during the 1950s. The communal hall was bright enough, with yellow walls and a row of fourteen lock-up boxes for post, one for each apartment. The pale stone floor, speckled like a hen's egg, had been freshly cleaned with strongly smelling disinfectant, and Mitsos held his breath as they slowly climbed the flight of stairs that led to his grandparents' door.

The stairwell was brightly lit compared with the apartment itself. Whenever they went out, the shutters were always closed but Katerina would throw them open on her return to try and let in the breeze. The net curtains across the windows allowed little light to penetrate. It was always dusk here, but this was how Katerina and Dimitri liked it. Direct sunlight made all the fabrics fade and bleached their wooden furniture, so they preferred to live with pale light filtered through gauze and the dim glow of low-wattage bulbs to guide them around their home.

Mitsos placed the shopping bag on the kitchen table, and his grandmother quickly unpacked their purchases and began chopping and slicing. Her grandson sat watching, mesmerised by the neatness of the tiny cubes of onion and the evenness of the aubergine slices. Having performed these same tasks ten thousand times, Katerina was as accurate as a machine. Not one shred of onion strayed from her board onto the flowery plastic table cloth. To the last atom they travelled without wastage into the frying pan where steam rose into the air as they met the oil. She had the dexterity of a woman half her age when she cooked, moving with the speed and nimbleness of a dancer around the kitchen. She glided about on the vinyl flooring, moving between an ancient fridge that regularly rattled and back again to her electric cooker, whose ill-fitting door had to be banged hard to make it shut.

Mitsos was completely absorbed, but when he looked up he saw his grandfather standing in the doorway.

'Are you nearly done, my sweet?'

'Five more minutes, and everything will be cooking,' replied Katerina. 'The boy has to eat!'

'Of course he does. Come, Mitsos, leave your grandmother a moment.'

The young man followed his grandfather into the gloomy living room and sat down opposite him on an upholstered wooden-framed seat. Every chair had an embroidered antimacassar, and every other surface was dressed with a white crocheted cloth. In front of the electric fire was a small screen on which was a finely appliquéd vase of flowers. All his life, Mitsos had been watching his grandmother sew, and he knew that every item was a product of her handiwork. The only sound was the low rhythmic thud of the ticking clock.

On the shelf behind his grandfather there was a row of framed photographs. Most of them were of himself, or his cousins in America, but there were also wedding pictures – his parents', and his aunt and uncle's too. And one other framed photograph, a very formal portrait of his grandparents. It was impossible to tell how old they had been when it was taken.

'We must wait for your grandmother before we begin,' Dimitri said.

'Yes, of course. It's *Yiayia* who would forego a sack of diamonds to live here, isn't it? She seemed so angry at the thought of ever leaving. I didn't mean to offend her!'

'You didn't offend her,' said his grandfather. 'She just feels very strongly, that's all.'

Soon enough Katerina came into the room, suffused with the aroma of the slowly baking vegetables. Removing her apron she sat down on the sofa and smiled at both her Dimitris.

'You have waited for me, haven't you?'

'Of course,' replied her husband lovingly. 'It's your story as much as mine.'

And in the low light of the apartment, where it could have been dawn or dusk, they began.

# Chapter One

*May 1917*

THROUGH A PALE gossamer haze, the sea shimmered. Onshore, the most vibrant and cosmopolitan city in Greece went about its business. Thessaloniki was a place of dazzling cultural variety, where an almost evenly balanced population of Christians, Muslims and Jews coexisted and complemented each other like the interwoven threads of an oriental rug. Five years earlier, Thessaloniki had ceased to be part of the Ottoman Empire and become part of Greece, but it remained a place of diversity and tolerance.

The colour and contrast of its rich ethnic meze was reflected in the variety of outfits paraded in the streets: there were men in fezzes, fedoras, trilbies and turbans. Jewish women wore traditional fur-lined jackets and Muslim men their long robes. Wealthy Greek ladies in tailored suits with a hint of Parisian *haute couture* were in striking contrast to peasants in richly embroidered aprons and headscarves, who had come in from the surrounding rural areas to sell their produce. The upper town tended to be dominated by Muslims, the area nearest to the sea by the Jews, with Greeks occupying the city's outer edges, but there was no segregation and in every area people from all three cultures mixed together.

Rising up the hillside behind a huge semicircular arc of coastline, Thessaloniki was like a giant's amphitheatre. High up on the hill, at the furthest point from the sea, an ancient wall marked the boundary of the city. Looking down from this height the landmarks of religion dominated: dozens of minarets rose into the air like needles in a pincushion, red-tiled domes of churches and dozens of pale synagogues dotted the cityscape in its great sweep down towards the Gulf. Along with the evidence of the three religions that all thrived here were remains from Roman times: triumphal arches, sections of ancient wall and the occasional open space where ancient pillars stood like sentries.

The city had improved in the past few decades, with the laying down of some broad boulevards, which contrasted with the ancient pattern of winding lanes that snaked like the serpents of the Medusa's hair up the steep gradient towards the upper town. A handful of large stores had appeared, but the majority of retailing was still carried out from small shops no bigger than kiosks, family run, thousands of them, all vying with each other for business and squeezed into the narrow streets. As well as the hundreds of traditional kafenions, there were European-style cafés serving Viennese beer, and clubs where people discussed literature and philosophy.

There was a density about this city. The volume of its inhabitants and their containment in a space enclosed by walls and water gave it a concentration of strong smells, vivid colours, and continuous noise. The calls of the ice-seller, the milk-seller, the fruit-seller, the yogurt-seller, all had their own distinctive pitch, but together made a pleasing chord.

Night and day, there was never a pause in the continual music of the city. Many languages were spoken here: not just Greek, Turkish and Ladino, the language of the Sephardic Jews, but French, Armenian and Bulgarian were also commonly heard on the streets. The rattle of a tram, the cries of the street vendors, the clashing calls to prayer from dozens of muezzin, the clank of chains as ships came in to the dock, the rough voices of the stevedores as they unloaded cargoes of necessities and luxuries to satisfy the appetites of rich and poor – all of these combined to make the city's endless tune.

The smells of the city were sometimes not as sweet as its sounds. A pungent stench of urine wafted from the tanneries, and sewerage and rotting household waste still flowed down into the harbour from some of the poorer areas. And when the women gutted the previous night's catch, they left the steaming, odorous debris to be devoured by cats.

In the centre was a flower market, where the fragrance of blooms still hung in the air for many hours after the stallholders had packed up and gone home, and in the long streets, orange trees in blossom provided not only shade, but the most intoxicating aroma of all. There were many houses where jasmine rampaged around the doors, its aromatic white petals carpeting the road like snow. At all times of day, the smell of cooking suffused the atmosphere, along with wafts of roasted coffee made on small stoves and carried through the streets. In the markets colourful savoury spices such as turmeric, paprika and cinnamon were shaped by the seller into small mountain peaks, and plumes of aromatic smoke curled up from narghiles, smoked outside the cafés.

Thessaloniki was currently home to a provisional government led by the former Prime Minister, Eleftherios Venizelos. There was a deep division in the country – known as the National Schism – between those who supported the pro-German monarch, King Constantine, and supporters of the liberal Venizelos. As a consequence of the latter's control over northern Greece, Allied troops were currently encamped outside the city in readiness for operations against Bulgaria. In spite of these distant rumblings, most people's lives were untouched by the world war. For some, it even brought additional wealth and opportunity.

One such person was Konstantinos Komninos and, on this perfect May morning, he strode in his usual purposeful manner across the cobbled dockyard. He had gone to check on the arrival of a shipment of cloth, and porters, beggars and boys with handcarts steered out of his path as he took his straight course towards the exit. He was not known for his patience with people who got in his way.

His shoes were dusty and some fresh mule dung clung stubbornly to his heel so when Komninos stopped at his usual bootblack, one of a row kept busy next to the customs house, the man had at least ten minutes' work to do. This *loutros* had been cleaning shoes for Konstantinos Komninos for decades and was well into his seventies, his skin as dark and leathery as the footwear he polished.

They nodded a mutual greeting but neither spoke. This was typical of Komninos: all of his routines were carried out without conversation. The old man worked at the leather until it gleamed, polishing both of the expensive brogues simultaneously, applying the polish, working it into the leather and finally brushing with sweeping strokes, ambidextrously, his arms flying left and right, crossing over, up and down, side to side, as though he were conducting an orchestra.

Even before the job was finished, he heard the tinkle of a coin dropped into his tray. It was always the same, never more, never less.

Today, as every day, Komninos wore a dark suit and, in spite of the rising temperature, kept his jacket on. Such habits were an indication of social standing. Going about one's business in shirt-sleeves was as unthinkable as taking off armour before a battle. The language of formal dress for both men and women was one he understood, and one that had made him rich. Suits lent a man both status and dignity, and well-cut clothes in the European style gave a woman elegance and chic.

The cloth merchant caught sight of himself in the gleaming window of one of the new department stores and the shadowy glimpse was enough to remind him that he was due a visit to the barber. He took a detour into one of the side streets away from the seafront and was soon comfortably seated, his face lathered and every inch except his moustache closely shaved. Then his hair was meticulously clipped so that the space between the top of his collar and his hairline was precisely two millimetres. Komninos was annoyed to see that there were hints of silver in the specks of hair that the barber blew from his clippers.

Finally, before making his way to his showroom, he sat for a while at a small circular table and a waiter brought him coffee as well as his favourite newspaper, the right-wing *Makedonia*. He dispensed with the news quickly, catching up on the latest political intrigues in Greece before giving the headlines on military developments in France a cursory glance. Finally he ran his finger down the share prices.

The war was good for Komninos. He had opened a large warehouse near the port to help deal with his new business – the supply of fabric for military uniforms. With tens of thousands being called up for military service, this was a huge enterprise. He could not employ too many people, or deliver the orders fast enough. Additional quantities seemed to be required on a daily basis.

He drank his coffee in a single sip and rose to go. Each day he experienced a profound sense of satisfaction from having been up since six in the morning. Today he enjoyed the idea that he still had another eight hours in his office before leaving for Constantinople. He had important paperwork to do before his departure.

★　★　★

That afternoon his wife, Olga Komninos, looked out from their mansion in Niki Street and gazed at Mount Olympus, just visible through a haze. The heat had been building up and she opened one of the floor-to-ceiling windows to let in some air. There was not a breath of wind, and sounds carried easily. She heard calls to prayer mixing with the clatter of hoofs and carriage wheels in the street below, and a ship sounding its horn to signal its approach.

Olga sat down again and put her feet up on a chaise longue, which had been moved closer to the window to catch the breeze. Since they had never been worn outside, there was no need for her to remove her dainty, low-heeled shoes. Being an almost identical match, her silk dress seemed to vanish into the pale green of the upholstery, and the blue-black of her braided hair accentuated the pallor of her skin. She could not get herself comfortable on this languid day, and drank glass after glass of lemonade, poured from a jug that her devoted housekeeper regularly appeared to replenish.

'Can I bring you anything else, Kyria Olga? Perhaps something to eat? You haven't had anything at all today,' she said, with gentle concern.

'Thank you, Pavlina, but I just don't feel like eating. I know I should, but today I simply . . . can't.'

'Are you sure I shouldn't fetch the doctor?'

'It's just the heat, I think.'

Olga sank back onto the cushions, her temples beaded with sweat. Her head throbbed and she held the icy glass against it to try to relieve the pain.

'Well, if you still haven't eaten anything later, I will have to tell Kyrios Konstantinos.'

'There's no need to do that, Pavlina. And besides, he is going away this evening. I don't want to worry him.'

'They say the weather is going to turn this evening. It's going to get a bit cooler. So that should help you a little.'

'I hope they are right,' Olga replied. 'It feels as though there might be a storm.'

Both of them heard something like a clap of thunder, but then realised it was the sound of the front door banging shut. It was followed by the rhythmic beat of footsteps on the broad wooden staircase. Olga recognised her husband's business-like pace and counted the standard twenty crotchet beats before the door swung open.

'Hello, dearest. How are you today?' he asked briskly, walking over to where she lay, and addressing her as though he was a doctor speaking to a simple-minded patient. 'You're not finding it too hot, are you?'

Komninos now removed his jacket and carefully hung it over the back of a chair. His shirt was transparent with sweat.

'I've just come back to pack a suitcase. Then I'll be going back to the showroom for a few hours before the ship leaves. The doctor will come if you need him. Is Pavlina looking after you? Have you eaten anything since last night?' Komninos' statements and questions blended together without pause.

'Make sure you take good care of her while I am away,' he said, directing a final comment at the housekeeper.

He smiled at his resting wife but she had looked away. Her eyes rested on the sparkling sea, which she could see through the open window. Both sea and sky had now darkened and one of the French windows was banging against the frame. The wind had changed, and she sighed with relief as a breeze caressed her face.

She put down her glass on the side-table and rested both hands on her swollen belly. The dress had been perfectly tailored to conceal her pregnancy but, in the final few months, the darts would be pulled to straining point.

'I'll be back in a fortnight,' Komninos said, kissing her lightly on the top of her head. 'You'll look after yourself, won't you? And the baby.'

They both looked in the same direction, out of the window towards the sea, where the rain now lashed in against the curtain. A streak of lightning cut across the sky.

'Send me a telegram if you need me desperately. But I'm sure you won't.'

She said nothing. Nor did she get up.

'I will bring some lovely things back for you,' he finished, as though he was talking to a child.

As well as a ship full of silk, he planned to return with jewellery for his wife, something even better than the emerald necklace and matching earrings that he had brought last time. With her jet black hair, he preferred her in red and would probably buy rubies. Just as with tailored clothes, gems were a way of showing your status, and his wife had always been a perfect model for everything he wanted to display.

As far as he was concerned, life had never been so good. He left the room with a lightness of step.

Olga stared out at the rain. Finally the intense humidity had given way to a storm. The darkened sky now crackled with lightning, and in the slate-grey sea a frenzy of white horses reared and fought and fell into the foam. The street below the Komninos house was soon submerged. Every few minutes a great arc of water curled over the edge of the promenade. It was a tempest of exceptional fury, and the sight of the boats rolling up and down in the bay was enough to bring back to Olga the terrible nausea that had blighted these past few months.

She got up to secure the window but, catching the strange but pleasing odour of rain on damp cobbles, decided to leave it open. The air seemed almost fresh after the stifling heat of the afternoon, and she lay down again, closed her eyes and enjoyed the gentle breaths of salty air on her cheeks. Within a moment, she was asleep.

Now she was the lone sailor in a fishing vessel struggling with the rage of the waves. With her dress billowing around her, her loosened hair stuck to her cheeks and the briny water stinging her eyes, the sunless sky and the landless horizon gave her no indication of the direction she was going. The sails were filled by a powerful southwesterly wind that carried the boat along at alarming speed, its steep pitch allowing the water to lap over its sides. When the wind suddenly dropped, the sails were left empty and flapping.

Olga clung on, one hand on the boat's smooth gunwale and the other on the oarlock, desperately trying to keep her head clear of the swinging boom. She did not know if she was safer in or out of the boat as she had never been in one before. The water was already beginning to soak her dress, and the spray on her face and inside her throat was starting to make her choke. Water continued to gush into the boat and, as the wind picked up again and filled the mainsail, a gust caused its fatal capsize.

Perhaps death by drowning would be painless, she thought, giving herself up to the weight of her clothes, which began to pull her down. As she and the boat began to slip steadily beneath the waves, she saw the pale shape of a baby swimming towards her and reached out for him.

Then there was an almighty crash as if the boat had hit a rock. The naked infant had vanished and now Olga's gasps for breath were replaced by sobs.

'Kyria Olga! Kyria Olga!'

Olga could hear a faraway voice, breathless and distraught.

'Are you all right? Are you all right?'

Olga knew the voice. Perhaps rescue was at hand.

'I thought you had fainted!' Pavlina exclaimed. 'I thought you had taken a tumble! *Panagia mou!* I thought you had fallen! It was ever such a loud crash downstairs.'

Covered in confusion and somewhere between the state of dreaming and waking, Olga opened her eyes and saw her house-keeper's face close to hers. Pavlina was kneeling right beside her, looking anxiously into her eyes. Behind her, she could see the huge floor-to-ceiling curtain furling and unfurling like a great sail, and even now the force of the wind was lifting the heavy satin drape and blowing it horizontally across the room. Its edge licked at a small circular table and swept across its empty surface.

Disoriented, almost giddy, Olga began to realise what had created the crashing noise that had woken her and brought Pavlina rushing into the room. She brushed away the strand of hair that had fallen across her face and slowly manoeuvred herself into a sitting position.

She saw the fragments of two porcelain figures scattered across the room, heads severed from bodies, hands separated from arms, thousands of drachmas' worth of *objets d'art* literally reduced to dust. The weight of the damask and the force of the wind had swept them to the unforgiving floor.

She wiped her damp face with the back of her hand and realised that she had not left her tears behind in the nightmare. As she struggled to catch her breath she heard herself cry out: 'Pavlina!'

'What is it, Kyria Olga?'

'My baby!'

Pavlina reached out and touched her mistress's stomach and then her forehead.

'He hasn't gone anywhere! No doubt about that!' she concluded cheerfully. 'But you're a bit on the warm side . . . and you seem rather damp too!'

'I think I had a bad dream . . .' whispered Olga. 'It seemed so real.'

'Perhaps I'll send for the doctor . . . ?'

'There's no need for that. I'm sure everything is fine.'

Pavlina was already kneeling on the floor gathering up pieces of china into her apron. Mending a single ornament in this state would have tested an expert, but the combined ingredients of the two together meant it would be an impossibility.

'It's only some porcelain,' Olga reassured her, seeing how upset she was.

'Well . . . I suppose it could have been worse. I really thought you had fallen.'

'I am fine, Pavlina, you can see I am.'

'And I'm the one supposed to be looking after you, while Kyrios Konstantinos is away.'

'Well, you are. And you are doing a really fine job. And please don't worry about those figurines. I am sure Konstantinos won't even notice.'

Pavlina had been part of the Komninos family for many years longer than Olga, and knew the high value placed on such collector's items. She hastened over to the French windows and began to close them. The rain had made a patch on the carpet and she could see that the edge of Olga's fine silk dress was soaked.

'Oh my goodness,' she fussed, 'I should have come up before. We're in a terrible mess up here, aren't we?'

'Don't shut them,' appealed Olga, standing at her side, feeling the spray on her face. 'It's so cooling. The carpet will dry out as soon as it stops. It's still so warm.'

27

Pavlina was used to Olga's occasional eccentricity. It made a change from the rigidity with which her late mother-in-law, the older Kyria Komninos, had ruled the house for so many years.

'Well, as long as you don't get too wet,' she said, giving her an indulgent smile. 'You don't want to be catching a chill, not in your state.'

Olga lowered herself into another chair further from the window, and watched Pavlina meticulously picking up the pieces of porcelain. Even if she had been able to bend, Pavlina would not have allowed Olga to help.

Beyond the bulky figure of the kneeling housekeeper, Olga could see the wild sea. A few ships were out there, just about visible through the storm, occasionally illuminated by a flash of lightning.

The ornate clock on the mantelpiece struck seven. She realised that Konstantinos would have been at sea for an hour or more by now. Such weather conditions rarely held up the bigger ships.

'If the wind is in the right direction, then I suppose it might even speed up Kyrios Konstantinos' journey,' Pavlina reflected.

'I suppose it might,' answered Olga absent-mindedly, now only aware of the gentle stirring inside her womb. She wondered if her baby had heard the storm and felt himself tossed by the sea. She loved her unborn child beyond all measure and pictured him swimming effortlessly around in the clear liquid of her womb. Tears and sea spray rolled down her face in equal measure.

# Chapter Two

ONCE THE FEVERISH temperatures of August came, the citizens of Thessaloniki looked back with wistfulness to the warmth of May. It was now forty degrees in the shade and people closed their windows and shutters to keep the fearsome heat outside.

There was a breeze of sorts, but even this provided no relief: the westerly Vardaris blew its hot breath over the city, bringing layers of fine, dark dust into people's homes. Streets were deserted in the hottest hours of the day and a traveller might mistakenly have imagined that these houses had been abandoned. Inside, it was equally silent as people lay in the darkness, their breathing shallow and inaudible as they tried not to take in the fetid air.

Air and sea alike were thick and still. When children dived into the sea, the ripples spread a hundred metres across the bay. As they pulled themselves out of the water they dried in an instant, leaving a stinging residue of salt. There was little variation at night and the air remained as motionless as the reading on the barometer.

Konstantinos Komninos had been delayed in his return from Turkey, but finally arrived home at the beginning of the month. By that time, Olga felt as though her pregnancy had lasted a lifetime. Her fine ankles had puffed up and her once neat breasts had swelled beyond the capacity of every dress that had been sewn for her confinement. Konstantinos discouraged her from having anything new made at this stage, so she wore a capacious white cotton nightdress, which would give her ample space even if she continued to expand in the final weeks of pregnancy.

A few days after his return, Konstantinos moved into another bedroom.

'You need more room,' he said to Olga. 'You won't be comfortable if I am taking up half the bed.'

Olga did not object. Every night was more restless than the previous one, and most nights she managed only an hour of sleep. For long periods she would lie on her back in the darkness staring into the inky void of her shuttered bedroom, feeling the strong kicks of the baby inside her womb. They were vigorous, regular movements. Sometimes all the child's limbs seemed to move at once and she formed a picture in her mind of what he would be like, how strong, how restless, how energetic. She never allowed herself to imagine the child as a girl. Konstantinos' reaction might be more than one of disappointment. Olga already knew she had not fulfilled expectations because of the length of time it had taken her to conceive, and her husband had not concealed his impatience. She had been in her mid-twenties when they married and more than a decade had gone by before the doctor had confirmed that four months of pregnancy had passed and all seemed stable. During the intervening decade, there had been many occasions when she experienced a heart-leaping moment of certainty but, time after time, had grieved over the telltale spill of blood that followed after a month or two.

Her hand rested on the protruding bump and she felt her fingers shift as the kicks came, one after the other. If only this baby would arrive, she thought, and sang as if to calm him, all the while giving herself more peace.

A clock ticked on the mantelpiece in her bedroom, another in the hallway, and on the quarter-hour the chimes of the clock in the drawing room told her how much time was passing, helping her to count the hours until she could get up. She wished each one away.

It was true that Olga needed more space in the bed, but for Konstantinos a more significant factor was his mild revulsion at her altered body. He scarcely recognised the woman she had become. How had the mannequin he had married, with her slim hips and a waist that he could enclose within his own two hands, have transformed into someone he found almost untouchable? He was repulsed by the spherical belly with its stretched skin and her huge dark nipples.

During these last few weeks, while she lay sleepless, counting the discordant chimes of the various clocks, she often heard the quiet padding of footsteps up the staircase and the almost inaudible closing of a door at the end of the corridor. She suspected that Konstantinos slipped out after she had gone to bed and discreetly visited one of the city's smarter brothels. Not even for a moment did she feel she had a right to protest. Perhaps she would win his attention back one day.

Olga knew that Konstantinos had married her for her beauty. She was under no illusions, and had been picked as if from a beauty parade of girls working as mannequins for one of the city's best tailors. Without a dowry – both her parents had died before she was ten years old – she felt herself in some ways fortunate. Many models who worked in Thessaloniki ended up in the burgeoning red light area of the city.

She did wonder, however, what it would have been like to marry for love, and realised that the possession of beauty had both saved and condemned her. Olga knew how it felt to be a commodity, like a roll of silk or a gilded statue, purchased and displayed.

As she grew older, she had begun to see how physical perfection could be a burden, but at the same time she was seized with anxiety when she lost it. Over the past months she had watched the expansion of her body with growing alarm: the engorgement of her veins, the protrusion of her navel and the bulging of her stomach until the skin was so stretched beyond its limits that the outer layer appeared to split apart, leaving dozens of pale streaks, like raindrops running down a windowpane.

Though the nausea she experienced meant that she ate almost nothing, her body continued to expand. Each morning, as Pavlina braided her mistress's ebony hair and wound it around her head, the women talked to each other's reflection.

'You are still as beautiful as you ever were,' Pavlina reassured her. 'You're just a little plumper round the middle.'

'I feel swollen, Pavlina. Not at all beautiful. And I know Konstantinos can't bear me any more.'

Pavlina's met Olga's glance in the mirror and saw her sadness. Olga looked almost more beautiful when she was unhappy. When they were moist, her molasses-dark eyes gained even greater depth.

'He'll come back to you,' said Pavlina. 'As soon as the baby has been born, everything will be back in place. You'll see.'

Pavlina could speak with some authority. She had borne four children before the age of twenty-two and after the first three births she was living proof that the dramatic expansion of the female body during pregnancy could be reversed. Following her fourth pregnancy, however, her body finally lost its elasticity. Olga glanced at the comfortable figure of her housekeeper, who looked more like someone on the point of giving birth than she did herself.

'I hope you're right, Pavlina,' she said, putting aside the cloth to which she was slowly and ineptly adding an edging.

'When exactly are you planning to get that finished?' teased Pavlina, as she picked up the tiny sheet to examine her mistress's handiwork. 'The baby is due this month, isn't he? Or is it next year?'

In six months, Olga's attempts at embroidery had scarcely progressed. The needle slipped through her sweating fingers and several times she had pricked herself and droplets of blood had stained the creamy linen.

'It's a mess, isn't it?'

Pavlina smiled and took it from her. She could not deny this statement. Olga's hands were not made for embroidery. Though her fingers were slim and elegant, she had no knack with a needle. For her, it was purely an activity with which to kill time.

'I'll launder it and then finish it off for you, shall I?'

'Thank you, Pavlina. Would you mind?'

During all these months of sickness, Olga had been uncomfortable, but in the early hours of that August morning these feelings of restlessness overpowered her. She could not lie still even for a minute. Her back ached more when she was sitting than standing and the pains in her abdomen, which had been mild for a week or so, intensified. Every few moments she almost passed out with the pain. Finally her time had come.

Although it was a Saturday, Konstantinos left for his offices at six thirty, as usual.

'Goodbye, Olga,' he said, coming into the bedroom during a moment when the contractions had receded. 'I'll be at the showroom. Pavlina can send for me if you need.'

She attempted a smile as he put his hand on hers. It was meant to reassure her, but it was as fleeting as a feather's touch, a perfunctory gesture that made her feel less loved rather than more. He seemed oblivious to her pain, and appeared not to have noticed the soft moans that she had been making when he entered the room.

Soon she was howling, as the waves of pain overwhelmed her, gripping on to Pavlina until the housekeeper's arm bore her fingerprints. Surely such terrible agony could only mean the end of life, not the beginning.

Passers-by heard the occasional agonising scream but such a sound was common in this city, and the noise was swallowed up in the general cacophony of trams, carts and street traders. At ten o'clock, Pavlina sent for Dr Papadakis, who confirmed that the baby would soon be arriving. Konstantinos Komninos' position in the community meant that the doctor would stay until the baby arrived safely.

In the final hours of labour Olga did not, for a moment, let go of Pavlina's hand. Without it she feared being drawn inexorably into a dark tunnel of pain that would take her away from the world.

With her spare hand, Pavlina mopped her mistress's brow with cool water, which was constantly brought up from the kitchen.

'Try to get her to relax a little,' the doctor advised Pavlina.

The housekeeper knew from her own experiences that when pain was ripping your body into two, this was an absurd suggestion. She would like to tell him what she thought, but there was no point. She bit her lip. The man was in his seventies. However many thousands of babies he might have delivered in his career, he could never even get close to imagining what Olga was experiencing.

The bed was wet with sweat, with water and with the liquid that burst from her body like a flood. Olga felt herself drifting almost out of consciousness, and thought of the nightmare she had had all those weeks ago – and which had often recurred in some form during the past few days.

The doctor had settled himself into a comfortable chair and sat reading a newspaper, occasionally consulting his pocket watch then glancing over at Olga. It seemed as though he was monitoring her, or perhaps he was just calculating how long it would be before he would be eating his lunch.

With the heavy curtains almost shut, the room was in near darkness. He held his newspaper up to catch the shaft of light that found its way in. Only when her screams seemed as though they might shatter the mirror did he actually get up. Without getting close enough to endanger the perfection of his pristine, pale suit, he began to issue some more instructions.

'I can see the baby's head. You need to push now, Kyria Komninos.'

Nothing seemed more natural to her. Every part of her being felt this urge, but at the same time, it seemed an impossibility, as though she must turn her body inside out.

Perhaps an hour went by. For Pavlina it seemed a day, and for Olga an unquantifiable amount of time during which her life was measured only by waves of pain. She entered a state of delirium. She did not know that she had been close to cardiac arrest, and that the baby's distressed heart was within a beat of failure. She was aware only of the pain. It was all that seemed real for these final moments of her labour.

A baby swam out of the darkness into the half-light of the room. And screamed. Olga's pains had ceased so she knew the high wail did not belong to her. This was a new sound.

She lay still and silent for a few moments. Breathless. Tears of exhaustion and relief coursing down her face. Olga became aware that the attention of the two people looking after her had shifted away and was focused on something across the room. Their backs were turned towards her and instinctively she knew not to disturb them.

She closed her eyes for a moment and listened to their quiet murmurings. She had no reason to be concerned. Olga felt the presence of a fourth person in that room. She knew he was there.

'Kyria Olga . . .'

Olga saw Pavlina at her bedside. Against the whiteness of her blouse and the ampleness of her bosom, the small white bundle was almost invisible.

'Your . . . baby.' She almost choked on the words. 'Here is your baby. Your son. Your boy, Kyria Olga!'

And there, indeed, he was. Pavlina lowered the tiny thing down into Olga's open arms and mother and son looked at each other for the first time.

Olga could not speak. A powerful surge of love flowed out of her. Never had she felt anything as strong as the unconditional adoration that she felt for this small being in her arms. In that moment of meeting eyes, an unbreakable bond was made.

A message was sent to Konstantinos Komninos and, when he arrived, Dr Papadakis was waiting for him downstairs.

'You have a son and heir,' he informed him proudly, as though he had been responsible for the entire procedure.

'That's excellent news,' responded Komninos, in the tone of a man being informed of the safe delivery of some Chinese silk.

'Congratulations!' added Papadakis. 'Mother and baby are both well, so I'll be leaving now.'

It was almost three and the doctor was anxious to be on his

way. He always hoped to have Saturdays free, and certainly did not want to miss the recital that was being given that afternoon by a visiting French pianist. It was an all-Chopin programme and Thessaloniki society was buzzing with excitement.

'I'll come by and see them next week, but let me know if you need me before then, Kyrios Komninos,' he said with his automatic smile.

The two men shook hands and before the doctor had let himself out of the house, Komninos was already halfway up the sweeping staircase. It was time to see his son for himself.

By now Pavlina had helped Olga wash and had freshly braided her hair. Clean sheets had been put on the bed, and the baby was asleep in the crib beside it. It was a picture of peace and organisation, exactly how Konstantinos liked to see things.

Without even looking at his wife, he walked across the room and gazed down silently at the swaddled newborn.

'Isn't he beautiful?' asked Pavlina.

'I can't really see him properly,' he replied, with a hint of dissatisfaction.

'You'll see plenty of him when he wakes up,' interjected Pavlina.

Komninos gave her a disapproving look.

'What I mean is, it would be better to let him have his sleep for now. And as soon as he is awake I will bring him to you. It would be better not to disturb him.'

'Very well, Pavlina,' he retorted. 'Could you leave us a moment?'

As soon as Pavlina was out of the room, he looked at Olga.

'Is he . . . ?'

'Yes, Konstantinos, he is.'

After all her years of failure to conceive, Olga had known her husband's greatest fear: that when she finally managed to produce a child, there would be something wrong with it. Her anxiety over what Konstantinos would actually do in those circumstances could now be put to one side.

'He's absolutely perfect,' she said simply.

Satisfied, Komninos left the room. He had business to attend to.

# Chapter Three

O<small>N THE SAME</small> sweltering Saturday afternoon, perhaps even at the very moment when little Dimitri Komninos emerged into the world, a woman began to cook her family's meagre dinner. She lived in a very different kind of house from the Komninos mansion. Like hundreds of others, her home was in a densely populated quarter, just within the old city walls, in the north-west of the city. It was where the poorest people of Thessaloniki lived: Christians, Muslims, Jews and refugees, crowded on top of each other in streets where there was little money, but plenty of life.

Some of these dwellings were built into the city walls themselves, and the space between them was hardly enough to hang out a single shirt for drying. Families were large, money was scarce and work not always easy to find, and in this home there were four almost grown up, but not yet married, children. Such a number was typical. The mother worked full time to keep her small tribe fed and clean, and when there was no cooking pot on the fire, there was a cauldron of hot water. There was a constant need for it, for washing the filthy clothes and bodies after each day's work at the port.

The three sons slept in the main living room, while she and

her husband occupied the only bedroom, along with their sixteen-year-old daughter, who slept on a couch at the end of the bed. There was no other reasonable arrangement until she could be married, which was highly improbable for a girl with no prospect of a dowry.

The mistress of the house bought wisely and never indulgently, purchasing most of her ingredients from the vendors who came in from the countryside with their baskets of onions, potatoes and beans. Meat was a luxury eaten only on special feast days, but often there were sheeps' entrails to float in the soup, given away by the butchers if they were unsold at the end of a day. That afternoon there was such a soup simmering, which they would eat later with chunks of coarse bread that her husband had been told to fetch on his way home. Sweat ran down her bare, muscular arms as she stoked the flames beneath the simmering pot. At the end of every Saturday, the men of the family met up with cousins and nephews in a smoke-filled kafenion to drink and chew over the week's events. With war raging all around them, in Europe and beyond, there was always plenty to discuss.

The family kept an old mule in the lower ground floor of the house, along with a goat to make them self-sufficient in milk and cheese, and, as well as a thousand uninvited flies, a few chickens shared the sordid living space, making their nesting places in the soiled hay. They knew to keep well clear of the mule's hind legs and instead picked at scraps between the goat's cloven hoofs. When the kitchen was not full of cooking smells, the odour of animal dung pervaded instead.

It was into this dark and fetid space that a small spark from the fire found its way that afternoon. A thousand times before, an ember such as this had been spat out by the crackling wood and then floated slowly down to the floor, where it glowed for a moment and then died. This one, however, flew with the accuracy of a well-aimed arrow through the narrow space between the floorboards and in its trajectory seemed to pick up heat from its own gathering speed.

It dropped onto the mule's rump, where it was instantly flicked off by its tail. Had the rhythm of the animal's continuously swishing tail wafted the ember to the left, it would have landed on the damp urine-soaked floor. Instead, it travelled to the right and landed on the straw bedding. It did not stay on the surface, but slipped a few layers down, close to where the hen sat incubating her eggs and creating the perfect conditions to nurture the warmth of the still glowing spark.

Upstairs, the pot continued to simmer. The long-suffering mistress of the house expected her menfolk in an hour or so and meanwhile went upstairs to rest. Her daughter was already there, lying in the darkness. It was much easier for her to get some sleep now, before her parents were both there in the same room. Most nights her father noisily and roughly manhandled her mother before they both fell asleep and then grunted and snored until morning.

Down below, a fire began to take hold within the pile of straw, but the smell of burning feathers and the squeals of the terror-struck livestock went unnoticed by mother and daughter, both now dozing two floors above.

It was a matter of seconds before the flames curled around the wooden beams and crept along the ceiling. Soon the whole ground-floor room was alight, and walls and ceiling became sheets of flame as the fire progressed with speed and efficiency, upwards to the next floor and then outwards to the adjacent homes.

Even the increasing heat of the house was not enough to rouse them. Summer temperatures in Thessaloniki were often intense. In the end, it was a noise, like a huge explosion, that disturbed them. It was the sound of the kitchen floor falling into the basement.

In a moment, both women were on their feet, wide awake, dripping from heat and terror, grasping each other's hands. The fire was already climbing the stairs so they knew their route that way was blocked, but they could hear familiar voices shouting their names in the streets below.

There was no time for weighing up the risks. Daughter first, then mother, they climbed onto the windowledge and threw themselves on the mercy of their menfolk below. Then, just as their house collapsed neatly in on itself, they ran for their lives, finding themselves part of a human river moving swiftly eastwards. Soon they blended into the crowd, quite unaware of their pivotal role in the conflagration.

Neighbours had quickly noticed the billowing smoke and smelled the appetising aroma of roasted goat, and all of them had been safely down the street before their own homes were consumed in the blaze. There was no time for speculating on the cause and certainly no time for spectating. The fire was travelling as fast as the fierce, warm wind would take it.

Within an hour of ignition, dozens of these homes were gone; their largely wooden construction and the summer drought had turned the city into a tinderbox. There had been no rain since June and there was nothing to stand in the way of the fire's spread. The city had a few fire engines, but they were old and inefficient and, in any case, much of the local water supply had been diverted to the vast encampments of Allied troops outside Thessaloniki.

In the centre of the town, where there was as yet no sign of the fire, Konstantinos Komninos was about to reach his showroom. He had a spring in his step. At last, he had a son.

There was no one to share the news with, apart from one man.

For longer than Komninos could remember, there had been a caretaker and night watchman who sat, night and day, in a small airless cubicle at the entrance of the showroom. Tasos had worked there for more than half a century. He walked up and down the rows of fabric once or twice a day, occasionally strolled out into the street to find a lemonade vendor, or some tobacco, but for most of the time he was simply sitting, watching and sleeping. He could glimpse the sky from a high window that faced the street. At night, this diminutive, dark-haired man curled up to sleep on the couch at the back of his small room. Komninos had no idea where he ate or how he washed. He was paid to be there for twenty-four hours a day, three hundred and sixty-five days a year, and he had never complained, in all the years he had known him.

When he heard the sound of the key in the lock, Tasos came out of his lair to greet his boss. He knew that Komninos had been summoned home earlier and was keen to hear the news.

'How is Kyria Komninos?' he asked.

'She has delivered safely,' replied Konstantinos. 'I have a son.'

'Congratulations, Kyrios Komninos.'

'Thank you, Tasos. Is there anything to report?'

'No, all as quiet as the grave here.'

Konstantinos had opened the main door to the showroom and was about to shut it behind him when Tasos called out after him.

'Kyrios Komninos, I forgot – your brother called in about twenty minutes ago.'

'Oh?'

Komninos was annoyed by the thought of his brother coming to the showroom on a Saturday afternoon. This was the time he always spent here alone when it was closed to customers, masterminding the incomings and outgoings, putting himself in control of the cash flow, profit and loss accounts, writing the correspondence and doing the deals that unquestionably positioned him as the head of the business.

'He'd heard that a fire has broken out somewhere up in the north and wanted to know if I knew anything about it. How I should know, sitting around in here all day, I'm not sure.'

Komninos shrugged.

'Typical of Leonidas to pick up rumours the minute he's back on leave!' said Konstantinos. 'Fortunately some of us have better things to do.'

Komninos liked to walk through his silent showroom and run his fingertips across his rolls of silk, velvet, taffeta and wool. He could tell a fabric's price per metre merely by touching it. This was his greatest pleasure. For him, these cloths were more sensual than a woman's skin. The rolls reached from the floor to the ceiling, and ladders ran along on runners the length of the fifty-metre room so that the top ones could be easily accessed. Everything was arranged by colour from one end of the room to the other, with crimson silk next to scarlet wool, and green velvet next to emerald taffeta. His salesmen were responsible for colour sections rather than specialist fabric types, and he could see at a glance whether any of them had been inefficient with their inventory. The symmetry and perfection of this space without the clutter of the staff pleased him inordinately. His father, from whom he had inherited the business, had always encouraged him to come in and enjoy the order and calm of the showroom without staff and customers.

'Think of this place,' he used to say to the five-year-old Konstantinos, 'as the Alpha and the Omega of our lives.'

Then he would point out the cutting shears neatly left at the centre of each of the polished cutting tables.

'There is the Alpha,' he would say, tracing the 'A' shape of the scissors. 'And here is the Omega.' He would point at the roll-ends made of perfect 'O's. 'In this family, those are the only letters you need to know.'

Each day, Konstantinos thought of his father's words, and now he was able to look forward to the time when he could repeat them to his own son.

On Saturdays he could enjoy being there without feeling the eyes of his employees on him. He was a man who knew he was not well-liked. It was not as though he cared, but it still made him feel uncomfortable. He was aware of the way in which people stopped speaking to each other when he walked by and could feel the heat between his shoulder blades as they observed his retreating back.

His office was raised, with windows on three sides and a clear view of the whole width and length of the enormous room. It was hard for his employees to see him through the blinds, but from his watchtower he could see everything that went on. Important customers were always invited up there and coffee was sent out for. Komninos would pull up the blinds on those occasions, knowing that the view of his vast rainbow never failed to impress. Customers came from every town and city in Greece to purchase, and few of them left without buying in bulk. There was no other cloth wholesaler with such a range, even in Athens, and he could hardly keep up with demand.

In addition, he was the sole supplier of wool cloth for most of the army regiments that had been mobilised in northern Greece at a time when, with thousands of Allied forces camped outside the city, the price of everything on the commodities market, from wheat to wool, had gone up. For the wealthy, there was money to be made. Komninos had always read figures better than letters, and had a nose for wise investments.

The business had been left equally to him and his brother, Leonidas, who was his junior by eight years, but the younger man had little interest in spending his days in this barn of a showroom, and even less in the complexities of speculation on the price of wool on the commodities market. Leonidas was an army officer and a life of action suited him much more than a life of commerce. These brothers had absolutely nothing in common except their parents, and now that the latter had gone there was more antipathy than love between them. Even when they were small it was hard to believe they were from the same family. Leonidas, tall, with fair hair and blue eyes, was Apollo to his brother's Hephaestus.

As Konstantinos sat in his office, studying his ledger and doing mental calculations of current weekly income versus interest rates and rising expenses, offset against a new order for fifteen thousand metres of wool for army greatcoats (which could be supplied from material he had had in stock for two years, but which he would sell at this year's price), his brother was running like a madman down the empty street.

Tasos was roused from his siesta by the sound of Leonidas bursting into the building.

'Tasos . . .' breathless, hardly able to speak, '. . . we've got to get hold of Kosta!'

'He's here. In his office,' answered the caretaker. 'What on earth is the matter? Don't normally see you in a hurry!'

Leonidas ran past him into the showroom and took the steps of the spiral staircase up to the office two at a time.

'Kosta, the city is burning! We've got to get some of this stock out!'

'Tasos told me you had gone off to look at some fire or other,' answered the older brother, without raising his eyes from his columns of figures. His sense of position and dignity would not allow him to react. 'Hasn't it been put out yet?'

'No! It's raging, Kosta! It's out of control! Come down into the street now and smell it! It's coming this way! For God's sake, I'm not making it up!'

Konstantinos could hear the fear in his brother's voice. It was not the voice he used when he played practical jokes.

Leonidas took him by the arm and led him down the stairs and out into the street.

'You can't see anything yet, but don't you smell it? And look at the sky! It's nowhere near sunset and it's getting dark!'

Leonidas was right. The reek of burning was palpable, and the clarity of the afternoon sky had been replaced by a haze.

'I want to see where it is, Leonidas. I don't want us to panic if there's no need.'

'Well, where it was ten minutes ago might be different from where it is now . . . All right, let's go and see if they've started to get it under control.'

While they hurried along, Konstantinos told his brother about his new nephew. It was an incongruous moment to deliver such news, but it gave Komninos great satisfaction to announce that there was now an heir for the business.

Leonidas was very fond of his sister-in-law and it was to see Olga rather than his brother that he made a visit to Niki Street a priority whenever he was on leave. If he ever settled down, he wanted to find a woman who was as beautiful and serene as she. Sometimes he wondered if such a cold character as Konstantinos deserved such a fine woman and tried to dismiss the question of what would have happened if he had met Olga first.

'That's wonderful,' he said. 'Are you sure you shouldn't be with her?'

'All in good time,' answered Konstantinos.

Leonidas shook his head with disbelief, thinking not just of Olga and the baby, but the wonderful Pavlina, of whom he was very fond.

The smoke thickened as they hastened northwards and Konstantinos stopped to tie his silk handkerchief around his face to protect himself from the particles of ash that swirled around them. When they turned into a main street, they were met by a crowd of people coming towards them. Konstantinos had seen plenty of mobs during the political upheavals of the past few years, but these people wore a different expression.

Many of them were struggling beneath the weight of their possessions – bulky items for which they had scrimped and saved – cupboards, mirrors, even mattresses. These were far too precious to leave behind. Every porter in the city had been attracted to the business potential of the disaster, and their handcarts, spilling over with people's motley collections of objects, now blocked the streets.

On the horizon, still some distance away, Konstantinos saw the unmistakably fierce glow of fire licking upwards into the sky.

'Do you believe me now?' demanded Leonidas, stopping to cough and catch his breath.

'We need to get back to the showroom,' said Konstantinos, his voice weak with fear. 'And we need as many porters as we can find.'

They were already too late for such a thought. All the able-bodied men who might sell their services had been hired out. Observing the mêlée, the two brothers realised that they were on their own. Tasos was the only one who could help them. As they turned back towards the showroom, their pace quickened to a jog.

'I reckon we've got no more than a couple of hours, unless they get it under control soon,' said Leonidas over his shoulder.

Konstantinos was trying to keep up with his brother, who was a head taller than he, and much more athletic. He responded with a grunt. It was at least twenty years since he had run anywhere and his chest burned. The thought of losing any of his stock spurred him on, however, and within ten minutes they were both through the door and explaining to Tasos what had to be done.

'I'll identify the most precious fabrics,' said the older brother, 'so that you and Leonidas can make them a priority for removal! Pile them up by the door and we'll take them a cartload at a time across Egnatia Street. We should be able to fit thirty in each load.'

Egnatia Street was the wide boulevard that ran west to east across the city.

'There's no chance of the fire crossing over it so anything we can get on to the south side will be safe,' said Leonidas.

The three men got to work. For the first time in a decade, Konstantinos ran up and down the ladders, pulling out bolts of fabrics and letting them drop to the floor. They were picked up by Leonidas and carried out of the building, where Tasos piled them on his cart. The first cartload was ready and together Tasos and Leonidas trundled it down the street. Five minutes later they deposited the rolls outside a customer's shop.

'Just keep an eye on these for us, would you?' Leonidas asked the tailor. 'We'll be back.'

There was no need to explain. Dozens of other merchants and traders were dumping their goods on the other side of the street. Everyone had the same thought: the fire would never cross it.

The streets were full of shouting and the suffocating smell of smoke on an already airless day.

By the time Leonidas and Tasos were back in the showroom, another hundred or so rolls lay ready for collection in the aisles.

'Take the purple silks first, followed by the red velvets. The wool should go last, but get all the *crêpe de Chine* on to the next load – whatever the colour – and try and make sure the creams don't get too soiled . . .'

As soon as he was handling the fabrics, Konstantinos' passion for them took over. His orders for their preservation and protection spilled out, one after the other, like silk coming off the roll.

In the past hour, since he had broken the news of the baby to his brother, he had not given a thought to his new son or his wife, nor to their safety. As long as they were south of Egnatia Street like his precious wools and silks, he knew they were safe.

Tasos and Leonidas had returned for their fourth load of fabric. By the time they were preparing the fifth, both of them had removed their shirts and were mopping their faces.

'Try to keep the pale ones clean, won't you?'

The lighter coloured fabrics were getting soiled with the men's sweat. It was one instruction too many for Leonidas.

'Look, Konstantinos, it's only a speck of dirt . . .'

'If we're going to save the bridal fabrics, they have to be usable and that one is worth thousands of drachmas a metre!'

'For God's sake, what does it matter? Personally I can't understand why you aren't at home with your wife and child!'

'Because I know they are safe. And this showroom may not be. I've worked seven days a week on this business, for the best part of my life. Even if you don't, Leonidas, I understand the value of what we have here. And so did our father.'

'None of them will be worth anything at all if we don't get them out of here,' interrupted the old man.

He had just been out into the street where the smell was now stronger, the crowds seemed larger and, unless it was his imagination, even the heat in the air seemed greater.

'I don't think we've got much time.'

The two brothers faced each other, both enraged by the attitude of the other.

Leonidas picked up a roll of dark velvet from the floor and went out onto the street. Tasos was right. They all had to get out of there.

He dropped the fabric on the cart, raced back inside and grabbed Konstantinos by the arm.

'We're going, *now*.'

Leonidas could feel his brother's resistance to his touch.

He pulled him towards the entrance and even then Konstantinos took a moment to triple-lock the doors. By this time, Tasos had struggled to the end of the street with the handcart and turned right towards Egnatia Street. The air was now thick with smoke and the sound of crackling fire was audible.

Within a few moments they had caught up with the old man and saw the pyramid of fabrics on the pavement. Passers-by steered themselves politely around the obstacle, preoccupied with their own journeys away from danger.

'We need to get everything inside,' urged Konstantinos.

'And who exactly is going to steal a piece of velvet?' snapped Leonidas.

The tailor was already helping Tasos to move the material inside his shop, and soon there was a solid stack of nearly two hundred rolls in the middle of his floor. Konstantinos stubbornly ignored his brother's question. He had plenty of people around him now who would carry out his instructions without challenge.

Suddenly the ground beneath them rocked and the tailor's shop was shaken to its foundations. A moment ago it had seemed a safe haven, but now everyone – the tailor, his family, the Komninos brothers and Tasos – rushed back out into the street. There had been an explosion somewhere in the city and, amidst mounting chaos and fear, there was another, and then a third.

People hastening away from the fire seemed to quicken their pace.

'It's foreign soldiers,' one man told them as he passed. 'They've started blowing up buildings.'

It was not an act of insanity, but the only possibility of halting the fire. With the dire shortage of water in the city, the creation of a firebreak was the only solution anyone could think of and Allied soldiers had come into the city to help.

'Hopefully that will do the trick then,' Konstantinos said. 'I think we should be going now. My wife had a baby a few hours ago.'

'Congratulations, Kyrios Komninos! What a day to remember!' said the tailor.

'Well, it has been so far!' he replied with a small smile. 'God willing, we'll be back tomorrow to get all this stock out of your way.'

Finally, he turned to Tasos.

'Will you check up on the showroom and bring me a report?' Tasos nodded.

'I think we should be going now,' urged Leonidas, perplexed by his brother's certainty that all would be well. 'Don't you want to go and reassure Olga?'

'I am sure she will be fine. She has Pavlina there. And don't babies sleep for a while after they're born?'

'I don't know,' answered Leonidas. 'I have no experience of them. But I'm sure everyone is aware of the fire by now.'

In the past hour or so, Leonidas had grown increasingly concerned about Olga. He had observed his brother's preoccupation with the business with incredulity. How could he be so neglectful of his beautiful wife and their newborn son? Were he married to someone like Olga, she would be at the centre of his life.

They headed towards the sea and walked along the front. Everything looked just as it always did, with the elegant villas on the esplanade and the ships in the bay silently watching each other.

A pungent odour hung in the atmosphere, but now that the sun had set, the sootiness of the air blended in with the night sky. Incongruously, a hotel was still serving dinner to its guests, and café tables were still occupied by people sipping their drinks. Thessaloniki seemed to have divided itself into two unrelated worlds. Those south of Egnatia Street knew of the fire, but were certain of their own safety. There was nothing they could do to help, and it was their duty to be calm.

Tasos was now making his way back northwards. When he smelled the strong aroma of roasting lamb, he knew the meat market must have gone up in flames and the sight of a few crazed sheep cantering through the streets confirmed it.

To see livestock running free was strange enough, but then he saw a giant bird flying through the air towards him. When it landed, only centimetres in front of him, he realised it was, in fact, a chair. Three of its legs were broken by the fall. The street was littered with abandoned possessions and even now, those escaping were tossing things out of their windows: sewing machines, tables, cabinets . . . People had accepted that they would never again be returning to their homes and desperation had set in.

With the blind obedience of a man who had owed his living to one family for more than half a century, Tasos was resolved to carry out his boss's request. When the volume of people coming in the other direction blocked his route, he retreated into a doorway, but eventually he reached the end of the long street where the business was situated. He could see the flames through an upper window but the front of the building was still intact.

'It won't take long,' he thought to himself, 'just to run in and grab the order book.'

He knew that this would be one of Kyrios Komninos' main concerns and he put his key in the door.

Inside, like a monster in need of a meal, the fire had been greedily devouring rolls of tulle and taffeta, before taking its time over a satisfying main course of wool and heavy linen. Bolt after bolt of fabric was reduced to ashes. Like matches in a box, they burned and each one became a taper that lit the next.

Observers saw the windows suddenly blown outwards by the great pressure of heat from the back-draught within. If sticks of gelignite had been stored in the building it could not have caused a greater explosion. Shards of glass were blasted into the air and came down in a lethal shower of splinters. The building and everything in it was utterly destroyed.

At the same moment that Tasos was consumed by the inferno, the brothers were almost at Niki Street.

They were only a few villas away from their destination when Konstantinos glanced to his left up a dark side street and saw a glow at the end of it. To his horror, he realised that the fire had done what nobody believed possible. It had crossed Egnatia Street. Everything was different now.

The wind had changed direction and was vigorously fanning the fire southwards towards the massive section of the city that housed most of the commercial buildings and the grandest homes of Thessaloniki. Nothing could stop it. Not only was his home threatened, but more seriously for him, he realised that his warehouse, the biggest storehouse of fabric in Greece, was in the path of the flames.

Although it had become clear that this fire was turning into a disaster for the city, he still believed it would not be a catastrophe for him, Konstantinos Komninos. While the cheap wooden-framed buildings in the rest of the city might be flattened, the massive warehouse that he had built with steel and bricks would survive.

Konstantinos grabbed his brother's arm. They needed to get to the villa, and quickly. When they reached the house, Olga was sitting in the hallway, pale and dark-eyed, with the tiny baby clutched to her chest. Pavlina stood next to her, a bag in each hand. The two of them were in tears but relief poured over their faces when Konstantinos and Leonidas appeared.

'We need to go, immediately!' said Konstantinos roughly, and without any delay ushered them into the street.

They hastened as fast as they could along the promenade, the newborn aware of nothing but the warmth of his mother's arms and the strong beat of her heart. The sea, only a few inches to the right of them, gave them small comfort.

The Greek army was using a few fire engines to try to hose down some of the flames, but it was futile, like throwing a bucket of water at a forest fire. The priority now was to get the inhabitants of Thessaloniki to safety.

People from every race had gathered in an area just east of the White Tower, and dozens of vehicles were ferrying them away from the flames and out of the city. Others were escaping by boat. Destinations were unfixed; flight was all that mattered. The whole of the seafront was now ablaze and falling buildings presented new dangers as iron balustrades began to melt and walls collapsed thunderously into the street. Even with the Babel's Tower of languages, bonds were briefly formed between those who rescued and those who were saved.

An orange glow had spread over the sky, as though the sun

had set and risen again within a few hours. The whole city was alight.

Leonidas helped Olga, the baby and Pavlina into an army vehicle. Olga was clearly very weak but Leonidas reassured Konstantinos that she was in good hands and would be well looked after. The cloth merchant had pressed a handful of notes into the army officer's hand, with a promise of many more should all go well, and told the driver to take them to Perea, where one of his best customers lived.

In spite of the little love lost between the brothers, Leonidas felt obliged to stay with Konstantinos. They walked eastwards, then sat all night and much of the following day at a safe distance along the waterfront, watching the cremation of their beloved city.

That day, many were convinced that a miracle took place.

The fire had cared little for any religion. There were a few minarets still standing, like tree trunks in a burned out wood, but almost every synagogue had been razed. Dozens of churches had been lost as well, but when the fire reached the ancient basilica of Agia Sofia, it mysteriously stopped. Some saw it as an answer to their prayers.

Whether through God's intervention or not, the fire no longer had the wind behind it. The flames needed its power to help it leap to the next area of the city and without this, the conflagration could not continue. Even though the city would continue to smoulder for some days, the fire had run its course.

By Monday morning, Konstantinos was eager to get back to the city. From where they stood, it was impossible to make out the extent of the destruction, and he was still certain that his main warehouse by the port would have survived.

'I need to inspect the damage,' said Konstantinos.

With growing trepidation, the brothers walked in silence towards their devastated city, the blackened silhouettes of the gutted build-ings becoming ever more apocalyptic, the closer they came to the centre. There was a palpable sadness in the air. The city was in mourning, its blackened remains its own widow's weeds.

A man in rags stood with Bible in hand raging to an imaginary congregation. He was reading from the Book of Revelation.

'Alas, alas, for the great city that was clothed in fine linen, in purple and scarlet, adorned with gold, with jewels, and with pearls. For in a single hour all this wealth has been laid waste.

'And all shipmasters and seafaring men, sailors and all whose trade is on the sea, stood far off and cried out as they saw the smoke of her burning, "What city was like the great city?" And they threw dust on their heads, as they wept and mourned, crying out: "Alas, alas, for the great city where all who had ships at sea grew rich by her wealth."'

'That seems to fit . . .' said Leonidas.

'Don't be so superstitious,' said his older brother angrily. 'Some idiot started a fire. It's as simple as that.'

All along the water's edge towards the city they noticed submerged remains of burned-out fishing boats. Against all odds, they had been caught by sparks from the flaming seafront buildings.

Many others were making the same silent pilgrimage to inspect the devastation, and the spectacle they faced was worse than any of them had imagined. Hotels, restaurants, shops, theatres, banks, mosques, churches, synagogues, schools, libraries – all were gutted, as were the houses. Thousands upon thousands had been destroyed.

A stillness hung over the city. The brothers saw many people picking over the ashes of their homes, unable to believe that nothing remained of their lives but the smouldering embers that might once have been furniture, clothing, icons or books. Everything was reduced to the same.

Close to the Komninos home, two women walked arm in arm towards the brothers. They looked so incongruously elegant and at ease, protecting their heads from falling ash with a parasol, like ladies taking an afternoon stroll, but as they passed, the brothers saw that both women wept, unashamedly.

When they arrived at their family home, they completely understood the women's grief. For a few minutes, they simply stood and looked, unable to believe that this vast, smouldering space had once been the magnificent house that their father had built with such pride. A strong memory of his childhood bedroom overlooking the sea swept over Leonidas and he recalled how he had woken every morning to the dancing patterns of the sea on his ceiling. Although he had moved out many years ago, every memory returned in a single flash of compressed recollection, as swift and unchronological as a dream. His eyes were stinging from the acrid fumes that hung in the air, but now his tears flowed.

Konstantinos immediately thought of the desk in his study, his personal papers, his priceless collection of clocks, his paintings, the magnificent drapes that had swept so elegantly from ceiling to floor. It had all gone, and all of it was irreplaceable. Fury swept through him like a flame.

'Come on, Leonidas,' he snapped, taking his brother's arm. 'There's nothing we can do. I need to see the showroom and then the warehouse.'

'It'll be the same story,' Leonidas replied, bleakly. 'Do you really need to see?'

'The showroom might have withstood the fire,' said Konstantinos optimistically. 'We won't know until we go there.'

They walked together along the devastated streets, with purposeful pace. Konstantinos was determined not to lose hope, but arrival at their destination only confirmed that Leonidas was right. The showroom had vanished. There was not a trace of the rainbow of which he had been so proud: red, blue, green and yellow, all were now reduced to shades of grey. They did not venture inside. Metal girders swung dangerously from the ceiling and who knew how sound the remains of the brick walls really were?

'The warehouse is of a much more modern construction,' he said. 'And that's where the bulk of the stock is kept, so let's not waste time here.'

Konstantinos Komninos turned away. The sight of these ruins was unbearable and he did not want his brother to see how their loss affected him.

Leonidas was still taking in this spectacle, when he realised that Konstantinos was already at the end of the street. He hastened after him.

They took a circuitous route as some of the roads were impassable, walking street after deserted street. Sometimes, as though the fire had not liked the taste, part of a building had survived. One of the big department stores still had a legible sign: '*Vêtements, Chaussures, Bonneterie*'. It seemed so cheerful but so untrue. No such things remained. In the same street, a twisted metal sign, '*Cinéma Pathé*', still hung from a beam. They already looked like words from another era.

Eventually they saw a sight that would have saddened the hardest of hearts: the burned out church of Agios Dimitri, the city's patron saint. The flames had consumed it. Both the brothers had memories of their parents' funeral services being held there, and it was where Konstantinos and Olga had been married. Now it was just an open space, a courtyard, its floor piled high with bricks, its painted apse exposed to light and air for the first time in its hundreds of years of history. It was naked, undignified. They saw a lone priest walk among its ruins. He wept. Another crazed individual called out the words that St Paul had written to the people of this very city. They had never had more resonance.

'"When the Lord Jesus is revealed from heaven with his mighty angels in flaming fire, he shall inflict vengeance upon those who do not know God and upon those who do not obey the gospel of our Lord Jesus",' he cried.

As well as churches, Konstantinos and Leonidas saw the ruins of synagogues and mosques, and it seemed people still found comfort in their places of worship. Where walls had survived people camped in their shadows; laundry was strung up between their pillars, kitchens had already been improvised in synagogue doorways and blankets were neatly arranged dormitory-style inside burned-out mosques.

The sight of two banks, the Banque Salonique and the Banque d'Athènes, almost undamaged gave Konstantinos a moment of optimism, as did a grand marble-fronted department store, but these buildings were miraculous exceptions.

The Hotel Splendide, where people had dined on the night of the eighteenth of August, totally confident that the flames would never reach them, was gutted. Leonidas' favourite haunt, a seafront café on the edge of Eleftheria Square, had met the same fate. The square, which had been the heart of the city's social life, was now silent.

The two men finally reached the area just north of the port where the main Komninos warehouse was situated.

Both stood and stared at what remained of the vast *apothiki*. It was completely gutted.

'My beautiful warehouse,' whispered Konstantinos after a few moments. 'My beautiful, beautiful warehouse.'

His younger brother looked at him and realised he was weeping copiously.

It was as if he was lamenting the loss of a lover, Leonidas reflected, shocked to see his older brother display such emotion. Even when their mother had died unexpectedly, his brother had not shed this quantity of tears.

As they stood surveying the devastation, a German aeroplane flew over. The pilot would report back to his superiors that Thessaloniki had made a good job of destroying itself. They could not have done it better themselves.

Meanwhile, a local, French language newspaper was preparing its first edition following the fire. Its stark headline said it all:

### *LA MORT D'UNE VILLE*

### DEATH OF A CITY

# Chapter Four

FOR FIVE DAYS, Olga heard nothing from her husband but she was so preoccupied with her baby that she hardly gave him a thought. Night and day blended into each other, all of them wakeful, all of them sleepless. Sometimes she managed to rock little Dimitri off to sleep, but usually it was only for half an hour or so.

Pavlina shared Olga's room in the grand home in Perea that belonged to Konstantinos' old friend, a wealthy shipper who imported many of his consignments of fabric. From their window ten kilometres away around the coast, they could see the pall of smoke still sitting above the city.

The devastation of Thessaloniki seemed distant to Olga but on Thursday she received the news from Konstantinos that virtually all he owned had been destroyed.

'I am so sorry,' said her hostess, with tears in her eyes. 'How awful for you . . . to lose everything!'

Olga appreciated her concern but could not respond to this with the emotion required. Yes, it would be terrible to lose everything, but she did not feel it was true. She held 'everything' in her arms. This baby was now the centre of her world and nothing else mattered.

The following day Konstantinos, who was staying in a hotel in an undamaged quarter of the city, went to visit his wife and baby. He was already salvaging what remained of the warehouse. The entire stock had been destroyed but the foundations of the walls were still solid and he was already starting to rebuild. He had sent out orders so that he could build up his inventory again and was going to need somewhere for storage as soon as the new fabric arrived. Within a few days of filing his insurance claim, Konstantinos had put his emotions to one side.

'I will build an even better, stronger business than before,' he assured Olga.

Work would not begin for many months on their home. It was not Konstantinos' priority. Meanwhile, Olga knew that the kind hospitality she was receiving in Perea could not be for ever. It was an arrangement that was meant to last only a few days and by then they had been there for two weeks.

Although the seafront, and most of the city north-west of it, had been destroyed, the section of the upper town where Olga had grown up remained undamaged.

The small house at 3 Irini Street that she and her sister had jointly inherited from their parents was currently empty and Olga thought it would be the ideal place to stay while repairs were being made. Her sister had moved to Volos two years earlier to live with her son.

The next time that Konstantinos came out of the city to visit them, she tentatively suggested that they move there until the villa could be rebuilt.

'It's small, I know, but there will be enough space . . .'

Her voice tailed off. She could already sense Konstantinos' resistance to the idea.

The entire house would have fitted into the drawing room of

their old home; for a man who had never lived anywhere but on the affluent seafront, the thought of dwelling in an area where you rubbed shoulders, quite literally, with the poorest of Muslims and Jews was slightly abhorrent. He found it amazing that such pure beauty and pale skin as Olga's could have originated in the squalor and filth of the city's upper town.

But Olga was determined.

'Please, Konstantinos . . . Pavlina can sleep in the attic room. She doesn't mind,' appealed Olga. 'And it won't be for ever.'

It seemed there was no better solution. Any house that might have been available for rent had been razed to the ground. With some reluctance and many reservations, he agreed.

Later that week, Olga and the baby returned to the city. Pavlina had gone a few days in advance to clean the place up and Konstantinos would arrive that evening.

Although the driver approached the city along a route that avoided the most badly affected areas, the extent of the devastation was obvious. A month after the conflagration had destroyed almost the entire city, the unmistakable stench of fire-damage still hung in the air.

Olga caught a glimpse of the haunted shells of the city's great buildings, their blank windows looking out blindly towards the sea, and saw the remains of the Komninos villa.

She arrived in Irini Street with the baby at around midday. It was halfway through September but the sun was as strong as it had been in August.

When she got out of the carriage at the end of the narrow street, she saw that Pavlina was talking to someone she recognised. It was Roza Moreno, her neighbour.

Roza was overjoyed to see Olga and leaned in close to admire the baby.

'My dear, I am so happy to see you, and congratulations!' she said. 'What a time for the little man to be born! But what a joy to have you back here again.'

'Thank you, Roza. I'm very happy to be here again,' said Olga.

Almost automatically, as a gesture of trust and affection, she handed her baby to Kyria Moreno, who held him close to enjoy the sweet baby smell. Her two sons were still small, but the unique scent of the newborn quickly disappears.

Although they had not seen each other for more than two years, they quickly exchanged pleasantries and caught up with the major events of their lives.

'You'll find the street hasn't changed very much,' said Roza. 'We were so lucky that the fire didn't come this way. We lost our synagogue, but to be honest, we'd rather that than lose our home – but don't tell anyone I said that!'

'And the workshop?' enquired Olga, as Roza handed back the baby.

'Badly damaged, but not beyond repair!'

The Morenos, who lived at number 7, were a Jewish family who ran one of the busiest tailoring and dressmaking business in the city and were customers of Konstantinos Komninos. Roza's husband, Saul, had inherited the workshop from his father and one day he would pass it on to his sons, Elias and Isaac. Even though they were only one and four years old respectively, his plan was already made.

Within hours of the fire, Saul Moreno had started cutting new patterns to replace those he had lost and had a few suits tacked together ready for fitting. Many people had lost everything apart from what they stood up in, so he foresaw a boom ahead and was industrious enough to find a way to take advantage of it. A merchant in Veria had given him six months' credit on some rolls of reasonable wool and he immediately got to work again, visiting some of his clients in their homes to take measurements.

'I think we'll manage here, Olga, won't we?' Pavlina said as they stepped over the threshold.

'Yes, I think we will,' replied Olga. 'It's more like home than home . . .'

The few possessions they had, most of them blankets, sheets, nappies and other baby paraphernalia, were carried into the house. Kyria Moreno then arrived with an adapted fruit crate that would do for a makeshift crib. She had padded it comfortably on the inside and embroidered sheets and a quilt with Dimitri's name.

At number 5, between Olga and the Morenos, lived the Ekrems, a Muslim family with three daughters. Mrs Ekrem called in that same afternoon with gifts for the baby and some sweetmeats for Olga. She was a very good-hearted woman and mostly communicated through smiles and gestures with her neighbours, so limited was her Greek.

Olga was happy being back in the warm familiar surroundings of the home where she had grown up, in a street full of gentle memories. All of the families she had known in her childhood years were still in the same houses and were happy to see her again. They soon forgave her for having been such an infrequent visitor since her marriage.

The warmth and closeness of the next few days would be joyful for Olga, but not for Konstantinos. He found the proximity of other people in the neighbouring houses, hearing them through the walls to either side and even in the street below, intolerable. Most houses had become home to several families after the fire. There were refugee camps for those who had been left entirely homeless outside the city, but if you had a brother or a cousin with a roof still over their head, you expected them to share their good fortune. For this reason, several houses in Irini Street, with their overhanging floors and livestock in the basement, became ramshackle homes for anything up to fifteen people, with all the additional noise and chaos that entailed.

Konstantinos made his feelings clear, and though Olga had always obeyed what was probably the most important of her marriage vows, namely a promise never to cross her husband, there was a moment when she let slip an unguarded comment.

'It's so claustrophobic,' he complained after one disturbed night.

'I know it's not on the seafront, but I like it here.'

'You grew up in this street, Olga,' retorted her husband. 'So you're used to it!'

'Well, we're much better off than most people,' she said quietly.

Olga had heard stories of the refugee centres that had been set up on the outside of the city for the tens of thousands left homeless by the fire. Though many of them were well-ordered and run by kindly foreigners, everything was rationed and, come the winter, life would be harsh there. The only other option for the seventy thousand homeless (if their relatives could not accommodate them) was to take one of the free trains to Larissa or a boat to Volos, where new housing was being built. The majority of those who had been left destitute were Jews, and thousands of them had no choice but to leave.

Whatever those people had lost, Konstantinos felt that his loss was greater. He was not interested in relative sums. He'd been one of the richest men in the city; now his personal fortune had been reduced more than anyone's. The insurance company had written to say that the scale of the claims they had received meant that they were unable to offer him the full compensation he had expected.

'I would rather not be preached at by my wife,' he retorted. 'You just can't see anything wrong with this street, can you?'

'And all you can see are its faults. So why don't you find somewhere else to live?'

Olga did not see the hand that flew towards the side of her face. She just felt a single, stinging smack.

Pavlina returned from taking the baby out and was astonished to find Olga sobbing on her bed. When her mistress eventually lifted her head off the pillow to explain, Pavlina was shocked to see the red mark that had been left on her cheek.

'It's a disgrace,' said Pavlina. 'His father would never have done such a thing. Nor his brother.'

'And I wasn't preaching at him, Pavlina. I was just giving my own view.'

'And then he left, did he?'

'Yes, and he told me that he is going to stay elsewhere.'

The baby was needing to be fed now, so they could not continue the conversation, but Olga knew that the relationship with her husband would never be the same again.

Once she had recovered from the initial shock of the slap, Olga admitted to herself and to Pavlina that it was a great relief not to have her husband's thunderous presence in the small house. He sent a message to say that he had returned to the hotel where he had stayed after the fire. It was closer to his rebuilding projects, which was a plausible enough reason to give anyone in Irini Street who might wonder why Kyrios Komninos had moved out.

All was peaceful until a few days later, when Dimitri began to cry a great deal more than usual, and even Pavlina, who prided herself on her skills with the newborn, could do nothing. For someone who had been in the world for less than a month, the baby seemed able to reach an extraordinary volume with his yells.

Olga and Pavlina took turns to hold him in their arms and for hours at a time rocked him back and forth but nothing would stop his crying and no amount of feeding seemed to calm him down.

Konstantinos arrived unexpectedly one morning.

'I can hear our child in the street!' he shouted, partly in anger but also to make himself heard above the baby's screams. 'He must be ill! Why haven't you called the doctor?'

'Babies often cry like that once they find their lungs,' said Pavlina defensively, noticing Olga wince slightly at her husband's wrath.

Konstantinos spun round to face her.

'I shall tell Dr Papadakis to come this afternoon,' he said curtly. 'I know you have some experience, Pavlina, but I think a trained medical view would be worth getting.'

After this, apart from occasional visits, Konstantinos kept away. He provided as much money as was needed for food but did not stay to eat. He could not feel at home in a street where the animals seemed to outnumber the humans and where he felt as cramped as a pig in a pen.

Dr Papadakis soon appeared in Irini Street. He had never before visited this area of the city and, like Konstantinos Komninos, did not bother to hide his distaste. For the short duration of his visit, he wore the expression of a man on his way to another destination.

He examined mother and baby, and immediately declared that the problem was the mother's milk supply. It was not adequate. They would need to find a wet nurse for Dimitri.

Olga accepted the diagnosis with some sadness. She had so much enjoyed the closeness of feeding her baby, but she would do whatever was best for him.

The beauty of living in an overcrowded street was that there was always someone close by that you could call on, whether to mend a shoe, catch a rat, or run to the other end of the city with a letter. The solution to the problem of feeding Dimitri was very close at hand.

'I have almost stopped nursing Elias,' said Roza. 'But I have plenty of milk. Do you want me to take over?'

It seemed the most natural thing in the world.

So, within a day, Dimitri was suckling at a different breast. His stomach was full again and he was once again growing strong under his mother's constant, smiling gaze of adoration. She did not tell her husband the identity of the wet nurse. She knew he would not approve.

Even in this street, which to the rich might seem poor, a strong community thrived. Living cheek by jowl with each other made everyone more tolerant rather than less so.

The children all played together, Christian, Muslim and Jew. Whether they were chasing each other around the nearby church or one of the many minarets that still towered over the city, or scrambling over the ruins of a synagogue, it did not matter to any of them that these were places of worship. The name of the faith they represented was even less important.

They knew there were some differences between them. 'Why can't you talk like us, Isaac?' one of the Christian boys teased. 'And why can't you come out to play on Saturday?' The Muslim boys got teased too. 'I heard my father saying that your uncle was drunk last night!' '*So?* My mother says that as long as he doesn't buy *raki* himself, then it's all right!' This was how they lived in Irini Street, with tolerance and the habitual turning of a blind eye.

★　★　★

In November, there was a trial in the city that everyone followed with great interest. The couple who lived in the house where the great fire had supposedly started were accused of arson. Konstantinos, who was now visiting his wife in Irini Street less than once a week, happened to call in on the day of the verdict and was vehement that the fire had been an illegal act.

The couple had been acquitted, but it was against Konstantinos' nature to believe that such a catastrophe could have been a random event and he needed someone on whom to focus his anger for such losses.

'So, we're supposed to believe that the destruction of our city was just an accident?' he said, banging his fist down on the table.

It was a question that required no response. Olga did not dare to disagree with her husband over anything at all these days, though she quietly believed that the fact that the couple had lost everything they owned suggested their innocence.

On that particular morning, Komninos scarcely acknowledged his wife and baby. He only had eyes for the newspaper. Olga stood at the stove stirring her husband's coffee and observed that it took precisely the same amount of time for his anger to reach boiling point as it did for the dark liquid to rise in the *briki*. She poured it into the tiny cup, put it on the table beside him and backed away.

The acquittal of the destitute refugees was not the only significant news that day.

All month, there had been daily bulletins of events that were the result of the bitter division within Greece. Just before the devastating fire, King Constantine had left the country and been replaced by his second son, Alexander, who had defied his father to support Venizelos. After purging the army of royalists, Venizelos, once again Prime Minister, had led a superficially united Greece into war on the side of the Allies. As a result, Leonidas Komninos had gone to fight on the Macedonian front in the north of Greece.

The supplying of cloth for army uniforms had proved to be good business for Konstantinos Komninos. Every day of conflict could bring him huge riches. If he could get the business back on its feet, millions of drachmas could be his, and even with the infrastructure of the city in chaos, he could work the situation to his advantage.

Olga watched her husband as he swiftly leafed through the newspaper, taking in the rest of the day's news with hardly a glance. He was not going to spend much time mulling over the events of the war, even though his own brother was on the front line commanding troops. The only thing that interested him now was getting back to the warehouse, where scaffolding was being erected that day.

Komninos downed his coffee in one gulp before getting up, pecking Olga on the cheek and touching the baby's head. Dimitri was draped across her left shoulder in a deep slumber, oblivious to all the troubles of the world. Roza Moreno had just left and it would be a few hours before the baby stirred. His contentment and innocence were absolute.

'Is everything all right here? How's the baby sleeping?' His questions tumbled out one after the other, none of them requiring an answer. He was in a hurry to go and Olga had no desire to detain him.

'The warehouse should be ready in a few months,' he said. 'And then there's the showroom to sort out. After that I'll see what we can do about the house.'

And then he was gone. Olga stood at the doorway and watched the dapper figure swiftly retreating down the cobbled street. His dark, well-cut suit and felt hat stood out among the outfits worn by the residents of Irini Street. What struck her most forcibly was that his walk had virtually broken into a run. He could not get away fast enough.

The months passed happily in Irini Street. The temperatures had dropped, so everyone spent more of their time inside rather than on the street. Roza Moreno came five times a day and, after the late afternoon feed, often stayed for an hour or so having brought her boys with her.

On other days, Olga and Pavlina went next door to the Morenos and Kyria Ekrem would join them, along with her daughters. By the light of a flickering candle, storytelling would commence. There was always a generous slice of *toupishti*, the honey and walnut cake Roza made from a traditional Jewish recipe, to go with their coffee, and, with Elias on her lap, she related the stories of how her ancestors had arrived in Greece more than four centuries ago. She talked as if they had stepped off a boat earlier that same day.

'There were twenty thousand of us thrown out of Spain,' she said with mild outrage, 'but when we reached Thessaloniki, the Sultan was thrilled. "How foolish the Catholic monarchs must be to throw out the Jews. Turkey is all the richer for having them here, and Spain all the poorer!" he cried.'

Occasionally she would drop in a Ladino phrase and then translate.

'And we thrived here, the largest section of the population! There were dozens of synagogues, and Thessaloniki became known as *la Madre de Israel*.'

How she loved to talk.

'We recreated the golden age that we had once had in Spain, right here in Thessaloniki, and we found a familiar mixture of religions here: Muslim, Christian and Jew. We all lived happily together with our separate religions. There was even the same climate and the same food – pomegranates!' she said smiling.

Saul's mother, who lived with her son and daughter-in-law, spoke not a word of Greek and only conversed in Ladino. She was always in the corner, wearing her traditional Sephardic outfit, a white blouse embroidered with pearls, a long skirt and apron, a thick satin top coat, trimmed with fur, and a headscarf, also stitched with pearls. Sometimes she would tell a folk tale, which would be translated by her daughter-in-law into Greek.

The Ekrem girls were enthralled by her tales of this faraway city called Granada, which used to have so many mosques and a castle with turrets and writing in Arabic script on its walls. As they nibbled on pieces of sweet, moist walnut cake, they imagined it as a fairytale place, somewhere unimaginably beautiful and exotic where they might one day go together on a journey. Mrs Ekrem often read from one of her volumes of *The Thousand and One Nights* and, in the soporific half-light, they imagined their mother as Scheherazade, telling her engaging stories of fate and destiny. She would read a phrase in Turkish for her eldest daughter to translate into Greek.

When they sat there together in the small living space of the Moreno house, there was a curious mixture of fragrances: the herbs and spices they used in their cooking, the incense from church, the narcotic scent from a narghile, candlewax, sweet pastry, the odour of a baby's nappy and the sickliness of a mother's milk. When Saul Moreno eventually came in, they caught the sourness of his sweat. He was working hard to keep up with the ever increasing orders for army uniforms.

Dimitri got used to being passed from hand to hand and dandled from knee to knee, hearing a variety of accents and gazing up into different faces. He breathed in the dozen different scents, and loved the embraces from all these different families. For his first few months, all he saw were smiles. And every time he saw one, he smiled back.

'*Mitsi Mitsi Mitsi mou! Mitsi Mitsi Mitsi mou!*' the other children would chant, playing peek-a-boo and using the diminutive of his name.

Throughout these months, Konstantinos continued to supervise the reconstruction of his massive warehouse near the dock, expanding it into the space that had been occupied by the adjacent building, which had been razed to the ground. His perfunctory visits to Irini Street continued, but he could not help showing his distaste at the number and nature of the people who were crowded into houses that were no bigger than wardrobes.

When he came back to his home city on leave, Leonidas found he had no such dislike of Irini Street, and seemed to prefer it to the area in the city centre where his own squalid apartment was situated. Pavlina always welcomed him with a warm meal, Olga with her smile and Dimitri with unconcealed delight. The little boy adored his uncle, who would spend hours singing him nursery rhymes or performing magic tricks, making toffees or coins appear from nowhere. There were squeals of excitement and laughter whenever Uncle Leonidas appeared.

There was an overall rebuilding plan for the entire city that was being drawn up by a Frenchman, Ernest Hébrard. It specified that the small streets would be replaced by boulevards and grand build-ings. These would be much more in keeping with the scale of things that merchants such as Komninos aspired to, but while he celebrated the transformation of his city, the Muslims and Jews he shared it with did not. The Moreno family saw with dismay that the area of twisted lanes south of Egnatia Street where many Jews had lived was not going to be rebuilt on the old model and most of the Jewish community was to be pushed towards the outer edge of the city. It was the same for the areas of the city where many Muslims had lived. They were being shunted away from the centre too.

Through the sheer good fortune of having been spared the fire, the quarter where Irini Street was situated was outside the area for replanning. It may have been overcrowded, but it was a harmonious way of life that suited its residents, and none of them ever wanted it to change.

Konstantinos completed the rebuilding of the warehouse, and even before the first anniversary of the fire it was functional again, with a monthly income as high as it had been before – and even greater profits. He would now commence work on the showroom.

In November 1918, the war which had drawn in nations from every corner of the globe came to an end. The Greek divisions fighting on the Macedonian front had helped break German and Bulgarian resistance and the general collapse of Germany had followed. When the Armistice was signed and the victors began to carve up the sprawling Ottoman Empire, Eleftherios Venizelos was hoping that the Greek contribution would be recognised. For many years, he had nurtured a great dream, his '*megali idea*': to reclaim huge areas of Asia Minor from the Turks and to re-establish the Byzantine Empire. At the time, there were over one million Greeks living in various locations across Asia Minor, many of them in Constantinople. A central part of Venizelos' dream was to recapture this city, which had been taken from the Greeks in 1453.

As the terms of a treaty were being drawn up, Venizelos was hoping for control of Constantinople and Smyrna, a city on the west coast of Asia Minor. For many Muslims in Thessaloniki it was an uncomfortable time. The Allies had beaten their fellow Muslims in Turkey and they quietly wished that the Ottoman Empire had been victorious.

Before a peace treaty with Germany could be signed, however, Venizelos' ambition brought about a dangerous new mission for the Greek army. In May 1919, while his brother was counting his profits from the trading of wool and khaki, and his little nephew was playing hide and seek with his friends in Irini Street, Leonidas Komninos was heading towards Asia Minor. With the support of French, British and American ships, twenty thousand Greek troops occupied Smyrna, which was regarded as one of the finest ports in the Aegean.

The ostensible reason for the invasion was to protect the city from the Italians, who had landed just south of it, but Venizelos also claimed to be protecting the hundreds of thousands of Greeks who lived there from the Turks. Five years earlier, nearly a million Armenian Christians had been forced from their homes in Asia Minor and marched barefoot into the desert to die. There was concern that the Greeks who had inhabited the region for generations might meet the same fate, and such thoughts strengthened the motivation of Leonidas Komninos and his men.

The occupation was carried out with relatively little bloodshed (the Turkish commander had been told not to resist), but some atrocities were committed and several hundred Turks were slaughtered.

The following summer, Leonidas' regiment marched successfully eastwards. The objective was to extend the area of occupation close to Smyrna. As the Turkish Nationalist movement grew, resistance became increasingly fierce, but nevertheless the Greeks succeeded in occupying most of western Asia Minor, systematically destroying Turkish villages and exterminating their inhabitants as they passed through.

The taking of Smyrna had triggered a wave of nationalism among the Turks and many of them dreamed of revenge. They now retaliated by slaughtering thousands of Greeks, including many who lived near the Black Sea. Brutality on a shocking scale was perpetrated by both sides, and villages and towns were wiped out.

During this time, Leonidas came home just once on leave. He visited his brother at the warehouse, but spent most of his week sitting quietly in the house in Irini Street. Olga found him changed. He seemed to have aged ten years in only one.

There was one way in which he did seem the same, however. In spite of the fact that he was exhausted he still had time and energy for little Dimitri. On this visit he had brought him a hoop and he kept his nephew amused for hours by trying to teach him over and over again how to balance it.

In early 1921, Leonidas' regiment was part of a new offensive. This time the aim was to reach Ankara. Although the Greeks were defeated in two significant battles, they managed to occupy some strategic positions in central Asia Minor and by the summer it appeared that victory over the entire region was finally within their grasp. Even at the time, Leonidas considered it an error not to press on to victory but the order was to halt and the regiment had no choice but to obey. Just as he feared, the Turks used this time to organise a new line of defence on the other side of the river Sakarya, one hundred kilometres west of Ankara.

The Greeks eventually advanced to the river. With their superior numbers, it might have been an easy victory, but after a bloody twenty-one-day battle against an enemy that occupied positions on higher ground, they began to run out of ammunition and had to retreat, withdrawing to the lines they had held two months earlier.

Even though they had not been entirely defeated, morale among the men was low and within the senior ranks many, including Leonidas, campaigned for withdrawal westwards towards Smyrna. Others persisted in their fantasy of taking Constantinople and so Greek troops were obliged to stay and defend their positions. For almost a year, there was a stalemate.

Meanwhile the Turks were busy organising their troops for a final battle. They were not interested in any kind of settlement with the Greeks. The man in charge of their campaign had been born in Thessaloniki, only a few hundred metres from Leonidas himself. Forty years old, the ice-blue-eyed Kemal Ataturk was now leading the Nationalist movement in Asia Minor, and with a government established in Ankara, he was hellbent on crushing the Greeks and driving them back to the Mediterranean.

At the end of August 1922, Ataturk attacked the Greeks' defensive positions and within a few days, half of the invading soldiers had been captured or killed.

The defeated men had no time to dig the sun-baked earth, and fields lay strewn with unburied dead, many of them stripped of their boots and weapons. Clouds of buzzing, blue-black flies hovered menacingly, waiting for the vultures to have their fill. There were no flowers or funeral rites, and the Greek heroes of battle lay unmourned and, before long, unrecognisable.

Survivors fled westwards towards Smyrna, intent on self-preservation. Many of them paused to commit appalling atrocities en route, raping, massacring and looting, before razing whole towns to the ground. In one Muslim village, all the inhabitants – men, women and children – were locked inside the mosque before it was ignited.

In the first week of September, thousands of Greek soldiers, Leonidas among them, arrived in Smyrna hoping to escape from the country by boat. Hot on their heels came the Turkish army, aflame with desire for revenge. Three years had passed since the Turks had lost the city, but they had always planned to take it back.

# Chapter Five

L EONIDAS LAY SLUMPED against the wall of a grain store. His head
had fallen forward onto his chest and his tattered uniform was
smeared with dried blood. Filthy, bruise-blackened toes protruded
through the ends of his boots.

A few hundred yards away, a woman and her daughter turned
into the street, fresh and clean in their pale summer frocks. The
little girl skipped, and chatted, as sweet as rose petal syrup, looking
about her eager and curious. She knew something was happening
in her city but she did not know what.

Close to her breast, the mother also carried a baby, dressed in
matching cotton lawn, embroidered with pink daisies.

The past few days had brought rapid change to their beautiful
city. In spite of recent events in the rest of Turkey, Smyrna had
been relatively carefree since the turbulent few days of 1919 when
the Greek troops had taken it over, and its residents were curiously
oblivious to the upheavals taking place elsewhere in Asia Minor.
The recent warm summer days had seen people on the streets
selling their harvests of figs, apricots and pomegranates, and bargains
had been struck for opium, satin and frankincense in a dozen
different languages by people in an array of native dress from

turbaned Persians to fez-topped Turks. In the previous month the opera had sold out every night, and open-air cafés had been full, their customers serenaded by string quartets.

Only a week ago this street had been suffused with the aroma of jasmine and freshly baked bread from a nearby bakery. Now it stank of unwashed men. A few days before, following the sudden arrival of thousands of Greek soldiers, waves of Greek civilian refugees had also begun to pour in from the interior. Like the soldiers, they were fleeing from the Turkish army and were destitute.

The population of Smyrna was now fearful, especially when they heard a rumour that the Turkish cavalry was on the outskirts of the city.

'Come on, *agapi mou*, let's walk a bit faster,' the young mother said with suppressed alarm.

As they passed, she cast a sideways glance at the row of Greek soldiers who lay there, all identically positioned, their heads uniformly angled, legs splayed. They looked as though they had fallen before a firing squad. Their state of semi-consciousness was the result of a relentless thousand-kilometre march, with few supplies except those they had pillaged from the towns and settlements along their route. They were comatose with exhaustion.

It was then that the woman noticed they were the object of the soldiers' stares.

'We have to get home. Now!' she said, almost breaking into a run and pulling the child along. The uncanny silence of the streets, the dead bodies that seemed to be stirring to life, the lurking dogs – none of this was normal for Smyrna and she was disturbed beyond all feelings of fear. Her senses were on alert. Like the mangy hounds in the shadows, she was aware of an unknown, but imminent danger.

Meanwhile, in the dark space of Leonidas' mind, memories and hallucinations swirled in a devilish dance. Though he did not yet know it, the foul recollections of what he had seen and perpetrated would never be washed from his mind. Sweet dreams would never come again. With his few surviving men, he had arrived on the outskirts of Smyrna a few days earlier, hoping to sail home to Thessaloniki. British, French, Italian and American warships basked in the harbour, but there was not a Greek flag in sight. They were too late. The Greek ships carrying thousands of their fellow soldiers had departed.

Exhausted from their journey, they had found somewhere to rest in a quiet street. There would be a solution but for now, on these lumpy cobbles, they succumbed to troubled sleep.

Several hours later, a grey blanket settled over Leonidas. It was not like the comforting counterpane that his mother used to spread over him for winter warmth. It was a layer of dark smoke, creeping up his nostrils and down into his lungs. He dreamed of the fire that had destroyed his family's business. His recollection of the temperature on that day and the strength of the blaze was so vivid. And then came the screams.

'*Fire! Fire! The city is on fire!*'

The cries awoke him and he realised that the acrid, bitter stench of smoke was not just in his dream. The situation in Smyrna had been relatively ordered, given that the city's population had swollen by several hundred thousand in the past few days, but chaos now took hold and shook the city like an earthquake. People ran through the streets screaming and crying. Fear was in the eyes of both wealthy and poor. The city had caught light.

All the men leaped to their feet. Panic swept away exhaustion. Streams of people swarmed past them towards the sea, a few with babes in arms, but most of them with nothing. There were groups of children who had disgorged from schools and orphanages, and a wealthy woman who had grabbed the most valuable coat she had and now stood incongruously dressed in sable. The refugees who had come into the city in the past few days clung on to their bundles of possessions with which they had already trekked for hundreds, if not thousands, of kilometres. All of them were heading in the same direction. To the harbour.

The Armenian quarter of Smyrna had been torched by the Turkish cavalry, who now rode through the city wreaking havoc and destruction. Greeks hiding in their homes would listen with terror from an upper floor as their doors were beaten down and their rooms ransacked. They would then smell petroleum being sprinkled about before their homes were ignited. The choice was this: to reveal their presence and be cut to pieces or to be incinerated and die in the fumes.

Stories travelled as fast as the fire: of rape and mutilation, of rows of heads from decapitated women on stakes, of rats feasting on entrails. Whatever crimes the Greeks had committed, the Turks were intent on exacting revenge a hundredfold. The only real hope was to get out to sea. Smyrna was melting around them.

'We have to try and get out,' said Leonidas to his men. He felt that he had already failed them, by being left stranded in this city.

'We're an easy target like this, aren't we?' said one of the youngest recruits, plucking at his army shirt.

'Nobody is safe from the Turks,' answered his captain. 'But it would probably be safest if we separate and take different routes to the harbour. It will make us less obvious.'

'Where will we meet?'

'Just get any boat you can. And we'll see each other again in Thessaloniki.'

After two years of being in each other's company it was a

perfunctory parting, but each of them had to look out for himself now. Leonidas watched the tattered remains of his regiment join the human flow that surged down towards the sea. Soon they became indistinguishable from the rest.

Before following, Leonidas looked behind him. Columns of fire and smoke plumed high into the air. The ground where he stood was suddenly rocked by an explosion and then he heard the crash of a collapsing building, the sound of shattering glass, the thud of falling masonry. Like hundreds of thousands of others, he sensed that time was running out to escape from this flaming city.

Down at the port, both residents and refugees were fighting for places on any boat they could. What had begun in an orderly fashion, with people quietly queuing and hopeful for a place, had descended into chaos. With the city on fire and atrocities being perpetrated just a few hundred metres away, panic was taking hold. The temperature of fear increased with every person who arrived to join the crowd, which was now enclosed in a space just one kilometre wide and a few hundred metres deep. It was a catastrophe.

Alone and unencumbered by possessions, Leonidas was able to manoeuvre himself towards the centre of the crowd. He could see small boats piled high with chairs, mattresses and trunks being rowed out to sea. Other vessels meant for one man and his fishing nets had twenty people on board. There was the sound of splashing as people threw themselves into the sea, intent on swimming out to one of the Italian boats to plead for refuge. Occasionally there was the sound of gunfire as a swimmer was picked off by a Turkish sniper.

Leonidas felt a wave of shame. Every Greek killed was revenge for a dead Turk. What a pointless game of numbers it seemed to have become. Death for the man he saw vanishing beneath the surface of the water was speedy but he knew there had been times when he and his men had ensured that a victim's suffering was long and painful before they allowed him his final gasp.

Flashes of the shame and horror of the past few months had haunted his dreams, but now plagued his every waking moment too. He turned away from the water and pushed against the tide of people to find his way to the back of the crowd. His eyes were stinging with tears from the smoke but sobs came from deep within. He could not leave. With all the crimes that weighed on his conscience, how could he push in front of any other man, woman or child? There was not one person here who did not deserve to live more than he. In all those months of the campaign, the soldiers had been swept along on a tide of hatred and self-justification, but now it was self-loathing that tore at his heart. Base acts of animal violence swam in front of his eyes, one after another, then another and another . . . The harbour of Smyrna had disappeared for him and in its place were dark images from the past weeks.

Anyone not entirely preoccupied by their own plans for escape would have noticed a skeletal, sunburned soldier walking as though in a trance away from the sea. His ragged hair was white with dust, and tears ran between the deep crevices of his prematurely aged and wrinkled skin.

Coming in the other direction was the woman with her two girls in their embroidered frocks. She was desperate for places for herself and her daughters. '*Athina*?' she asked repeatedly, as she followed directions towards the queue for a ship to Piraeus, the closest port to Athens. Her politeness and her elegance were a passport through the crowd and people parted to let her and her infants through. The baby's pitiful cries were enough to arouse sympathy in even the hardest heart.

As the woman continued on her way, a building went up in flames close by and sparks flew. She was only metres from the front of the queue.

At that moment, a glowing ember dropped onto the little girl's sleeve. The fabric immediately melted away, burning the skin beneath, and she shrieked in pain, pulling away from her mother to extinguish the flame. Meanwhile, her mother was being relentlessly swept forward, and in the next moment had been ushered onto a small boat. It would take her to the Piraeus-bound ship that was safely anchored some distance away.

Realising that her daughter was not with her, the woman began to scream.

'Where's my Katerina? Where's my little girl? Katerina! Katerina! Katerina! My little one!'

She clamoured to be allowed off but her desperate attempts to stand up caused the little vessel to rock precariously and her panic was clearly putting everyone in danger.

'People are fighting to get *on* these boats, not off!' insisted a burly man, grabbing her wrists and pulling her down. 'Now just bloody well sit down so we can get out of here! Someone else will bring your kid.'

A wall of people now stood between the five-year-old and the water, obscuring the sight and sound of her sobbing mother.

The little girl was preternaturally calm. This was her home city and she was certain to find someone to help her. Surrounded by the maelstrom of shouting, fear and burning, she wandered away from the port. The agony of her raw skin now began to torment her.

Meanwhile, Leonidas continued to meander blindly away from the crowds. There was an intense throbbing inside his head, as though the screams around him were within his skull. He sank down in a doorway and buried his head in his hands, wanting to block out the chaos around him.

Eventually he looked up, as if he could feel the child's eyes on him. In her white dress, she looked like an angel without wings, and behind her pale silhouette the distant fire surrounded her with a supernatural glow. She was a fairy, a spirit, but she was crying.

This vision stirred him to action and he stood up.

This little angel made him feel brave. He saw that she was clutching her arm.

'It hurts,' she said, bravely.

'Let me look.'

The vulnerable patch of raw skin needed protection and, without a moment's hesitation, he ripped off his shirtsleeve.

'You must get it bandaged up properly, but this will do for now,' he said, tying the fabric round her arm. The heavy cotton khaki looked incongruous next to the fine white muslin, which he noticed was embroidered with delicate flowers.

'So where are you going? Why are you wandering about alone?'

'My mother and sister have gone . . .' she turned and pointed towards the sea, '. . . on a boat.'

Her innocence was transcendent.

'We have to get you on a boat, then, don't we?'

She held her arms out so that he could pick her up and together they went back towards the clamouring crowds.

'What's your name?' he asked her. 'And where do you come from?'

'I'm Katerina. And I don't come from anywhere.'

'You must come from somewhere,' he teased, happily distracting her with their conversation.

'I didn't have to come from somewhere. I was already here.'

'So this is where you live. In Smyrna?'

'Yes.' Almost impossibly, Leonidas found himself smiling. Her childlike detachment from her situation seemed almost mystical. His own despair seemed to lift.

Katerina was weightless in his arms. As light as a fairy, he mused. He had only ever lifted one other child, his nephew, Dimitri, and that was more than a year ago. Even then, Dimitri had been heavier than this little person. In spite of the rank odour of sweat and smoke around him, he could smell that the child who wrapped her arms so tightly round his neck gave off an aroma of clean linen and fresh flowers.

The dense crowd responded to his authoritative voice and what remained of his soldier's uniform, and parted to let them through. He could feel the crunch of broken glass and had to avoid tripping on all the abandoned domestic objects underfoot. A small child, especially a barefooted child, as so many were, would not have survived for a minute all alone in this chaos.

Leonidas spoke to a woman who seemed in charge and explained that the child was injured. Soon she was being helped into a boat.

'Look after my sleeve!' he shouted cheerily. 'I'll need it back!'

'I promise!' the little girl called out.

Hers was the first smile he had seen in a year. In all his time in active service, he had rarely seen such stoicism.

Leonidas waved until she was a speck on the horizon. Then he headed back to the flaming ruins of the city.

# Chapter Six

As each stroke of the oars took them closer to the big ship anchored out in the bay, Katerina grew excited at the thought of seeing her mother. When they drew up alongside, she grasped the metal steps and began to climb. Her arm was throbbing and when strange hands reached down towards her and lifted her onto the deck she winced with pain as one of them touched her arm. A well-meaning woman patted her on the head, gave her a piece of bread and a cup of water and settled her onto a bench. The ship was crammed full of women and children. Husbands and fathers were away in the army and thousands of them had died in recent months. Almost all of these women were widows.

'Are you alone?' enquired a woman who seemed to be in charge.

'My mother's here,' Katerina replied. 'But I don't know where.'

'Shall we go for a walk then, and see if we can find her?'

She took Katerina's hand and together they walked the length and breadth of the ship. Many people were in great distress. Some were wounded, others rocked back and forth, traumatised by the events of the past twenty-four hours.

Katerina's grip on the woman's hand tightened.

'Can you tell me what she looks like?' the woman asked. 'What was she wearing?'

'She had on a dress like mine,' answered Katerina with certainty. 'When she makes a dress for herself she always makes one for me that's the same.'

'It's a very pretty dress, then!' she said smiling. Although the little girl's dress was grubby, she could see it had once been beautiful. It was covered with embroidered daisies and edged with lace but now, rather incongruously, one of the sleeves appeared to have been made out of a different fabric.

'But what have you done to your arm?'

'It caught fire,' answered Katerina.

'Oh dear! Well, as soon as we've found your mother, we'll have it looked at,' continued the woman with a concerned voice. 'Now, can you see her on deck? If not, I'm sure she will be inside.'

'She's with a baby,' Katerina said chattily, 'who's only a few months old.'

It was beginning to dawn on the woman that this search might be fruitless, so she tried to distract Katerina with conversation, asking her questions about her sibling, whether it was a boy or a girl, her name and so on. After a twenty-minute search, it was becoming obvious to the woman that the mother was not going to be found. She was loath to crush the child's cheerful spirit, but sooner or later she would have to tell her that they had run out of possibilities. Her mother was not on this boat.

'I am sure we will find her, but for a little while we'll have to ask someone else to look after you . . .'

Another rowing boat had arrived to offload its human cargo onto the ship. There was precious little space left and the woman who was helping to arrange the evacuation looked over anxiously.

'Excuse me!' she said to a woman who was sitting between two children, on a huge bundle that now contained everything they owned. 'Would you mind keeping an eye on this little one for a moment?'

The mother held out her hands towards Katerina.

'Of course, come and sit with us,' she said kindly. 'Move up, Maria.'

Katerina heard a slightly strange accent, but it did not make the woman too hard to understand. One of the two children snuggled closer to her mother to make space for Katerina.

'Make yourself nice and comfy,' said the mother. 'I'm Kyria Eugenia and these are my daughters, Maria and Sofia.'

It was dusk. The engines began to throb and the heavy clank of the anchor being pulled up alerted everyone to the ship's imminent departure. Katerina's head lolled onto Maria's shoulder and with the motion of the ship the three little girls were soon asleep. They were among the last of the two hundred thousand people evacuated from Smyrna in those terrifying few days.

By sunrise, the ship had docked.

The night before, Katerina had been so tired that she had not taken in that the two girls she was now travelling with were identical twins. She looked from one to the other and rubbed her eyes, wondering if they were playing tricks on her. Both of them giggled. They were well accustomed to such a reaction and played on their uncanny similarity.

'Who is who?' asked Sofia.

'You're Maria!' answered Katerina.

'Wrong!' cried Sofia with delight. 'Now hide your eyes!'

Katerina did what she was told and when Sofia shouted 'Ready!' she opened them.

'What's my name?' asked Sofia.

'Maria!'

'Wrong again!'

She had never seen such similitude. To the millimetre their hair was cut the same length and their red dresses were indistinguish-able from each other. Even the freckles on their noses matched. It was an hour or so before they were all allowed to disembark, and during that time they played lots of games with Katerina, all based on their similarity. By the time they were allowed onto land, they were firm friends. The three of them followed Eugenia down the gangplank, holding hands like paper dolls.

A soldier threw Eugenia's bundle into a waiting truck and they climbed in after it.

'Where are we going?' Katerina heard Kyria Eugenia ask, but the soldier's response was inaudible. They were somewhere she did not recognise and, for the first time since their parting, the certainty that her mother was close by left her. It already seemed a very long time since she had seen her. Was it a day? A week? A month? She sank back against some crates, pulled her knees in towards herself and cried quietly so that no one would notice. She knew this was the best way.

Not so long ago, her mother had sat her down and said, 'You must be brave, my little one.'

She remembered that her mother had been weeping herself at the time, so Katerina felt it was for her sake that she must refrain from crying too.

'Your father won't be coming back from the war. He was very courageous and died saving someone else.'

Katerina had felt proud of her father and, even at her young age, she knew how to bury her sadness and to make sure that it did not make anyone else feel unhappy too.

When they reached the camp where tens of thousands of others had already settled, her confidence returned and she began to ask questions of Kyria Eugenia.

'Where have they brought us? Why are we here? Are we going to see my mother?'

'Well, Katerina,' she said, in her gentlest voice, 'we're on an island called Mytilini now. But I am sure they will try to find—'

'But my mother wanted to go to Athens!' the little girl said with alarm. 'Is it far away?'

'It's not such a big distance from here,' Eugenia replied reassuringly, squeezing her hand.

There was no point in telling the child the truth. Those who had been in charge of organising the evacuation from Smyrna were interested only in shifting the huge number of people to safety. Getting them away from the flames and the vengeful Turks had been their priority, not keeping records of who went where and with whom. There were a million or more people on the move and the chances of tracing Katerina's mother were virtually non-existent.

'I'm sure we'll find her later on, my sweetness.'

'I'm hungry,' whined Sofia, passing a queue for soup. 'Can't we have something to eat?'

'Let's find somewhere to sleep first and then we'll get something,' answered her mother. She could see from the sheer volume of humanity milling around that only a percentage of the refugees would be sleeping under canvas that night. There was not enough accommodation for them all.

For several hours they waited patiently for a tent to be allocated to them, and all the while Katerina's eyes darted left and right, eagerly hoping for a glimpse of her mother. No one told her that Mytilini was nearly two hundred and fifty kilometres from Athens.

Once in their tent, Sofia continued to whine. Though they

looked the same, Katerina was already noticing that the twins were very different in other ways.

While they were still on the boat, Sofia had proudly told her that she had 'come out first'. Maria had protested that it was only by a matter of minutes, but clearly her earlier emergence into the world had given Sofia the confidence that made her the leader of the two. Her twin, Maria, was her reflection. Like an echo she often repeated Sofia's views rather than having her own and she was certainly the gentler of the two.

Eventually, the exhausted trio of children lay down on a straw mattress and sank into a deep slumber, their hunger forgotten.

Eugenia stood outside and looked up and down the row of tents. Most of these refugees had lost every possession they owned, as well as members of their family. Many of them were in a trance-like state, as though sleepwalking, their lined faces without expression. When she saw one of the occupants emerging from the adjacent tent, she greeted her. Living less than a metre from each other, with nothing more than thin canvas to divide them, this woman was now her close neighbour but she gave not even the slightest acknowledgement that Eugenia was there.

Almost immediately, Eugenia understood why. Wrapped within the folds of her voluminous dress, typical of the style worn by the more rural Pontic Greeks, the woman held a sick child. Eugenia noticed that she was weeping, but the child itself was limp and silent.

The woman drew her headscarf across her face and hastened away without meeting Eugenia's eye. Dysentery. There had been rumours in the accommodation queue that it was wiping out hundreds of people every day and a knot of fear tightened in Eugenia's stomach. She hoped they would be out of this place soon.

★ ★ ★

The girls woke up to a feast of bread, tomatoes and milk. It was more than a day since they had eaten. The twins had quickly accepted that Katerina was part of yet another change in their lives. In the past few months, everything had altered so dramatically that having an additional person with them seemed a small detail.

As soon as they had eaten, Eugenia took Katerina to the first-aid post. The nurse carefully removed the 'bandage' that had been protecting her arm. Beneath it, the flesh was raw from shoulder to elbow.

'We'd better get this cleaned up and dressed straightaway,' she said, with no attempt to conceal her surprise at the extent of the wound. 'Does it hurt?'

'Yes, but I try not to think about it,' answered the little girl.

Katerina winced as the nurse applied ointment, but within moments, the stinging flesh was hidden away beneath a gleaming bandage and the little girl looked down proudly at the flawlessly bound arm.

'Bring her back to see me in four days' time,' the nurse told Eugenia. 'I want to make sure it's still clean. There are enough bacteria around here to wipe out the whole lot of us in the blink of an eye . . .'

Eugenia took Katerina's hand and led her quickly out of the tent. She was angry with the nurse for saying such things in front of a child.

The two of them walked along the narrow 'streets' of the refugee camp, working their way towards the row where the twins awaited their return. Suddenly Katerina remembered something. The sleeve.

'Kyria Eugenia! We've got to go back! Please! I left something there.'

The anguish in the child's voice gave her no option. Within minutes, pulling on Eugenia's hand, Katerina had dragged her back to the medical tent. The little girl went straight up to the nurse, who was attending an injured woman.

'Do you still have my old bandage?'

The nurse paused in her work and gave the child a withering look.

Katerina looked around. The floor had been swept and she spotted a pile of debris by the tent flap.

'It's there!' she said triumphantly, running over to pick it up.

'But, Katerina, it's filthy. Wouldn't it be better to leave it behind?' pleaded Eugenia, mindful of what the nurse had said about the virulent bacteria rampaging through the camp.

'But I promised . . .' She held on to it tightly.

Eugenia knew how stubborn little girls could be and she could see the determination on Katerina's face.

'Very well, but we will have to give it a good wash as soon as we can.'

Before they left the tent, Eugenia noted the look of disgust on the nurse's face. There seemed no harm in keeping a child happy in these circumstances, she mused to herself. Katerina's contented expression showed how much it meant to her to have retrieved the rag.

'I promised to give it back to the soldier,' she explained. 'It's still got one of his buttons.'

Eugenia took a closer look and sure enough there was a button still attached to it. It was tarnished, but there it was, still hanging by a thread.

Katerina put it away in her pocket and they returned to their tent to find the twins.

The task of tracking down her mother still preoccupied Katerina, and she and Eugenia spent many hours walking up and down rows of makeshift tents to see if they could find her. Many of the families they met were Pontic Greeks, like Eugenia and her daughters – people who had lived near the Black Sea – and Eugenia even found some from her village near Trebizond. In the one-thousand-kilometre flight from their homes to Smyrna, families and friends had become separated and she was overjoyed to re-establish contact with some people she knew.

Katerina did not see one familiar face from Smyrna and the camp organisers confirmed to Eugenia that no one named Zenia Sarafoglou had registered with them.

Silently, Eugenia accepted that she might need to keep Katerina with her. All around there were similar situations and depleted families were being formed into new shapes by loss and adoption. Maria and Sofia were beginning to regard the newcomer as a permanent sister. Like many nine-year-old girls, they had strong maternal instincts. Until now, they had shared a single doll between them, but now they had a bigger than life-size version. Katerina basked in their attention and even allowed them to rebandage her arm whenever it was necessary. It was beginning to heal, but the arm would be badly scarred.

The mild October weather encouraged them to play outside for most of the day, and with plenty of children all around, the three girls made new friends. But as weeks turned into months, and the temperatures dropped, they retreated more and more into their tents. Among the possessions she had carried with her across the plains of Asia Minor, Eugenia had brought some of her embroidery silks and some wool left over from a rug she had been weaving. Under her guidance, the girls began to fill their days making patchwork blankets from scraps of material they found in the camp. Sometimes there was a delivery of old clothes from a philanthropic organisation in America and they would be given something 'new' to wear, which could be embellished with colourful stitching, appliqué and plenty of imagination. On one particular day, in a moment of boredom, Maria had pushed her needle through the canvas of the tent-flap and soon they had covered their 'door' with stitches, 'writing' their names in red, green and blue and decorating them with flowers and leaves.

For a final flourish, Eugenia traced the words '*Spiti mou, spitaki mou*' in large stitches. This was what the tent had become: 'Home Sweet Home'.

For the children at least, the traumatic departure from their homes began to fade in their memories and dreams became sweet once more.

Even though the efforts of the adults to keep the children happy were largely successful, they were all too aware of the ever-deteriorating conditions of the camp and were growing weary of the stultifying inactivity.

Eugenia knew that their old life in Asia Minor could never be recovered, but she could not begin to contemplate the thought of a permanent life in Mytilini's unfriendly landscape. They were playing a waiting game. Many had died of disease in the camp and there was always the possibility that it would be their turn next. What an irony, thought Eugenia, to have survived such hardships to reach Smyrna and then to die here.

There was enough food but winter was beginning to bite, with plummeting temperatures and torrential rainfall.

Rumours began to reach them that diplomatic efforts were being made to resolve their situation. That at least was a comfort. Even if time had no real meaning for the children, most adults felt the relentless passage of the days and wondered how much of their lives were to be squandered in this place.

One day they heard the welcome news that they were all to be taken to the mainland. Though the numbers were massively imbalanced, there was to be an official exchange of populations between Greece and Turkey.

After the catastrophic wars of hatred and violence of recent years, the politicians considered this the only solution. Muslims could no longer live in safety in Greece, and the Greeks could no longer live comfortably with the Muslims in Turkey. With its vast land mass and large population, the exchange would make relatively little impact on Turkey, but it would change Greece beyond recognition, swelling the number of people living in the small, under-resourced nation from four and a half million to six million in a matter of months. The effect of increasing the population by twenty-five per cent would be particularly dramatic since the majority of the newcomers would arrive with little more than the clothes they stood in.

In January 1923 a convention was drawn up in Lausanne. Within a year this unprecedented migration of populations from one country to another would be complete.

# Chapter Seven

Throughout the spring, there was great anticipation in the camp before arrangements for departure were finalised. Katerina overheard one conversation after another about where they might go and a single word kept spinning round and round in her head: Athinathinathinathina. It was the last word she had heard her mother say: '*Athina*'. Athens.

Katerina was excited at the renewed prospect of finding her mother and sister, and began to count the days. Each day she put one small cross-stitch on the hem of her dress. Before she had sewn all the way around, she hoped to be with her once again.

The adults seemed excited at the prospect of going. Homes were promised there and Katerina was sure that this was where she would be reunited with her family.

Finally, a huge ship docked in Mytilini and everyone waited to hear whether they were included on the passenger list. As soon as she had confirmation, Eugenia and the girls began to pack up.

Many more families had flooded into the camp in the past few months and conditions had deteriorated badly. With the rising spring temperatures, disease spread rapidly and healthy children were often snatched away from their despairing parents in a matter of hours.

As Eugenia and the girls gathered their possessions, they were not sorry to be leaving. The embroidered tent-flap, now adorned with flowers and foliage around the words 'Home Sweet Home', seemed less appropriate now.

Down at the dock, there was plenty of noise and bustle. It was like a large-scale excursion with the atmosphere of a *panegyri*, a saint's day feast, and for the first time they felt the warmth of the spring sunshine on their faces.

Friends who were already on board called out and waved. They were thrilled to be on the move, and full of excitement and anticipation. At last, there was the possibility of a new life, with all the opportunities that Athens promised.

With one twin on each side of her, Katerina stood behind Eugenia. They were right at the front of the line now, and the grubby odours of diesel fumes and engine oil could not have smelled sweeter.

Eugenia looked up; one of their neighbours from the tented 'street' waved and called out from the upper deck. Passengers were crammed onto the boat, and the familiar face soon disappeared into the crowd that surged around her. The boat was packed on every level.

The uniformed official began to draw the barrier across.

'I'm sorry. It's full. In fact, it's over full, Kyria. They have given passage to one hundred more people than this old crate should take.'

'But surely it can take another four! What difference will it make?'

'You will have to wait for the next one.'

'But when will that be?' protested Eugenia, trying to hold back her tears.

'We're expecting another one. I can't say when. But everyone here will be moved off the island in due course,' the official replied in the polite, dispassionate tone of one who would return to his own bed that night.

The only way in which the man's life had been affected by these events had been the increase in his salary. He had made a killing in the past few days, accepting bribes from those who could afford a payment to get to the top of the list.

They watched with dismay as the boat pulled out of the harbour and Eugenia saw the faces of her friends diminish to invisibility. The official stood with his back to them, as though he wished to block the view of her vanishing hopes.

She dropped her bundle of possessions down in front of her, almost on the official's feet.

'We will sit here, then,' she said. 'Then we'll be at the front of the queue.'

'Be my guests,' he said superciliously, and walked away.

Less than an hour later, a second boat was spotted on the horizon. After what seemed a painfully long time, the ship docked and once again, the tedious process of registration had to be gone through. Eugenia sent the three girls off to see if they could find something to eat and gave the names of herself and the children to a new official. The previous one had disappeared and this new one seemed more sympathetic.

'How long will it take to get to Athens?' she asked him.

'You aren't going to Athens,' he replied matter-of-factly, without even glancing up from the form he was filling out with Eugenia's details. 'You're going to Thessaloniki.'

'Thessaloniki!' Eugenia felt a surge of panic. 'But we don't want to go to Thessaloniki! We know nobody in Thessaloniki. All the people from my village have gone to Athens!'

'Well, it's up to you. There are plenty of people in the queue right behind you who would be happy to take your places on this boat. And I can't keep them all waiting.'

Eugenia made one last plea: 'But Katerina is not my daughter. And her mother is in Athens! We need to get her there.'

The official was unimpressed. Such separations and misplacements were a common occurrence at these times.

'Well, there is no boat going to Athens, but there is one going to Thessaloniki.'

'When will there be one for Athens?'

'I have no idea and nor does anyone else. Look, Kyria, this is not a pleasure excursion so you'd be wise to make up your mind sooner rather than later about whether you want your names on the passenger list.' He moved her form to one side of his desk. 'If you'll just step to one side now . . .' he added impatiently. 'There are hundreds of people behind you who don't look as if they will be so particular about where they are going.'

Eugenia watched as the breeze lifted the edge of the paper. A strong gust of this wind, and her entitlement to a place on the ship could be floating away.

She had less than a second to decide. Though Athens was the destination of all their fellow villagers, Thessaloniki was closer; but the one really decisive factor was that there were no other guaranteed options.

'We'll go!' she said, slapping her hand down on the form. 'Please. We'll take these places.'

'Very well,' the official responded. 'Could you sign your name here, confirming you are mother to the two girls and . . . here, confirming you are responsible for the third?'

Eugenia did not hesitate now and wrote her name, clumsily, on the two lines. She had never doubted, even for a moment, that she should look after Katerina until the child's mother was found. Nothing had seemed more natural. From the moment when this bonny child in her torn white dress had been given to her on the boat from Smyrna she had loved her as her own. If the misfortunes of conflict against the Turks had not taken her husband away – he was officially missing – she would probably have had several more children. Perhaps this was why she had welcomed this 'addition' to her family with such a ready embrace.

The four of them were the first on board, so it seemed like many hours later that the ship was finally full and ready to leave. There was the clank of chains and the children, who had been running up and down on deck, excited at the thought of the new journey, returned to Eugenia.

She did not tell them where they were going. Her daughters would be distressed that they were not going to join their old friends, and Katerina would know that her mother would not be waiting at the end of their journey. In other ways, perhaps none of them would ever know the difference between Athens and Thessaloniki.

The boat drifted through the night, the waters illuminated by a full moon. The children slept soundly. Their possessions became their pillows and the blankets they had been given in the camp protected them from the salty breeze.

Eugenia lay awake all night listening to the sounds of the sick, hoping that her girls would escape illness. A few people had boarded the boat with dysentery and were now in the grip of fever, and five or six times someone stepped over her legs carrying a sick or even lifeless body. They were trying to put those who were ill in one area of the boat as it was the only way of reducing the possibility of an epidemic. Sound carried in the stillness and Eugenia could hear the constant murmur of the two priests on board as they comforted the dying or quietly chanted the words of the funeral oration. Several times, she heard the distinctive dull 'splash' of a corpse being thrown overboard.

She watched over the trio of children, studying their wisps of dark silky hair, the unblemished skin of their foreheads and the long lashes that brushed their cheeks. The three innocents who slept so peacefully beside her seemed luminescent in the moonlight. They had done no more to bring misfortune on themselves than the angels they resembled. Even a moment of misery was more than they deserved.

She prayed to the *Panagia* to protect them all and whether or not the Virgin heard, the boat continued inexorably across the inky sea.

As she gazed at them, Eugenia's eyelids became heavy. By the time the coastline of the Greek mainland began to take shape in the distance, she was sound asleep. When she awoke they would be in a new country, and a new life would be about to begin.

# Chapter Eight

FOR KONSTANTINOS KOMNINOS that May morning was like most others. He rose early and prepared himself for the day's work. His warehouse and showroom had reopened two years previously and he was already in the process of expanding into a third building. Although many businesses had never recovered from the fire, Konstantinos had used the destruction of the premises built by his father to create something bigger and stronger and more of his own making. He had contested his insurer's inability to pay and had won the case, so the opportunity for him to rise like a phoenix from the ashes of the city had been his. In addition, the prolonged period of mobilisation of the army, and the continuing conflict in Asia Minor, had provided him with unparalleled commercial opportunity.

War had given but it had also taken.

At the end of October, he had received notification that his brother was missing. Leonidas had reached the outskirts of Smyrna following his regiment's retreat across Asia Minor but after that nothing had been heard of him. According to some who had managed to survive, the majority of the soldiers in Leonidas Komninos' regiment had been cut down and massacred.

Reconstructing the premises and making business improvements had taken priority over the rebuilding of Konstantinos' seafront mansion, and although the latter had been started, it was an undertaking to which he gave less time. The entire house had to be demolished before it was rebuilt. The only parts of the original that could be reused were the foundations themselves.

While Olga and little Dimitri Komninos had continued to live in Irini Street, Konstantinos had stayed in a hotel. He rarely got home from his office until midnight, so it was a valid excuse that he did not want to disturb the sleeping household.

Olga loved life in the old town with its constant activity, and was in no hurry to move her happy and contented child elsewhere, but the dramatic changes brought about by the exchange of populations had already begun to transform the city. Even Irini Street was about to be affected.

The Ekrem family were shortly to move out. For several weeks they had prepared for departure, packing their belongings, saying goodbye to their beloved friends and giving small presents to the people they had come to love in this street. They were promised some compensation for the home they were obliged to leave, and a new place to live in Asia Minor, but it was somewhere completely foreign and strange to them and they had no desire to rip themselves from their happy life in Thessaloniki.

The night before they left, the Ekrems were invited in by the Morenos for a farewell meal and brought with them as a gift a treasured volume of poems by Ibn Zamrak, whose work was carved onto the walls of the Alhambra Palace.

The two families were all agreed: they had so many things in common. Expulsion of their respective races from Spain was just one of them.

'"*Granada!* Ever the home of peace and fondest hope. Just

being there is both desire and satisfaction",' translated one of the Ekrem girls.

'You never know what life will bring, do you?' said Kyria Ekrem in her broken Greek.

'When that was written no one had the remotest idea that all the Arabs were going to be chased out, I suppose,' said Saul wryly.

That morning, Olga had risen early to say her final goodbye. If Komninos had passed by on the way to the barber he would have been appalled to see his wife's sentimentality over the departure of some Muslims. He had never understood why she had been so friendly with the Ekrems.

By seven forty-five, he had already visited his barber for a close shave and his boot-black had received his daily tip. At seven fifty he was seated in the kafenion close to his new offices by the docks, and by eight o'clock he was on his second coffee, having scanned three of the city's many dozens of newspapers. Now he ran his eye over the financial pages and assessed the approximate value of his stocks and shares.

Availability and demand for wool were dependent on many factors over which he had no control, but there was a skill in predicting when to buy and from where. It was the same with other fabrics, and for those he had to be in tune with what was considered '*à la mode*', not just currently but for the future, both in fashion and in furnishings. Whether or not they were aware of it, the majority of the well-heeled citizens of Thessaloniki were clothed and their houses 'draped' by Konstantinos Komninos.

The politics of his country, and this city in particular, had pre-occupied Konstantinos more than ever during these past few months.

A million Asia Minor Greeks had arrived in Greece even before the final treaty with Turkey, due to be signed in July, and each day more came.

Different statistics had been floating about for months but all of them caused alarm. For many months, refugees had been streaming into Thessaloniki and how to feed and accommodate them was a major cause of anxiety. The newspapers had been happy to stir up discontent. 'MORE THAN A MILLION,' shrieked the headline of one. 'THESSALONIKI TO BE SWAMPED,' predicted another. 'WHERE WILL WE PUT THEM?' another one asked, when the news came that one hundred thousand refugees were to be settled in Thessaloniki itself.

Like many of the affluent citizens of Thessaloniki, Konstantinos Komninos was watching the effects of this huge influx of destitute refugees with great concern. There were many who had been living in shacks or sharing their homes since the fire, and even his own family was not properly housed.

He was not the only merchant to start each day in this kafenion. He shared the habit with one of the most successful tailors in the region, Grigoris Gourgouris. They each occupied their usual tables, both of them smoked the same brand of cigarette and both read the same right-wing newspapers. Although their acquaintanceship went back thirty years, their relationship rarely strayed beyond the impersonal world of commerce. Gourgouris bought most of his fabrics from Komninos but, in spite of their interdependence, they nurtured a healthy dose of distrust of each other, based on the notion that the other was usually getting the better deal.

'As far as I am concerned, we shouldn't have allowed so many of them through here. They should have gone straight to Piraeus,' hollered Gourgouris across the room, his double chin wobbling as it always did when his passions were aroused.

'There should be a little more space to breathe quite soon,' commented Komninos phlegmatically, without glancing up from his newspaper, 'when all the Muslims have gone.'

'Personally, I shan't be sorry to see those fezzes disappear off the streets,' said Gourgouris. 'But the numbers are hardly going to balance, are they? We're gaining more than we are losing.'

'But think of it, Grigoris! With a new wave of Christians coming into this city, there'll be more suits needed to put on their backs! So it won't be all bad . . .'

They both laughed and then Komninos tossed a few coins on the table and got up to leave. It was eight o'clock and he had work to do.

Touching the brim of his hat, he said a curt 'Good morning' to his customer and went out into the morning sunshine.

He strolled down towards the docks. He was expecting a shipment in that day and hoped for news on what time the boat was going to arrive. There were always dozens of waifs hanging around in the dockland areas, some of them looking for work, some begging, some simply hanging around idle, staying close to their bundles of possessions, which they had left in doorways. Komninos never dipped his hand into his pocket. It was his rule. Once you gave to one, all the others would come running. His tactic was to look right through them, to treat them as though they were not there.

He was a familiar figure to the harbour master.

'Good morning, sir,' he said, striding towards Komninos. 'How are you today?'

'Extremely well, thank you. Any news of my boat?'

'We have something rather larger coming in this morning,' the harbour master responded, 'so I'm not sure we'll have the manpower for unloading, even if she does come in today.'

Komninos glanced over the man's shoulder and saw what he

meant. Only a few hundred metres or so outside the harbour entrance, a ship was approaching. It was a huge vessel and he could already see that this was not a cargo ship. The decks were dense with people. He turned on his heels, hot with irritation.

On board, everyone had got up with the sun and now jostled for the best view of their destination. Through the morning haze they could make out a few shapes and outlines, a tower, a slope, a wall that seemed to split the city from the hill to the sea, some minarets spiking up into the sky, a spread of sizeable villas to the east.

For Katerina, standing eagerly at the prow, the city that grew larger and clearer with every passing minute meant the end of the search for her mother. For so many weeks now, she had been sewing the hem of her dress and it was now edged in a multicoloured row of little crosses, with space for only one more.

As the mist lifted, the city did not appear to be nearly as big as she had imagined. She had seen pictures of Athens in a book and this was not what she expected. For the most important city in Greece, it was disappointing. Where was the Acropolis?

She then noticed something else. Along the waterfront were shells of burned-out buildings, and for a moment she believed they had been brought full circle and returned to the chaos of the city she had grown up in.

'Kyria Eugenia! Kyria Eugenia!' she said, tugging at her sleeve. 'We're back in Smyrna!'

The three girls had been clinging on to the railings of the ship and now they all turned their faces away from the view. Eugenia found three eager, anxious faces looking up at her.

'No, my dears, it isn't Smyrna,' she replied. 'They have brought us to Thessaloniki.'

'Thessaloniki?' they choroused, like three birds in a nest. 'Thessaloniki? We thought we were going to Athens?'

Katerina found herself gulping back tears. This was not where her mother had gone. All those months of hope and expectation seemed to sink to the bottom of the sea.

Eugenia bent down and hugged Katerina to her, feeling the little girl's sobs banging against her shoulders. The twins then joined hands and made a circle around them. Not one of them was where they wanted to be.

The four of them stayed like this for some time while the ship moved towards its destination. Then they felt a strange stirring beneath their feet as the engines went into reverse. The vessel was slowing, and soon afterwards they heard the metallic clanking of the anchor being lowered. They were not inside the harbour, but still some way out to sea.

They watched the captain going ashore in a small tug and an hour or two then passed by. Rumours began to circulate that they were not going to be allowed off. Disease had spread rapidly around the ship, with a huge section of it now roped off as a makeshift quarantine, and everyone knew that this would not make them welcome arrivals.

Those who were healthy were eager to get off the ship, and when the captain finally returned, many were clamouring to disembark. He made the announcement that he had been given permission to dock but those with dysentery and tuberculosis would have to stay on board for the time being.

At last, after many hours, they came into the harbour and felt the walls wrap themselves around the ship.

'*Mana mou*, look at all those people,' cried Maria with excitement when she saw the crowd. 'Look how many there are waiting to welcome us!'

'I'm not really sure that's what they are doing, darling . . . But they seem pleased to see us, don't they?'

In reality, the people at the port were not there to welcome the arrivals from Turkey. They were Muslims who were there to try to grab places for the return journey. They were pleased to see the ship rather than the people on it.

If embarkation in Mytilini had seemed chaotic, it did not compare with the near breakdown in law and order that took place with disembarkation in Thessaloniki. In spite of the numbers of sick that they knew were still on board, people fought to get on the ship. Eugenia was leading the girls off when someone pushed past them, almost causing Katerina to fall under the gangplank and into the dark waters below.

'Excuse me! Can't you wait for one more minute?' Eugenia shouted with indignation. The woman glanced round. It was clear that she had heard the fury in Eugenia's voice, but her muttered reply in Turkish suggested that the actual meaning of the words was lost on her.

As they moved into the surging crowd, Katerina held on so tightly to Eugenia's hand that her fingers went numb. Maria and Sofia gripped on to each other and on to their mother's skirt to make sure they were not separated. All four of them were mindful of Katerina's history and did not want it to be repeated. It would be all too easy in this crowd.

The quartet forced their way through the surging mass of humanity and once they were clear of it they paused to rest. Eugenia dragged their bundles of possessions a few more metres and then told the three girls to sit tight on them. She was confi-dent that someone, somewhere in the vicinity would be waiting to tell them what they had to do next. This was supposedly an organised exchange of populations and they had all been promised that arrangements had been made for their accommodation.

Katerina and the twins did as they were told and sat watching the comings and goings of this human traffic. One of the very significant differences between those who were arriving and those who were leaving was that the latter seemed to have huge quantities of possessions: crates, boxes, bags, trunks and mattresses. Even small children had something balanced on their heads as well as grasped in both arms. Katerina looked in amazement at all these worldly goods. It was a long time since she had owned more than what she stood up in. With one hand she absent-mindedly touched the stitches on the hem of her dress and with the other felt the piece of fabric she still kept in her pocket. These were all she had.

Above the noise that swirled around them, there was a sound that reminded Katerina of somewhere far away: the muezzin. It was so many months since she had heard it.

'Is this really Thessaloniki?' she asked Maria, who looked at her blankly and shrugged.

Even in the midst of the chaos, men got out their mats and kneeled to pray. This meant turning their backs against the sea, towards which they had been so eagerly rushing. They seemed no longer to care about time as they bowed repeatedly towards the earth, up and down, up and down, praying for the last time on Greek soil.

Much to their amazement, the girls saw the tears of grown men and heard their sobs. They also looked at the resigned faces of the women and the numb expressionless faces of children smaller than themselves.

By now, Eugenia had returned to them and was watching the spectacle too. As the men finished praying, a group of people who were clearly Christians approached one family to say goodbye. Their farewell was tearful and the embraces long and heartfelt.

'No one said goodbye to us like that, did they?' Sofia asked her mother.

It was not a question that required answering. All such things were beginning to fade in the children's memories, but Eugenia would never forget that there had been no such love between Christian and Muslim in the village they had come from. The nature of their departure from home had been terrifying and sudden. She had had just enough time to seize her twin daughters before fleeing for her life in order to escape the band of Turkish soldiers who had arrived.

For a time, they had to wait. Eugenia shared a sense of resignation to her fate with most of those around her. Until the dockside became less crowded, she knew it was pointless to try to find anyone responsible for helping them.

A man passed by with a cart of sesame buns, but she had no money. Hunger had begun to gnaw at her patience. Why had nobody come to their aid? Why was no one bringing them food?

'I'm sorry, girls,' she said, unable to hide her own hunger and frustration. 'Perhaps we should have stayed in Mytilini.'

The twins looked at her blankly. Only Katerina spoke.

'Look, the ship's going. There won't be so many people now.'

She was right. As evening fell, everything changed. The ship had drawn out of the harbour and now only the newcomers remained.

Moments later, a woman, taller than any Eugenia had ever seen before, came towards them. Wearing a crisp white shirt, an immaculate pale beige skirt, flat, brown leather shoes and her fair hair worn in a neat chignon, it was clear that she was neither a 'local' nor a Greek from Asia Minor. She looked like a chic French woman, but when she stooped down to speak to the children, her faltering Greek revealed an American accent.

'Would you mind coming to fill in some forms?' she said, with a note of apology in her voice. It was said as though she was inconveniencing them. 'You need to go over there,' she continued, pointing towards the customs house.

They joined a queue that snaked forty deep out of the door and waited patiently. Talk in the queue was that their final destination was not this city after all, but a new 'village' west of Thessaloniki, which was being specially constructed for refugees on agricultural land. They were told that land was being reclaimed from the swamp and that there would be jobs and a livelihood for everyone who went there. The main crop, tobacco, was a hugely valuable one.

It sounded tempting and was much more than Eugenia had hoped for during all the months of living on hand-outs, but her skills were in rug weaving, not on the land, and she had hoped to be in a city where there might be an appropriate opportunity. She was without a drachma to her name, an outsider, a refugee, a woman with neither status nor money. Perhaps she had no right to boast about her skills and to remind others of what she had once had. Whatever life might have promised, this was what it had delivered.

As she was giving the official the children's ages, Eugenia noticed a second queue where people were differently dressed. Seeing a few men wearing fezzes, she realised that the Muslims were being made to stand in line for something as well.

The American woman looked towards Eugenia and something connected in her mind. She came over to her.

'Look,' she said, 'there is a Muslim family over there who has just given us the details of their home. They have three daughters, just like you, and a house in the old town – but this means staying in Thessaloniki rather than going to one of the new villages.'

Eugenia's reaction was not difficult to read.

'So you would prefer to stay in Thessaloniki?'

'Yes, I would! I truly would.'

'Well, let me see if I can secure that house for you. There are a few people ahead of you in the queue but your family seems to match the one that's leaving – and you would fit in so well there.'

The American spoke with real concern and clearly wanted the best solution for those she was helping.

Eugenia did not contradict her assumption about Katerina being her daughter. She did not want to jeopardise their chances of staying in the city.

This was the population exchange in action. Lives were literally being swapped. One family was leaving and another arriving. If Eugenia could have the Muslims' house, she could finally settle and begin her new life. It was all she wanted now. A chance to start again.

By nightfall, the sorrowful Christians they had seen embracing their Muslim friends would have new neighbours. The Muslims who had left on their ship were well on their way to Turkey now, leaving behind them a life that they had loved and shared with every part of the community.

The balance of Thessaloniki had already altered. Over the space of a few months, the city had become predominantly Greek, and the Jews were now a minority.

Finishing his paperwork that night, Konstantinos Komninos contemplated this notion and did a rough calculation of what gains this would bring to him.

Meanwhile, Eugenia had settled the girls under a blanket in a doorway close to the customs office. She sat watching them. It was not the unevenness of the cobbles that prevented her from sleeping, it was her almost uncontainable excitement that they might soon have a roof over their heads.

Katerina lay between Maria and Sofia, still but sleepless. They had come a long way but she had still not found her mother and sister. Tomorrow her search would have to begin again. At least they were on the mainland of Greece now. Athens could not be so very far away.

# Chapter Nine

THE FOLLOWING MORNING, Eugenia was the first in the queue for a hand-out of bread before returning to her position in sight of the customs office, determined to confront the American woman who had made a promise to them the night before. Another boat might arrive today and the house that she had already occupied in her dreams might be taken by someone else.

Several hours passed. The girls ran around the dockyard, playing games, teasing stray cats and briefly encountering other children, but Eugenia stayed rooted to the spot. She was not going to let this opportunity get away.

At about midday, she saw the statuesque American walking briskly down the street. She was even more perfectly and improbably dressed than on the previous day, wearing a white muslin shirt, a floral skirt and pale blue suede brogues that were now grey with dust. Eugenia had never met anyone quite like this, someone with the authority of a man but the grace of a woman.

Her heart pounded. She was so fearful that the American might have forgotten them but, with great joy, she realised that she was heading straight towards her.

'*Kalimera, Kyria Karayanidis,*' she said.

120

Eugenia smiled. She even remembered her name. With tens of thousands of other refugees that alone seemed miraculous.

The woman was brisk and businesslike, and her manner was not simply that of a woman wanting to pass the time of day.

'Look, you remember the family I told you about yesterday . . . ? I've been to their house . . .'

Eugenia swallowed hard. The girls had gathered round her now. Whether they were to be sent to one of the new villages in the agricultural area north of Thessaloniki, or to a house in the city itself, she must react as though she were glad. Under no circumstances must the children sense any disappointment.

'. . . well, I think it would be ideal for you. You are a perfect match. Do you want to come and see it before you make a decision?'

'No, no,' replied Eugenia, almost inaudibly. 'I'm sure it will be fine.'

Katerina was hanging back. 'What about my mother?' she asked Eugenia.

The American looked at the child, then back at Eugenia, a quizzical expression on her face.

'I'm not her mother,' explained Eugenia. 'I've been looking after her since we left Smyrna in September—'

Katerina interrupted, 'Because my mother and sister went to Athens and I got left behind and I thought we were being taken to Athens and then the boat went somewhere else and then it looked like we had sailed back to Smyrna, but we hadn't, it just looked the same because it had burned down, and now I need to go to Athens to find them because they still don't know where I am and . . .'

Katerina's flow of words came out at such speed that the American struggled to understand.

121

'Can you tell me all that again,' she asked her.

Eugenia listened nervously. Without Katerina there would only be three of them and this might jeopardise their chance of securing the house. If only the child had kept quiet for a few hours longer about her mother. Eugenia found it hard to suppress her feelings of irritation.

'. . . so can you help me find her?' Katerina had repeated her breathless spiel, but this time a little slower.

The American took in everything she had said, made a speedy assessment and gave her verdict.

'The best thing is to stay together for now, and meanwhile we will look into your mother's whereabouts. Some records have been kept, but they are not accurate enough just to allow us to send a little girl off to Athens! Your mother could be there, she could be here, or she could be somewhere else entirely. But we will do our best to reunite you.'

She had taken both of Katerina's hands in hers and looked into the child's bright, believing eyes as she spoke. The little girl absorbed every word she said and accepted all of it unquestioningly.

'Let's go, shall we?' she said briskly. 'Come along. Give your mother a hand with her things.'

Eugenia almost wept with relief that they seemed to have secured the house and the four of them followed, the little ones struggling to keep up. For every one of the American's strides, the girls took two paces.

They walked up and up and up, taking the road that climbed away from the sea. They saw every kind of building: ancient, modern, abandoned, burned-out, scaffolded, some palatial, others little more than hovels. They saw churches, mosques and synagogues. They walked past bathhouses, bazaars, department stores, indoor and outdoor markets and the state of these public buildings was as bafflingly varied as that of the homes. Devastation by fire, overcrowding and poverty, redevelopment by the wealthy and ambitious: evidence of every influence and event was written in the streets.

The city was built on a slope and their destination seemed to be at the very top of it. The streets, both big and small, thronged with people, trunks, carts, furniture, and even animals. As well as the boats that arrived with regularity, bringing people in, there was a constant flow of people departing. Like the movements of ants around a hill, the scurrying about and the bearing of burdens looked random and yet it had purpose. Everyone here was going somewhere. Though they did not all know precisely where their journey would end, one thing was certain: the Christians were coming and the Muslims were going.

Once or twice the American was obliged to pause to allow a group of people to pass. If they did not, she and her little group could all be swept back whence they came.

'Here we are, at last,' said the American, with a smile. 'Irini Street.'

They were at the end of a narrow street that was touched by the sun only in high summer. The unsurfaced road was dusty and, Eugenia imagined, muddy in the winter. It was not unlike the centre of her village, where the upper floors of the buildings over-hung the street, and chickens roamed looking for scraps. It felt almost like home.

To Katerina, the environment seemed less familiar. Back in Smyrna, the street where she had lived had marble paving stones and the only animals she had ever seen near her home were horses that were attached to carriages.

Unlike all the other streets they had passed on the way, this one was quiet. There was a dog lying in the middle of the road and a few chickens relentlessly pecking at the earth. Not a soul stirred at siesta hour.

'We're almost there,' the American said encouragingly to the girls. 'Look, here's the house and . . . here's the key!'

She produced it from her pocket like a magician and they all stood looking at the front door, its dark paint chipped and in need of repair.

It took her a few moments of fiddling with the lock before, with a big 'clunk', the mechanism within it turned.

One by one they followed the American over the threshold, Eugenia first, followed by Maria, Sofia and then Katerina. A match was struck to light the oil lamp that stood in the corner. Strange shadows danced about in the ochre glow.

'Let's get some daylight in here,' said Eugenia brightly. 'We need to see where we are!'

She marched over to the other side of the room and pushed open the heavy wooden shutters. A shaft of strong sunlight slanted in, illuminating a table that was the central piece of furniture. The room seemed to breathe.

Katerina stood very still. She had not been inside a house for more than six months and the solidity of the walls around her felt unfamiliar. She had got used to the flimsy living space of the camp in Mytilini. It had felt right to be somewhere so temporary when she woke every day in the hope of a surprise reunion with her mother and sister. It was different here: wooden furniture, a stone floor and, on the table, a vase of flowers. They had been fresh many days ago but dry petals now lay in a circle round the base of the vase. The daisy skeletons were almost sculptural and cast a crisp shadow on the table.

'Well, girls,' said Eugenia, with unnatural cheeriness, 'here we are. Home. This is home.'

Not one of them spoke. It was beyond comprehension that a house could suddenly become a home just by being given the name, just by having a vase of dead flowers.

'And look!' she went on. 'Here's a letter for us!'

On a shelf was an envelope and next to it a small book. Eugenia opened the letter with care.

Inside was a single sheet folded in half. In the half-light, Eugenia blinked at the script that covered it.

'Do you read Turkish?' she asked the American.

'I'm sorry, I don't,' she replied. 'Not a word.'

After a lifetime of hearing Turkish each and every day, Eugenia understood a great deal, but could not read a word of it. The script was unintelligible to her.

'Well, girls,' she said, returning the letter to its envelope and tucking it inside the book, 'we'll keep these safe and one day perhaps we will find someone who can read them to us.'

Katerina was rooted to the spot. A stranger's house, a stranger's letter. A strange city. And – for the first time in many months, the awareness of it overpowered her – a strange family. Perhaps if she closed her eyes, everything would change back to how it had been.

'Well, I shall be leaving you now,' said the American, breaking the awkward silence. 'Come back to the customs office later on and we should be able to help you with a small loan, but mean-while I can get you some more clothes for the girls. We have had so many donations from America, it's just been a matter of sorting them.'

She was a woman with a mission and keen to get on with her

next task. There were hundreds of thousands of refugees in exactly the same situation as Eugenia, and she was not to be held up with any further questions.

'Thank you for all you have done,' Eugenia said. 'We really are grateful to you for this house. What do you say, girls?'

'Thank you,' they chorused.

The American smiled and was gone.

Maria and Sofia were full of excitement, running up and down the stairs, chasing one another, grabbing each other's skirts, shrieking and laughing. Once they had got used to the idea of this place being their own, they dashed about, opening cupboards, lifting lids of boxes and shouting information down to their mother.

'They've left a mattress!'

'There's a big trunk up here!'

'It's got a blanket inside . . .'

'. . . and there's a rug on the floor!'

Meanwhile, as Katerina sat quietly in the corner on the floor, Eugenia was investigating every drawer and cupboard downstairs to see what the previous owners had left. She had acquired a few things on the way: metal drinking vessels and plates, and three blankets. Except for one, all her possessions, both workaday and sentimental, had been left behind in the terrifying haste of their departure. With a small prayer, she placed on a shelf her icon of Agios Andreas, which had once belonged to her grandparents. It was said in her old village that the saint had preached close by on the shores of the Black Sea and Eugenia had grown up under his constant gaze.

Every cupboard contained some kind of eloquent remnant of the former owners. As well as pots and pans and plates and cutlery, there were bags of ground spices, a jar of oil, honey and herbs. There was a trunk that still held blankets and even an inlaid box containing some papers.

The different scents of these residual possessions – the sharpness of the turmeric, the mustiness of the rug – seemed to spirit the previous occupants back into the house and filled Eugenia with unease. Who was to say that they would not return? Would there be a sudden knock at the door? Perhaps they even still had a key and were going to walk in any minute. She was full of trepidation.

She told herself to be calm. There was no evidence of a scramble to leave, and the house felt ordered and warm from the owners' presence. It was as though they had eaten a meal and quietly left, taking what they needed, but leaving carefully selected items for their successors. There were still crumbs on the table but these were soon wiped away along with the shrivelled petals.

It was a long time since Eugenia had needed to keep a tidy house and the *nikokyra*, the housewife, readily reawoke in her. She found an old broom leaning against the wall and went to work with a vengeance. A desire to erase every trace of the previous occupants overcame her. One day, perhaps, she would even be able to replace the things in this house with her own: chairs, cupboards, cups and cushions. Though she had almost forgotten how, she hummed as she worked.

Upstairs the twins had found a treasure-trove. Some abandoned clothes along with a fez, whose felt had been eaten away by moths, suggested a new activity and, with joyful hysteria, they appeared at the foot of the stairs draped in their voluminous robes. They began to march up and down like sultans with great solemnity in front of their mother, and all three of them had difficulty suppressing their giggles. Maria was wearing the characteristic Turkish hat and Sofia had wrapped her head in a silk turban.

Katerina remained quietly sitting in the shadows. She did not have happy memories of people wearing such a style of dress.

Beside her there was a drawing in the dust. With her finger she had outlined a boat, with a thumbprint for each of the occupants: a captain and two passengers. Her mother and little sister were never far from her mind.

# Chapter Ten

Oɴ ᴛʜᴇɪʀ ꜰɪʀꜱᴛ night in Irini Street, they curled up together on the same mattress. So accustomed were they to the comfort and proximity of each other's warmth and breathing, they would not have it any other way.

The following morning, Katerina woke before it was light. She could see a silhouette moving about in the semi-darkness and sat up.

'Kyria Eugenia!' she whispered. 'Is that you?'

The shadow came back towards the bed.

'I am going out to find us some bread.'

'Can I come with you?' Katerina asked quietly. 'I can't go back to sleep now.'

'Yes, but you will have to be as quiet as a mouse. I don't want the twins to wake up.'

Katerina slid out of bed, put on her shoes and followed Eugenia out of the room.

It was almost impossible to get lost in Thessaloniki and Eugenia followed her nose back to the port. The sea was at the foot of the hill, the old town was at the top and everything else was in between.

By the time she got to her destination, the customs house, there was already a queue but she was determined to remain there until she could speak to an official. She had four mouths to feed and needed to know if anyone could help her.

Everyone involved with the refugee effort was doing so out of the goodness of their hearts, and the manner of the man in charge was kind and concerned. He explained that she should come each day with her family to receive hand-outs and to see about employment. There were plenty of opportunities in factories and in tobacco grading, he explained.

Eugenia wanted to tell him that neither of those things would suit her. The prospect of sorting tobacco leaves made her heart sink. She did not know whether she had any rights to refuse such work but did not want to seem ungrateful for what was being offered. The most important thing for now was that milk and vegetables were being handed out just along the street, so they went to get some before hastening back to Irini Street.

On her way back, they passed a row of little shops. One of them sold fabric, another every kind of upholstery trimming, and the window of the third was stacked from top to bottom with thread. Seeing the skeins of wool in every colour made her think, for the first time in many months, of the loom that she had left behind and she felt a surge of hope. She had been an expert weaver in a place that now seemed almost unbearably far away, but perhaps she could pick up that piece of her life once again? She stopped for a moment to feast her eyes, to dream, to fantasise about which colours she would buy. As well as the threads, she saw another image in the glass: a woman, twice her age, thin and ragged, with wispy, unkempt hair. She looked at her with sadness and disbelief.

'Kyria Eugenia! Kyria Eugenia! Come and see!'

Katerina tugged at her hand excitedly and Eugenia was willingly led from the reflection of the woman she had become.

'Look at all those buttons! And all those ribbons! Can we go inside?'

Eugenia knew that Katerina's mother had been a seamstress and that the child already had her own passion for sewing and embroidery. The child's excitement was almost as great as her own in seeing these displays of colour and luxury.

'Not now, Katerina. But we'll come back another day.'

In the past hour or so the rest of the city had woken up. Several other people milled about in Irini Street, some sweeping their front doorsteps, others on their way to market or to their work. Eugenia knew she was the stranger and received, without embarrassment, the unabashed stares of the residents. The sight of her reflection in the haberdasher's window had shown her how thin and ill she looked after all those months in Mytilini, and she was ashamed of her ragged clothes.

At that moment, she wondered if it would have been a better option to go to the rural area outside Thessaloniki, where at least she would have been with other refugees, perhaps even with someone from her village. It might have been a great comfort to have the company of people who had shared the experiences of fear and flight. Instead of that she felt marginalised.

Was the prickling sensation on her back caused by resentful eyes, or was it entirely in her imagination? She tried to catch the eye of one or two people as she passed, but received back nothing but blank looks. Even the presence of little Katerina by her side failed to arouse a friendly smile.

A voice close behind her interrupted these thoughts.

'*Kalimera!* Good morning!'

Eugenia started.

The owner of the voice caught up with her. She was holding

the hand of a small boy, who kicked at the ground with his heel as they spoke.

'Good morning,' the woman repeated. 'I think you are our new neighbours?'

'Good morning,' said Eugenia politely, for the first time self-conscious that her accent made her sound very different from the residents of Thessaloniki. 'We're living up there on the left.'

Eugenia pointed at a house just up the street from where they stood and even now was slightly ashamed of its state of repair.

'I'm Pavlina and we're living next door to you, so if there is anything we can help you with . . . ?'

'Thank you so much,' said Eugenia, smiling. 'I'm sure there will be lots of things I need to know. We are trying to settle in, but it's all very new to us.'

'And what's your little girl's name?' she asked, stooping down to Katerina.

'I'm Katerina,' Katerina answered. 'But this isn't my—'

'I am sure you and Dimitri will be the best of friends,' said Pavlina, interrupting.

The children looked at each other with mutual suspicion. Dimitri continued to dig at the dust with his heel and Katerina retreated into the folds of Eugenia's skirt. It seemed unlikely to both of them.

It would take more than a few days for Eugenia and the girls to settle into their new environment. They had cleaned the house and rearranged all the objects they had inherited from their Turkish predecessors, but the smell of their dust and spices had infused the floorboards themselves. It would be many months before she forgot that the table, chairs, pots and pans had once belonged to someone else and Eugenia wondered how long it would be before she did not feel the presence of another woman in her kitchen.

The curious looks from neighbours soon turned to smiles. The next day on her way back from collecting the daily hand-outs at the dockyard, Pavlina spoke to Eugenia again.

Feeling bolder, Eugenia asked who the house used to belong to.

'Didn't they tell you that?' asked Pavlina. 'Seems odd to me that you don't even know whose house you are living in.'

'But the house isn't theirs any more, is it?'

'Well, they say they can't come back. But who knows these days? Politicians say one thing one minute and then they change their minds. Mind you, it would be a long way for them to come . . .'

She seemed happy to supply her with information, so Eugenia pushed her a little further.

'What was their name?'

'Ekrem. She was a lovely woman. He was all right, but he used to get drunk down at the kafenion sometimes, and you could hear him giving her a thrashing. And you know that Muslim men aren't meant to drink! But she had a good soul. And there were three girls, all beautiful, with eyes as dark as coal. And do you know what, I think if they had been older, they would have run away rather than leave this city, so happy they were. It was a cruel business. I think they hoped nobody would notice they were still here. They went off to somewhere in central Turkey. She was dreading it; wept buckets the day they were leaving. She couldn't stand the idea of going off to some town in the middle of nowhere to live with his family. Wouldn't surprise me if she threw herself in the sea on the way. "You'll drown in your own tears," I said to her. "I'll drown myself one way or another," she said to me. Well, she started packing everything they had and then he said there was no point. They would have things in their new house. And she said she wanted to have her familiar things. And he said no. And on it went. With their windows open you could hear everything. You didn't need to speak their language to know what was going on.'

Pavlina would have been happy to keep talking but Eugenia had heard enough. The more vivid the image of her Turkish predecessors became, the less she felt this was her home.

A week after they arrived in the city, Eugenia got lost on her return home from the port and the family found themselves outside a small church. Like ducklings, the girls followed Eugenia through a gate and across the little yard. She pushed open the door and gradually their eyes adjusted to the darkness. Inside, an oil lamp flickered, dimly illuminating the face of the saint, whose dark, ovoid eyes gazed down at them. After a few moments, they realised that the ancient walls and ceiling were covered with beautiful paintings in deep earthy colours; dozens of saintly faces with pale halos seemed to hover over them.

They took it in turn to light a slim, tapered candle and plant it in a trough of sand. Eugenia guessed that Maria and Sofia prayed for their father. She also made a request to the *Panagia* concerning the family in whose house they now lived. She hoped for their wellbeing, but also that they would never return.

It was easy to guess what Katerina prayed for. Her lips endlessly repeated the words '*Mitera Mou*', confirming what Eugenia already knew: that Katerina's thoughts rarely strayed from her mother.

Their candles had given the church enough light for Eugenia to appreciate its size and beauty. A saint was portrayed performing various miraculous feats, and in this intimate space she felt as though a thousand pairs of ears might be listening to their prayers. Though she had brought with her an icon from her village church in the hope that a new one would be built in the name of their local saint, she now questioned if she would ever need such a church, when this perfect house of God was so close by.

The four of them stood in a circle watching the candle flames dance. The warmth and atmosphere were so embracing that they had no incentive to leave. Perhaps they had been there for ten or even twenty minutes, when they heard the creak of rusty hinges and the church was suddenly filled with daylight.

The huge man in black robes and a tall hat who entered seemed to fill the church. He boomed out a greeting, his voice too huge for the space, and they all jumped, as if caught misbehaving. It was the priest.

'Welcome,' he boomed, 'to Agios Nikolaos Orfanos.'

Eugenia crossed herself several times. She had not noticed the name of the church as they came in but knew that Nikolaos Orfanos was the patron saint of widows and orphans. All those months of uncertainty, and now she suddenly felt sure. Her husband, the father of her twins, must be dead, otherwise why would God have drawn them to this place? It must be a sign.

In these past few years, so many women had been widowed and so many of their offspring orphaned. Greece was full of solitary wives and fatherless children, and she knew that the death of her husband was almost a certainty.

'Good morning, *Pater*,' muttered Eugenia, hastening past him and out of the church. The girls followed unquestioningly, sensitive to their mother's change of mood.

Katerina was dazzled by the sunshine. *Orfanos*. She was so sure that her mother was waiting for her somewhere that the idea of being an orphan did not seem possible. Even so, a shiver went down her spine. She was puzzled by the tears streaming down Eugenia's face but decided they were caused by the brightness of the light into which they had emerged.

They soon turned back into Irini Street, and as they came down the hill towards their house, Pavlina was coming up the hill towards them. This time she was with another woman, taller than herself and strikingly beautiful.

'Hello,' said Pavlina. 'How are you today, Kyria Karayanidis?'

'Very well, thank you,' answered Eugenia.

Katerina found herself staring at the beautiful, dark lady. She had not seen such an expensive dress for a long time and it reminded her a little of one that her mother used to wear, with a little pleat at the hem, that flapped in and out as she walked.

Olga introduced herself and asked the children's names. They exchanged pleasantries and shortly afterwards were joined by another neighbour.

'And this is Kyria Moreno,' said Pavlina. 'Her family lives at number seven.'

'And that's my son Elias over there, playing with Olga's Dimitri,' said Roza Moreno proudly.

Eugenia looked at the two dark-haired little boys whose heads were pressed close together in discussion. If they had not been so differently dressed, they could have been brothers.

Many more comments passed to and fro as they exchanged information about their lives, their children and how they made their living. Eugenia realised that all of them in some way were connected with clothing and fabrics and textiles, and she gingerly mentioned that she had once been a carpet weaver.

'My husband might know someone who is looking for weavers!' exclaimed Kyria Moreno with enthusiasm. 'Let me ask him tonight. With all the Turks gone, you'd be surprised what a dent has been made in some trades. I don't believe they really thought too much about what we would lose from this city when it was all signed and sealed.'

'It's been an upheaval but I am sure Kyria Karayanidis knows that better than anyone,' said Olga quietly.

The children had all evaporated away during this adult conversation. Maria had gone inside the house but Sofia, the more confident of the two, remained outside, leaning against a wall and watching Dimitri rolling a hoop down the slope with the other boy. With each attempt, it stayed upright for longer. He was aware of her fascination with his progress and as a consequence began to show off. Ten minutes later Sofia was chatting with the boys and joining in their game.

Katerina wandered to the end of the street. The search for her mother must begin there and then, and the only way was to ask questions and to look. Was that not what her mother had always said to her: 'If you don't look, then you won't find.' So this was what she must do.

Once again, she found herself outside the little church and knew that if she kept walking downhill she would get back to the port. Perhaps there would be someone there who had a list of people from Smyrna. Who was to say her mother was in Athens? Perhaps she had come to Thessaloniki instead. Until she asked, she would never know.

Before she got too much further, she found herself at a familiar row of shops. It was the one selling ribbons that attracted her.

In his window, the vendor had created a vivid rainbow of satin, and Katerina stopped to stare. A *zacharoplasteion* stacked from floor to ceiling with pastries would not have had greater allure. It evoked a memory that seemed from a thousand decades ago of a dancing skirt her mother had made for her, using rows and rows of ribbon hand-stitched together in a continuous spiral of gradually changing colour, from red to orange, then through shades of yellow to different hues of green to blue. Whether by hand, or with her precious sewing machine, Zenia Sarafoglou had sewn all Katerina's dresses with love and originality.

This shop would be a paradise for my mother, Katerina thought. If she was in this city, she would be drawn here. It was the kind of place she used to go every day. With a boldness that did not belong to a child, she pushed against the door of the shop and walked in.

As she opened the door a small bell rang. It was intended to alert the shopkeeper that someone was entering but nobody appeared. Contrasting with the brightness of the exterior, the inside of the shop was gloomy but the chink of light through the door illuminated the pale gleam of the jars of beads. They sat on the shelf like candy.

Katerina closed the door behind her and ran her fingers along the spools of ribbon that lined the shelves. The sensation of satin beneath her fingers was luxurious and she could not resist picking one up and allowing it to unfurl into her hands. Then she heard a cough. The ribbon fell to the floor with a thump and the next moment, a match was struck and the shadow of a giant suddenly loomed over her.

Her heart beating with terror, she ran for the door but as she reached it she saw someone now stood at the counter. He was no giant, but an ordinary man with glasses on the end of his nose and white hair.

Her instinct to flee the shop vanished. What harm could he do her from behind his counter? Her desire to track down her mother overcame any timidity she felt.

'Can I help you?' The tone was kind, soft. The voice of a grand-father. 'I suppose you would like something for your hair?'

She was still too afraid to speak.

'You can have a little snippet, but any more than that and I will have to charge you.'

Katerina lifted her hand to her hair. It was straggly and not very clean. Perhaps a little piece of ribbon might keep it in place better.

'What colour would you like?' he asked, picking up a huge pair of scissors.

'Blue . . .'

'Blue?' he chuckled. 'I have a few of those. Perhaps three hundred different blues. Baby blue, indigo blue, aqua blue, cerulean, cobalt, sapphire, navy, turquoise . . . Which is your favourite?'

Katerina could see that he was smiling, proud of the extraordinary range of colours that were crammed into this small shop.

'I don't know. Which is your favourite?' she asked.

'Do you know, I have never been asked that before,' he replied, more amused than ever by this child. 'When my customers come in here, they usually have a fixed idea about what they want, so I don't normally give my view.'

'My mother is like that,' answered Katerina. 'When she is making a dress for me she always knows what she wants. I never get to choose. So you tell me which one to have.'

'Well, in that case, as you ask, I will give you my favourite colour. I don't have much of it left, but it's special and some of the wealthy ladies have taken to edging their hats with this one.'

He tucked his scissors into the pocket of his apron, slid his wooden ladder along the shelving, climbed right to the top, reached up to the very highest shelf and removed a reel.

'It's what we call a navy blue,' he called down to her. 'But this one has a gold thread running through the middle. I added it myself. And the ladies seem to love it.'

Balancing on his ladder, he snipped off two pieces each about fifteen centimetres in length and replaced the reel.

Back on the ground, he held out the pieces of ribbon to Katerina, who meanwhile had tried to plait her hair.

'Thank you,' she said, tying them into untidy bows. The flashes of gold in the ribbon were incongruously luxurious against her dirty dress. 'Thank you so much! It's beautiful.'

She examined it closely, fingering the gold stitching in admiration.

'I'm looking for my mother. She makes dresses. Did she come in to buy ribbon?'

The way she asked the question made the shopkeeper think that this girl and her mother had become separated on their shopping errands.

'Where were you when you last saw her?' he asked helpfully. 'I am sure when you make your way home, you'll find she is there. She must be getting anxious about you.'

'She won't be at home. She doesn't know where I live. I haven't seen her for ages and ages.'

The old man looked quizzical.

'We were in Smyrna,' she added. 'And I lost her.'

She did not really need to tell him any more. The world now knew about the destruction of Smyrna and the consequences for its population.

'Whatever happens, I'm not going to give up looking,' she added.

Her childish optimism pained him. She obviously had no idea how big and chaotic this city was, and did not realise how much confusion the current influx of people had created. The haberdasher was lost for words. He did not want to destroy her hope, but nor did he feel it should be false.

As if to conceal his fear for her, he said brightly: 'Well, tell me what she looks like and if anyone like that comes into my shop, I will send her to see you.'

Slowly and meticulously, Katerina gave the names of her mother and sister and watched as he wrote them down:

'Zenia Sarafoglou, brown hair, brown eyes, with a baby called Artemis.'

Her sleeve had ridden a little way up her arm and the huge scar on her arm caught his eye. He felt even more pity for her than before. There was nothing distinctive about her mother's name and this child had little hope of finding them so all he could do was to be kind. Her obvious delight in these small pieces of ribbon touched him deeply.

'I promise to keep an eye open for her and you must come in for some new ribbon whenever you like. How about that?'

Katerina smiled from ear to ear, distracted a little from the task of finding her mother.

'Thank you,' she said. 'My name's Katerina, by the way.'

'And mine is Kyrios Alatzas.'

She was back in Irini Street even before Eugenia had noticed her gone. Sofia was now being taught some hoop-balancing skills by Dimitri, Maria was still indoors and Eugenia was still engaged in conversation with their neighbours. Some other women had joined the group.

For the next few days, accompanied by one or both of the twins, Katerina made a more concentrated search for her mother. She poked her head inside churches, mosques and synagogues, many of them burned out by the 1917 fire. In some of them, groups of refugees were still sheltering.

The streets in Thessaloniki were full of trees, planted there to provide shade in the searing heat of summer. Nowadays they had become notice boards for desperate relatives who had put up appeals for missing family members. Though Katerina herself could not decipher them, Maria and Sofia read her the names. Her mother's Christian name was quite common, so that a hundred times a day her heart would lift, but when they read out the family name that followed her hopes came crashing down.

The three girls became more adventurous in their exploration of the city and walked away from the twisting streets of the old town towards the commercial centre of the city. On their way they passed the fragrant smells of the flower market and the groups of barrows that had been trundled for many kilometres by the farmers and their wives from smallholdings outside the city. Crouching down in the shadow of their own wheels, they waited for customers to come and buy their tomatoes, melons, potatoes and aubergines.

When they reached the grand neoclassical building that was home to the biggest bank in Thessaloniki, they knew they were almost at the sea. Katerina loved to sit at the water's edge with her legs dangling down almost into the water and for a moment she liked to let her eyes lose their focus until she could only see the dancing sparkle of the water. After a few minutes, the twins would tug, one on each arm, to pull her up and away.

'Come on, Katerina! It's time to go! Mother will be anxious!'

In reality, Eugenia knew that they would not get lost and was happy to have them out of the house for a while. What the twins really wanted was to go and feast their eyes on their favourite sight: the department store. Here the window displays provided a free and everchanging picture show. It was one of the first such shops in the city and the owner skilfully displayed everything from dresses and shoes to glassware and chinaware. It seemed to them a palace, a place where a princess would shop. They saw well-coiffed women and their beautifully dressed children going inside, and dreamed.

Even when they became a familiar sight, shopkeepers and stall-holders always smiled when they saw the girls coming; the spectacle of the twins' uncanny similarity and the way in which their gestures mirrored each other fascinated everyone. They looked like a pair of rag dolls with their long plaited hair. Even the wrinkles in their socks seemed to match and their shoes were identically scuffed.

Most days when they were out in their street, they saw Dimitri and Elias. Sometimes they were trying to play *tavli* and on other occasions they were kicking a ball. One day Dimitri was alone with his hoop.

'Where's your friend?' Katerina asked him.

'I don't know.'

'Don't you have any brothers and sisters?'

'No.'

'Or a father? I don't have one.'

'Yes. I do have a father. But he's working on a new warehouse and a new home for us as well.'

He explained how his father was rebuilding a house on the waterfront and that one day they would go and live there.

Katerina listened, her eyes round with disbelief. Sometimes she and the twins had looked at the homes by the sea and wondered if they were for the royal family. Perhaps this explained why Dimitri looked so different from the other children in the street. The three girls often giggled when they saw him with his pressed trousers and gleaming white shirt. Sometimes his knees were dirty, but the rest of him always looked shiny. Even his friend Elias used to tease him. Saul Moreno tried to make sure his sons were neatly dressed, simply because it was a bad advertisement for his tailoring business if his own children were not turned out smartly, but even if they began the day looking well turned out, they both looked scruffy by lunchtime.

'We sometimes go and look at the boats,' said Katerina, 'all on our own. Why don't you come with us?'

Dimitri had overheard his father talking about these 'new'

Greeks and knew that he was not meant to get too close to them. He heard the words *prosfiges* – refugees – and *Mikrasiates* – people from Asia Minor – and they were not spoken kindly. Even worse, thought Dimitri, he heard they had been 'baptised in yogurt', which sounded very unhygienic to him, and it was only years later that he realised this was a derogatory term to describe the Christians who had arrived as part of the population exchange. Now that he was standing up close to this girl he realised that she did not smell at all. His father must be wrong. These new girls seemed the same as the girls in his school, even if they were much scruffier.

Dimitri wanted to explore Thessaloniki with Katerina, but his mother was anxious for two reasons. Over the past few months, a strong but irrational fear of the city had grown inside her. Although she felt safe in Irini Street, anywhere beyond the end of the cobbled road terrified her. Pavlina had urged her not to communicate such feelings to her son.

The other reason for wanting to keep Dimitri close by was that his father might pay one of his visits. Even though he never stayed long, he usually called in to the house twice a week. Dimitri knew this was why he was always kept so clean, why his mother insisted on him wearing a clean shirt every day, why he had to wash his face morning and night and why his fingernails had to be scrubbed. These ablutions were 'just in case'.

On the occasions when he did appear in Irini Street, Konstantinos Komninos always had two duties. If it was the evening, he stopped to pass the time of day with Saul Moreno, who was one of many Jewish tailors who bought his cloth. His main purpose, though, was to inspect his son. He looked him up and down, and once even pulled at his ear to see behind it.

One day Konstantinos came for another reason. Dimitri was

sent upstairs where he sat on his narrow bed and listened to the noises from down below. Cutting through the silence, he heard an unfamiliar sound. An adult was sobbing. Dimitri knew it was his mother. He crept to the top of the laddered staircase and listened.

It was like two lines of piano music: in the right hand, the sound of Olga's crying, and in the left, his father's voice. They interwove, neither louder than the other, both of them equally audible. There were many words Dimitri did not understand or could not make out, but a few were familiar to him. 'Smyrna' and 'Asia Minor' were among them.

The sound of his mother's crying drew him down the staircase. His father sat opposite Olga, reading from a sheet of paper. He stopped when he saw his son appear at the foot of the stairs.

'Dimitri!' he shouted angrily.

'Dimitri,' echoed his mother's quiet voice. 'Go back upstairs, my darling, quickly now.'

The child was frozen to the spot. He was mesmerised. He had never seen his mother look like this. Her usually perfect hair was hanging loose. Her eyes were swollen.

'Well, I suppose the boy should know,' his father said, folding the paper and putting it into an envelope.

There was a moment of silence. Dimitri stood on the step, unsure whether he was allowed into this adult tableau of announcements and tears. He wanted to run to his mother, but feared his father's reaction.

'Your uncle Leonidas was reported missing some time ago in Turkey, but his body has now been found.'

It was a solemn fact, stated by Konstantinos without emotion. Dimitri listened. He had such strong and happy memories of his uncle, but this was not what upset him most. It was the sight of his mother so badly affected by what she had just heard that he would never forget.

Later that afternoon, when his father had left, his mother's hair was once again in place and Kyria Eugenia came to the house to see her neighbour, Dimitri went out into the street and found Katerina and the twins.

'Next time you go to the sea,' he said, 'I want to come too.'

# Chapter Eleven

A FTER MUCH PERSUASION from Pavlina, Olga eventually agreed to let her son explore the streets where she had grown up herself.

'Even if you're too afraid to walk them,' the trusted housekeeper argued, 'there's no reason to keep your son locked up inside. He's got to learn.'

Having conceded, there was one stipulation she wanted to make: the outings must remain a secret from his father.

These were carefree times for Dimitri. As well as the three girls, Elias and Isaac usually came too. There were plenty of other groups of children on the street so their own small gang, strolling, chatting and playing hide-and-seek, turned no heads. Dimitri always had a few coins so they were able to buy *koulouria*, the circular sesame buns, from the street vendor. These kept their stomachs full until they went home.

Once or twice they found themselves close to one of the Komninos warehouses and so they took a detour away from it towards the sea. Many times they caught a glimpse of the huge seafront mansion that was under construction. The scaffolding was still up but the windows were now in.

'You'll soon be going to live there, then?' asked Katerina, one afternoon.

Dimitri did not answer. He looked blankly at the enormous house with its fluted pillars and grand stairway to the front door. It did not seem to have anything to do with him. The house in Irini Street had always been his home and he feared the day when he would be leaving it to live with a father he hardly knew.

'Will we be able to come and see you? Will we be allowed in?' teased Sofia.

They may have been physically identical, but Sofia and Maria had little else in common. Maria noticed that Dimitri seemed to blanch at Sofia's teasing questions.

'Stop it, Sofia.'

'But will your father let us in, with our scruffy clothes and holey socks?'

'Sofia!'

Katerina saw that Dimitri was uncomfortable and it seemed a good moment to change the subject.

'Come on, Dimitri,' she said, pulling on his hand. 'Let's go now.'

'And let's find a new way home,' suggested Maria.

They took a small road that led them northwards, away from the sea, and kept walking up and up and up until they met another big road, which they crossed, careful to avoid the huge rattling trams that hurtled towards them in both directions.

'Where are we?' asked Katerina timidly after twenty minutes or so of their ascent.

'I know! I know!' sang Sofia. 'I know where we are!'

'So where are we?' challenged Maria.

'We're . . . near the cemetery,' answered her twin, looking about her and seeing that they were now opposite the entrance to the big municipal *nekrotafio*.

'Come on! Let's go and see . . .'

'See what?' asked Maria.

'What's in there, of course!' cried Sofia.

'You mean "who"?' chimed in Dimitri.

'I suppose I do,' she said curtly, annoyed as ever by the younger boy's almost precocious and pedantic correction.

Confidently, they filed in through the iron gate. They were not alone in this village of the dead. Several women who were tending a family grave looked up at them and smiled. They were going about their tasks as though they were purely domestic ones, cleaning and shining a family tomb just as they would polish a step or a window at home, arranging flowers as they would for their kitchen table, and sweeping leaves just as they had in their back yards earlier that day. There were several sizeable monuments where people had erected life-size statues of their departed loved one, and in the twilight they looked as if they might come to life.

Katerina looked at the letters and poems that people left for the deceased and saw that many of the graves were newly decorated. She looked at Maria.

'You don't think . . . ?'

'No,' Maria said firmly. 'I don't think your mother is here.'

Sofia was sitting on a marble step at the top of one of the cemetery's dozen or so main 'avenues'. She had found a family of kittens living behind one of the slabs that was an entrance to a family tomb and one of them sat on her lap purring. Their mother seemed to have disappeared. Dimitri and Elias were close by, aiming stones at a circle that they had drawn in the dust.

'Shall we take one of them home?'

'Don't be silly, Sofia,' said Maria. 'We've got enough cats in our street. Come on. It's time to go. I don't think Katerina likes it here.'

They were relieved to have Katerina as an excuse. None of them was comfortable here in the fast-fading light with so many shadows and so many ghosts.

Eugenia had been back to the offices of the Refugee Settlement Commission. The elegant American woman who had been so kind to them a few months earlier was still there, dispensing hand-outs and advice to those in need.

'How are the girls?' she asked.

'You remember us?'

Eugenia was incredulous. So many thousands of refugees had arrived in Thessaloniki since they had and most of them had passed through this office.

'Of course. You, the twins, the little one. Every family sticks in my mind for some reason or other. Even without your twins, I would remember you. The youngest isn't your daughter, is she?'

'No,' answered Eugenia. 'And that's why I am here. We still need to try to find her mother and sister.'

'That's understandable,' smiled the American. 'And some records have been kept. But your best starting point might be the camps close to here.'

'But she went to Athens!'

'The little one thinks she did, but it's quite possible that her boat came to Thessaloniki. I think it's worth trying the nearby camps first.'

There were several camps on the perimeter of the city and over one hundred thousand refugees were accommodated in them. The promised new housing was yet to be built. Eugenia would have to take Katerina with her in order to identify her mother, so the following day they took a bus to the outskirts of the city and began their search.

The tin town was a strange sight. Empty five-gallon kerosene tins had been flattened out to make walls, and packing cases had been broken down and reused as wooden frames. They were makeshift, but they also had a permanence about them, which was reflected in the presence of pots planted with flowers and herbs outside their entrances. When she poked her head inside, Eugenia could see cleanly swept earthen floors and the usual layout of a simple home in Asia Minor, with heavy, woven blankets for bedding and an image of a saint tacked onto the wall.

For hours and hours they walked up and down the rows of these silvery homes, repeating the same questions over and over again. There was the occasional moment when it looked as though someone recognised the name. An old man scratched his head as if, somewhere inside his skull, he had vital information. A woman folded her arms and rocked back on her heels as if on the point of an inspired pronouncement. On both occasions, Katerina's spirits were raised, only to be dashed when it became apparent that neither of them had the slightest idea. Everyone else immediately shook their head, or shrugged or simply ignored the question, too demoralised to be interested in someone else's lost relative.

Eugenia always began by asking people if they knew of anyone from Smyrna. Initially, many of those they met seemed to have come from close to the Black Sea, and Eugenia even came across some families who had lived in Trebizond. There were tears and smiles of recognition between them and a few moments of reminiscence about the old life in Asia Minor, but ultimately no recognition of Katerina's family name. None at all.

By the time they had trekked through the camp for some days, Eugenia no longer had any illusions about whether their lives would have been happier in this community of refugees. She realised that they had had immense good fortune on the day they were taken to Irini Street. Mytilini had been civilised compared with some of the scenes of squalor they had seen in this camp, and Eugenia returned to the house in the old town, full of new appreciation that they had a front door of their own.

It was looking as though Katerina had been right after all and that her mother and sister were in Athens. The American advised Eugenia that there were hundreds of thousands of refugees there too, many as yet without fixed addresses, but she would see what she could do to help them. Meanwhile, Eugenia assured Katerina that they would not give up their search. The following week they travelled to another of the camps, which was a little further away.

Maria and Sofia were not short of people willing to take care of them. Some days they went to eat with Olga and Dimitri, and on others Kyria Moreno invited them in to hers and they would eat a different style of food. Saul Moreno was usually home from work by five in the afternoon and they would sit tucked shoulder to shoulder around a table in the kitchen, the little grandmother, sometimes in her fur jacket, quietly chewing in the corner. The chaos was a pleasing one, and the food even better.

For a few days after Eugenia and Katerina returned from their fruitless search, tired out from their travels and lacking anything to eat in the house, the Moreno family continued to invite them in for meals. They enjoyed the atmosphere inside their house, with the grandmother in her traditional dress and the snatches of her lyrical Ladino.

Saul Moreno loved an audience and enjoyed repeating the stories of the Jews' arrival from Spain. One evening in particular he was caught in a state of nostalgia for a time he had not lived through but whose legacy he enjoyed. He quietly admitted to Eugenia that the twentieth century had not, so far, been their best time and that life had been better before 1912, when the city was still part of the Ottoman Empire. The Muslim authorities had been more tolerant of the Jews than the Orthodox Greeks, who had made Sunday the official day of rest and disregarded the importance of the Sabbath.

The children were fidgeting now, coughing, shifting in their chairs and bored with his meanderings.

'I'm not saying it's bad now,' he said, leaning across to Eugenia. 'But it's not quite what it was before we had the Fire. And then all the Muslims left, as you know. That didn't help. All these changes have made us the minority, which has given us a few problems, of course.'

'Come on, dear, don't dwell on it too much.' Kyria Moreno patted his arm. 'It isn't so bad now. You mustn't bore poor Eugenia with it all.'

Elias stifled a yawn and was nudged in the ribs by his older brother.

'He's not boring me at all,' responded Eugenia. 'It's reassuring to know that we weren't the first people to arrive here without homes.'

'You certainly weren't. Perhaps you will have a golden age, just like we did.'

'I doubt that,' said Eugenia. 'But things will do as they are for now. Though perhaps with a few more husbands coming back . . .'

The domestic tasks had piled up while Eugenia had been away. After washing the floor, she made her priority the laborious process of laundering the sheets. Seeing the opportunity to make a game of slapping each other with wet fabric, Maria and Sofia were happy to wring out the great expanses of white cotton. Katerina then helped Eugenia to hang them up. Once the job was completed, they all went inside.

'Katerina,' said Eugenia, 'shall we sit down and write a letter to your mother? The American lady says she will help to deliver it.'

Out in the fresh air, their sheets fluttered from the balcony.

Many miles away in Athens, Katerina's mother was also hanging up her washing. In the plush setting of the Athens Opera House, she spread a damp blouse over the edge of a balcony.

All around the capital city, refugees were being accommodated in schools, theatres, churches, and anywhere else where they could find room for their children and themselves to store a few belongings and to sleep at night,

The Opera House was the latest building to throw open its doors to the refugees. At night, people slept in rows on the hard, raked stage or across the creaking velvet seats in the stalls. Bigger families were given one of the Grand Circle boxes as a temporary home. They were the envy of the whole theatre, with their privacy and their carpeted floor.

The once elegant building now looked like a rubbish dump and stank like an open sewer. There was no running water and occasionally someone tried to light a fire for cooking, adding the stench of smouldering velvet to the already repulsive repertoire of smells.

Zenia and her baby had been allocated a space in the Dress Circle, along with other mothers and small children. In the same section, there were some of her old neighbours from Smyrna. They had managed to stay together since they had fled their homes. These women comforted Zenia in the loss of her daughter and reassured her that they would be reunited, promising to do everything they could to help her. She found it hard to forget that they were the same ones who had prevented her from leaving the little boat when she realised that Katerina was not with them. To this day she wondered why she had listened to them. She found it hard to forgive and the bitterness remained with her.

Over the months, Zenia had learned why they had been so anxious about the risk of her capsizing the boat. They were not concerned for their own lives. They had managed to save the relics and a few icons from their neighbourhood church in Smyrna and were, even then, planning the new church they would build with the fragments of the old. These irreplaceable remnants of their past life had been lying in the bottom of the rowing vessel and they would have done anything they could to prevent her jeopardising their survival. For that reason alone they had stood between her and Katerina.

Zenia tried to put these thoughts out of her mind. She grieved for her dead husband and her vanished daughter, and once a day left the noisy squalor of the Opera House for a nearby church. As she kissed the glass panel that stood between her and the icon of the *Panagia*, she wondered how many of the lip-prints were hers. Each day she came to ask for the same thing: knowledge. She was in mourning, without even knowing if her loved one was dead.

Had Katerina escaped the vengeance of the Turkish cavalry? Zenia had no desire for more than a 'yes' or 'no'. The stories of organised rape and decapitation had quickly spread outside Smyrna. All she wanted was to know whether her child was alive or dead, however painful the discovery might be.

There was talk of some permanent new homes for the inhabitants of the Opera House, which elicited a stirring of excitement. Zenia fantasised: there would be a hearth, an outdoor toilet, a table and chairs, a cot for the baby and a couch for Katerina. As if to fuel her daydream, one of her neighbours in the Dress Circle told her about some people who might be able to put her in touch with her daughter.

'They might be able to locate her and deliver a letter. Why don't you write and see what happens? There's no harm in trying, is there?'

The next day, she found her way to the offices of the Refugee Settlement Commission.

'My little girl is too young to read properly,' she explained to a woman sitting at a desk, 'but someone, somewhere might know her name and know where she is . . .'

'Yes,' said the woman, repeating Zenia's words, parrot-like but with a thick French accent. 'Someone, somewhere might know . . .'

The woman looked at the letter with indifference and tossed it onto a pile on her desk.

'Katerina Sarafoglou,' read the envelope. 'Once of Smyrna.'

Zenia had little hope that it would reach its destination but what other options did she have? It was like an arrow shot blindly into the darkness.

# Chapter Twelve

FOR SEVERAL YEARS, Katerina diligently continued to write her letters but received no replies. This did not deter her. It was a good way of practising her handwriting. Every few months, even though her desperation to find her mother diminished, her ability to form her letters increased. The one-way correspondence recorded what she had been doing and related how she spent her days. They were the diary of a very happy child.

Each letter was taken by Eugenia to the office of the Refugee Settlement Commission, who in turn passed it to the Post Office. Eugenia noticed that the American was no longer there and realised that the number of staff had been reduced. Life for the refugees was no longer in crisis. Even though many were still in camps, the majority were now properly rehoused in purpose-built villages in the north. Soup kitchens remained open but most people were now making a living, sorting tobacco or raisins, weaving or tailoring. Those with skills were at long last in gainful employment.

Olga had lent Eugenia the money to buy a loom and her little house was filled with the rhythmic sound of the shuttle passing to and fro.

'I don't want to be paid back with money,' Olga had told her, 'but one day, when my house is ready to move in to, you can weave something for me in return.'

Eugenia smiled. The money she earned with her weaving was just enough to cover their food and clothing, so Olga's kindness was hugely appreciated. The mansion was slowly taking shape but it would be a while before Eugenia needed to complete her 'commission'.

Katerina loved to watch the rugs growing before her eyes. The twins were less interested. Weaving reminded them of their home back in the old days before they came to Greece. The click–clack sound and the sight of the skeins of wool in mounds around their mother's feet took them to a place that was now mostly forgotten and they were not sure if the vague memories they had were bitter or sweet. Their most vivid recollection was of when they had fled. Moments before, their mother had been weaving.

Eugenia resisted Katerina's requests to let her play with the loom. The rugs needed an even hand and any inconsistencies would lower their value. So Katerina sat by her side and contentedly worked on some embroidery, which she was doing under the instruction of an expert, Kyria Moreno.

Although she did not go every day to the Moreno workshop, Kyria Moreno sewed at home doing the hand-finishing on some of the garments produced by her husband's business. With two sons and no daughters, she was thrilled to be able to pass on to Katerina some of her favourite stitches and to inspire her to make pictures with coloured silks, just as she had done herself when she was nine years old. Over the months, Katerina's small fingers and sharp eyes began to create even more delicate designs than she could manage herself.

The families of Irini Street grew closer. Their houses may have had doors but they were never shut. In winter a thick curtain hung down to keep the heat in and, during the summer, it was replaced by a slightly lighter one so that the house might catch a little of the breeze that blew in from the sea. These curtains meant that adults and children alike could pass in and out of each other's houses without invitation. The children went round in a pack and the mothers found that they either had six children in their home or none. The relationship between them was more like one of siblings than of friends.

It was a street that hummed with activity. Only Olga sometimes found herself without a task. She was a lady in waiting to resume her role in the mansion, but was in no hurry even to do that. Once a week she was taken to the house to make decisions on paint colours, and had spent the past year instructing tradespeople in the decoration of her new home. Painters, curtain-makers, furniture-makers, rug-makers, all of them filed through the house on the seafront. As they signed a contract to confirm an order, they would all be given a surprise.

'There's no hurry,' Olga would say, smiling sweetly at them.

Everyone in the upper echelons of Thessaloniki society wanted things yesterday. Except for Kyria Komninos. In a place where the rich got richer and the poor appeared to get poorer, the ones with money seemed to make increasingly stringent demands. The trades-people all commented on it. They were puzzled by this woman who wanted them to work at a leisurely pace and went away scratching their heads.

The Komninos warehouses were thriving. The business had grown exponentially and Konstantinos was now impatient to be in his new home. Nearly ten years had passed since the fire and, though his life with Olga and Dimitri had settled into a pattern that suited him perfectly, one that had allowed him to focus entirely on his business, he now wanted the status of a spectacular home with a family installed within it.

Dimitri had been taken to the new house several times. To him, it seemed dauntingly large. The huge rooms were bigger than his classroom, and the lofty ceilings reminded him of church. It seemed cold and dazzlingly light, and had a strange odour that he could not define.

When he was telling Pavlina about it, he simply said, 'It smelled white.'

She tried to make him more enthusiastic, but her words fell on deaf ears.

'You'll have ever such a big bedroom,' she told him. 'And I'll be cooking up some lovely treats for you in my new kitchen!'

Dimitri began to dread the move to the grand house that was not his home, knowing that living there would bring about some major changes. For so many years, he had seen Elias, Isaac, Katerina and the twins every day. He knew there would be no more games of *pares y nones* or his favourite, *los palicos.*

His father had also told him that he would be going to a new international school, where he would be learning French and meeting different children. Neither of these prospects filled him with great joy. He liked the friends he had and he did not want to learn the language of a strange country.

Olga did not relish the notion of returning to her lonely life on the seafront either: she dreaded the solitude, the *monaxia*, and would miss the wonderful people who had taught her that loss, separation and expectation of hardship could make people stronger rather than weaker. Pavlina felt the same way and would especially miss the flow of harmless gossip, the *koutsombolio*, with the women of the street.

The day came when they were finally packing to go. Although it was less than twenty minutes by foot, they may as well have been leaving for a foreign country for the emotions that stirred inside them. A handcart came to the door to collect the boxes that they had accrued over the years, and a shiny black car waited for them at the end of the road. The narrow width of Irini Street prevented it from being driven to the door but everyone was aware of it lurking there, waiting to take Olga to her old life and Dimitri to a new one. Dimitri solemnly shook the hands of his friends, but Elias, his 'milk brother', he hugged in a firm embrace. The women wept without shame as they said their farewells.

Perhaps for the last time, the boy allowed his mother to take his hand as they walked away from their happy home.

Although she had no certainty that Katerina was even alive, Zenia had continued to write to her. It was more than four years since they had both fled from Smyrna and their correspondence to each other lay undelivered in a sorting office in an Athens suburb. Tens, perhaps hundreds, of thousands of other undelivered letters lay stacked in piles, evidence of the huge number of people separated from their families or without permanent addresses.

The operation was run by a meticulous, almost obsessional, postmaster who did everything he could to help correspondence reach its destination. An unmarried man of fifty-five who lived with his widowed mother, he had dedicated his life to the learning of foreign languages. He could read French, Italian, Bulgarian and English, and had learned several alphabets in order to decipher some other languages, all of them picked up from books studied by candlelight in the same gloomy room where he had been born many years before. Beneath his mop of thick silver hair was a brain of such multilingual brilliance that he was sometimes consulted by university professors and politicians for translations. He had no other ambition, however, than to carry out the task to which he was officially assigned: to make sure letters reached the right recipient. With the sheer volume of new arrivals into Greece and the general movement of population, he faced a great challenge.

When space ran out, he had no choice but to take drastic measures. For him this was to open an envelope and invade the privacy of the writer. For a man with such meticulous manners, it was a last resort. If this was not successful, however, he was obliged to go one step further and dispose of the correspondence, which for him was acceptance of such total failure that he would not be able to sleep that night.

Inside the massive warehouse with boxes stacked from floor to ceiling (each one with a place name), the postmaster always worked long into the night, usually reviewing the oldest mail. One day, his mind was working particularly lucidly, making connections and recalling letters that he knew were in the warehouse.

Some of them were labelled according to postmark, some by destination, some by the name of the writer's original home in Asia Minor. Occasionally he had a flash of inspiration and recalled precisely where he had seen a letter that might match with another name.

Katerina had addressed her envelopes: 'Zenia Sarafoglou, Athens'. The postmaster had also noticed letters to 'Katerina Sarafoglou, Once of Smyrna'. Were these two connected? There was every chance they were not, as the name was not unusual, but he carefully opened letters from each package and noted the address from which they had been written.

He saw that the letters written to Katerina were written from the area of Athens which predominantly housed the refugees from Smyrna and was known as 'New Smyrna'. He then carefully slit open the top of one of the letters that had a Thessaloniki postmark. Inside, he saw the large but legible characters written by a child. At the top was an address, '5 Irini Street', and at the bottom, a signature, 'Katerina'.

His heart lurched a little. There was no certainty that they matched, but like a detective who follows an inspirational hunch to solve a crime, he found his palms were starting to sweat. It was worth trying. He forwarded the letters for Katerina to a colleague in Thessaloniki with the instruction: 'Try this address.'

A few weeks later, Eugenia heard a knock on the door.

'I know the surname isn't yours,' said the postman, 'but . . .' He held the package towards her without letting it go. 'Do you know a Sarafoglou?' he asked.

She looked at the name and nodded.

'Someone's got some reading to do then!' he said cheerfully, before turning away.

There were at least thirty or forty letters bound together with string. Eugenia scrutinised the elegant handwriting. She sighed. It was what Katerina had been waiting for all these years. Eugenia had encouraged her to keep the memory of her real family, but now that she held the key to their reunion in her hand, she realised how desperately fond she had become of the little girl. For weeks at a time she forgot that Katerina was not her own flesh and blood. The letters were put up on a high shelf next to the icon where a small lamp permanently glowed and for several days they sat there, untouched.

One afternoon, a few days later, Eugenia went into the nearby church of Agios Nikolaos Orfanos, racked with guilt that she had not yet given Katerina the letters. The excuse she made to herself was that they might upset the little girl. She begged the *Panagia* for guidance.

Back in the house, she began to prepare an evening meal but all the while the letters were at the forefront of her mind. She glanced up to make sure they were still there but something else immediately caught her eye. For the first time since she had lit its flame some four years before, the oil lamp next to the icon had gone out. It was a sign. God must be angry with her for withholding the correspondence.

The girls came in an hour or so later. After the long walk back from school they were all hungry. As soon as they had eaten, Eugenia told the twins to go upstairs and, trying to conceal her anxiety, she told Katerina she had something for her.

'Some letters have arrived for you,' she said. 'I haven't opened them, as they are addressed to you, but I think they might be from your mother.'

'My mother!' Katerina cried out. 'Where are they? Where are they?'

Eugenia had already cut the string and put the letters in order of the dated postmark.

'Here they are,' she said, placing them on the table in two piles.

Katerina stared at them, suddenly seized with fear. They were from a woman she no longer knew and at that moment she realised she had no memory of her mother's face. If they collided in the street, she might not recognise her.

Eugenia began to read the correspondence to her, occasionally omitting a line or two if she felt it was the right thing to do. Although Katerina's reading was improving, it was beyond her to read the uneven scrawl that ran across these hundreds of pages.

The first dozen or so of her mother's letters were written with cheerful breeziness, full of trivial observations about the journey they had made from Smyrna to Athens. They had been written without belief that they would ever reach their destination and the tone was as if they had taken a pleasure trip and were soon to be reunited. Each page contained chatty references to things they would do when they were together again, descriptions of the dresses she was planning to make for Katerina, the bonnets and bibs she was going to edge for the baby and new themes for her embroidery.

She described what had happened to herself and Artemis when they had arrived in Athens. It was very different from Katerina's experience with Eugenia, except for one factor: the hands that reached out to them from the humanitarian organisations.

'Without those,' wrote Zenia, 'life would have been impossible.'

'You can't imagine where they have taken us! It's not like an ordinary home at all. It is called the Opera House and it's one of the grandest buildings in the whole of Athens. This is where they put on plays, but instead of saying the words, they sing them. And the singers all wear big gowns and the people who come here to watch them wear very fine clothes too (except that while we are living here, they are not putting on their shows). Everything is red and gold: red carpet and red chairs and huge red velvet curtains with golden embroidery and the biggest tassels in the whole world. Just imagine what a giant's house would look like if that giant was a king and that's where we are. Everything is huge and we are going to stay in this fancy building until they find somewhere more permanent for us!'

Life in the Opera House, according to these letters, was vibrant, sociable and comfortably cushioned. Enthralled, Katerina listened to her mother's descriptions of this palace that was inhabited by ordinary people who had been invited in by a benign but outsized monarch. The image of the colossal cauldrons from which their meals were ladled completed this picture of a life lived under the friendly patronage of an invisible giant. Not once did Zenia mention the squalid reality.

'Of course, we are not inside our Opera House all day. Sometimes we go out into the street and explore the city of Athens.'

Zenia also avoided a truthful description of the streets in the overcrowded capital. She was careful to leave out the details of the begging and prostitution, although they would not have been unfamiliar to Katerina. Thessaloniki had many of the same problems. Instead she talked about the big squares and monuments that even children who had been brought up in Smyrna had seen in picture books.

'Up on a big rock overlooking the city is one of the most ancient and most important buildings in the whole world. It's called the Parthenon and was once a temple. It was on the cover of a picture book you had when you were little. When the sun sets it is bathed in an amber light and seems to be on fire.'

Katerina sat at the little table around which everything in this house revolved and savoured every word. Sometimes the voice seemed so close, it was as if her mother were speaking. At other times it was like listening to such distant music, she had to strain to catch its notes.

The correspondence was peppered with names of people from

Smryna and Katerina had a vague recollection of a few of them. Within the story of Zenia's current life, they became familiar once again.

After the first dozen or so relentlessly cheerful letters, which were written in the months immediately following their departure from Smyrna, there was a break in the correspondence.

Following this hiatus, the letters described a new 'village' that they had moved to. Zenia admitted that they were all happy in the end to move out of the giant's home.

'He allowed it to become too crowded,' she wrote, 'and a new place has been constructed for us, with much more space. It's like a normal village, with streets of small houses. We have to share with a mother and her daughter but our girls are getting along reasonably well with each other.'

Eugenia picked up the nuance – that the children played with each other happily and naturally, but the mothers were not sure about each other. Such enforced coexistence was rarely happy for strangers.

One of the very few men in this widow-heavy community asked Zenia to marry him. Angelos Pantazoglou lived in the next-door dwelling with his three children (his wife had died at the birth of the last).

With more than twice as many women as men among the refugees, Zenia knew that this was a unique opportunity to provide her daughters with a father and so, one Friday, for the second time in her life, she drank from the common cup and felt the fleeting touch of the wedding crowns, the *stephana*, on her head. In her letter to Katerina, she described to her daughter the obese priest who wheezed so much that he could scarcely walk the compulsory three laps of the altar.

Letters written less than a year later reported news of a son, 'a brother for you and your sister,' she wrote with enthusiasm, 'and of course your other siblings too.'

Eugenia read the package of letters almost without pause. Its narrative seemed to demand a continuous flow. Katerina did not interrupt once, except when Eugenia repeated the names of her step-siblings and she repeated them back at her: Petros, Froso, Margarita, and now, a half-brother, baby Manos.

The letters always ended with the words: 'If this letter finds you, Katerina, I hope it will bring you to join us. I tell Artemis about you and she asks about you every day. I think it's hard for her to understand that she has a sister who is not here.'

When Eugenia came to the end of the final letter it was nearly midnight. Usually Katerina would have been asleep by this time but that night she was wide awake, almost beside herself with excitement.

'We've found her!' she said. 'I'm going to see my mother again!'

Eugenia forced a smile. Inside she was weeping.

Within days, a postman had found Zenia in Athens and delivered the package of letters from Katerina that she had been writing for years. They did not need to be put in date order, the development of the handwriting from the very early stages to almost adult fluency guided the reader as to which letters came first and which last.

They were full of contented ramblings about her life in Thessaloniki and when Katerina described the woman who had been looking after her all this time, Zenia felt a sudden, urgent pang of jealousy. The feeling recurred each time she saw the name 'Eugenia' written on the page; she could not help it.

During the course of the correspondence she came to know the Karayanidis, Komninos and Moreno families and many others who peopled the colourful old street in which they lived. The child's passion for the vibrant and colourful city of Thessaloniki leaped from every word of every page.

In Katerina's final and most recent letter she had even enclosed a handkerchief on which her mother's name was carefully embroidered. Zenia smiled, glad to see that her daughter carried on a family tradition. Her own sewing skills were now confined to putting buttons on cheap shirts, which were then packaged up for a wholesaler and sold to a market stall.

'Can we write, can we write?' Katerina nagged for the next few days, excited that she would finally be sending a letter that she knew was going to arrive.

Her letter was a list of questions. She wanted to find out more about her brothers and sisters, how to find the house and when she might come. Eugenia enclosed a letter with Katerina's, formally introducing herself and asking Zenia what arrangements they should make.

Now that they had the full address, the letter did not take long to reach its destination, and within a few weeks the postman was knocking on the door again in Irini Street.

Zenia had addressed her reply to Eugenia but inside the envelope there were two letters: one for Eugenia and one for Katerina.

Before the child returned from school, Eugenia read hers. Zenia explained the facts of her situation. She now had five children to look after. Her husband gave preferential treatment to the four that were his own, but little Artemis was pushed around not only by her stepfather but by some of the other children too. When Zenia tried to point out this unfairness, she was given a sharp slap. This had begun to leave her bruised but the marks were always under her clothes. Although the walls that separated their flimsy accommodation were thin, there was no interference in such matters between families. Behind their own front door, everyone's business was considered their own.

I need you to know the truth of my situation, Kyria Karayanidis. Nothing would make me happier than to see Katerina again, but I believe she may have a better future staying in Thessaloniki with you than coming to Athens. I know times are difficult but would you care for her a while longer?

When Katerina came home, her own letter was waiting on the table and she picked it up with great excitement.

'Will you read it to me?' she cried. 'I can't read her funny writing.'

'Of course, sweetheart,' said Eugenia. 'Let's sit down.'

She took a deep breath and began.

'My darling daughter, I was so pleased to receive all your letters. Your life sounds so happy and contented and Thessaloniki must be a wonderful city. Life in Athens is not as easy. We have very little space and it is a struggle to get enough food to feed us all.'

Eugenia paused. She knew what must surely follow.

'Much as I yearn to see you, I want you to think twice about coming to live with us. Consider what you have in your life now and if what it contains is good, with good people, perhaps that is what you should hold on to. The things you know are sometimes much better than the things you don't know.'

Eugenia looked up and saw the child's eyes were full of tears. She also noticed that Katerina was inadvertently stroking her scarred arm, an action that had become automatic whenever she was anxious or upset. Eugenia could feel the writer's anguish and knew what it was she was trying to say to her child. She pitied them both equally. Katerina was too young for such a choice, but there it was, in black and white, written on the letter that now lay before her.

Even before Eugenia had finished reading, Katerina had realised something herself. She no longer knew which of these two women was really her mother: the woman who had been reading to her or the woman who had been writing to her. She kept this thought inside, but the desire to get to Athens, which she had felt so deeply and for so long, had begun to melt away.

# Chapter Thirteen

FOR A WHILE, sadness was Katerina's constant companion. It was there waiting for her each morning when she woke and stayed with her all day as she went to and from school and played with her friends. Sometimes it followed her into her dreams and she woke with her face in a pool of tears. She had learned to be brave when she was small, though, and she was determined to shrug off this unwanted friend. Eugenia kept a careful eye on her and after many weeks saw her slowly rediscover her smile.

At around the same time as losing the dream of seeing her mother, she had lost one of her closest companions. Irini Street did not seem the same without Dimitri. Both he and his mother, for different reasons, had not kept their promise to visit.

Dimitri was missing his friends too. His new school took him in a new direction beyond the White Tower and towards the huge mansions on Olga Vasilis Street. Many had turrets and domes and double-sweeping staircases that presented a choice on how to reach the front door. They had been commissioned by the affluent merchants who wanted to advertise their success, if not their good taste, and made even the Komninos house look modest.

On Sundays, Katerina, Elias, Isaac and the twins would stroll down to the sea, and Dimitri would look out of the huge drawing room windows on the first floor of his house and see them.

'Can I go out for a while?' he would ask his mother.

'As long as you are home for dinner,' she would answer. 'Your father is coming back at eight.'

Her husband would often be out during the day at the warehouses or his office. She knew Konstantinos would disapprove, but Olga was happy for Dimitri to take a break from his studying. As well as a dozen other academic subjects, he was learning French, German and English, and his father had great ambitions for his fluency, as long as he worked hard enough.

'If we are going to take our business forward, Dimitri, those are the languages you have to learn. We are looking towards Europe and America now. Buying from the East and selling to the West. This is where we will make our fortunes.'

Olga sometimes wondered what he meant by that. How much more of a fortune could he possibly want?

In their first days back in the refurbished home, Olga could see how much Dimitri missed the company of his old friends and urged him to see them again. Even if her growing fears were keeping Olga away from Irini Street, she did not want her son to lose touch with his old playmates.

One day he spotted them on the promenade and ran out to find them. Olga watched the group from the balcony.

Looking down at the crowd moving in both directions along the esplanade, she had an overpowering sense of her own solitude. Part of her yearned to be with them. The sight of her son with his friends and a thousand other people milling about in the weekend sunshine, enjoying the intoxicating combination of warmth, breeze and light, was a familiar one. Her sense of being shut, not merely within the walls of the house but inside her own skin, created an invisible barrier that kept them apart.

She was totally unable to leave the house nowadays. In the summer she found the heat oppressive and in the winter the dampness made her bones ache. These were not the only excuses, though. The four walls of her magnificent house were like a cage, within which she was safe. Food was brought to her, clothes were sewn for her, the hairdresser attended to her hair at home and now her son came and went without need for guidance or help. Since returning from Irini Street, the outside world had become a place of irrational fear and a reluctance to leave her home had turned to full-scale terror for Olga.

Konstantinos Komninos was unaffected by his wife's silent phobia. He often brought significant clients to the house for dinner, and on these occasions Olga was always impeccable, both in appearance and mood. In winter, she wore a tailored dress that showed off the quality of the heavier luxury fabrics in which Komninos specialised, and in the summer, she changed to lighter ones. Sometimes, if the client was very important, a tailor would be commissioned to make something bespoke for the occasion. For example, when a French couturier visited, Olga greeted him in an outfit of red, white and blue. Dimitri even appeared that night to recite a French poem.

Olga stopped watching when the children disappeared from sight. She imagined them eating sweet *trigona* pastries with their fingers and sipping lemonade purchased from the street vendor, just as she had done when she was a child. She closed the shutters and retreated inside the darkened room to rest. In due course, Dimitri would return, his face flushed with sunshine and laughter.

Isaac always made sure that the girls were back in good time too. He took responsibility for them all and Eugenia was happy to know that the strong capable boy would make sure they were safe.

Sofia and Maria were fourteen now and almost of the age where they should not be out on their own, unaccompanied.

The twins would soon be leaving school and both of them had already declared that they did not want to follow in their mother's footsteps and become weavers. They wanted to be outside. To their mother's dismay the twins announced to Eugenia that they wanted to grade tobacco leaves. An agriculturalist had been to the school to start signing up pupils and Sofia and Maria were on his list of recruits.

'But why don't you want to learn a skill?' their mother appealed. 'If you start learning something now, you will be an expert in it before you are twenty. Don't you want that?'

'We don't want to be sitting inside a dark house for the rest of our lives,' answered Sofia.

'And we would be with lots of other people,' said Maria.

'And we would get paid by the amount we process.'

'But that's the same with weaving,' said Eugenia. 'I get paid for every rug I finish.'

'But it takes you months to make a rug!'

'That doesn't mean to say that I don't get paid more each month than the girls who are paid every week for their tobacco sorting!'

It seemed that someone had already done a good job of persuading the girls that their future lay in the enormous tobacco trade that thrived in northern Greece.

Katerina cowered in the corner. She was still too young to have been targeted by the farmers who had been allowed access into the school, and in any case she would not have been open to their propaganda. Whenever this argument was brewing, she slipped away next door.

Roza Moreno loved it when Katerina appeared in her house. She was always busy, whatever the time of day, but she happily chatted while she worked. There was generally a close-packed rack of jackets that she had finished that day, their immaculate button-holes completed and buttons sewn on (as many as a dozen if it was double-breasted and had small buttons down each cuff). Finally she had stitched a label onto the satin lining: 'MORENO & SONS, Master Tailors of Thessaloniki'.

'Every time I finish a garment and read those words,' she told Katerina, 'I feel proud.'

The original Moreno had been Saul's great-grandfather, and the skill had now been passed down through three generations. With their two sons, there would be a fourth.

Much of Roza Moreno's day was spent working with suiting fabrics: wools and tweeds in the winter, and sometimes linen in the summer. More than a thousand times, Katerina had watched her neatly and rhythmically stitching a buttonhole. It mesmer-ised her to see a human being working like a machine, but this was not really why she came.

As well as the finishing touches on suits, Roza specialised in the fine crochet work and embroidery that people wanted for their trousseaux. She had a high reputation among the very wealthy Europeans for this, and to teach a little girl, with the finest fingers she had ever seen, was a joy. She taught Katerina everything, from the basic requirements to keep the skin on the hands smooth so that nothing would catch, to the importance of threading silk correctly so that it ran along the weft of the fabric. The minutiae of the craft were crucial and, once learned, never forgotten.

Very soon, when Katerina copied some of her stitches, Roza could not tell the difference between those of the child and her own. Kyria Moreno was a virtuoso, but Katerina, her pupil, was a prodigy.

On the evening when the row over the tobacco factories was

in full swing, Kyria Moreno was, as ever, delighted to see her. It meant she could put the man's jacket to one side and indulge her real passion.

'Hello, Katerina!' she said. 'How are you today?'

'Very well, thank you, Kyria Moreno. And how is Kyria Moreno today?'

She nodded her head in the direction of the corner where Kyria Moreno's mother-in-law always sat. The elder Kyria Moreno was very silent these days and most of the time appeared unaware of her surroundings. She was like a waxwork, dressed in the finery of traditional Sephardic dress, to be admired like a work of art.

'We're very well, aren't we, Kyria Moreno?'

Roza Moreno was in the habit of speaking to her mother-in-law as well as speaking for her, so a strange monologue would often go on in front of the apparently comatose old lady.

'Shall we get the box down, then?'

Katerina pulled a chair over towards a high shelf and climbed up to get a wooden box. It seemed almost as big as she was, but she managed to slide it off the shelf and pass it down to Kyria Moreno, who put it in the centre of the table.

Katerina ran her hand over the lid, enjoying the patina of smoothness, and traced with her finger the delicate image of the pomegranate, which had been inlaid into its surface. The box was oval, lined with pale pink silk, and the lid itself was padded. The interior space was divided into tidy compartments, within which were spools of white cotton for lace, lengths of fine gauze edging, skeins of silk in pastel colours, tiny spools smaller than a little finger and, in the padding of the lid itself, needles ranged in size order.

From a smaller box, Roza Moreno got out some silk lingerie, which was being kept pristine betwen layers of tissue. It was for the daughter of a wealthy client and to be worn on her wedding day. There was to be no expense spared on either the gown, which was being produced in the workshop, nor on the garments that were to be worn beneath it.

They both sat down at the table, next to each other so that Katerina could follow Roza's hands and copy.

'Can you pass them to me?'

When Katerina picked up the weightless silk culottes they ran like cool water through her fingers.

'Here you are,' she said giggling, as they landed on the linen table cloth. 'It's as though they aren't really there!'

'This is the flimsiest fabric that you can actually sew,' said Kyria Moreno. 'Any finer and there's not a needle in the world that would be small enough.'

Katerina had her own scrap of silk *crêpe de Chine* to work on. She had already embroidered the edging and was now starting work on some lettering. Her plan was to complete a whole name in the same scripted style that her teacher was using for the under-clothes. It took huge skill and concentration to place the point of the needle correctly so that it did not snag the fabric, but the child was determined and her skill seemed innate.

'Can you thread a number eight for me?'

A number 8 was very fine and would smoothly slip through fabric without leaving a mark. First of all, Kyria Moreno split the silk into two 'filos' and further subdivided one of those so that they would be sewing with something finer than human hair. She then relied on Katerina's eagle-sharp eyesight to thread the silk. She made no knot in the thread as the ends would be hidden invisibly within the fabric.

Then they both began to sew. The art was to 'inscribe' the name in stitches, and to make it look as though it was spontaneously written like a signature, a style which made the garment completely personal for the wearer.

They worked for an hour or more, with the muffled sound of the continuing argument coming through the wall. Roza hummed as she sewed, very quietly and under her breath, every so often looking down to her left where Katerina was studiously working her way along the name, each stitch taking her closer to the flower with which she was going to finish it off.

'That's perfect, *glyki mou*, flawless, sweetheart,' Roza said. 'Don't you think you should be going home soon, though?'

'I want to finish this first,' Katerina said without a second's hesitation. 'And anyway, Kyria Eugenia will call me when it's time.'

'I should stop now, my eyes are so tired, but I'll keep you company! When Saul comes in, I'll stop.'

Kyria Moreno had finished the name in pale pink on the culottes and now folded them carefully and replaced them in the box, which she then tied up with ribbon. They would not come out until the wedding day.

Then she picked up the sewing that she did purely for her own pleasure. It was a piece of embroidery that was both finished and unfinished, a work in progress that she might be adding to for the rest of her life: an embroidered quilt that was already in use on her bed with appliquéd birds, fruit, flowers and butterflies. She would always find a space to add another tiny bunch of grapes, a sprig of jasmine or, as she was doing today, some orange blossom.

'It's my own little paradise,' she said.

For Roza Moreno, the quilt that kept both her and her devoted husband warm at night was a profoundly symbolic work.

'Even if I live for another thousand years,' she said, 'it will never be finished. It had a beginning but it will never have an end.'

Roza's words lodged themselves in Katerina's mind. For ever after, love and sewing would be linked.

Not many minutes before Saul arrived home, Katerina completed her final stitch and proudly put her finished work down on the table, replacing the tiny needle in the cushioned lid of the sewing box.

'This is beautiful, Katerina,' said Roza putting her own sewing aside to admire it. She had been watching the child working on this piece for some weeks now, and without doubt it was the best thing she had ever done. 'Shall we find some tissue to wrap it in?'

Once it was wrapped, it was time for her to go home. The smell of Eugenia's stuffed vegetables, *gemista*, was wafting in from next door and telling her that dinner must be almost ready.

The debate over the twins' future was still raging and continued at the supper table.

'But Isaac has left school already!' whined Sofia.

'So why can't we?' continued Maria.

Eugenia calmly continued to chop the tomatoes for their salad. Her twins had never enjoyed being at school and she knew that they often skipped lessons. It appeared that they had not really seen the purpose of an education in the classroom and wanted to be in the outside world, enjoying their freedom.

'It's different for Isaac. He has a family business to go into. And he is an apprentice,' she responded calmly.

The three girls sat at the table waiting for their dinner. Maria was breaking a piece of bread into tiny pieces, agitated. Sofia, always the spokesman for the pair of them, was determined to pursue the subject.

'So why can't we be apprentices?'

'You can be. We can try and find an apprenticeship with a weaver. Or I could teach you.'

'But we don't *want* to do what you do.'

Eugenia knew as well as both the twins did that neither of them had the patience for either weaving or sewing. Sofia had once produced a very crude sampler, but Maria's fingers were not nimble enough even for the most basic of stitches. Nevertheless, Eugenia did not want them to become 'tobacco girls'. She had no idea where such a life would lead.

The argument went round in circles. Katerina sat quietly, ate what was put on to her plate and then crept up to bed. She took the gift-wrapped package out of her pocket and put it under her pillow.

The next morning, before she left for school, Katerina put her present on the stool next to the loom. It was Eugenia's name day and the child knew that when all the household chores were done, she would be sitting down to weave.

When Eugenia unwrapped the package and the handkerchief fell into her hand, her eyes widened with amazement. There was something that astonished her even more than the delicate perfection of her name and the shaded petals of the rose. Hovering above the perfectly embroidered flower was a butterfly with wings and antennae. The detail was extraordinary. Still holding it in her hand, she hastened next door.

'Roza,' she said, as she lifted the curtain and walked into the Moreno house, 'have you seen this?'

'Yes, of course. I watched her doing it.'

'I don't know what to say . . .'

'This child has a great gift. Like you, I was amazed to see what she had been doing.'

'But how can a child of ten sew like this?'

'I don't know. Even Saul says he has never seen anything like it. I taught her the basics, but she is in a league of her own.'

'It really is hers, then? I thought for a moment that you must have helped her . . .'

'I didn't touch it! It's all her own work, believe me. My own embroidery looks clumsy next to hers.'

'I wish my twins had some of her talent . . .'

The two women laughed together and chatted for a while, before Eugenia got up to leave. She had a rug to finish that month and needed to put in as many hours as she could that day.

'*Xronia Polla, Eugenia,*' said Kyria Moreno. 'Happy Name Day.'

'Thank you,' said Eugenia. 'Come to us later on and share some *glyko,*' she smiled.

She returned to the house and spent the rest of the morning weaving, alternately daydreaming of a secure future for Katerina and worrying about what the future held for her stubborn twins.

Her reverie was interrupted by a sharp knock on the door. It was the postman. His visits to 5 Irini Street were relatively rare now, as Zenia's letters had become less frequent, but they greeted each other and Eugenia held out her hand, expecting to be handed the usual small, pale envelope with its familiar spidery handwriting.

This time, however, the letter was typewritten and the name on the outside of the envelope was hers.

It was clear from its style that the government had sent out thousands of such letters, identical in every detail but the name itself. It simply recorded that Eugenia's husband, 'Mikaelis Karayanidis' (the name was handwritten in a space), had not been seen for five years and, although there was no definitive proof, he must now be presumed dead.

Months had gone by during which Eugenia had not even given him a thought, so now it was hard to grieve. She had done that a long time ago.

When the three girls returned from school that afternoon, the twins began to make a cake. It was a messy and chaotic concoction of ground almonds, honey and sugar, which would be big enough for the whole street to celebrate their mother's name day.

She would have to choose her moment to tell the girls, but as they laughed and chattered over the mixing bowl, she felt that now was not the right one.

Later that evening, when the Moreno family had left and the big plate that had held the cake had been scraped clean, Eugenia gave the girls the sad news. They received it with equanimity. Neither of them had any recollection of their father.

'I knew he was dead,' said Sofia.

'How?' challenged Maria.

'I just did. Ages ago.'

'You always know everything,' said Maria, resenting her sister's gift of prophecy.

'Once you forget someone's face and know that you are never going to see them again, they are dead, aren't they? Or at least they might as well be.'

'Yes, but you still didn't *know*. You couldn't have done. And anyway, no one knows, even now. That's what the letter says.'

Katerina thought of her mother. She could hardly recall her face now and wondered if that meant that she was dead too.

The twins continued their argument for some time, bickering about whether or not their father was dead. Eventually Eugenia had had enough.

'Girls, please stop. Now! It's time for bed.'

The two of them stomped up the stairs, leaving Katerina to say good night to Eugenia alone.

Katerina gave her a hug. She saw that Eugenia had the handkerchief she had embroidered for her on her lap.

'Thank you for this, Katerina,' she said, laying it out to admire the rose and the butterfly. 'You must have worked so hard to make it and it's so beautiful.'

Katerina saw there were tears in Eugenia's eyes and assumed that they were for her lost husband. She was not quite sure what to do.

'It took me a little while,' she said brightly. 'Do you like the edging? I made that stitch up myself. And did you see the butterfly?'

What really caused a lump in Eugenia's throat was not the news of her husband. That already seemed like something in the past. What stirred her was the utter flawlessness of this embroidery and the innocence of its execution. While there was an urge and an instinct to create such beauty there was hope. In those five years since their flight from Asia Minor, there had been so many dark times, but such moments, such gestures as these, gave it light. The artistry and perfection created by these small hands had moved her beyond words.

'Yes,' she managed to say quietly. 'I love the butterfly.'

# Chapter Fourteen

BY THE TIME Katerina was thirteen, her prodigious talent for needlework had grown and her passion for it was obsessional. She had been spending more and more time with Kyria Moreno.

She was now embroidering antimacassars, table cloths and pillow-cases with inset panels of hand-crafted lace. The edges were crocheted with a hook that was no thicker than a tapestry needle. Once a week, Eugenia would pack them into a bag, walk to one of the wealthier parts of the city and sell them door to door. They were high-quality work and worth far more than people paid for them, but when she returned her bag was always empty and her purse full. Katerina's talents meant that they were never hungry.

Eugenia had lost the argument with the twins. They had already started work at the tobacco factory on the edge of the city and were happy with their new daily routine. It was demanding but sociable, and kept them busy from seven in the morning until four in the afternoon with a bonus if their manager was impressed by the speed and quality of their work. Sofia often got a few extra coins on pay day, even though her sorting was no different from anyone else's, and Maria noticed how flirtatious her sister was with their supervisor. She concluded that the two things were probably connected but said nothing, knowing that her sister would be ready with a sharp rebuke.

Life at number 5 Irini Street was very quiet without the twins. Eugenia worried about them being so far away and remained unhappy about the work they were doing. At least she knew that Katerina was unlikely to follow them. Her extraordinary talent would take her on another path.

'Eugenia,' said Roza one day, 'Saul says that as soon as you are ready for her to leave school, Katerina is welcome to come and work with him. Elias started last week and it would be nice to have another youngster joining the business.'

'I think it should be soon, Roza. It's what she wants.'

'He is interested to see how her skills will apply to ladies' fashions,' she continued. 'He has high hopes for her, you know.'

'Shall we talk to her about it later?'

That evening, the two women raised the idea with Katerina. The child leaped at the idea of leaving school with enthusiasm. The mathematics she had learned would be useful as there were always calculations to be done with patterns, measurements and numbers of stitches, but the other subjects, such as science, history and geography, had always seemed tedious to her. She had never understood how they connected with her life.

The following day, the three of them went to the Moreno workshop in Filipou Street, a fifteen-minute walk from Irini Street. Kyrios Moreno was in the entrance hall to greet them.

'Ladies, welcome!' he said with a great flourish.

The workshop was arranged like a school, with big rooms off either side of a corridor. First was the showroom, where the fabrics were displayed and different styles of gentlemen's suits were worn by headless mannequins. In the corner they saw Isaac engaged in intense conversation with a customer, holding up swatches of fabric towards the light as he helped an elderly gentleman make his selection.

In the next room were the pen-and-ink drawings of the women's fashions, and these were displayed on the walls like pictures in a gallery. Katerina walked along the row of images and smiled. Every dress illustrated was made to measure, so closely did it fit the wearer's shape.

'This is where our lady customers come, to see our designs and to be measured up, but they often want something more bespoke. So on every garment we can create something unique, whether it's beading, or lace, or a particular shape of collar. We are known for two things here, Katerina: our quality and our detail. They are never less than perfect.'

There was a single, spotlit dummy in the room and both Katerina and Eugenia stopped to stare. It displayed a bridal gown of such luminosity that it hardly seemed destined for a human being.

It was long and straight, as was the fashion of the time, and the palest cream *crêpe de Chine*. The bodice was sewn all over with tiny seed pearls that were no bigger than raindrops, and the same pearls had been used to edge the hem. Attached at the shoulders was a gently billowing cape of gauze with little rivers of even finer pearls running through it. The overall effect was of a fairy's costume and, but for the pearls, which gave it substance, it might have floated away on the wind. It was impossible to imagine a bride beautiful enough to wear it.

Kyrios Moreno saw them admiring it.

'Isn't it exceptional?'

Neither of them needed to answer.

'It has taken three weeks of full-time work just to sew on the pearls,' he told them proudly. 'And each one is in its perfect place.'

The light caught their opalescent sheen. It was a magical dress.

'The bride is coming in this afternoon to take it away,' said Kyria Moreno. 'But there's often a wedding dress on that dummy, and sometimes they are much more elaborate than that. You'd be amazed what the wealthy people of this city dream up for their daughters!'

'And we try and help them realise their fantasies!' added her husband. 'Which is why we need the kind of skills you have.'

'But I could never make a dress like that!' said Katerina.

'Well, you couldn't yet. But I guarantee that in a few months' time, you'd be able to sew on those pearls with no trouble! Come on, let me show you the rest.'

In the next room, there were huge cutting tables, and both men and women at work with pairs of shears. Katerina spotted young Elias with a tape measure draped around his neck being shown how to line up the fabric before starting to cut. Like her, he was a new apprentice.

In the room after that, there were rows and rows of people sitting at long benches, each of them with a gleaming Singer sewing machine. The noisy clatter as the needles were treadled up and down precluded further conversation. Everyone looked completely engaged in their work and several of them raised a hand to greet Kyrios and Kyria Moreno. There was a great range of ages, from girls who looked younger than Katerina, to women who might be in their eighties, and the same with the men.

The penultimate room was known as 'The Store' and it was where the buttons, threads and edgings were kept in gleaming glass-fronted cabinets and wooden chests, all clearly labelled on the outside so that it was easy to locate the required item. Katerina smiled, reminded of Kyrios Alatzas' beautiful, ordered ribbon shop that she loved so much.

In the last room, there was a more informal layout. Several dozen women worked with garments on their laps, doing the same kind of finishing work that Kyria Moreno often did at home: buttonholes, beading, hemming, edging and all sorts of complex embroidery stitches. Each of them had a small table and a wooden box by her side and there was a hum of convivial chatter, which continued even when Kyrios Moreno entered the room.

'Good morning, ladies,' said Kyrios Moreno, over the hum. 'May I introduce you to my neighbour, Kyria Karayanidis, and to Katerina Sarafoglou, one of our city's rising young needlework stars.'

Saul Moreno's manners were impeccable and his introduction made Katerina feel taller than the White Tower.

'Good morning,' they all chorused without interrupting the flow of their work.

Katerina studied the various things these women were doing. If she could get some more experience with buttonholes, she would be more than capable of joining them.

When they were back in the showroom, Kyrios Moreno turned to face Katerina.

'Well, young woman, what do you think? Would you like to join us at Moreno and Sons?'

Without a second thought, Katerina nodded.

With warmth and humour, Kyrios Moreno took her hand and shook it firmly.

'I am so pleased,' he said. 'When can you start?'

'Next week?'

'There will be a chair waiting for you in the finishing room,' he said, smiling.

As he turned to show them out, they saw a face they recognised: Konstantinos Komninos. His greeting was formal.

'Good morning,' Eugenia said quietly. 'How is Kyria Komninos?'

'She is well, thank you. I came to look at some new fabrics for her.'

Eugenia was about to ask why she did not come and look at them herself but stopped. It was five years since Olga had lived in Irini Street, but even then she remembered that she rarely ventured outside her house.

'This is Katerina, do you remember her?'

'Not really,' he said, abruptly. 'But children do change, don't they?'

'And how is Dimitri?'

It was many months since Katerina had seen Dimitri and she was missing him very much. She and the other children had always teased him for being serious, but he was clever and kind, and his absence had left a space.

'He is doing well at school and working hard,' responded Konstantinos grandly. 'He has important exams coming up and then he'll be starting his law studies.'

'Please say hello to your family from us,' Eugenia asked him.

Komninos replaced his hat and nodded.

'Good day,' he said turning away and walking out through the main door.

Eugenia was certain that Kyrios Komninos would not pass on any such message and resolved to call on Olga herself. She knew she would be ill at ease in the Niki Street mansion, but felt guilty that she had left it so long without visiting.

Katerina wondered if it was Dimitri's ambition to study law or just his father's. As far as she remembered, he had always wanted to be a doctor. Either way, it was not hard to imagine her clever friend deeply immersed in his books.

They said their final goodbye to Kyrios Moreno and the three of them walked back to Irini Street in the sunshine. The city teemed with people and they passed several cafés where elegant women sat enjoying their coffee and sweet pastries.

'You see those ladies, just to our right,' whispered Roza. 'They are all wearing "Moreno" outfits.'

'How do you know?' asked Katerina.

'I can just tell from the fit. You'll begin to recognise the style too – the generosity of the fabric, the detail. I remember sewing the buttons on the mint-green jacket,' she said.

Eugenia laughed.

'You remember everything?'

'No, not everything. I can't remember most of the names of the people at the synagogue. They just don't stay in my head. But stitches – I remember almost every one I've ever done!'

Katerina wondered if she would be like that one day. She felt so like a grown-up, so like a woman walking along with Eugenia and Kyria Moreno. Her days of dolls and make-believe were over and she was more than ready to start her working life.

The two women began to gossip.

'Do you think we should call on Olga?' mused Eugenia, who had been thinking about Kyria Komninos since their encounter with her husband.

'I have delivered bits and pieces to her occasionally but usually Pavlina comes to pick things up for her. Apparently she hasn't been out of the house since she left Irini Street,' said Kyria Moreno.

'That's awful! So who does she see?'

'Kyrios Komninos invites his clients to the house, which is the reason he keeps her so well dressed.'

'So he still treats her like his mannequin?'

'I suppose you could see it that way. They are always working on something or other for her in the workshop but I doubt many of her outfits are worn more than once or twice.'

Katerina's eyes widened. The idea of wearing something only once was beyond imagining. For most of her life she had one dress on and one that was hanging up to dry, and from the day that she had been looked after by Eugenia, she had worn clothes passed down from the twins. The white cotton frock sprigged with daisies in which she had fled Smyrna was the last brand-new item of clothing she had ever possessed.

'And what about Dimitri? Has he ever been there when you visited?'

'No. He's usually at school,' Roza mused. 'Elias goes round there sometimes. You remember how much those two used to love playing *tavli*?'

'I do,' replied Eugenia.

'Well, they haven't changed. It's as competitive as ever – a long-drawn-out campaign that neither of them will ever win outright – and if Kyrios Komninos comes in when they are playing, Elias has to leave straight away. He is so ambitious for that poor boy. If he isn't fluent in five languages before he leaves school, there'll be trouble.'

Eugenia laughed. 'Poor child.'

Katerina listened. A vivid image of Dimitri's strange life in his privileged home came to her.

A question began to form in her mind about the Morenos. With their huge business and all its rich customers, why did they live in Irini Street with people like themselves? She could not help wondering. Surely they could have a huge mansion, like the Komninos family?

She plucked up the courage to ask.

'Why don't you live somewhere like Dimitri? Somewhere bigger and grander?'

'Why would we want to do that?' Roza answered, feigning surprise at the question.

Katerina was a little embarrassed, but felt compelled to continue. 'Well . . . you have such a big workshop . . . and such an important name in this city. And all those grand ladies wear your clothes, and so do their husbands.'

Roza Moreno knew exactly what the girl was getting at. The handful of people who visited the workshop and also knew where they lived were usually bemused. The Moreno family had prospered but had never moved from their small house in a scruffy street in the old town.

'I'll tell you, my dear. And it's very simple,' she said. 'My husband runs the business as much for the people who work there as for himself. We only employ the best tailors and seamstresses in Thessaloniki, so we pay them more than the average salary.'

Katerina nodded as Kyria Moreno continued.

'Lots of them are related to us, so they are as determined as we are to keep the reputation of the company that bears their family name. But,' she paused, 'we don't only employ Jews – there are a couple of Greeks! We have always made sure of that. There used to be plenty of Muslims with us too and we still miss them.'

'I shouldn't think many other workshops have as much light and space as yours,' said Eugenia.

'Most of them are much smaller,' answered Roza. 'Saul has spent all the profits from the past ten years on improving conditions, so instead of having a bigger home, we have a bigger workshop!'

'And the new sewing machines must have cost a lot of money,' said Eugenia.

'Yes,' Roza said. 'It was a big investment, but everyone looks after their own as though it actually belongs to them.' She took Katerina's hand. 'So you see, we don't need to live like our customers any more than we need to dress like them,' she said, gesturing to her own clothing, a full skirt and plain blouse, which bore no relation to the new European styles.

By now they had turned into Irini Street. Here was the rest of the answer: the street where nobody looked down on anybody, whether they were old Greeks, 'new' Greeks from Asia Minor, Greek-speaking Jews or Jews who spoke only Ladino.

Simultaneously, all three of them had the same thought. Why would any of them want to swap their lives or their homes with Olga Komninos? They pictured her, unsmiling and alone, in her mansion on the sea.

A week later, Katerina went to school for the last time. The following day, Eugenia woke her at six thirty. In ten minutes she was washed, dressed and ready to leave the house.

Her heart beating with excitement, she stepped out into the street. Kyrios Moreno and his sons were waiting for her in the pale dawn light.

'Here she is!' Elias said, enthusiastically. 'Ready? Shall we go?'

Today was the beginning of Katerina's life in the working world, her first day as a seamstress, a *modistra*.

'Yes,' she said, proudly. 'I'm ready!'

# Chapter Fifteen

KATERINA BEGAN HER full training under the wing of Saul's aunt, who was a strict but knowledgeable teacher. For forty years, Esther Moreno had been working in the business and it was her life as much as it was her nephew's. An unmarried lady, she had not missed a single day of work in four decades.

The first stage of the apprenticeship involved learning about the fabrics, what were their limitations, strengths and uses, from the men's tweeds and twills through to the ladies' silks and cottons. She was given swatches from more than one hundred rolls of fabric and told to experiment on them and to try different sized needles and varying thicknesses of thread so that she would know which was best to use.

'Only by feeling these things between your own fingers and seeing the result for yourself will you know which is the most suitable. There is no room for error once you are working on a garment. So you have to make your mistakes now.'

Esther Moreno's knowledge of customers' expectations was based on decades of unbroken experience. She was humourless but usually right, and the novice hung on her every word.

For three entire weeks, Katerina sat quietly in a corner with a pile of materials of every weight, from velvet to toile, and saw what was possible with each one, which weight of silk or yarn worked best. Never before had she had such an opportunity to feel so many different variations of texture, quality and thickness. Nothing distracted her from this task.

After that she was sent to observe the measuring and fitting process (ladies only, of course) and then for two days she sat in the cutting room. This was where every drachma of profit could be lost. With the price of good fabric being so high, every square centimetre of it had to be well used. If there was an error with the direction in which the fabric lay, a careless slip with the shears, or the arrangement of pattern pieces was not economical, they would make a loss on the garment.

'If a mistake is made at this stage, the garment will cost us more than we can sell it for to the customer,' Esther said bluntly.

Katerina picked up a pair of the unwieldy, man-sized shears and hoped she would never be involved in cutting.

Next was the sewing room, where Katerina was greeted by the deafening but rhythmic clatter. They sat down together at one of the machines and Katerina ran her fingers over its cool metal curves. They were a work of art, each of these Singers, with fine etching on the silver plate that concealed the mechanism and exquisitely painted flowers and fronds over the main body. Esther Moreno demonstrated to Katerina how to thread the machine and work the treadle with her feet, but she was alarmed by the sensation that the needle was running away with her and hoped that her days at Moreno & Sons were not going to be spent among these machines.

'So now, the finishing room,' Esther said. 'This is where your imagination can take you anywhere you allow it.'

Katerina had dreamed of this room since her last visit. All the women looked up as they came in, and smiled.

'Now, there are rules when you are tailoring and fitting,' said Esther. 'You are almost governed by mathematics and rules of proportion and, to some extent, the unique and often curious shape of the human body, but . . .'

Katerina was trying to focus on what the woman was saying, but found the scientific way she spoke about the body rather curious. After a few moments her concentration returned and Esther was still talking.

'. . . there are no limits, no rules on what you can do to embellish a dress,' she was saying. 'There are certain things that need to be established with the customer beforehand. You have to estimate the amount of time you will need, ascertain the price of materials, do a cost calculation and submit that to me so that I can assess the profitability.'

Katerina had no idea what she was talking about. All she wanted to do was sew, and she was transfixed by the row of bows that one of the women was attaching all the way down the back of a full-length ball gown.

She nodded. It seemed the correct response. Clearly Esther Moreno did not expect her to say very much.

'I understand that Kyrios Moreno is putting you in here, so I'll leave Kyria Raphael to look after you now.'

'Thank you so much, Kyria Esther,' Katerina said politely.

Esther Moreno was already opening the door to leave. She was much more at home in her office, where she dealt with the estimates and invoices for the business, and everyone in the room breathed a sigh of relief when she had gone.

Katerina was immediately put to work on some beading. Only young eyes and small fingers like hers could pick up the tiny crystals and grasp the size 9 needle that was needed to sew them. By the end of the day she had run them all round the hem of the gown and the other women gathered to admire how well she had done.

'It's so neat!'

'And even!'

'Perfect, Katerina!'

She was almost embarrassed by the lavishness of their praise, but it told her what she needed to know. She was good enough.

From that day on, she thrived, and was always called on to do the tasks that required the finest work. She could do embroidery, appliqué, edging and ruching with stitches that were almost invisible to the naked eye, and the evenness of her stitches, whatever the size, was remarkable. Whether she was doing satin stitch, feather stitch, herringbone or chain stitch, in and out went her needle with the same mechanical beat as the machines in the adjacent room.

Sometimes even the act of threading a needle evoked powerful feelings of nostalgia within her and it was during these long hours in the workshop that she thought most of her mother. It was always the same moment that returned to her, one in which their lives had been, in her childlike view of the world, perfect. In that frozen particle of time, her mother was sitting in a very upright chair next to a window, and her back was straight and stiff. She was embroidering something with gold thread and, as the light streamed in through the window, it glistened. Her work, an ecclesiastical robe, was spread across her lap.

'Never slouch,' she had always told Katerina, and whenever this image came to her, she automatically adjusted her position.

Day to day, Katerina was protected from the seediness of much of Thessaloniki. The cobbled alleyways that led to and from the Moreno workshop in Filipou Street did not take her past the makeshift shacks that still housed many who had lost their homes in the 1917 fire. Nor did they take her anywhere near the wooden huts that were incongruously squeezed between magnificent apartment buildings and rows of middle-class villas, where a few refugees from Asia Minor still lived like gypsies. Nor did she ever find herself near the railway station, which was possibly the worst area of all. In the crowded 'streets' of tin huts, sewage and rats ran along side by side and every other door opened into a hash den or brothel.

Though the houses were simple and close-packed, as if carelessly erected by a child, Irini Street was affluent compared with many other parts of Thessaloniki. Never more so than at this time, this was a city of extreme wealth and extreme poverty. At one end of the scale were the affluent bankers and merchants, the kind of people who comprised the Moreno clientele and the Komninos customers, and at the other, the abjectly poor who dwelled in slums and relied on soup kitchens. The families of Irini Street were somewhere in between.

Unemployment was high, but even among those who had jobs, dissatisfaction continually bubbled to the surface. Unlike Saul Moreno, most employers did not bother to keep their workers happy and the late 1920s had seen continual protest. Tobacco workers were a huge source of labour militancy and fought over conditions and pay, but they were not alone. Transport workers, printers, bakers and butchers all took industrial action. This unsettled atmosphere of poverty and exploitation was a perfect breeding ground for communism.

The Nationalists were vehemently hostile to the growing Left, but they had another target as well: the Jews, whom they accused of not assimilating into Greek life.

Throughout the decade, the right-wing newspaper, *Makedonia*, had stirred up hatred and suspicion against the Jews, promulgating rumours that they planned to take over the state. It reminded readers that in 1912, when the city ceased to be part of the Ottoman Empire and became part of Greece, the city's Jews had given the Greek army a cool welcome. Some did not even speak the Greek language and continued to use Ladino. In other words, they were neither patriotic, nor truly Greek. The list of their 'crimes' was a long one, according to *Makedonia*.

It was a time of brewing resentment, and widespread poverty among the Asia Minor Greeks had helped to foment it. One day, Saul Moreno arrived at the workshop very early, as usual, and found the word 'JEW' splashed across the door in red paint. Before the first of his staff had arrived, he had bought a can of black paint and repainted the entire door. Everyone was puzzled by his sudden desire to change its colour but he did not want to disturb his staff by giving them the real reason.

'I just felt it would make a change,' he said, but in a few weeks he would repaint it his favourite green.

Kyrios Moreno tried to protect his wife. Each day on his way to work, he bought one of the plethora of newspapers that crowded the newsstand, but if there was a reference to anti-Semitic activity he quickly got rid of it. He also kept very quiet about the hostile stares he sometimes noticed and did not tell Roza that one or two of their customers had taken their business elsewhere.

At the end of June, there was some major news that reached him even before he read it in a newspaper.

Two of his tailors lived in a predominantly Jewish neighbourhood known as the Campbell district. On the previous night, their homes had been torched. The men were still in shock but wanted to tell the story to their colleagues. Twenty people gathered round in the cutting room, appalled by what they heard but hungry for a first-hand account. It seemed that a crowd of Asia Minor refugees, mostly from the down-at-heel areas nearby, had been responsible.

'To start with, we barricaded ourselves in. It seemed the best thing to do, if we wanted to protect our homes and keep safe as well.'

'But it didn't turn out that way . . .' said his neighbour.

'They were on the rampage.'

'Like mad men!'

'As soon as they set light to the first building, we had to get out. Fast. So everyone ran. Literally fled with what they could carry.'

'Some people lost everything! Workshops, homes, everything!'

'We were lucky to get out alive!'

'And they attacked two other areas as well, you know!'

The incident shocked Jews and Greeks alike. There was a trial of some of the perpetrators, including the editor of *Makedonia*, who had whipped up so much ill will against the Jews. Many Jews made plans to emigrate, even one of the Moreno tailors. If he could no longer feel secure in his own bed, he was leaving. The following month, with a few dozen other families, he departed for Palestine.

Saul Moreno was determined not to allow these events to affect his business. He took out full-page advertisements in some of the most right-wing newspapers and, with their permission, reproduced testimonials from some of his wealthy and high-profile clients.

Each of the advertisements ran the line: 'Let us dress you top to toe.' They used an illustration of an elegant couple, the man in evening dress and the woman in a long, beaded gown. The woman in the picture bore an uncanny resemblance to Olga Komninos.

At the foot of the page, in large, confident letters, were the words: 'MORENO & SONS, THE TOP TAILORS IN THESSALONIKI.'

The advertisements were a display of confidence, a gesture of defiance directed against those who wished them ill.

There were other ways in which Saul Moreno kept the morale of his workers high. He bought a gramophone player. It was played for an hour at the end of each afternoon, and the women loved the moment when he came in to wind it up. From the second the needle landed with a 'crump' on the record and the sound crackled into the room, the atmosphere lightened.

The collection of recordings was limited, but they usually began with one of Haim Effendi's Sephardic songs from Turkey and always ended with their favourite, Roza Eskenazi. Their busy hands worked in time to the rhythms of this music.

Over the clatter of their sewing machines, the workers in the adjacent room smiled when they heard the women singing at full volume.

Esther Moreno disapproved of the music and the holiday atmosphere it created, convinced that productivity slackened off when it was playing. She was wrong. If anything it made the women in less of a hurry to pack up and go home. Katerina was among those who particularly loved the music and became word-perfect in every song. There was no gramophone at home.

Katerina's slim fingers were becoming increasingly nimble and her execution of some of the most difficult techniques improved. Sometimes, on the finer fabrics, there were seams that could not be adequately done by machine and she would do them by hand. The handiwork on her gowns became the most sought after in the city.

'You can wear her dresses inside out,' her wealthy customers boasted.

It was true. Her seams were perfect, and even the pattern on the reverse of her beading was sometimes as beautiful as the beading itself.

One day she was asked to finish a pale yellow crêpe dress. It had been tailored for someone with the narrowest waist and Katerina had been asked to sew on the twenty-five or so self-covered buttons that ran down the front, and to make the looped buttonholes. The challenge would not have been so great if they were not the size of glove buttons.

'It's for Kyria Komninos,' Saul Moreno told her.

Katerina knew she was not meant to make personal comments about clients or their choices. Discretion and tact were prerequisites of the job, but Katerina could not help making a comment.

'She is so slim! Slimmer than ever!'

It shocked her to imagine how thin Olga had become. In her mind, such slimness was usually associated with illness or starvation, but she knew the latter could not be the cause. Even if there were thousands of people without enough to eat in this city, everyone knew that the Komninos business was going from strength to strength.

'Is she . . . ?'

'What?'

'In good health?'

'One of the fitters went to her house to measure her, and didn't mention anything about her being ill. In fact, when you've finished, would you mind delivering it for me?'

'Of course,' said Katerina, trying not to look overeager.

'Kyrios Komninos wants her to have it by Saturday.'

This gave Katerina less than two working days to complete the task.

She began straight away, and in time to the music of Markos Vamvakaris, the last button was sewn on at three o'clock on Friday afternoon. The dress had its final inspection from Kyrios Moreno and was then wrapped up in several layers of tissue and carefully laid in a large flat box that was tied firmly with yellow ribbon.

With the package tucked under her arm, Katerina put on her hat and coat and nervously set off for the Komninos house, a place she had seen and thought of so many times, without ever once going over its threshold.

It was already drizzling when she left the workshop, and by the time she reached the sea, there were waves crashing over onto the esplanade. As a tram passed, she felt the splash of water round her ankles and quickened her step. The rain was getting heavier now and, knowing that the dress must be worth more than half her year's salary, she fretted that the contents of the unwieldy box might get damp. She grasped it with both arms.

The streets were quiet that afternoon, as most people were waiting until the rain stopped before venturing out, but through the drizzle she saw a solitary figure coming in the other direction. He carried a leather briefcase like a businessman and she wondered which of them would step aside to allow the other to avoid the puddle that lay across the pavement.

She then realised that they were both turning into the same entranceway.

In the past year or so, she had only ever seen Dimitri in the distance and it was strange to see him now so close up. Though he dressed like a man, in a smart suit, he still looked just as he had done since boyhood. Age sixteen seemed young to start emulating your father, was the first thought that went through her head.

Dimitri did not, at first, recognise Katerina. He had been looking down at the pavement, his vision partly obscured by his hat, but, when she spoke, his response was immediate.

'Dimitri . . . hello. How are you?' she said, her heart hammering.

'Katerina! What a surprise! What are you doing here?'

Before she had time to answer, Pavlina had opened the door. 'Come on in,' she said. 'Quickly. It's horrid out there!'

'I'm delivering a dress for Kyria Komninos,' Katerina explained, handing the box over to Pavlina.

'You must give it to her yourself!' Pavlina exclaimed. 'Take off your wet things and come upstairs. She's in the drawing room.'

Dimitri and Katerina took off their damp coats and followed Pavlina up the broad staircase. Katerina tried not to gawp at the grandeur of the house, the scale of the rooms and the lavishness of the drapes. She had never seen anywhere like it. There were huge oil paintings in gilt frames on the walls and most of the highly polished European furniture seemed to have a touch of gold.

Dimitri tapped on the double doors at the top of the stairs. They heard a quiet 'come in'.

Olga was sitting by the fireplace on a big chair, with her feet up on another. She was reading. She looked up, surprised and slightly quizzical to see her son with a young woman whom she did not at first recognise.

'Mother, it's Katerina! She's come with a package from Moreno.'

'Katerina! I almost didn't recognise you.'

The roundness of her face and eyes was unchanged, as were the openness of her expression and the broadness of her smile, but her hair, which she had once worn in plaits that reached her waist, had been cut into a bob.

Olga looked just the same, if a little thinner.

Perhaps she has been ill, thought Katerina, which would explain why she never comes to Moreno & Sons herself.

She put the box down on a chair next to Olga and was surprised by her lack of interest in opening it.

'Would you like me to take it out? I think it needs hanging up.'

'Don't worry. Pavlina can do that in a minute. I want to know what you have been doing. How is Eugenia? And the twins?'

Despite her understated manner and her quiet voice, Olga Komninos seemed thirsty for information. Katerina began to tell her about all the evenings she had spent with Roza Moreno and how she had been invited to work in the business.

'Every single day, when I wake up it's as though the sun is coming up right inside me,' she enthused. 'And each morning I walk to the workshop with Isaac and Elias. Their father generally goes much earlier than we do . . .'

For ten or fifteen minutes she continued without a pause, describing how she spent each day, the people she worked with, what they listened to on the gramophone and so on. Her excitement and enthusiasm for her life and work were enviable. She even managed to provoke sympathy for the lugubrious Esther Moreno, who wore her sourness like a dowdy dress.

By the time she had finished, Olga had a full picture of Katerina's working life, as did Dimitri, who had been standing in the doorway for some time, listening, mesmerised, to every word. He could not help comparing Katerina's pageant of colleagues with the staff of the private college he attended. It was usually with weariness that he got out of bed, put on his formal clothes and picked up his bag of books to walk eastwards in time for lessons. He woke up already tired, having worked until late the night before, so the feeling of joy that Katerina experienced when her alarm clock went off was entirely unknown to him.

When Pavlina appeared behind Dimitri with a tray of coffee, he knew he could no longer linger in the doorway.

Katerina stopped talking when he entered, suddenly self-conscious.

'It sounds as if you like your work,' said Dimitri.

'Yes, I do,' she replied.

Both of them were almost overcome with shyness.

'Coffee, Katerina?' Pavlina asked.

'No, thank you,' she said. 'Just some water, please. And then I must go.'

'That's such a shame, Katerina,' said Olga. 'I was so enjoying hearing about what you are doing. And you haven't even told me about Irini Street yet. Please stay a little longer.'

For a while, Olga had felt stirred to life, as though someone had fanned the dying embers of a fire. Although the idea of the outside world was terrifying and the thought of going there almost paralysed her, she still yearned to be part of the normal day-to-day life that went on in the streets, in the cafés, in the workplaces. Her husband did not bring that to her, and nor did the people he invited to the house, whose politeness and formality only increased her sense of loneliness and isolation.

Katerina had altered the room. If someone had lifted the formal arrangement of roses and chrysanthemums from the vase and replaced it with a bunch of freshly cut wildflowers, with the bees still buzzing round the blooms, it would have made a similar transformation.

Dimitri crossed the room and sat down next to Olga. Mother and son continued to be charmed by the young woman's tales and anecdotes, and the good humour with which she told them.

When he arrived home, Konstantinos Komninos was greeted with a sound that was unusual in this house: gales of laughter coming from the first floor. His cough and the thump of his ascending footsteps silenced them, and by the time he walked into the drawing room Katerina had already stood up to go.

'This is Katerina, from Moreno and Sons,' said Dimitri hurriedly, as if to excuse her presence. 'She was delivering something.'

'I know who she is,' he said rudely. 'And where is it? Where is the dress?'

He saw the box still lying on the chair. Pavlina had not returned to hang it up and as Komninos took it out of its wrapping and held it up, they could all see there was a crease down the front.

'But you're meant to be wearing this tonight!' he exclaimed, not hiding his annoyance. Holding the dress with one hand, he strode over to the little table next to Olga's chair, picked up the bell and rang it angrily. Seconds later, Pavlina was in the room.

She did not need instructions and silently took the dress out of his hands.

'I'll make sure it's perfect for tonight,' she said cheerily. 'It just needs to be steamed.'

Katerina was covered in shame. She was supposed to make sure the garment was taken out of its box as soon as she arrived. That had been Kyrios Moreno's precise instruction and unfortunately it would get back to him that she had failed.

The atmosphere in the room had changed completely. Katerina glanced through the big French windows and noticed that the sea and sky were both still a threatening grey. In spite of that, the atmosphere out there looked more inviting than the one she found herself in.

'Dimitri,' said Olga with artificial good cheer, 'show Katerina out, would you?'

'Of course,' he replied.

'And thank you so much for delivering the dress, Katerina. It was very good of you to finish it on time.'

'Goodbye, Kyria Komninos.'

Katerina followed Dimitri downstairs. He was embarrassed at

the way in which his father had demonstrated his anger in front of the young woman. He and his mother had enjoyed seeing her again, he said, and hoped she would come again. Katerina smiled and said she very much hoped so too. He let Katerina out of the front door, then went straight up to his bedroom on the second floor.

Some hours later, he heard his father's guests arrive. He pictured his mother, her pale skin skilfully brought to life with some rouge and her dark hair piled elegantly high to accentuate her long slender neck. The pale yellow silk crêpe of her dress would be skimming her body and swaying perfectly as she walked. She outshone all the other wives and soon the affluent invitees, who were from Athens on that occasion, would have made the decision to purchase all their fabrics in the future from Komninos. They would be particularly impressed by Olga's outfit. Five years earlier, Konstantinos had purchased 20,000 stremmata of land in the agricultural area north of the city and planted it with mulberry trees. The silk worms had been doing their work and Komninos was now producing his own silk. The quality of it was going to push his business into a new sphere.

All evening, Dimitri's head remained bent over his books. If he passed his forthcoming school exams he would be guaranteed a place at medical school and although his father was against it, he was determined to stand his ground.

It was not only the constant hum of human voices and endless clattering of plates and crockery that disturbed his concentration. As the words of his textbook swam in front of him, he thought of the stories that Katerina had told and remembered her childlike voice, ringing like a bell across the room. It had been so long since he had heard such care-free laughter from his mother. Even if she did not want or need them, he hoped very much that Katerina would be coming to deliver more dresses.

As he struggled to memorise the periodic table, the only thing that seemed to have lodged in his memory was the image of Katerina's smile.

# Chapter Sixteen

WITHIN THE YEAR, Dimitri passed his exams and joined the medical faculty at the university. His father was furious. Business these days seemed increasingly to involve contracts and written documentation, so Dimitri's expertise and qualification in Law would have strengthened the business even further. His son's knowledge of medicine would contribute nothing.

Konstantinos swept his son's disobedience aside, just as he did most obstacles that came in his path. His great pleasure in life was to overcome challenge, whether in the form of competitors, suppliers or, nowadays, his factory labourers.

He had come through the financial slump of the early thirties, when most of his competitors had disappeared beneath the weight of their own debts, and was stronger than ever before. If he was enjoying such financial success during times of political and economic uncertainty in this city, it was almost unimaginable how much he would be able to achieve in future years.

He greeted each morning with expectation and confidence. Everything seemed to be going his way. He was a giant in his hand-made size five and a half shoes.

Dimitri, meanwhile, was meeting a new world, a place of ideas and views based on other principles than economic necessity. Unlike the teachers at his school, who had been paid by the parents to hold certain opinions and to instil particular principles and beliefs into their pupils, the university professors who taught Dimitri were more independently minded. As well as his anatomy and pharmacology classes, he began to attend a philosophy class and was soon engaged in debates on the nature of right and wrong, the exploration of belief versus knowledge, wisdom versus truth, and so on. Political theory classes soon followed and his own views on society swiftly began to develop.

He had never been oblivious to what he saw around him, and his early days in Irini Street had given him more experience of the tattier parts of Thessaloniki than most of his fellow students had ever had. Even so, he had not seen for himself the true depth of poverty that existed in his city. He had supposed that the street traders who peddled cigarettes and combs probably lived in the shanty settlements near the railway station or in Toumba, but now he knew there were places considerably worse than those. He had to confront the fact that he had been brought up in a way that bore no relationship to the lives of the majority.

It was perhaps a good thing that he did not see very much of his father during those times. They would have come to blows. Dimitri was being exposed to every kind of new political idea and soon realised that his father did not live by any definable ideology, either political or spiritual. Konstantinos' true God was money. He believed in the Greek Orthodox Church as an institution and as a cornerstone of the nation, but only worshipped when it suited him. He did not have any real 'faith' and merely observed the rituals because they defined him as a Greek citizen. His one true 'belief' was in his own ability to expand the profits of his business empire.

Nor did Konstantinos Komninos have a firm affiliation with any political party. He was a natural conservative. He had been nervous about the influx of refugees that had spilled into his city in the previous decade and resentful of what it had cost the city as much as the impact it had on the streets. He had had few friends among the departing Muslims, so he was quite happy to see them disappear. In some respects he had approved of the veteran statesman, Eleftherios Venizelos, because he had made Greece more Greek. In other respects, he was pro-Monarchy. He voted pragmatically but was a conservative with a small 'c' and a royalist with a small 'r', and had never hung a portrait of either the exiled King or Venizelos. Law, order and control of the working classes were good for business, and he had fully supported some purges that had taken place in the army and the university after a recent, failed, military coup.

For Dimitri a rapid sense of unease was developing. He lived in a luxurious mansion and yet instinctively sympathised with the majority who were poor. It was a conundrum that was hard to solve but he hoped his medical training would at least give him the opportunity to help some of the city's less fortunate inhabitants.

'Just try to live the best life you can,' Olga said simply to Dimitri. She had been listening to her son's dilemma, knowing that she must keep it from her husband.

Dimitri assiduously avoided his father. It was not difficult as Konstantinos was rarely at home.

Early one morning in his second term at the university, he saw Katerina and Elias on their way to work. When he spotted them coming towards him down the street they seemed self-contained in a world of shared laughter and contentment. They did not even notice him until they were only a few feet away.

'Dimitri!' exclaimed Katerina. '*Ti kaneis?* How are you?'

Within a few minutes they had exchanged dozens of life's details, interrupting each other with questions, exclamations and answers.

'How is Eugenia?'

'Weaving in a workshop now. It's hard work but more sociable.'

'And the twins?'

'Maria is married now and has moved to Trikala with their baby.'

'A baby! So young!'

'And Sofia is supposed to be getting married too . . .'

'"Supposed"?'

'Well . . . They've already been engaged for two years. It seems a long time to me . . . And Kyria Komninos?'

Katerina was finishing some beading on a new gown for her, so she had been on her mind.

'She is well,' answered Dimitri, knowing that this was the expected answer. 'Perhaps you'll be asked to deliver the dress?'

'I would love to. But do you remember last time? I got into such trouble over that yellow dress. In any case, we're so busy now that there is a special delivery service. Kyrios Moreno even has his own van now!'

What a pity, reflected Dimitri. He remembered the afternoon, two years earlier, when Katerina had delivered the yellow dress and how much gaiety she had brought into the house. He was not sure that he had seen his mother smile since then. He watched her every day, pale and beautiful, and knew that she never left the Niki Street mansion. Her only conversation was with Pavlina and himself, and he was certain that his parents rarely spoke. His father came in when she had already gone to bed and left before she was up, and Olga's only contact with the outside world was to watch, from the safe distance of the drawing room, the comings and goings along the esplanade. She was always eager to hear about the university, hungry for the details of Dimitri's day: where his discussions had led him, who his friends were. She lived her life through him, because she had no other.

'Let's go for coffee some time!' enthused Elias. 'We have unfinished business, don't we?'

Dimitri laughed. Elias was referring to the *tavli* tournament they had begun over half a life-time earlier. They had played countless games and neither had ever been ahead by more than one win. It had been obsessional. Both of them had improved since that time and added new versions of the game to their repertoire.

Sending warm regards to their respective families, they agreed to meet again the following weekend.

Dimitri could not resist a glance over his shoulder. With a pang of envy, he noticed that Katerina's head was inclined towards Elias'. Hardly a breath of air came between them.

Integral to Dimitri's life at the university was his group of new friends. When they had finished their essays, they often met up again in the evening. There was always much to debate and the kafenion was a more appropriate place than the library.

Vassili was the clear leader of their group, not just because he was the most physical (he played soccer for one of the city teams), but because of his loud voice and lack of self-doubt. His background and upbringing had been very different from Dimitri's. His father, a refugee from Asia Minor, was a trade union official, and socialist beliefs ran through his veins, as red as blood. A few months earlier he had met the charismatic Communist leader Nikolaos Zakhariades who, like Vassili's own family, had come from Asia Minor. Vassili had fallen under his spell.

Here was a set of beliefs with well-defined aims, and idealistic youths such as Vassili responded to the hugely powerful personality who promulgated them in this city. In days gone by, they might have followed Venizelos, but his beard had long since turned white and his powers were spent. Vassili's new cause was more obsessive than a fresh love affair and more frenzied than a religious conversion.

The only thing that distracted him from politics was music. Late one Friday evening, or perhaps even in the early hours of the following day, when five of them, Dimitri, Vassili, Lefteris, Manoli and Alexandros, had emptied a bottle of *tsipouro* and they had almost run out of ideologies to debate, Vassili told his group of friends that he was taking them to hear some music. There was a popular rebetika singer performing downtown and they must all go.

Dimitri's father was scornful of most music so there had never been a gramophone in the Komninos house. In spite of this, Dimitri had heard plenty in the past few months. There was music on every street in this entertainment-hungry city, and crowds would gather in the sunshine as well as in the snow to hear klarino players from the mountains, mandolin bands and gypsy drummers.

Most café owners now had radios, and from the crackling sets normally screwed to the wall behind the bar, Dimitri had, of late, become acquainted with rebetika, the popular 'music of the under-ground', the music of suffering. He enjoyed the nostalgic oriental sounds of those who mourned their lost origins in the East but had not yet been to any live performances. There had always been work to complete, books to read.

'Come on, Dimitri, your essay will wait. This *rebetis* won't.'

They walked towards the railway station into a street filled with *tekhedes*, rebetika clubs, hashish bars, and brothels, and Dimitri thought how angry his father would be if he knew he was here. How else could he learn about life without exploring places other than the well-washed paving stones of the city's bourgeois pavements? Vassili purposefully led them through a low archway into a dingy room, dimly lit and dense with smoke. The place was packed out and they squeezed their way through the crowd to the one table that was still free. Within seconds, a bottle of clear liquid was slammed down on the table with six small glasses.

Three musicians were already playing, one on bouzouki and two on baglama, its higher-pitched sister. The music was rhythmic, insistent, repetitive and the atmosphere charged with anticipation.

Eventually the big attraction emerged from a back room and made his way through the crowd. It took some time. He stopped to shake hands with a dozen people on his way to the area that was slightly raised to create a stage. At each table he accepted a *tsipouro* and after clinking glasses with everyone close by, he downed it and moved on. He was smartly dressed in a suit and a gleaming white shirt, handsome, charismatic, smiling.

'That's Stelios Keromitis,' Vassili shouted above the noise. He was a rebetika star from Piraeus and for a few nights he was in Thessaloniki.

When he finally reached his fellow musicians, he picked up the bouzouki that was waiting for him and took his seat. He fiddled with the pegs for a moment to tune his instrument, tucked his cigarette neatly between the little finger and third finger of his left hand and, with a nod at the others, began to play. After a few introductory bars he started to sing. It was a growl, like a lion, deep and full of pain and anguish, matching the lyrics, which spoke of death, disease and separation. Such themes were the reality of day-to-day life in the sordid alleyways through which they had walked to reach this place.

A large proportion of people in the room, Vassili included, were refugees from Asia Minor, and a yearning for the land of their birth was ever-present. The half-Eastern, half-Western sound of the music embodied their sense of separation and longing, and they inhaled the pathos of the music as deeply as they took the hashish into their lungs.

As the night wore on, the audience began to sing and occasionally Keromitis' voice was almost lost. By now he was smoking a narghile and only sang the odd burst between inhalations. The air was opaque with smoke and noise, and alcohol had thickened their sensibilities.

About three in the morning, a man close to the front stood up and the nearby tables were pulled back. Slowly he began to revolve, his arms outstretched, cigarette in hand, his head angled to the side. Dimitri thought of the dervishes he had once been taken to see. This man's trance-like state reminded him of theirs, though he looked earthwards rather than to heaven.

The dancer was lean and strong, his unbuttoned shirt revealing a glimpse of powerful torso. His friends began a slow rhythmic hand-clap as he rotated, gradually dropping closer to the ground and never losing his balance as he turned on his haunches and rose again. He seemed in a state of extreme introspection and occasionally, as if pulling energy from the earth, he leaped high into the air.

Dimitri noticed that the few women at the back of the room close to the bar, probably prostitutes, craned their necks to watch. One of them even stood on a chair to see over the crowd.

These women who were paid for sex by the hour would willingly have given their services for nothing to this unselfconscious human being. His sinuous body and apparent oblivion to their admiring glances enthralled them.

His performance aroused them all, men and women alike, and for six and a half minutes, no one looked at Keromitis. The power of the *zeibekiko* held them all spellbound. Eventually, when a few glasses had shattered at the dancer's feet, a sign of approval and encouragement, the music changed from the mysterious, counter-intuitive 9/8 beat and the man returned to his seat, blending once more into the crowd.

Around five in the morning, when Keromitis had finally exhausted himself, Dimitri and his group drifted outside. The streets were filled with the hazy orange light of a newly risen sun and they made for a nearby café.

'Let's eat,' said Vassili, who was at the head of the group.

The combined effect of the hashish and the rebetika, even though it was full of suffering, had left them feeling high. It was the first time in his life that Dimitri had lost an entire night of sleep and he was surprised by the sense of heightened alertness it gave him. The overpowering ambience of the *teke*, the stridence and sincerity of the music, and the strong camaraderie within this group of students had all given him a different sense of what it was to be alive. He found the scent of the city's subculture unexpectedly alluring and wondered how the bourgeoisie could be so contented with dinners in expensive Europeanised restaurants or with soirées in grand houses, when close by was a culture of such emotional rawness.

When he had time and was in a state of greater sobriety to reflect, he would know the answer to this. That dawn, sitting in front of his *patsas* soup, spooning warm and nourishing lumps of lamb's guts into his mouth, in a childlike way he could not imagine how anyone would not want to be in this moment, in this place, with him.

'I'm going back to get some sleep before our class,' announced Vassili.

There was a low-toned murmur of agreement from the others and each of them put a few drachma on the table before leaving the café and going their separate ways.

Dimitri had a vague notion of the route that his father took to work and in his bleary-eyed state made a note to avoid the same streets. Fifteen minutes later, he arrived back home, let himself in and slipped up to his bedroom. On the previous evening, his father had assumed that his son was behind the closed door, studying hard for the forthcoming examinations.

After that night, visits to rebetika bars became more frequent and the griminess of the city's subculture brought him closer to the heart of Thessaloniki. The evocative lyrics of broken hearts and broken lives may have had no connection with his own experience, but they gave Dimitri a chance to wonder and to dream.

The pimps, *rebetes* and hashish dealers seemed as integral to the city as the bankers and owners of the department stores, and there was something appealing about the rawness of this alternative life, away from the order and perfection of the house in which he slept. For a decade or more, Konstantinos Komninos had issued dark warnings to his son about the areas of Thessaloniki that he claimed were too dangerous to frequent. 'They're full of low-life and whores,' he told Dimitri. 'Keep away from them.'

Elias Moreno began to join the group on their evenings out. This usually followed a fierce and noisy *tavli* contest with Dimitri. For an hour or so, they worked their way through a repertoire of games: *portes*, *plakoto* and *fevga*, playing in a fast percussive rhythm whose beat neither of them ever missed. Not a second passed between the fall of the dice and the making of a move, and every action had its sound. First, the crack of the dice as they were hurled against the side of the board, then the whirl as they rotated like spinning tops and finally the quick slide and clack of the counters, before the dice were once again seized and thrown. The counters were constantly chattering, but between the moment when the game began and the final satisfying slam of the loser's counter on the central ridge of the board, the players did not speak a word.

Occasionally an expletive would be muttered at the dice for failing to land as a double. For the duration of the game it was war and, for an hour or so, with eyes focused on the board, they did not give each other so much as a glance. Dimitri mopped his brow with a handkerchief and Elias used his cuff. Only once the game had ended was conversation resumed. This was when Dimitri would enquire after Elias' parents and also after Katerina.

He knew that, now the twins had left home, and Eugenia was working long hours in the carpet factory, Katerina had almost become a member of the Moreno family. She often went for dinner and took the place at the table that had once been occupied by Saul's mother, who had died a few months earlier.

Most evenings Katerina would stay for a few hours afterwards, working on some embroidery and enjoying the company of Roza Moreno. For both of them it was not work, just the continuation of a pleasurable activity that they were lucky enough to do in the day as well as in the evening.

Elias spoke of Katerina with admiration and affection, and, even though he thought it wrong to be jealous of his 'milk brother', sometimes Dimitri could feel a slight prickling under his skin.

Elias had taught himself to play the oud and occasionally performed in one of the bars. Whenever he did so, Dimitri, Vassili and the others would go along. Elias had become a welcome part of their group. Unlike them, he was a working man, connected with a world of commerce that was far removed from their academic sphere of libraries and lecture halls, but they were all bound together by their attachment to rebetika.

The music and the men who played it were the backdrop to

the many evenings spent together and politics were often the subject of their discussion.

The country continued to see widespread poverty and political and economic uncertainty. Unrest was brewing. In just over a decade there had been a dozen coups and nearly twice as many governments, and the pendulum had continued to swing between those who wanted the return of the monarchy and those who did not. The place of the monarchy in Greece had continued to be a matter of great controversy and debate. In 1920, when King Alexander had died of a monkey bite, his father had returned from exile only to be driven out of the country again two years later. He had been replaced by his eldest son, George, who was in turn obliged to leave at the end of the following year. For nearly twelve years King George had remained in exile, finally returning after a rigged plebiscite.

Close-run elections were held in January of 1936 and although the Royalists gained the most seats, the Communists held the balance of power. This made for an uneasy climate, with no clear centre of authority.

The police had new powers and were now able to arrest people simply for disagreeing with the government or protesting.

Vassili felt that it was time for action. He tried to stir up his friends.

'These prisoners have done nothing *wrong*!' he ranted. 'Usually they have just expressed the truth: that they are being underpaid and exploited. Which is factually *right*!'

'It's illogical, unjust . . .'

'Intolerable!' bellowed Vassili. 'And we should be doing something about it!'

Dimitri knew that if he got into a discussion with his father over the rights and wrongs of how the Left were being treated, they would come to blows. Most of the time he managed to hide behind the urgency of his studies, a need to go to the laboratory, pressing engagements with his professors and so on, but once a week, largely for his mother's sake, Dimitri had dinner with both his parents. To spare Olga, as her disposition would patently not deal well with a huge row between father and son, he steered clear of controversial subjects, kept conversation light, talked of his anatomy classes, enquired after the business and generally kept the illusion going that he would one day join the Komninos business.

It was one Saturday evening just after Easter and the weekly ordeal was planned for the following day. Dimitri and Elias were playing *tavli* and had arranged to meet up with Vassili later for a night in their favourite *teke*. It was after eleven when they left the kafenion, but the musicians they were hoping to hear would probably not begin playing until midnight.

Dimitri had drunk only one beer as he had to study hard the next day in preparation for some exams. If he had not been so clear-headed, he would have had trouble believing his own eyes as they walked through the seedy streets. For a while, they were walking fifty or so metres behind the shadowy and indistinct figure of a man. Then he stopped at an entrance in front of them and turned to look behind him before walking through the doorway, which had been opened for him from inside. He did not see Dimitri and Elias, as they were obscured by shadow, but both of them saw him quite clearly.

'Wasn't that . . . ?' Elias stopped, embarrassed, wishing he had not spoken.

'My father. Yes. I'm certain it was.'

Without discussing it further, they both continued walking. Dimitri was in a state of shock. It was one of the less filthy whorehouses but, even so, it was a known brothel. His father was visiting a prostitute.

Dimitri's first thought was to wait until his father emerged, and to confront him there and then.

Elias linked his arm through Dimitri's, reading his mind in an instant. He could feel his friend's anger and dismay.

'Perhaps it's best not to make a scene here, Dimitri,' he said. 'Perhaps you shouldn't say anything at all.'

Dimitri knew he needed time to absorb what he had seen. For the moment, his only thought was that everything his father seemed to stand for was based on a lie. He was more connected with the dark side of Thessaloniki even than himself. He was a hypocrite.

When Dimitri got home that night, he was almost insensible with alcohol. He fell against the hall table and sent an ornament crashing to the floor. His father appeared with such alacrity at the top of the staircase that Dimitri wondered if he had been waiting for him.

'What time do you think this is?' He was half-whispering, half-shouting, as he ran down the stairs at great speed towards his son. 'Where on earth do you think you have been?'

Dimitri thought he was going to strike him, otherwise why the hurry? He stood very still as his father came flying like a raven in his black silk dressing gown towards him. He held on to the hall table with one hand to steady himself.

'Didn't you hear me? Where have you been?' Konstantinos' voice had risen out of a whisper to full volume now. 'Answer me!'

Pavlina had been disturbed by the noise and was standing at her bedroom door on the ground floor, her face full of bleary-eyed concern.

Maintaining his control, Dimitri leaned towards his father and, with an inch between their faces and in a low voice so that Pavlina could not hear, answered his father's question.

'I've been in Dionis Street.'

Komninos went pale. There was a distinctly triumphant edge to his son's voice.

Pavlina had disappeared and now returned with a broom to sweep the shattered remains of the figurine. As she guided the shards into a neat pile, her eyes stayed on the two men.

Konstantinos quickly regained his composure. Olga was now standing at the top of the stairs.

'What's happened?' she called down. 'Dimitri, are you all right?'

Her first thoughts were maternal ones. She knew that Dimitri frequented some of the unsafer parts of the city and she had read that there were often knife fights in the *tekhedes*.

'I'm fine, Mother,' he called up to her.

'It's time for everyone to be in bed,' barked Konstantinos. 'Pavlina, finish doing that in the morning, please.'

Olga had melted away and Pavlina silently backed into her room, leaving the broom leaning against the wall. Konstantinos turned his back on Dimitri and retreated sedately up the stairs.

Dimitri waited until his parents' door closed and then, gripping tightly onto the banister rail, staggered up to his room.

The following lunchtime, Dimitri, Olga and Konstantinos assembled round the large circular dining table, their places laid, as usual, at 'twenty-minute' intervals. The stiff flower arrangement at the centre of it reflected the mood. Pavlina came and went with the different courses and conversation was stilted. Each time she cleared a plate, she saw that Olga had scarcely touched the food. Dimitri had not done much better.

Olga knew that there was a problem between her husband and son and tried to keep conversation light. Throughout the meal, Dimitri tried to avoid looking at his father.

Only a week earlier it had been Easter and they had attended a service together. Fresh in Dimitri's mind were images of his

father kissing the icon, crossing himself and obsequiously genu-
flecting as he touched the ring on the priest's outstretched hand
with his lips. He winced as he thought of his father's front-row
position in church, a seat that he now realised recognised his
financial contribution to the building, rather than his closeness to
God. He looked at his sweet mother and wondered if she had
any idea.

More than ever, Konstantinos Komninos seemed to take a
masochistic pleasure in exploring the depths of political difference
between himself and his son, and always worked on the assumption that ultimately Dimitri would come round to his way of
thinking. A son always took over the family business. It was never
any other way. He had still not accepted that his son had other
ambitions.

Konstantinos knew that Dimitri would not betray him in front
of his mother and used this knowledge to play an even rougher
game than usual with his son, goading him into inexpressible fury
about the current state of affairs in the country. The King had
just appointed an army general, Ioannis Metaxas, as prime minister
and Metaxas was allowing the police to crack down heavily on
worker protests, which were an increasing threat to law and order
in the city. Some trade unionists and Communists had already
been exiled and, as a factory owner, Komninos was gratified to
see that something was being done to prevent workers stepping
out of line.

'As far as I'm concerned, the tougher the measures, the better!'

He directed this comment straight at Dimitri, certain that he would
get a reaction.

For Olga's sake, Dimitri did not respond to this provocation. He
was afraid of saying something regrettable that he might not wish
his mother to hear but he knew his father was testing him, pushing

him to the limit. While Olga was there, Konstantinos Komninos knew he was safe.

Dimitri cut into his meat, fantasising that its glinting blade was being driven into his father's flesh. Still chewing, he got up.

'I must go,' he said.

'Where are you going on a Sunday afternoon?' asked his father aggressively. 'Won't the library be shut?'

'I'm meeting some friends.'

'What a shame, *agapi mou*!' Olga said. 'Pavlina has made your favourite *glyko*.'

'Will you save me a piece, *mana mou*?' he said, leaning down to kiss the top of her head. 'I'm sorry I have to go.'

He was out on the street within a second and was soon hastening towards the kafenion where he had agreed to meet Elias and Vassili. As he passed the window he could see there was someone else with them. Katerina.

Dimitri had been walking fast but his heart was beating more furiously than normal as he opened the door.

It was not so common to see women in this kafenion, so Katerina hastily explained why she was there.

'I had to do a dress-fitting at a customer's house,' she told him, 'just one street from here, and Elias persuaded me to come here for a coffee afterwards.'

'On a Sunday? Isn't that a day of rest?'

'Not always, when you're working for Kyrios Moreno,' she said laughingly, picking up her bag. 'Anyway, I hope to see you again soon, Dimitri.'

'Shall I walk you home?'

The words came with complete spontaneity and Dimitri was immediately embarrassed by his offer. It was obvious that Elias should accompany her. He lived in the same street.

'No, but thanks,' she laughed. 'It's still light. I am fine on my own.'

'Are you sure?' he said.

Much to his surprise, she changed her mind.

'Well, actually, it would be nice. You aren't coming home yet, are you, Elias?'

Elias shook his head.

It was not far to Irini Street, and Dimitri found himself trying to slow the pace.

As they walked, Katerina talked of the Moreno family. Kyria Moreno had taught her almost every technique she knew now, and each day she was given new opportunities to extend her skills. She spoke about her craft with passion.

'I think of those girls in the tobacco factories, doing the same thing day in, day out and I know I would die if I had to do it,' she said. 'Every single hour is different in my work. There are dozens of different kinds of stitch and every time I do one of them it's in a different colour, on a new fabric, in a new combination. The result is never the same twice.'

'A bit like music?' reflected Dimitri.

'Yes! I suppose it's just like that,' she laughed.

'There are only eight notes, but they can be put together in thousands of different ways! So you're like Mozart, but with threads rather than notes?' Dimitri smiled at this image of Katerina. 'Elias says you were a child prodigy too, just like Mozart.'

Katerina blushed. Perhaps because of the mention of Elias. Dimitri was not sure and tried not to think about the amount of time they spent together.

'I don't know very much about Mozart, but I think he might be exaggerating.'

Their walk home was over all too quickly. Katerina's lively, unselfconscious conversation had charmed him. It seemed to him that something lit her up from inside. Her eyes smiled as much as her mouth and even the way she walked seemed to suggest happiness.

During the following days, he realised he was thinking of Katerina and hoping to see her. An image of her sat in the back of his mind and he did not push it away. Katerina exemplified something to him that he probably already knew: that there was not always a link between happiness and wealth. His own ill ease and the knowledge of the fortune that waited for him was proof in itself of that.

There was, however, a link between starvation and unrest. In Thessaloniki, many were on the breadline and trouble was inevitably brewing.

Vassili was bringing daily updates via his father. Temperatures in the street were rising as they moved into the month of May; the sweetness of spring was turning into the sizzling heat of summer and with that, the population was losing its patience and making demands. There was talk of a widespread strike.

'Thessaloniki is on the edge of revolution,' reported Vassili to his *parea*, in a state of high excitement. 'The tobacco workers are going out on strike! Tomorrow! We have to be there to support them.'

They had no choice. They had to support the exploited, the underdog, the people who were being paid less for a week's work than the wealthy were paying for a meal in the city's expensive hotels. Vassili had taken Dimitri around plenty of the areas where they lived and now it was time to show some solidarity.

They met the next day at the university and then set off in a group towards the town hall. Within minutes they found themselves in the flow of a mighty human river. There was a sense of excitement: a sunny day in the country that had invented democ-racy, an open protest on the street. It seemed right.

'This is how we show them what we feel!' said Vassili. 'The government can't ignore this, can they?' He had to shout above the noise of the crowd to be heard by his friends.

Word was going round that they had been joined by workers from the trams and railways as well as dock and electricity workers. The desire to protest had spread like an epidemic and there were more than twenty thousand people on the streets.

Vassili was euphoric. 'This could work, you know,' he said. 'This is people power!'

Eventually, the demonstrators went their separate ways.

In an untimely encounter with his father that evening, Dimitri heard something unwelcome.

'Well,' he said, handing his hat to Pavlina, but looking directly at his son. 'You'll be pleased to know that Metaxas has given the police freedom of action!'

Dimitri tried not to react. He did not want his father to know that he had been out on the street that day.

'That seems excessive,' he replied.

'Not in my view, Dimitri, not in my view.'

Dimitri said nothing.

'Even better, he has imposed martial law. It's the only way, with those sort of people.'

Even the way his father said 'those sort of people' made Dimitri want to spit, but his strength was in being able to restrain himself. He always allowed his father the final word. It was almost a joke with himself that he permitted it.

'Stay off the streets, tomorrow, won't you?'

Konstantinos knew that he had demonstrated that day. Some spectator had spotted Dimitri and reported it to him.

The following day began in the same way. A group of students, Dimitri included, gathered and set off towards the centre of Thessaloniki to join various other groups.

The atmosphere was very different. In the centre of the city, protesters shouting 'Long Live the Strike' stood in a phalanx opposite police and soldiers. For a while they just looked at each other. The atmosphere was strangely still, but full of aggression.

Vassili, eager to be at the centre of the action, slithered his way into the heart of the crowd. Dimitri tried to follow but his way was blocked by the sudden surging density of protesters. There was a roar as they moved forward in one concerted action.

Then, as if to acknowledge that they might be losing control, the police opened fire.

From where he stood, Dimitri did not see anything but the reverse motion of the crowd as they moved backwards, some of them turning round in an attempt to escape. There was chaos, panic, utter confusion, total disbelief. The police had opened fire on an unarmed crowd.

People fled in every direction, screaming, punching out with their arms to escape, Dimitri's student friends among them. There was no time to look out for each other.

No one knew what was happening, nor what was going to happen, but they had an animal instinct for self-preservation and one or two people got knocked down in the stampede. Dimitri found himself in an alleyway. All the nearby shops and cafés were shuttered so there was nowhere to retreat to. He ran blindly and kept on running. The police would be arresting demonstrators and he knew they would behave brutally to their prisoners.

With his legs almost buckling beneath him from exertion and

fear, he noticed he was close to Irini Street. He knocked on Kyria Moreno's door.

There he stayed for a few hours, feeling safe but all the while anxious for the friends he had been with. Eventually, when he thought that the police would have given up trying to find perpetrators, he got up to leave. He took a glance up and down the street to check it was safe, but also, as he admitted to himself, to see if Katerina might be there, and then walked briskly back to Niki Street.

His mother was overjoyed to see him.

'Dimitri!' she said, hugging him. He could feel her warm tears dripping down her face and on to his shirt. 'You were there, weren't you?'

'I'm sorry, Mother, I'm really sorry. You must have been so worried.'

'All I know is that people were killed,' she said. 'Pavlina just came in with the news . . . I thought one of them might be you.'

'Oh my God!' said Dimitri, pulling away from his mother. 'None of us had weapons.'

'And lots of others were badly wounded,' she added. 'I'm just so glad you are here.'

'Vassili was at the front of the crowd. I need to see if I can find him.'

Dimitri bolted from the house and ran through the streets towards the hospital. There was debris everywhere, evidence of the panic that had ensued after the police had turned their guns on the demonstrators.

A search through the wards told him that his friend was not among the wounded and, in trepidation, he went to the nearby morgue. A doctor at the hospital told him that this was where the dead had been taken.

As he approached the building, he saw a familiar, haggard face. It was Vassili's father.

'He's not there!' he cried, hugging Dimitri and weeping with relief. 'He's not there!'

'And he's not in the hospital, either!' said Dimitri.

'He's not? I was just about to go there.'

'You don't need to. And he hasn't been home?'

'No,' said Vassili's father. 'There's only one other place I can think of.'

They realised that Vassili must have been arrested.

'I shall go to the gaol,' said the older man. 'But you mustn't come. It's an unnecessary risk.'

The following day saw an outpouring of grief for the dead. Thousands came to mourn. Twelve flower-strewn corpses were carried on open biers through the streets and people wept copiously for the martyrs and for the dozens of wounded who lay in the hospital. Those who were in the funeral procession came to lament the demise of their freedom, as well as the death of their friends. Petals carpeted the place where the protesters had been mown down.

When further strikes were scheduled, it was the excuse that Metaxas had been waiting for. He informed the King that the country was facing a Communist plot. On 4 August, he was given permission to declare martial law. Greece was now a dictatorship.

The heat was oppressive and that evening the mercury had still not fallen below thirty-five degrees. Olga had retired to bed early.

Dimitri found his place at the dinner table had been moved round so that he was opposite his father. Pavlina was yet to serve the first course but the wine had already been poured.

Konstantinos Komninos picked up his glass.

'I would like to raise a toast,' he said.

For once, Dimitri met his father's look.

Stubbornly, he did not reach for his glass but continued to stare into the cold eyes that were locked onto his.

'To law and order,' said Komninos. 'To the dictatorship.'

He was not smiling, but there was a triumphal glint in his eye.

Was it self-control or cowardice, wondered Dimitri, that prevented him from smashing the decanter into his father's face?

*Come on! Do it!* Komninos' expression seemed to taunt.

Wordlessly, carefully, Dimitri got up and left the room. Although flames of pure hatred licked at his heart, he would not allow his father the satisfaction of a reaction.

Konstantinos Komninos heard the distant slam of the front door and continued to eat his dinner, alone. Out in the street, Dimitri vomited into the gutter.

# Chapter Seventeen

Exactly as dimitri feared and precisely as his father hoped, Metaxas introduced further suppression of the unions and gave the police additional powers. Communists and left-wing activists were rounded up and put into prison camps. Torture was used to extract confessions or to make prisoners name other Communists.

For several months, Vassili remained in prison. No one had been allowed to see him, and Dimitri and his friends met up with his father on many occasions to discuss what they could do. His warning was always stark.

'I know you aren't party members,' he said, 'but if you go to visit they'll still mark you down as Communists. Keep away – that's the best thing to do.'

One of the law professors campaigned for his release, even testifying that his student had been on the way to his class when he was caught up in the demonstration. Six weeks after his arrest, Vassili's father received a letter. He opened it with excitement, expecting it to contain news of his son's release.

'Dear Kyrios Filipidis,' it said. 'We wish to inform you that your son passed away on 14 June. Cause of death: tuberculosis. If you wish to collect his personal effects, you may do so by the 18th of this month.'

He received the letter on that date.

Vassili's father was too stricken by grief to visit the gaol, so Dimitri and his friend Lefteris went on his behalf. Dimitri knew that to sign his name on the form incriminated him, but he was proud to be the friend of such a martyr.

Tears of sadness coursed down his face at the funeral, but inside a fury was raging. Beyond any doubt, the authorities were responsible for Vassili's death and Dimitri promised himself that he would never take the side of a government who encouraged such action. Surely Greece deserved something better.

On the surface, life in the city remained unchanged. Dimitri continued to attend classes at university and businesses such as the Morenos' carried on as normal. From time to time Katerina joined Elias and Dimitri for a coffee but the tone of their conversation had changed. They were in mourning for Vassili and all three knew that beneath the normality of the city, anxiety was festering.

These days, Dimitri did his best to avoid his father. Even the occasional meal with him was more than he wanted. He was full of fear when his father was around, not because he was afraid of Konstantinos Komninos, but because he was afraid of what he might say to this man whom he now despised.

His mother seemed to understand everything without discussion. Never once did she question Dimitri when he left the house only moments before his father was due to return, or when he ate meals at strange times.

Olga understood Dimitri's feelings for his father, and Konstantinos' feelings for his son. From the day he was born, there had been no hint of love. She remembered how her husband had looked down at the sleeping child as though he were a specimen rather than his own flesh and blood. Then there had been the fire, and their circumstances had changed so drastically. The moment when a father first holds his son, looks into his eyes and sees a reflection of himself had been missed.

During those first two decades of Dimitri's life, she often raised the same question with Pavlina.

'Did I do something wrong?' she would ask her, wringing her slender hands.

Pavlina had her own ideas about Komninos but her instinct was to protect Olga.

'I think it just happens sometimes,' she would say. 'There are lots of men who don't find their children interesting. They think they're woman's work.'

'Perhaps you're right, Pavlina . . .'

'And then when they reach a certain age, they realise they have turned into men and start talking to them. You'll see.'

In some ways, Pavlina's theory was borne out by Konstantinos' behaviour. He seemed only to be waiting for one thing: his son's contribution to the growing business empire. He still believed he could force Dimitri to become the son he wanted, but Dimitri knew he would never do his father's bidding.

Though he despised the grandeur of the house itself and climbed the steps to the door in one bound, like a thief, not wanting to be seen, he looked forward to the moment when he stepped inside and his mother made her appearance at the top of the stairs. Dimitri never questioned the fact that Olga was there, every time, always waiting. It had been thus ever since they had moved back into Niki Street and he never wanted it to change. Her beauty and her quiet presence were the constants in the home. Dictatorship or republic, the political regime made no difference to the smiling embrace that Olga Komninos gave her son.

★　★　★

In Irini Street, Katerina often came home to a similarly warm welcome. Eugenia, having worked all day at the factory, still returned home to her own loom and picked up the shuttle. When Katerina appeared at the door, she was invariably there to greet her. The little gas flame beneath the *briki* was then immediately lit and their home filled up with the aroma of coffee. The evening meal would come later. While there was still an hour of daylight, both of them wanted to exploit it, since working by the light of an oil lamp strained their eyes. They cherished every last second that the sun remained in the sky.

Sometimes, while they sipped coffee, Katerina would stand behind her and massage Eugenia's exhausted shoulders as they talked of their respective days.

One day Eugenia received a letter from Maria asking her mother to go and live with her and her new family in Trikala. Sofia lived only a kilometre or so from them, in a nearby village.

'I've moved once in my life,' she said. 'That was quite enough . . . though I do miss the twins so much.'

'Of course you miss them!' said Katerina.

'It's not right to be separated like this, is it?'

'No, no! Of course, it's not right to be apart.'

The irony of their conversation struck them both, at the same moment. Eugenia turned to look at Katerina.

'I'm sorry,' she said. 'I wasn't really thinking . . .'

In silence, Eugenia resumed her weaving and Katerina opened her embroidery box and took out a camisole she was edging.

'Really, I didn't mean to—'

'It's all right, Eugenia,' said Katerina. 'Sometimes whole months go by, and I realise I haven't thought of my mother at all.'

Katerina put her sewing down and leaned forward. Eugenia could see that her eyes glistened.

'It's a strange feeling. Deep down, I know I am separated from something. But I can't really grasp what it is I am separated from any more. A place? A person? I can't even find the words . . .' Tears ran down her face as she tried to describe the almost indescribable. 'Whereas, here . . .'

Eugenia handed Katerina her handkerchief and the young woman dried her tears.

'Here is . . . Eugenia, I don't even know how to say it! You must know what I am talking about?'

'Yes, of course I do, *agapi mou*. This is home, isn't it? I feel just the same.'

Katerina struggled. She was torn between feelings of loyalty and betrayal.

'Thessaloniki is where I belong now,' she said.

'I feel just the same way as you,' agreed Eugenia. 'And I don't intend to leave.'

Letters from Zenia to her daughter had become less regular. She was now open with Katerina about the harsh reality of life with her new husband, and told her very frankly that she was better off staying where she was. Her last letter described the subdivision of her home. It was now shared with her two stepdaughters' husbands, and their widowed mothers. There were twelve of them using one latrine. Their living conditions were squalid. Only Zenia had a job.

Katerina had ceased to struggle with her conscience, and her sense of separation changed. It gave her a new feeling of loss, but a new sense of belonging too. As she still often did, Katerina subconsciously ran her hand along her left arm. The scar had not faded these past years.

They sat quietly for a few moments before Eugenia broke the silence.

'It's getting harder to remember the old places. People still talk about them, but they are the past for us now, aren't they? And Thessaloniki has been so kind.'

'*So* kind,' Katerina echoed. 'I don't really remember everything now, but did people welcome us when we came?'

Eugenia threw back her head and laughed. Katerina had never really seen her react like this to anything. She rocked back and forth, almost incapable of answering.

'Yes, my dear, they did welcome us. Not everyone in the whole city did, mind you. And lots of people had a very different experience. But the people of Irini Street. How they welcomed us!'

Eugenia was smiling at the memory of it all.

'I do remember coming into this house for the first time,' said Katerina. 'People were staring at us in the street.'

'Ah, but they were so nice. The Moreno family brought us food and spare clothes. I don't even know why they had little girls' dresses as they only had sons. But now I think of it, Kyria Moreno must have made them specially for you all. I had never even thought of that before tonight . . . And Pavlina came in with honey and some vegetables. You remember that Olga and Dimitri were living there just while they were having that vast house rebuilt?'

'Yes, of course.'

'And I bet Olga Komninos was much happier living here in this street than where she is now.'

'I've heard Kyria Moreno say that she hasn't been out of that house since the day she left Irini Street. She must be exaggerating, mustn't she?'

'Who's to say?' Eugenia shrugged. 'But don't they make all those fine clothes for her in the workshop? They aren't only to decorate the wardrobe, are they?'

'Elias says that they are just for Kyria Komninos to wear in the house. For when they have grand people to dinner.'

'Well, I don't know. None of us knows what happens behind the closed doors of those big houses and we never will.'

It made Katerina smile. In streets where the houses were small, the doors were rarely shut, and on the occasions when they were, it merely took a gentle push to open them. In the mansion on Niki Street, no one knew what took place. Except for the owners. Katerina had never forgotten her visit there and could picture Olga alone in her high-ceilinged drawing room, with its elaborate architraves and cornicing. Their entire house in Irini Street would fit comfortably into the hallway.

The two women chattered on in the darkness. Katerina's sewing remained unfinished, and the shuttle lay idle.

Their only tears now were those of laughter.

Several times over the next few months, Katerina bumped into Dimitri and they developed a habit of going to the same pastry shop each time they met. It was close to the dazzling haberdashery shop, which she had been visiting on an almost weekly basis since her arrival in the city. She had become firm friends with old Kyrios Alatzas who owned it, though he no longer had to give her lengths of ribbon for her hair.

While the weather had still been hot Dimitri and Katerina had drunk lemonade out on the pavement, but when the days shortened they went inside and Katerina would choose a pastry from the glass cabinet. Dimitri always ordered her an additional one, which she would take home, teasing her about her passion for sweet things. Their conversation was a strange mix.

'I shouldn't really tell you this, but . . .' was usually how her anecdotes began.

There were rich women in Thessaloniki, 'of a certain age', as she described them, who came in to be measured up for the latest fashions. They brought illustrations and photographs cut from magazines and were convinced that they could be made to look the same as the women in the pictures.

'It's Kyrios Moreno's job to break the news, without offending the customer, that the outfit in question might not be suitable. It always goes the same way. You have to find him and say: "Kyrios Moreno, could you come and speak to a customer about Chanel?" It's something like a code. So, off he goes, and with the greatest tact you can imagine, he has to think of a way to adapt what the customer wants so that it will suit her. He'll say anything to make them agree, pretending that there are already twenty similar dresses in production or that the style will age them – that usually works. And colours too. Sometimes there will be a vogue for canary yellow, and yellow just doesn't work on everyone, does it? Most people look more dead than alive in it!

'I'm lucky,' she said, sighing. 'I don't have much to do with rich and difficult women, but sometimes I have to do some fittings, so I know what they can be like.'

Dimitri smiled knowingly. Many of those rich and difficult women were probably regular guests at his parents' dinner table. He listened, charmed by her gently satirical descriptions of them.

Katerina did not realise that Dimitri went out of his way to meet her. It was never a coincidence. Once or twice, when he had seen her walking home with Elias, he had avoided them and taken another route, giving himself the excuse that he would not want to interrupt what seemed to be an intimate conversation.

Katerina was equally keen to hear about the world that Dimitri lived in. She always listened eagerly when he told her of any rebetika musicians he had seen and sometimes she recognised their names. Dimitri had gone less frequently since the death of Vassili and the birth of the dictatorship, which had brought in new censorship laws. Rebetika was considered subversive and the police regularly raided the places where it was played.

He talked a little about his studies and the professors who supervised him. He tried to add some amusing touches, but it was hard. There was little humour in a medical degree.

Naturally, Katerina always asked after Olga.

'I wish she sometimes went out,' he said. 'I don't really understand it, but perhaps I will one day, if I study medicine hard enough.'

'I might be asked to visit your house soon,' Katerina told Dimitri one day.

His eyes lit up. 'Why's that?'

Kyrios Moreno had recently told her that, in due course, he would be asking her to do final fittings for Kyria Komninos. His oldest seamstress was about to retire after sixty years of working for the Moreno family and Kyrios Moreno saw Katerina as her successor. Martha Perez was renowned in the city. Her seams were invisible and her darts and tucks were more perfectly executed than by any modern machine. Her tailoring lay against the body like a second skin. She was his top *modista* and, ever since he had married Olga, Konstantinos had insisted that her clothes were made by Martha. At the age of seventy-five, tiredness was beginning to get the better of her.

Dimitri had sometimes seen Kyria Perez come and go, but he loved the thought that soon it would be Katerina instead.

'I am sure my mother will look forward to seeing you,' he said, smiling.

Katerina's world was a place of silks and satins, buttons and bows, embroidery and embellishment, a factory of beautiful things. Hers was a world of colour while Dimitri's was in monochrome. The university environment had always been austere, but had become an even more sombre place under the dictatorship. A mixture of fear and defiance hung in the air, and sourness too, as students with different political affiliations mixed together, creating tensions and rivalries of their own. Leftist militancy and communism were forced deeper beneath the surface, but this only seemed to strengthen them.

For a while, one aspect of life for the Morenos themselves seemed to improve. The dictatorship had suppressed the organisation that had encouraged the anti-Semitic attacks of the early part of the decade, so the Jews of the city felt a new sense of safety.

'It's been a whole six months now,' reflected Saul Moreno to his sons, 'since we've had graffiti on the walls. Not one word.'

They were on their way to the workshop. Katerina was with them, as usual.

'That's just as well,' said Elias. 'Because sooner or later, we would have had to tell Mother why we were always buying paint.'

Isaac, who was always less optimistic than his younger brother about things, and had seen for himself the destruction in the Campbell district only five years earlier, felt obliged to add his comment.

'You can lock a few people up,' he said, 'but if there are people who hate us, believe me, they'll find a way to show it.'

'Oh, come on, Isaac, don't be so pessimistic!' said his father.

'I want to be wrong, but those feelings don't just come from the Left. Didn't you see the paper yesterday?'

'No, I didn't.'

'There have been some attacks on Jews in Germany. Brutal ones. And not carried out by the Left.'

'But how far away is Germany?' scoffed his father. 'Eh? It's not Greece, is it?'

'Father is right, Isaac! Who cares about Germany? Let's at least stick to talking about Thessaloniki!'

'You can stick to talking about anywhere you like,' said Isaac, 'but I think you're being very naïve.'

'Well, let's not argue about nothing,' said Saul Moreno. 'Especially in front of your mother. You know how she hates to hear you two bickering.'

'Do you really think people would come to us for all their lavish clothes if they hated us as you say they do?' persisted Elias, wanting to disprove his brother's theory.

While his sons were still pursuing their argument, Saul Moreno had opened up the door to the workshop. Even if he had lost a handful of customers, his order books were full. As never before, people were waiting for baptism and bar mitzvah clothes, ball gowns and bridal gowns, and suits – always suits. Even if the fashion for width, turn-up or trouser-leg flare changed by a centimetre, there were plenty of men in this city who would immediately come for new measurements.

Life in Thessaloniki carried on largely as before, with the rich continuing to be rich and the poor to be poor (but with fewer outlets to express their discontent). People were largely unaffected by the fact that life in other parts of Europe was changing dramatically. Then, in September 1939, Germany invaded Poland and another world war began.

There was no shortage of news in Thessaloniki as the months passed. Though some of the left-wing titles had been closed under the dictatorship, there were still hundreds of newspapers and many different views on the war. The dictatorship's position was ambivalent. It was politically aligned with France, commercially dependent on Germany and friendly with Mussolini, a position of uneasy neutrality that could probably not be sustained for long. The good relations between Greece and Italy, which Metaxas had managed to sustain, began to deteriorate when Italian planes began to fly over Greek territory.

Dimitri and his friends constantly debated their positions.

'What is Metaxas waiting for? Why doesn't he think that we'll go the way of the rest of Europe? I can't stand his apathy!'

'What do you want him to do?'

'Get the country ready!'

'Perhaps he knows what he's doing,' suggested Dimitri. 'Maybe it's a more complex game of diplomacy than we know.'

'I don't believe it. I think he's just afraid to fight.'

'An army general, afraid to fight! Whatever your politics, you're a coward if you won't fight for your country.'

The students had been stretched intellectually but not physically, and they were ready for action. They knew that Greece was a sitting target.

In the early hours of 28 October 1940, the Italian ambassador delivered a message to Metaxas at his home in Athens. Mussolini wanted to occupy certain strategic positions in northern Greece.

The Greek Prime Minister responded with a resounding '*Ochi*' – 'No!'

Within hours, the Italians invaded through Albania.

'IT IS WAR!' stated the headlines, quoting Metaxas. Everyone knew that the Greek army was unprepared and ill-equipped.

'I'm joining up,' said Lefteris, one of Dimitri's fellow students. 'Our studies can wait. If we don't get the Italians off our soil now, there might not even be a university soon.'

'What? You, the arch-enemy of an army general, are going to join the army?' Dimitri asked with incredulity.

'We have a common enemy, don't we? How else do we fight him? We wait until Mussolini turns up here on our doorstep and then hit him over the head with a book?'

The others laughed, but it was not really a moment for humour.

'Look, if we join up today, we'll be on a train to Ioannina by tonight and in forty-eight hours we'll be part of the action. We'll be doing something, for God's sake.'

Whatever the political leanings of these students, ultimately they were all patriots at heart. They were determined to protect their *patrida*, despite the fact that not one of them had ever held a gun, and passion rather than good sense would lead them to the front.

'I'm with you,' said Dimitri. Everyone round the table concurred. 'And I'll let Elias know what we're doing.'

Everything moved quickly after that. On his way home to collect a few things, Dimitri stopped at the Moreno workshop. He had never been inside and Kyrios Moreno was surprised to see him.

'Can I have a word with Elias?' he asked with confidence, knowing that his appearance here in the middle of the day seemed strange.

'I'll send him out to see you in a moment,' said Saul Moreno. 'He's with a customer at the moment. You'd think people might have other things on their minds than a new suit. But it's business as usual, today. Perhaps they think that the invasion will push prices up.'

As he went through the door that led from the reception area into the workshop he left it half open behind him. Dimitri was transfixed by what he saw. A girl in a long, cream dress, covered in sequins that glistened like fish-scales, was standing on a chair, while another girl pinned the hem. With her arms held upwards and outstretched inside the full sleeves, she looked like an angel or a dervish, but when she rotated to aid the pinning, Dimitri realised it was Katerina. Wisps of hair had fallen across her face. It seemed as though her thoughts were a million miles away.

Suddenly the door swung open and Katerina caught sight of him.

'Dimitri!' she cried, with surprise and unconcealed delight. 'What are you doing here?'

Before he had time to answer, Saul Moreno returned.

'Elias is just coming,' he said.

Katerina now stood in front of him. She looked like a small goddess.

'It suits you,' was all he could think of to say.

'I'm exactly the same size as the customer,' said Katerina. 'So it saves her coming in for fittings.'

Dimitri was lost for words. He had only ever seen Katerina in simple, day-to-day clothes and the transformation was astonishing.

Elias then appeared.

'Dimitri! What are you doing here? My father said you wanted to see me. What's happened?'

Dimitri quickly recovered his composure. 'The invasion . . .'

'Yes, I know. We said it was going to happen, didn't we?'

'Well, some of us are going.'

There was not a moment's hesitation before Elias responded.

'I'm coming too.'

'I knew you would. But we have to go almost immediately. There's a train leaving for Ioannina at seven tonight.'

'That soon! All right. I'll tell my father, go home for some things and then meet you at the station.'

There was determination in Elias' voice. Dimitri knew he would be there in good time before the train rolled out of the station.

While Elias went to tell his father, Dimitri was on his way to break the news to his mother. Konstantinos Komninos would not find out until his son was well on his way.

It was as though Olga half expected Dimitri to be going. When he knocked on the door of the drawing room, she was standing by the French windows that looked out over the sea. The water was rough that day.

'You've come to say goodbye, haven't you?'

'How did you know?'

'I know my own son,' she said, with a catch in her throat. 'That's how I know what he will do.'

Dimitri put his arms around his mother.

'I hope you think what I am doing is right.'

'You're going to protect Greece, Dimitri. Of course it's right. And you are young and strong. Who else is going to do it, if not you?'

'I'm going with some friends too, I won't be doing it single-handedly,' he said, almost jokingly.

Olga tried to smile, but she could not manage it, so she turned away and walked towards the gilded bureau that stood against the wall. She opened one of its many drawers and took out a brown envelope.

'You'll need this,' she said.

Dimitri took the envelope without shame. From its thickness he could tell that there were millions of drachma inside. He and his friends would be needing them and he accepted them without hesitation.

'Thank you, Mother.'

There was no merit in delaying a parting that was unbearable to both of them. Olga stood erect, with her arms tightly crossed. She was squeezing herself so tightly that she could scarcely speak or breathe. Such a posture was the only way she could prevent herself from losing control. Under no circumstances must she allow herself to cry.

She looked at her son with pleading eyes and gestured with a nod of her head that he should go.

He kissed her on the forehead, then he was out of the door. Pavlina thrust some food into his hand and, with some spare clothes and a few books, he left the house at a run.

The following day, the Moreno workshop buzzed with the news of Elias' departure. Kyrios Moreno was impressed by the bravery of his son, and announced to all his young male workers that he would support them if they chose to make the same decision. Two of them did not return to work the following morning. They had followed Elias' example and signed up. Everyone was proud of them, knowing that they were joining thousands of other young Jewish men who were going off to fight.

Soon there were news reports from the front. The army suffered from a dire shortage of equipment and supplies, and weather conditions were becoming severe, with deep snow and sub-zero temperatures in the mountains. Most soldiers lacked experience, but soon acquired it.

Katerina wondered how Kyria Komninos had taken her son's departure and imagined that she would be as anxious as Roza Moreno. On her way home that night, she took a detour to the little church of Agios Nikolaos Orfanos, and lit two candles. She stared into the flames and prayed long, hard and equally for the safety of Dimitri and Elias. Elias and Dimitri. It was hard to know how to order their names.

The days went by and everyone waited for news. In the Moreno workshop they continued to sew. Sewing had always been a distraction for women when their men went away to war and never more so than now.

Katerina had just begun to do the edging on one of the most lavish commissions of her career, a wedding gown for the daughter of a wealthy Jewish family who lived in one of the largest mansions in Thessaloniki, one that outshone even the Komninos home for grandeur.

The white peaks and folds of the wedding gown on her lap took her imagination to the rugged mountains where the fighting was taking place. Stories of conditions on the front were circulating and everyone with loved ones there feared as much for the effects of frostbite as the Italian bullet. Katerina's mind had wandered hundreds of kilometres from Thessaloniki and her unfocused gaze saw only the white blur of a blizzard. She realised that her eyes were swimming with unshed tears.

Suddenly she felt a sharp stab of pain. In her reverie, she had pricked her finger, jabbing the needle deep into the flesh, and before she knew it, a drop of blood had fallen onto the fabric. In this otherwise pure landscape of virgin white that spread across her lap and cascaded to the floor, there was now a red spot. Katerina was aghast. She quickly bandaged her finger with a scrap of discarded fabric and the bleeding stopped, but she could do nothing to shift the mark. She had been told by Kyria Moreno, very early on in her training, that nothing in the world could remove a blood stain. The only solution was to cover it up. This was why all the *modistras* must learn to avoid ever pricking their fingers. The mark would have to be carefully concealed so she began to create the first of a hundred pearl-bead flowers, hoping the bride would be happy when she saw this unexpected embellishment.

As she continued her work that morning, she reflected on her 'accident' and realised why she had lost concentration. She cared for Elias like a brother but it was her fear for Dimitri that had brought her to the brink of tears. It was Dimitri whose image she had seen in those mountains.

Good news then came from the front. In spite of the awful conditions, the Greek army began to push the Italians back. Within a month, they had captured the Albanian town of Koritsa. They then transferred their offensive to the coast, which gave them access to supplies from the sea, and meanwhile continued to advance into Albania.

It was the first victory against the Axis powers. The Italians had now been chased from Greek soil. The troops were heroes and their survival of the harsh conditions had become legendary.

In the Niki Street mansion where a dinner was being given, a toast was raised. At last, Konstantinos Komninos felt he had a son he could boast about.

'To our army! To Metaxas!' he said. 'And to my son!'

Olga raised her glass, but did not drink.

'To my son,' she repeated quietly.

There was excitement in the Moreno workshop too.

'How long will it take them to get home, do you think?' Katerina asked Kyria Moreno.

'A few days, I expect. Perhaps a few weeks. We don't know where they are exactly, do we?'

The Morenos had received letters from Elias, so they knew that he was in a unit with Dimitri.

It was, of course, naïve to think that they would be returning so soon. Soldiers were now needed to protect the border and Elias' next letter informed his parents that he was obliged to stay. Katerina tried to conceal her disappointment.

If the main concentration of the army had not still been in Albania, then perhaps there might have been a stronger front to resist the next attack made on Greek territory. This came with terrifying and irresistible force at the beginning of April.

Sweeping over the border from Yugoslavia, the German troops came with such speed that the Greek and British forces could not stop them.

The people of Thessaloniki held their breath. Even the spring leaves seemed not to stir. The streets were silent as everyone waited. Theirs was the first major city that the Germans would reach.

'Isn't there something we should be doing?' Kyria Moreno asked her husband, tearfully wringing her hands. It was an extraordinary situation to know that it was only a matter of time before the Germans arrived.

'I really don't think so, my dear,' he said calmly. 'I think we just have to see what happens. We've all got work to do, haven't we?'

'Yes, I suppose that will keep our minds off it all.'

Kyrios Moreno was right. There was nothing that anyone could do.

Though many had loathed the man, the death of Metaxas three months earlier had left the country without strong leadership and resolve, even within the army itself. The strength to resist the German invasion was lacking.

On 9 April 1941, the tanks rolled in.

# Chapter Eighteen

IN THESSALONIKI, people were well used to hearing different languages: Greek, Arabic, Ladino, French, English, Bulgarian, Russian and Serbian were all distinguishable to people even if they did not speak them. These sounds were like musical compositions that flowed around their streets. They did not need to be understood, but their intermingling notes were part of the city's texture and, like chords, made music that was pleasing to the ear.

Now there was a sound that was less familiar to most ears: German. As soon as the occupying troops arrived, the people of Thessaloniki heard the orders barked between Germans to each other, and then at themselves. It added to their sense of unease.

'I think we just carry on as normally as we can for now,' said Kyria Moreno to Katerina, a few days after the occupation.

It was not really as though they had a choice, but in the Moreno workshop there was so much work to be done that they had little time to worry about what might be taking place outside in the street. The Morenos, as all Jews in Thessaloniki, were not unaware of the way in which the Nazis had persecuted the Jewish population in Germany. It made them anxious, but not unduly afraid. They felt some level of safety in numbers.

There were, after all, nearly fifty thousand of them in Thessaloniki. The Moreno workshop was a cocoon within which they could very happily continue as though nothing had changed and, once bent over their various tasks, the act of concentration helped distance them from the outside world.

'Perhaps Elias will come back soon?' Katerina ventured.

She knew that her employers were losing sleep over their younger son and, now that the Germans had invaded, Katerina hoped that both he and Dimitri might come home. After all, what was there for them to do? The Germans were on their way to Athens and the Greeks were as good as defeated, even if most people did not like to admit it.

'I hope so, Katerina,' Roza said, with the hint of a smile. 'I hope so.'

Meanwhile, it was important to keep their spirits raised, and that week, in spite of Esther Moreno's obvious disapproval, they did not wait until the end of the day to put on the gramophone. Sofia Vembo's sweet and tuneful voice sang out every day over the finishing room. It cheered them all as they stitched to the rhythm.

For the first week after the invasion, life continued almost as normal except that olive oil and cheese became almost immediately unavailable.

'I'm sure they'll reappear on the shelves again soon,' Eugenia said to Katerina optimistically. She had lived through plenty of shortages before.

For Katerina, the first significant indication of change was when she got to the workroom and the magnificent wedding gown that she had almost completed was no longer hanging on the dummy. It had been removed.

'Where's . . . ?' Katerina started to ask, with a hint of indignation in her voice, striding up to the naked tailor's dummy.

She turned to Kyria Moreno and realised that she was in tears.

'I've put it away for now,' Kyria Moreno answered, dabbing her face with a handkerchief. 'The wedding has been postponed.'

Katerina was speechless. She had been working on the dress for four months and she knew it had to be completed by the end of May.

'But why? What's happened?'

Katerina was dry-mouthed. Something awful must have happened to the poor bride.

Kyria Moreno was wringing her hands. A few other workers had arrived in the workroom, and all of them asked the same question.

'Where's the dress?'

The wedding gown had become a great focal point. Even in the Moreno workshop, it had pushed the boundaries of ambition and extravagance. The bride, Allegra Levi, who had been in for a fitting the week before, had wanted to look like a European princess, and this was what they had achieved for her.

Kyria Moreno began to explain. She spoke quietly, as though she did not want to be heard outside the room.

'They've arrested Kyrios Levi.'

She faced a barrage of questions: 'When?' 'What for?'

'He is not the only one. They have arrested other council members and community leaders. For no reason.'

Isaac had come into the room.

'There is a reason, Mother, and we all know it,' he said bluntly. 'It's because they're Jewish.'

There was silence in the room. The spectre of anti-Semitism had returned, and the hope that they could 'carry on as normal' ended there. Within a month, other anti-Jewish measures had been implemented. The Jews were obliged to hand in their radios. Kyrios

Moreno rarely bothered with the music that was played on the radio, but he always listened to the news.

'Let's simply *not* hand it over,' said Isaac. 'They aren't going to know, are they?'

'It's too much of a risk,' said his father.

'Well, they haven't said we can't have gramophones, have they?' said Kyria Moreno. 'So I'm going to hide that away. They're not going to take away our music.'

Three days later, they had their first visit from two German officers. They were accompanied by a young Greek man, who interpreted for both sides.

Having carried out the order to hand in their radio, the Morenos were unsure of why the Germans had come.

'They are here to inspect your premises,' said the interpreter. 'And you appreciate that a lot of Jews have had their businesses taken out of their hands.'

The young man's confidence that the Germans spoke not a word of Greek allowed him to be very free with how he talked to Kyrios Moreno.

'I don't think that's what they want to do here. If you're careful, you should be all right,' he added.

The officers asked to see every room. The tailors and seamstresses automatically stopped what they were doing and stood up when they entered. It was not out of respect, it just seemed the safest thing to do.

The younger of the two officers ran his hand along the rolls of wool in the storeroom. He seemed particularly interested in some fine woollens and stopped to examine them. Finally, he pulled out a roll and dropped it with a thump on the cutting table.

'*Dieser!*' he barked. 'That one!'

'They want suits, you see,' the interpreter told Saul Moreno.

'With your skills, you should be safe. There's no point in them kicking you out of here. It's not just the fabric – they could get that elsewhere – but your workmanship. Your reputation has already reached them. You're lucky!'

'So, better get measuring.'

Saul Moreno called in his top men's tailor and, with almost obsequious attention, began to note their measurements.

The interpreter skilfully moved between German and Greek, speaking with obvious respect and formality to the two officers.

A conversation of sorts began between Kyrios Moreno and the more senior of the two officers.

'Let me tell you how we heard about you . . .' the officer said.

He described, gloatingly, the house they had requisitioned for themselves to live in.

'It is somewhere close to the White Tower,' he said. 'A marvellous place and the family are very cultured and give us such excellent hospitality. They have two daughters and a very fine Steinway – and an excellent cook in the house.'

There were not many people in Thessaloniki with a Steinway piano. Isaac, who had not left his father's side, exchanged a look with Saul.

In the next breath, the officer confirmed what they had already guessed.

'I complimented Kyria Levi on her dress. It looked like something from the best couturier in Berlin or even Paris!' he said. 'So she took us on a little tour of her wardrobe, and there they were! Rows and rows of beautiful gowns – all with your labels! I hope to bring my wife over in the next few months, so I know this will be her first port of call. May we congratulate you!'

The younger officer then joined in. 'And then we had a look

at Kyrios Levi's suits. Pity the trousers end halfway up our shins. We wouldn't be here now if he wasn't so short!'

Something followed that the young Greek did not bother to translate and the two officers laughed together.

The thought of these two rifling through the cupboards and dressing room of one of their best customers, who was currently imprisoned, sickened the tailor.

The interpreter then spoke to Kyrios Moreno: 'I gather that they will be recommending this place to all their colleagues. So, if you work well for them there is no reason for them to shut you down. They aren't planning to pay you the going rate, but I think you're safe enough. They're a vain bunch, these officers, so make them look as dapper as you can.'

As soon as they had left, Kyrios Moreno gathered his staff together. Everyone had seen the German officers.

'We have some new customers,' he told them, 'and we must make sure we produce only our best work for them.'

They all went back to work, but the tension was palpable. Everyone in the workshop was Jewish except for Katerina. In the finishing room, someone put on a new rebetika record, with the volume turned down low.

Despite the strange tranquillity at night, parts of the city teemed with life during the day. Tens of thousands of refugees began to flood into the city from Bulgaria, swelling the huge number of people who were already on the breadline. Wheat, cheese, nuts, oil, olives and fruit were being shipped out of the country by the Germans, so the shortages deepened and the queues at the soup kitchens lengthened. Commodities that had disappeared from the shelves never reappeared and even basic foodstuffs were only available on the black market.

The evening of the day the Nazi officers had visited the Moreno premises, Katerina walked home with Kyria Moreno. As they passed one of the pastry shops close to Irini Street, she noticed a new sign in the window. Perhaps it had been there for days – she was not sure – or possibly she noticed it because there was not much else in the window. With the ever diminishing supply of raw ingredients available, the usual range and quantity of sweets no longer filled the display shelves.

'JEWS NOT WELCOME HERE.'

There it was, in big, black, unapologetic letters, shockingly cold and rude. It was as much as Katerina could do to stop herself marching in to protest.

Kyria Moreno was looking in the other direction and had not noticed it. Katerina linked arms with her and the two women continued to walk up towards the old town. They talked about the news that Athens had fallen and a swastika now flew from the Acropolis. It was the ultimate symbol of defeat.

The streets were quiet. People were less inclined to be out, even in the early evening, and the sound of their footsteps on the cobbles of the empty street was an eerie one.

'Whatever happens to our country, my dear,' said Kyria Moreno as they approached Irini Street, 'we will still have each other.'

The two officers soon returned to have their suits fitted. They were delighted with the results and ordered four more apiece. Then began a steady flow of other German customers. For every order that had been cancelled by a Greek customer, it seemed that a German order replaced it. The officers often browsed through the fashion magazines and examined the drawings on the walls. Once they had given their wives' and girlfriends' measurements, the cutters got to work. There were no fabrics to match these in Germany and they sent the gowns home, like tourists sending postcards. They were particularly impressed with the Komninos silk and though they did not pay the prices that Moreno was used to, they nevertheless paid a fair price. At least no one in this workshop was going to starve.

The *modistras* had little enthusiasm and inspiration for this work. They invented nothing new or imaginative, but did the most basic embroidery stitches they knew, with standard ruching, and none of their finest beads or braiding. Nevertheless, the Germans were always thrilled with the results and the women felt pleased with themselves that they had held something back. They were not used to working without passion. It felt empty, but it kept them from going hungry.

They sat closer to the gramophone now and had the volume on low, so that nobody outside the room could hear it. If they had a visit from a German, someone would knock loudly on their door and the gramophone would be wheeled into a cupboard and covered over with a blanket.

In a city where people were beginning to sell anything they owned in order to buy food, the employees of Moreno & Sons were among the privileged few. If an oil painting or a carpet would fetch enough for a loaf of bread, then it was sold without sentimentality. Such possessions no longer had any value.

There were some objects in the city, though, that were beyond price. After 1917, when much of the city had been razed to the ground, very few synagogue treasures had survived. Entire contents of libraries and archives had melted in the flames, and with few exceptions, ancient Torah and rabbinical writings that were said to have been brought over from Spain in the fifteenth century had been lost.

At the end of June, a month or so after the arrest of the city's chief rabbi, two smartly suited men arrived in Thessaloniki and paid a visit to two senior members of the Jewish community. One of them spoke enough Greek to make himself understood and they gathered that he had studied Ancient Greek at university. They introduced themselves politely as representatives of the Jewish Affairs Commission, which, they explained, had been set up to study world Jewry. The head of the Commission, Alfred Rosenberg, was a very cultured and educated man and wished them to gather any relevant documents or manuscripts and return them to the Commission's headquarters in Frankfurt.

It sounded both plausible and academic, and even the name of the person who had established it sounded Jewish. The rabbis nodded, smiled and feigned great interest and approval of such a scheme. As the men from Frankfurt presented it, the idea certainly had an intellectual credibility.

'So when will you start collecting?' enquired one of the Jewish elders with interest.

'Tomorrow, at dawn,' replied the one with the slicked-down hair. Though his thin lips curled into a smile, his blue eyes remained cold. 'And within the next week we hope to have completed the process of cataloguing and expect to have packed up everything we need. This does, of course, depend on the total co-operation of the Jewish community. And we are relying on you to ensure that.'

'Of course,' the Jewish community leaders both said in unison.

'Shall we see you back here in the morning?'

They both nodded. They were standing in the synagogue that was home to some of the few treasures that had survived the fire over two decades earlier. While one of the Germans did most of the talking, his colleague had been walking about, scrutinising the synagogue. He paused in front of the Ark, the tall cupboard where the holy scriptures were kept.

'I assume the Torah lives in this one,' he said. 'Any chance we could have a look inside?' He ran his fingers with almost sensuous greed over the curtain that hung in front of it.

'The key isn't kept here,' explained one of the rabbis. 'But I'll have it by tomorrow.'

As soon as the Germans had gone, they began to speak in low, hurried tones. Shortly afterwards they left the synagogue, and within fifteen minutes they were in Irini Street. It was now seven o'clock in the evening.

The moment he saw their bearded faces, drawn and anxious, at the door, Saul Moreno felt a sense of dread that he had not experienced since the day the tanks had rolled into Thessaloniki.

'We have to hide things. Not all of them. But some of them,' explained one of the rabbis breathlessly.

'Otherwise it will arouse suspicion, obviously,' said the other.

The two of them were seated, while Saul Moreno paced up and down.

'So what can I do? You aren't asking me to hide things in the workshop?'

'Not exactly . . .'

'Because Germans are coming in almost every day. It would put my staff in great danger.'

'Well, we're not asking you to do that. We wouldn't do that.'

'And obviously we can't hide all the scrolls. It would be impossible. But we need your help concealing a piece of manuscript and a fragment of one of the scrolls. And the curtain. We have to try,' pleaded the younger man. 'And you are the only people that can help us.'

Saul Moreno listened. He wanted to help very much. Nothing was greater than his duty to his synagogue, but he greatly feared endangering his wife, sons and all those good people who worked for him.

The rabbi had a battered leather suitcase with him.

'Let me show you what we have. Then you can tell us if our idea is mad.'

Kyria Moreno was standing looking over her husband's shoulder now and in the flickering candlelight they watched the rabbi open the case and begin to remove the contents. One thing at a time, he placed the contents on their table, as the Morenos watched, open-mouthed.

'This is a fragment of the Torah scroll that's believed to be the oldest surviving one in Thessaloniki.'

He then unfolded a familiar huge swathe of velvet.

It was the *parochet*, the curtain that was said to have been hanging in front of the Ark for hundreds of years and may not even have been new when it was brought over from Spain. The thread with which it was embroidered was tarnished now, but was pure gold.

'I've sat and gazed at it so many times,' said Saul. 'It's strange to see it in my own house.'

'Look at the embroidery, Saul. Nobody could do that now. The workmanship is from another age.'

Roza ran her fingers over the relief pattern, with a mixture of reverence and admiration.

'And these are some rabbinical teachings that were brought over from Spain. They are hard to decipher now. There is just one page that has survived. Ladino, look, written so lovingly.'

Finally, he took from the case a tallit. It was the finest, most fragile thing of all, a length of striped silk perhaps five hundred years old, with its compulsory tassels.

'We think it might have belonged to someone who came over in that first boat from Spain,' he said.

Nobody spoke as Saul Moreno surveyed the treasures and wondered where on earth they could hide them. Kyria Moreno eventually broke the silence.

'Saul, we have to help. I think we can do it.'

'How?'

'We're going to sew all night.'

Saul looked at her with some astonishment. Roza had known immediately what had to be done, even if her husband had been slow.

'I know exactly how to do it,' she said. 'It will involve some puncture marks in the paper, but it can't be helped.'

'Your wife is right. We've got to allow some minor damage. If we don't, we'll lose them altogether.'

'That's why we came to you.'

'Oh, there's this too. I forgot.'

The older man unwrapped a pointer, a yad, that was run along the lines of the Torah instead of a finger, to avoid any damage to the holy writings. At the end of the silver pointer there was a tiny, perfect hand with outstretched forefinger.

'It's not as old as these other things. But we can't let them take it.'

'I don't think there is anything we can do with that,' said Kyria Moreno. 'I think beneath your own floorboards might be the best place for it . . .'

Unusually, Kyrios Moreno allowed his wife to take over the situation. She clearly had a plan.

'And you can take away the suitcase,' she said. 'Once we have done our work, we won't be hiding anything. It will all be on display.' She turned to her husband. 'Can you get Isaac, please?'

Their elder son was upstairs but soon appeared.

'Isaac, I want you to go next door. Bring Katerina and Eugenia here. And then I need you to do a quick run around the city. I need Allegra, Martha, Mercada, Sara, Hannah, Bella and Esther. Tell them all to meet here. Say it's urgent. Saul, can you go to the workshop? These are the things we need.'

Even faster than she could speak, Roza was scribbling a list of the items she needed: various yardages of silk and padding, a score of different colours of thread, various lengths of braid.

The two synagogue elders were hastening away down the street when Katerina and Eugenia appeared on the threshold.

'What's happened?' asked Eugenia with concern, looking around at the strange miscellany of objects. 'Who were those men?'

Roza explained. Within fifteen minutes, the other women had arrived and soon they all knew what needed to be done. Roza had allocated individual tasks and had sketched out the designs that they should work to. Having spent the past fifty or so years of her life embroidering things for the synagogue, she was full of ideas for designs and patterns.

Eight of them were going to work on the quilt to conceal the *parochet*. In one night, they would make a quilt that would normally take several months. In the centre there would be an elaborate motif of pomegranates and around the edges a pattern of stitches into which they would sew their own names in Ladino. As well as being a popular image for embroidery, with its symbolism of fertility and plenty, she was 'planting' a clue. In Ladino, the word for pomegranate was '*granada*' and she wanted to reveal to anyone who possessed this knowledge that what lay beneath the layers of crimson satin had originally come from Spain, from Granada, to be precise.

It had to be spread across the Morenos' bed to be worked on and this is where it would stay, covering the quilt that Kyria Moreno had been embroidering for her entire married life. Four of them worked on the central pattern, inspired by words from Exodus: 'Thou shalt make pomegranates of blue and of purple and of scarlet . . . and bells of gold in between.' Four of them worked on the edges, one on each side. The urgency of the task seemed to inspire them and their fingers worked fast and accurately.

Downstairs, Esther worked carefully on the concealment of the fragile tallit. The silk from which it was made was so fine that it would not stand being pierced with a needle. She concealed it within two slightly larger pieces of quilted fabric and carefully stitched a seam around the perimeter. Round the edge, she embroidered what appeared to be an abstract pattern, but in reality it spelled out a few words she knew in Hebrew, telling the reader what was hidden inside. The swirls and curls of her design meant that no one would ever think of unpicking her elaborate stitching.

'We need to do something different with these, Katerina,' said Kyria Moreno. 'Something so ordinary that no one will even look at them twice.'

They both stood at the table, looking down at two frayed scraps of parchment.

'What I would like you to do, my dear, is to imagine you are a child again. I hope it won't be difficult, but you need to get the style right. I want you to embroider one picture that says "*Kalimera*" in big letters – you know the sort of thing, with the sun rising and a bird or a butterfly or some such creature in the sky. And then, a second one with "*Kalispera*".'

'With the moon and the stars?'

'Yes! Exactly that. But don't make them look like the work of a clumsy-fingered child,' she said smilingly. 'I've got to live with them on my walls!'

Katerina had done very similar pictures many years ago, under her mother's instruction, and the memory came back sharply.

Her *Kalimera* was filled in with big loopy stitches, in a glossy, yellow thread, and *Kalispera* was in midnight blue. She enjoyed the simplicity of the task and smiled at the result. No one would be suspicious of something that was found on the wall of every Greek home. Even if they got stripped out of the frame, the precious pages they had to conceal would be encased inside a calico backing. It was normal to hide the untidy mess on the reverse side of the stitching.

Although there were a dozen people in this small house, there was uncanny silence. Their concentration was absolute, their clandestine activity urgent. They were saving the treasures that connected them with their past.

From time to time, Katerina glanced up at Esther Moreno. For the first time since she had known her, the elderly woman looked contented.

All night long they sewed without ceasing. Everything had to be finished by morning.

As was general practice with such traditional pieces, Katerina embroidered dates in the corner. On the first she put '1942'. Then, in the second she carelessly transposed the figures. '1492' she wrote with her stitches. It was the date of the Sephardic expulsion from Spain. Anyone who knew the history of the Jews in Thessaloniki would spot this deliberate mistake.

Not so far away, the two Jewish elders waited at the synagogue. At seven thirty precisely, the two representatives of the Commission walked in. Outside, two porters leaned against their handcarts smoking and chatting. They had been hired to transport the contents of the synagogue to the railway station.

Even though they were speaking between themselves in rapid German, it was obvious what one of them was saying. He had noticed that the curtain in front of the Torah Ark was missing and was shouting and gesticulating. One of the elders quickly produced the huge key that unlocked the slender door, and when the German saw what was inside he was immediately distracted. His expression changed to one of salivating interest. He reached in and pulled out one of the scrolls, wrapped in its *mappa*, its ancient velvet mantle, and held it lovingly, like a baby. Then he placed it on the desk nearby and carefully unrolled it. He ran his finger tips across the words as though they were in braille and then replaced it in the mantle. The other German started to carry things outside to the waiting porters.

The synagogue elders, who had prayed all night in order to prepare themselves for this quiet but terrible ransacking, stood silently by. They showed no emotion. It felt as though they were being stabbed a thousand times without being able to put up any defence.

Having cleared out the Ark, the Germans removed several dozen other books. Finally, they wrapped the menorah in the heavily embroidered cloth that covered the desk and carried it outside into the street, where they placed it on top of one of the carts. It was all done with surprising care. The second in command had meticulously and ostentatiously made a note of everything they had taken. Perhaps it was to give the impression that things would be returned. This charade was the only aspect of the operation that kept the elders from breaking down in unmanly tears.

The Germans' task was complete. The synagogue was stripped bare.

There was a strange moment when the more senior figure offered his hand, as if he might want to shake those of the Jewish elders. Both of them instinctively took a step backwards.

'*Danke schön und guten Morgen,*' he said.

With those words, they set off down the street, the carts trundling noisily behind them.

Several dozen members of the congregation now emerged and stood in a group, with the two elders, watching the receding figures. As soon as the Germans were out of sight, they went inside the synagogue and began to pray.

Once the Commission had completed the task of stripping the Jews of their holy treasures and archives, the occupying forces more or less left them alone. They had already taken over the homes of most wealthy Jews, and had shut many businesses down.

Anti-Semitic feelings, which had lurked below the surface of the city for some years, were now acceptable.

Some things in Thessaloniki were the same for both Jew and Christian: lack of food. As cold weather approached, the shortages deepened. The Germans had shipped out everything they could to feed their own population and nothing could be imported.

That winter, people fought in the street for scraps or sorted through piles of rubbish, in the hope that someone might have tossed away a crust of bread. Shoeless children queued with emaciated parents outside soup kitchens, but there was little of any nutritional value in what they served. The Red Cross did what it could, but their efforts were almost futile. People in Thessaloniki began to die.

Every day, Katerina saw some new horror. One day, walking down Egnatia Street, the city's main boulevard, she noticed two bowed figures with distended bellies and protruding ribs. This in itself was not an uncommon sight, but with their hollow eyes, and apparently enlarged heads, it was hard to tell if they were young or old. They seemed to be somewhere in between, a horrifying mixture of baby and octogenarian.

Only the following day, she saw someone lying on the pavement. She hardly gave him a second glance since there were many refugees sleeping on the streets as they had nowhere else to go. When she emerged from the workshop a few hours later, she realised her error. The body was being lifted onto a cart. A brief conversation with a woman who was standing close by confirmed what she had feared. The man Katerina had assumed was sleeping was being collected for burial. He had died of starvation. She crossed herself several times, mortified with shame.

The situation in Athens was known to be a hundred times worse. Katerina hoped her mother was managing to survive. She had not heard from her for some time now.

Everyone who worked for Moreno & Sons was aware of their strange good fortune. The Germans continued to visit the Moreno workshop with great regularity, and the income they provided gave the employees access to the black market. It was the only way to survive and meant that not only did they eat, but so could their neighbours.

Saul Moreno's fabric was almost exhausted so his German customers went to the Komninos showroom and selected from his vast inventory. Konstantinos Komninos' supply seemed to be unaffected by the shortages from which almost every other business in the city suffered. His silk production had continued, and his range of wool and linen was only minimally reduced. After the measurements were taken at the Moreno workshop, a messenger was then dispatched to collect the correct quantity of fabric.

'Well, at least sewing takes our minds off what might be happening to our menfolk,' said one of the seamstresses, to no one in particular.

'Speak for yourself,' answered another. 'Every time I stick the needle into this dress, I imagine myself jabbing it into the German who has ordered it.'

'Or the fat little wife who's going to wear it,' added another.

Katerina did not join in. She whiled the hours away in a reverie, wondering where and how Dimitri was. She knew that Kyria Moreno thought of Elias during these long stretches of work and the two women often speculated on where they might be and hoped that they would still be together. There had been no news. Katerina had been sent a few times to fit a dress for Olga, but it seemed that she had not received a letter in many, many months.

Time went slowly in the workshop now. A German 'customer' had arrived one day and caught them singing along to one of their rebetika records.

'These are subversive!' he shouted. There was no need for translation. One by one he picked up their precious records, smashed them over his knee and dropped them contemptuously to the ground. Fragments of Bezos, Eskenazi, Papazoglou, Vamvakaris and many more lay scattered over the floor for the terrified women to gather up later. On his next visit, he brought them a recording of Wagner *Lieder*. His 'gift', which was proffered with great politeness, was put away in a cupboard. They all agreed that silence was infinitely preferable.

As well as the tailoring of suits for German officers and gowns for their wives, there was other work which they had all begun to do. Even with ration coupons, few people could afford fabric for new clothes, so the making-do and adaptation of what people already had in their wardrobes turned into a huge industry. Girls' dresses could be fashioned out of something their mothers had worn, and for men and women who had lost ten or fifteen kilograms in weight, there were waistbands to be resewn, and new darts to be made. Many children had nothing more than the rags they stood up in, so every evening was spent unpicking and adapting garments donated by wealthy Greeks.

As Katerina's fingers wove her needle in and out of fabrics old and new, the winter turned to spring. Orange trees burst into blossom, filling the streets with dense fragrance, oblivious to the grime beneath and the death in their shadows. Katerina looked at the white blooms and knew at least that Dimitri would no longer be in the snow.

She and Roza speculated each day on where he and Elias might be, and when spring had turned to summer and many other soldiers had returned, they concluded that they had joined the resistance. Though the Greek army could no longer oppose the Germans, there were still many men brave enough to continue a campaign of obstruction and sabotage.

# Chapter Nineteen

KATERINA AND ROZA were right. Dimitri and Elias were among the thousands of soldiers who had attached themselves to the resistance as soon as the occupation had begun, and were now in the mountains of central Greece, living rough and eating little. They had survived the greatest enemy of all, the cold, but the months of almost sleepless discomfort left them both fitfully dreaming of a night in their own beds.

When the Germans had invaded, army officers had been ordered not to resist, but many within the ranks remained determined to subvert the enemy and became members of the Communist-backed National Liberation Front (EAM). It seemed the only way to be part of a continuing war against the occupiers.

King George and his government had withdrawn to the Middle East, together with some of the armed forces, an armistice had been signed with the Germans and a collaborationist government had been established in Athens. The major political parties had chosen not to back the resistance movement which, in the view of Elias and Dimitri and their fellow *andartes*, was tantamount to accepting that their country now belonged to Germany.

Initially, EAM concentrated on relief work to help feed the

starving populations in both villages and towns and, at the beginning of the occupation, Dimitri and Elias had been drafted in to help raid a number of warehouses where food supplies had been hoarded by the Germans to feed their own troops.

Sometimes, they were heavy handed in their actions, but if it meant that their countrymen were fed, they believed that this was justified.

'At least we're *doing* something,' said Dimitri. 'We may not be fighting hand to hand, but this is still war, isn't it?'

'Personally, I would rather have a gun in my hand,' said Elias. 'I think we should be trying to get the bastards out of our country. Stealing their food isn't enough. It's tame.'

'You have a point,' conceded Dimitri reluctantly. 'The way things are going, we're more likely to die of starvation than a gunshot.'

'So why not fight?'

'Because we're helping other people. And for now that might be enough.'

Dimitri was rational and measured compared with his friend. 'EAM is doing everything it can to keep hospitals and pharmacies open as well. You know that, don't you?'

'Yes, I've heard,' responded Elias. 'At least with your medical knowledge you can do something constructive. What I'm doing just doesn't seem enough.'

'It would be impossible to fight when people are so hungry. Can you imagine anyone trying to conduct a campaign when half the troops are too weak to hold a gun? Come on, Elias, think about it.'

'There's a rumour going round that some proper guerrilla action is going to start. If that's the case, I'm in. Active rebellion. It's the only way. It's what Vassili would have done! Fight!'

Dimitri and Elias often had similar conversations. As a member of EAM, Dimitri believed in the same communist principles as his friend, but in the situation in which the country found itself, he could not see how they were ever going to rid Greece of the Germans. The war in the rest of Europe was not going the Allies' way. France and Belgium were occupied and there were rumours that Britain would be next.

News of the organised guerrilla action that Elias had heard about turned out to be true. In February the armed resistance movement within EAM, known as the National Popular Liberation Army, had begun operations. Its other name was ELAS.

'We're joining,' said Elias.

Dimitri was silent.

'Dimitri? What's wrong with you?' he shouted. 'What about all those Greek heroes? Aren't they supposed to be your ancestors?'

Dimitri looked up at his friend and felt ashamed. Many still did not regard Sephardic Jews as true Greeks, but here was Elias more than willing to risk his life to liberate his *patrida*. How could he, Dimitri, not follow such an example? He must continue the fight. It seemed to him that this was the only way to be a true Greek. Elias was right. Putting aside your weapons and submitting to an enemy occupier was not the way for a proud nation to behave.

'I'm with you, Elias,' he said eventually, meaning it in every way.

For some while they had enjoyed great success, attacking gendarmerie stations and Italian posts in remote mountain areas. They felt that they were achieving something and slowly but surely were regaining control of their country. Even if the central government had done nothing, ELAS was proving itself.

More than eighteen months had passed since the two friends had left Thessaloniki and they now had a few days' leave. They yearned to see their loved ones. They had fake papers, which were easily come by, but still had to be careful to avoid road blocks and the occasional gendarme, whose suspicion would be easily aroused. Travelling mostly at night, taking lifts with farmers who still had fuel supplies, Thessaloniki was in sight within five days.

It was June and the two men kept assiduously to the generous shadows created by the trees on the city's main streets. Their families and homes were almost within reach.

They were pleased to be there but Thessaloniki was not the same city that they had left. A pall of sadness hung over it. Gone was the hustle and bustle that had characterised Egnatia Street and the small roads on either side of it. Many shops were boarded up and the others that still functioned had nothing in their windows. Street vendors who used to add vibrancy and music to the general scene, with their cries and calls, had vanished, and near the station there were only two boot-blacks where there used to be at least a dozen. They saw several German soldiers in the street, but they took not the slightest interest in either Dimitri or Elias.

Dimitri watched a group of children overturning a bin. The hunger he had experienced in the mountains and villages had never looked as desperate as the famine here. At least, away from the city, there was always some kind of vegetation that could be made into a soup, or even fruit, nuts or roots. With guidance from trustworthy locals who taught them which ones to avoid, even berries had been an important part of their diet. Nature nearly always provided, but in the city the cobbles yielded nothing but mud in winter and, now that temperatures were rising, a choking dust. The urban landscape was a barren place for the starving.

They came to the grand space of Aristotelous Square where cafés still buzzed with activity just as they always had done. Customers were enjoying the afternoon sunshine and the sight of the glistening Gulf and far-off Mount Olympus, a view that had not changed. Many of the tables were frequented by German soldiers, and there were even a few Greek girls sitting chatting with them. Additionally, there were groups of sleek and well-fed Greeks. Dimitri realised that some of his father's wealthy friends and customers could easily be among them.

'We'd better separate now,' said Dimitri, knowing that he must avoid being recognised by any of these people. With their heavy boots and unshaved faces, they felt conspicuous.

'Do you think we look like *andartes*?' asked Elias, almost jokingly.

'Unfortunately, I think we probably do.'

Alone, it would be easier to blend into a crowd, vanish into a shop doorway or melt into a crowded kafenion. Dimitri and Elias had been warned that they must trust no one. In the cities, Germans were employing waiters and concierges and anyone else who might lead them to subversives or resisters. All of those who eavesdropped on their fellow citizens had families to feed, and consorting with the enemy could mean a day or two without the cramping pains of a hollow stomach and a child's endless whining for food. Hunger had made Thessaloniki a dangerous place.

The gendarmes, the military police, who had been feared and despised in the past, were detested even more now because they were serving the Germans. Theirs was a bleak choice. If they refused to co-operate with the occupying force, they would be tortured and executed. Some of them remained in their positions and took the risk of helping resisters, but it was hard to tell who was a 'good' gendarme and who was a 'bad' one. It was best to avoid them, just in case.

'Let's meet up again in twenty-four hours,' said Dimitri. 'I'll come to Irini Street at six o'clock.' He was hopeful of catching a glimpse of Katerina.

He checked his watch. It was a miracle that it still worked after all the months of rain and snow and dirt to which it had been exposed. It was an expensive Swiss make, a present from his father for his twenty-first birthday, which he had worn with great reluctance at first. It symbolised his father's love of money and status, and Dimitri had been embarrassed to wear it during his time at the university. It seemed to single him out. On the night when he had left the house, he had grabbed it at the last moment. He knew it would be useful, perhaps even something that he could sell. Now that the face was scratched and the gold around it dull, he had grown to love it and even to rely on it. Many times, the accuracy of its mechanism had been invaluable, when he and his fellow *andartes* had needed to orientate themselves in the mountains.

'See you tomorrow then,' Elias said. 'Give my regards to your parents.'

'And mine to yours,' said Dimitri.

Elias turned away and walked north towards the old town, slipping into one of the network of alleyways that would eventually get him to Irini Street.

Dimitri took a quiet street that ran parallel with the seafront. He saw no one. There was an unnerving deadness about the city. Ten minutes of brisk walking brought him to Niki Street. The size and grandeur of the house were even more impressive than he had remembered. He rang the bell and his heart began to beat furiously. Many such houses had been taken over by German officers and it suddenly dawned on him that he might be seconds away from arrest. He had not felt such fear in all those months in the mountains. Having had no communication with his parents for a long while, he had no idea at all who stood behind the door.

Before he had time to make a decision on whether or not to flee, he heard the heavy latch being pulled up, quite slowly, as though the person behind it was as nervous as Dimitri. When

Pavlina saw who was standing on the doorstep, she clasped her hand across her mouth in shock.

'*Panagia mou!* Dimitri!' She was half-choked by surprise. 'Come inside! Come inside!'

She pulled him into the hallway, stood back and looked at him with both pleasure and concern.

'Look at you!' she said, crossing herself many times. 'What have they done to you?'

It was not a question that needed answering. Dimitri knew that he looked gaunt and exhausted. He had caught sight of himself in the hallway mirror, the first he had seen in many months. He was not really sure who Pavlina meant by 'they'. Some kind of enemy, presumably. The Germans? Other Greeks?

'Your mother will be so pleased to see you! She is upstairs.'

'And my father?'

'Still at the showroom, I expect.'

Dimitri took the stairs three at a time, stopped for a moment at the top and knocked timidly on the drawing room door. Without waiting for an answer he walked in. Olga did not look up from her reading, presuming it was Pavlina coming in with her tea.

'Mother. It's me.'

Dropping her book, Olga got up and found herself locked in her son's embrace.

'Dimitri . . .'

There were no words, just tears, unashamedly wept by both of them. Eventually, she stood back in order to look at her son.

'I can't believe it's you. I've been so worried. I thought I might never see you again! We haven't had a word from you! Not for over a year . . .' Tears continued to flow down her cheeks.

'I couldn't get a letter to you. It wasn't possible. I am so sorry, Mother, I really am.'

'I'm just so happy to see you . . .'

They continued to embrace for some minutes. Eventually, Olga became calmer and mopped her face. She wanted to enjoy the moment of her son's return.

'Sit down,' she said. 'Tell me everything. Tell me what you have been doing. Tell me where you've been!'

They sat side by side on the chaise longue.

'Look, there's something you need to understand,' Dimitri said seriously. 'Something really important I must tell you now.'

'But can't it wait, *agapi mou*? Your father will be back later,' she said dutifully. 'And surely now you're home, there'll be plenty of time,' she smiled.

'That's the thing, Mother, I don't have plenty of time.'

'What do you mean, darling?' she said, her voice full of disappointment. 'You've only just got here. And the war is over now.'

'Oh, *mana mou*, you know that's not true,' he responded gently. 'The war is far from over.'

'As far as your father is concerned, it is.'

'Well, that might be where we differ. The fight continues. Thousands of us haven't given up. The Germans and Italians are still our enemies and while they remain on our soil, we will keep attacking them.'

Olga looked at her son with a mixture of love and pure dismay. He had been brought back to her and yet she could sense he was about to be taken away once again.

'And who are "we"?' Olga asked.

'ELAS,' he replied.

'ELAS?' she repeated in a whisper. 'You've joined the Communists?'

'I have joined the organisation that is putting up a fight against the Germans,' he answered defensively.

'Oh,' she said, going visibly pale.

281

'We're fighting for people who are not able to defend themselves, Mother,' he continued.

Then she saw a movement out of the corner of her eye. Neither of them had noticed the slight breeze of the opening door.

'Konstantinos!' she exclaimed, surprised to see him back so early. 'Look! Look who's come home!'

Dimitri got up, and father and son faced each other. Dimitri was the first to speak.

'I'm back.' He could think of nothing else to say.

Konstantinos cleared his throat. The tension was palpable. Dimitri could already feel his father's simmering anger. In spite of his time away, nothing seemed to have changed and he knew that the conversation would now take a polite course before the inevitable explosion.

'Yes, so I see. And where have you been?'

Komninos' tone of voice was the one that you might use when someone had returned after a week of absence. Dimitri had been away for eighty-four weeks and four days precisely. Olga had counted.

'In the mountains, mostly,' Dimitri answered with honesty.

'We were expecting you back some months ago . . . the war finished last April,' he said in a clipped tone. 'You could have let us know where you were.'

'I explained to Mother that it wasn't possible to send any mail,' he answered in his own defence.

'So what exactly have you been doing in the mountains?'

His father's questions were both persistent and disingenuous. Olga had already deduced that her husband had been in the room before they noticed him.

Dimitri looked down at the floor. He saw his boots, white with dust, their cracked leather almost split to reveal his feet. They had taken him an incalculable number of kilometres. His eyes strayed to his father's pristine brogues, so shiny they reflected the pattern of the rug on which both men stood.

He was proud of how he had spent the past months since he had joined ELAS.

'Olga. Please would you leave the room now.'

Dimitri had spent many nights half frozen to death in mountain caves, watching icicles form on the ceiling, but nothing had chilled him as much as his father's voice at this moment.

It froze Olga's heart too. She left the room and retreated to her bedroom, fearful for her son.

Dimitri remained standing. He was the same height as his father, to the millimetre, and tonight he wanted to look him in the eye. He inwardly castigated himself for feeling such fear. After some of the situations he had faced during his time as a soldier, it was absurd to find himself trembling. And yet he could feel his heart almost bursting through the walls of his chest.

As soon as Olga had left the room, Konstantinos spoke again.

'You are a disgrace to this family,' he said calmly. 'I overheard what you told your mother. When I have said what I wish to say, you will leave this house. And for as long as you are still fighting with ELAS you will not return. No one with such beliefs is entitled to be a son of mine. *No one with such beliefs* is permitted within these four walls. You are to go straight from this room and out of this house. I don't care where you go as long as it is out of this city.'

Konstantinos' voice rose ever higher as he spoke. Dimitri looked blankly at him. There was no more he wished to say to this man with whom he shared nothing but a name.

'If I did not want to bring this family's name into disrepute, I would report you this very minute to the authorities.'

Komninos wanted a response from his son and left a moment's pause. His son's silence infuriated him.

'Why don't you see sense, Dimitri, and admit that fighting is not the way forward for this country?'

'And what is the future?' Dimitri finally responded. '*Collaboration.*'

There were no raised voices in this encounter between father and son, but the suppressed anger was palpable. Konstantinos Komninos had the final word.

'Get out of my sight, Dimitri,' he said.

Walking past the closed door of his mother's room, Dimitri felt a terrible grief. How could his mother, whom he loved so much and missed each day, be married to this monstrous ego, this Fascist? With this question and the terrible guilt at the sadness he must be causing her, he went slowly down the stairs. Pavlina was standing in the hallway.

'Goodbye,' he said, kissing her. 'Say sorry to my mother . . .'

Before she had time to tell him that dinner was nearly ready, he was gone. She touched her cheek and realised that it was wet with tears that were not her own.

Once in the street, Dimitri was not sure what to do. He was not scheduled to meet up with Elias again until the next day, but there was only one place where he would feel safe. Irini Street.

He was there in twenty minutes, nervously ducking in and out of doorways, carefully avoiding the attention of the gendarmes. Irini Street was quiet, apart from two women sitting outside at the top of the street. Pushing aside the curtain that hung in the doorway, Dimitri slipped into the Morenos' house. Although it was dusk, it was even darker inside than it was in the street.

'Dimitri!'

It was a familiar voice. After a moment, his eyes became accustomed to the darkness and he could make out the silhouettes of four people sitting around the table. They all rose from their seats and came towards him.

'Dimitri! What are you doing here?' Elias asked.

'But what a nice surprise,' said Saul Moreno. 'We're so happy to see you!'

'Come! Come and sit down. You must eat! You must eat!'

Roza Moreno was guiding him towards the table where Isaac had already pulled up another chair.

Soon he was eating. It was the first wholesome meal he had eaten in many, many months. The normality of it was joyful.

'So, tell me. Did you see your father?' asked Elias.

'Yes,' said Dimitri, his mouth full. 'I should have known what he would be like.'

The whole family understood without needing any more information. There was a pause.

'So tell us. Tell us everything,' Saul Moreno urged. 'We want to know everything.'

Kyria Moreno went tirelessly to and fro keeping their plates filled with her special *quieftes* and *fijón* and their minds with questions. Until the early hours of the morning, the two weary men told them where they had been, of their campaigns, of their encounters, of how Dimitri had stitched wounds, applied tourniquets and learned how to extract shrapnel from wounds. Kyria Moreno wanted details of what they had eaten and she was shocked at their answers.

Dimitri and Elias not only talked, they also listened and asked questions. There had also been huge changes in the Morenos' lives in the past eighteen months. What was it like to live in an occupied city? How did the Germans behave? How were they treating the Jews?

Kyria Moreno painted a positive picture of it all, but Isaac was more honest.

'We have to sew suits for Germans,' he said sulkily. 'We would like to put razor blades into the seams, but that would be bad for business.'

'But we've been so fortunate,' said Saul. 'So many Jewish businesses have been taken away. At least we still have ours. And believe me, we're busier than ever.'

'But not with the business we would like to have . . .'

'Isaac!' said his father. 'Please stop. People died of starvation in this city last winter. Did we ever go hungry?'

'Let's not argue,' said Kyria Moreno, who was thrilled to see her youngest son and did not want this brief family reunion to be blighted by angry words.

'Mother's right, Isaac,' said Elias. 'We have so little time together.'

Kyria Moreno went to the sink and began to wash the stack of plates. Saul Moreno went upstairs, to sleep under the sacred quilt. As his mother clattered crockery at the sink, Elias had the chance to ask his older brother a question.

'Look, we're leaving again tomorrow. Why don't you come with us?' he asked in a low voice. 'We've lost a few men in our unit, and we could do with some more.'

'No more making suits for the Hun,' whispered Dimitri, encouragingly.

Isaac looked from one to the other. 'Let me sleep on it,' he replied.

Kyria Moreno looked over her shoulder. She saw her two sons and Dimitri leaning forward, heads almost touching. They looked as though they were engaged in some kind of conspiracy.

'Boys,' she said, smiling, 'don't you think it's time for bed?'

'Yes,' her sons said, in unison, and laughed.

'Elias, why don't you stay a little longer?' she asked. 'It's so wonderful having you back. And Dimitri can stay as long as he likes too.'

'We wish we could, Mother. But we only have seven days' leave, and it took us four of them to get here . . .'

That night Dimitri slept soundly on the stone-built couch in the living room. A bed had never felt softer and he was soon enveloped in vivid dreams that kept him asleep until well after twelve the following day. He then had a thorough wash outside in the courtyard, scrubbing the ingrained dirt from around his neck and bathing the sores that had been left by lice. Kyria Moreno had left fresh, clean clothes for him (he was exactly the same size as Elias) and the slightly starched cotton rustled as he put it on, its coolness soothing his skin. Standing in these laundered clothes, he felt reborn.

Elias had left a note for Dimitri on the table. He would be back at the end of the afternoon, in good time for them to leave for their return journey, but meanwhile had gone to the workshop to try to persuade Isaac to join them.

Dimitri felt a stab of jealousy. He could not pretend to himself that it was anything else: Elias would see Katerina.

In the past months, he had tried not to think of her. There had seemed little point. Up in the mountains, away from everything that was civilised and kind, it had seemed almost wrong to carry his thoughts of her, but now that he knew where Elias was, he wanted to run to the workshop himself.

It was not the right thing to do. He knew that. Instead, he went out into the street, suddenly desperate for fresh air, and began walking in the direction of the sea. Emboldened by his clean clothes, he went inside a kafenion he had never been to before and ordered. He could feel strange eyes on him, and looked up into the face of a gendarme who was staring at him with some interest.

'Konstantinos' son?' he asked.

Dimitri did not know how to react. To deny such a thing might seem ridiculous if this man knew his father. To admit it might have different repercussions.

'You are! Aren't you?' persisted the man, who was with a group of half a dozen colleagues.

Dimitri felt his face flush. Perhaps his father had already reported him as a Communist. He went rigid with fear. In the mountains there had always been somewhere to run if you were face to face with an enemy. He glanced past the gendarmes to the door behind them and realised there would be no escape.

'You must be Dimitri. You look so alike. Do give my regards to your father!'

He hated the idea that he resembled his father, but for now he felt a surge of relief.

'Yes . . . of course,' he said, forcing a smile to his lips.

He finished his coffee, swallowing some of the bitter grounds, got up and left. What a disgusting thought that his father was on first-name terms with a gendarme, he thought, but how predictable.

Dimitri hastened back to Irini Street. Elias was due back soon. Would Isaac be with him?

He had to wait only ten minutes for the answer to that question. Elias returned alone.

'He won't come,' said Elias with a note of disappointment. 'He says that someone needs to stay here with Mother and Father. He is probably right, you know.'

'Pity,' responded Dimitri. 'We could do with him.'

Elias had run upstairs to get a spare shirt and they both picked up the packets of bread and cheese that Kyria Moreno had left for their journey.

'Having just said goodbye to Mother, I doubt she would survive if we were both going. It would break her heart,' added Elias.

'Well, he knows what's right for him,' said Dimitri. 'Let's get going.'

He could not bring himself to ask Elias whether he had seen Katerina.

By nightfall, Thessaloniki was not even a speck on the horizon. Within two and a half days the two men were back with their unit in the mountains.

In Thessaloniki, two women cried themselves to sleep that night. The fleeting encounters with their sons had left them feeling almost more bereft than before. Olga could not even discuss her son's visit with Konstantinos. Dimitri's name was not to be mentioned. At least Roza Moreno had had the opportunity to kiss her son goodbye.

For the fourteen months since the invasion, apart from seizing synagogue treasures, businesses and homes, the Germans had done little to harm the Jews themselves. In mid-July, this changed. They suddenly announced that Jewish men between the ages of eighteen and forty-five must present themselves for registration. They were to be used as civilian labour in building roads and airstrips.

Kyrios Moreno tried to cheer Isaac up.

'Well, they need someone to do their hard work for them,' he said. 'And it's not only the Jews. They've got Greek men doing heavy building work as well.'

'But why can't the Germans do it themselves?' protested Isaac. 'I'm a tailor, not a builder.'

'It's just the way it is,' said his mother. 'I'm sure it won't be for long, *agapi mou*.'

Temperatures had risen that week to the hottest of the year and, that Saturday morning, nine thousand of them were made to stand in rows in Plateia Eleftheria. Its name seemed ironic that day: Freedom Square. The midday sun beat down on their heads and there was not a breath of sea breeze to cool them.

'I thought we were going off to start building roads,' one of the other tailors said to Isaac. 'Why are we all standing here?'

'I think we are about to find out,' he answered.

Orders were being barked from across the square. If the Jews were too slow to understand what they were being told to do, the German soldiers helped them out with the use of sticks. It seemed they were being told to perform a series of keep-fit exercises.

Isaac and eight others from the workshop tried to remain close to one another. Had it been a few months later, Jacob, the oldest of their group at forty-four years old, would not have been obliged to register. He was small, with a portly figure, and found the exercises more difficult than Isaac and the younger ones. The Germans noticed this and he was picked on and made to do a somersault, not once but five times in a row, so that he could be photographed.

One of the city's newspapers had been stirring up anti-Semitic sentiments during the previous few weeks and a crowd, including respectable citizens of Thessaloniki, had gathered to watch the spectacle of these young men being forced to do ridiculous exercises in the midday heat. There were encouraging claps and mocking catcalls to add to their humiliation.

For several hours, they were made to perform for the assembled mass, without water, shade or rest. After four hours, his bald head exposed to the fierce sun, Jacob vomited and collapsed. He was still unconscious an hour later, but none of his friends was allowed to come to his aid. Eventually, he was unceremoniously dragged away by the feet by two German soldiers, and when Isaac tried to protest, dogs were set loose on him. The crowd seemed to like this. The more terror and humiliation they witnessed, the louder they cheered. Christians being fed to lions had never pleased the braying horde like this. Eventually, the novelty wore off, even for the tormentors, and at this point the Jews were herded together, most of them in a state of collapse, and loaded onto trucks.

The following morning, Isaac and his group, who had managed to stay together, found themselves outside Larissa, south-west of Thessaloniki. Jacob was not with them. He had died without regaining consciousness.

This was where their torture really began. Thereafter, for ten hours each day, they laboured without a break, exposed to the unforgiving sun and the relentless interest of the mosquitoes. At night, while they slept, the vicious insects continued their work and within a fortnight many of them showed the symptoms of malaria. Even then, there was no respite and the soldiers in charge drove them from their beds each morning and forced them back to work. Once or twice, local villagers took the risk of bringing them additional food or a change of clothing, but this was the only kindness they ever received. Many collapsed in front of the guards, who prodded their emaciated bodies with rifle butts to see if they could get another hour of labour out of them. Only death gave them an excuse to stop working.

When the fourth of their close-knit group from the workshop had died as a result of the Germans' bestial cruelty, two in the group began talking of escape.

'We're going to perish here, so we might as well give ourselves a chance!'

'You don't know they aren't planning to let us go when the job is done,' said Isaac. 'And anyway, they'll shoot you if you try to get away.'

'But they won't see us trying to get away . . .'

'You can't guarantee that! You might just make things worse for the rest of us.'

Although there was a guard permanently on duty outside their makeshift tent, they always felt that their language created a place where they could not be touched. To the Germans, Ladino was a smudge of incomprehensible sound.

Back in Thessaloniki, a controversy was raging. Although Isaac was watching his fellow Jews collapsing and dying on a daily basis, there was a sudden glimmer of hope that they might all be released.

The Jewish community had been offered the chance to buy back the labourers, and a price of three million drachmas had been set. In sheer desperation, people began to try to raise the money.

A suggestion was then put forward. Instead of finding this unattainable sum, the Jewish community could pay in kind, by handing over their cemetery. The municipal authority had long wished to get its hands on this vast and valuable piece of land in the heart of the city and now they had their chance: the cemetery was given a value that exactly matched the ransom figure.

The Jewish community was in uproar. In the Moreno workshop, where most people had buried their relatives in this ancient and historic cemetery, there were tears of anger and frustration.

'But the value of our ancestors is beyond monetary value,' protested one of the older tailors. 'We can't let this happen!'

'And some of those graves are more than five hundred years old!'

'Look, the buried are already dead, and my sons are still alive,' said one of the older tailors, who had three boys at the labour camps. 'How can you even regard it as a choice?'

Everyone had a point of view, and no one was wrong.

Katerina noticed that Kyria Moreno always found an excuse to leave the room when the issue was raised. Once or twice she had followed her and found her weeping quietly in one of the storerooms.

'Every time I think of Isaac, I have this terrible feeling that I will never see him again,' she said. 'And here we have this chance to get our son back from the camps and people complain!'

Katerina put her arm around Kyria Moreno and hugged her.

'I can't bear to listen to them,' she said. 'There's nothing I can do about Elias, but at least I might see Isaac again.'

'Have you had any news of Elias?' asked Katerina, hoping for a snippet of information.

'Nothing,' said Roza. 'But they say that most of the resistance are in the mountains, so I assume he's there. Still with Dimitri, I expect. And the weather is on the change, isn't it?'

'Snow. Yes. I've heard they've already had a fall of it there.'

The older woman nodded and both of them sat in silence for a few moments. Kyria Moreno wanted to compose herself before she rejoined the others. Katerina was thinking of Dimitri. She shuddered, imagining him going through another winter without food or proper clothing.

The debate over the cemetery went on for some time, but the reality was that the Jews did not have a choice. The municipality had already lined up a workforce to destroy it, and in December more than three hundred thousand graves, including those of their great rabbis and teachers, were ripped up. Relatives rushed there to try to rescue the remains of family members, but most were too late, finding that bones had already been pulverised and gold dental work ripped out. A few were fortunate and got there in time to save their late, loved ones and would later reinter them in new cemeteries to the east and west of the city.

Marble headstones were taken away to be sold and later reappeared as part of a building or even underfoot, as a pavement slab. The Morenos, like most other Jews, were distraught when they saw the desecration of their historic and sacred burial ground. If it had been at the epicentre of an earthquake, greater damage could not have been done. The destruction was cataclysmic.

Within a few days, however, the Morenos' tears of sorrow turned to tears of joy. A skeletally frail man appeared at their door. It was Isaac. The bones of several hundred thousand dead had been successfully exchanged for a few thousand of the only just alive.

# Chapter Twenty

As 1943 BEGAN, the city descended further into a state of famine. This took over as the main preoccupation of all those who lived in Thessaloniki.

The Moreno workshop was managing to retain all of its remaining employees (as well as Jacob, three others had died in the labour camp) but there was now little work. The Germans no longer came in for their suits and even the wealthier people of the city – 'who must all be collaborators,' Kyria Moreno concluded – could not get the fabric for their new clothes. Konstantinos Komninos had put up his prices so much that only the very rich could afford to pay.

One of the few women who continued to have new gowns was Olga. Anxiety over her son, rather than a shortage of food, had caused her to become even more painfully thin. Some might have mistaken it for elegance, but underneath her expensively lined *crêpe de Chine*, her bones were as pronounced as those of the most deprived people of the city. Nowadays, her husband entertained German officers and when they were at the dining table, Olga lost her appetite completely.

Along with all the other *modistras* and tailors, Katerina continued to keep busy with alterations. Cuffs may have frayed and fabric turned shiny with age, but people found dignity in trying to keep up standards in their appearance. The Moreno workshop charged very little for this service, and when the customers were friends, they charged nothing at all.

There had been rumours that Jews were being deported from their respective countries across Europe, but as yet there had been no such action in Greece, so the Morenos had no reason to think that this was going to happen to them. As though it was someone's new year's resolution, all this changed in January 1943. One of Adolf Eichmann's deputies was sent to Thessaloniki with the order to plan 'the final solution' for the city's fifty thousand Jews. Within a month, one hundred German police had arrived to implement new measures.

'What's this about a star?' asked Isaac. He came into the workshop each day, even though he was still frail and his once dextrous sewing fingers had been wrecked by the months of hard labour.

'It has to be yellow, that's all I know,' said Kyria Moreno. 'And some of our customers have asked us to sew them on.'

'And it has to be ten centimetres in diameter and with six points,' said Katerina, who had already started sewing stars onto coats and jackets. Isaac stood and watched her.

With her fine, rhythmic stitching, Katerina managed to make her stars look like pieces of the finest appliqué. She had seen one or two people in the street with these ugly stars tacked on with crude stitches. If her Jewish friends had to wear these things, then they should at least look neat.

'I don't see why we should wear them,' said Isaac. 'I've done my service for the Germans. And as far as I'm concerned, that's all over.'

'Isaac,' said his father, 'we don't have a choice.'

'Who exactly has instructed us to wear them? And how can they make us?'

'Rabbi Koretz has told us to wear them,' said his mother quietly. 'The Rabbi!'

'He hasn't made the rule up, Isaac,' appealed his father. 'He is simply the intermediary.'

'And what else has he been told to tell us?'

Isaac's hatred of the Germans was much deeper than his parents'. He had been on the receiving end of their cruelty for many months and had known the extremes to which they could go. He had kept most of the details from them.

He saw his parents exchange glances.

'It looks,' said his father, 'as though we have to move house.'

'From Irini Street?' said Katerina, aghast.

'We think so,' said Kyria Moreno, in tears. 'We don't really know the details yet.'

'But why would the Germans want you to move? Are you sure it isn't just a rumour?'

Isaac had left the room, unable to conceal his anger, and Katerina and Roza continued to sew the stars in silence.

Within a few days, the news had been confirmed. The Moreno family, along with every single one of their employees, apart from Katerina, would be moving to an area near the railway station.

'Well, I'm sure they have their reasons,' said Saul Moreno. 'And I expect they will explain it all to us in due course.'

Kyrios Moreno's blind faith in those who guided his life, particularly the chief rabbi, was unwavering. He believed in good sense and was quite certain that at the heart of this new directive, there would be an explanation.

The Jews had been instructed to make a list of their possessions and most of them began, dutifully, to carry this out.

'It's for some kind of tax they're going to impose on us,' muttered Kyrios Moreno. He was beginning to have his suspicions, but still hid them from his wife.

None of his employees came into the workshop the next day. They were all at home, gathering their possessions, surveying their valuables and wondering what to take with them to their new homes. They had been told that the accommodation was likely to be more limited than where they currently lived.

Katerina and Eugenia had visits from several of the Moreno employees that night.

'Can you keep this safe for us?'

'Will you look after this for me, just until we're back in our homes?'

'Would you mind hiding something? Not for long, I hope!'

There was false cheer and a level of light-heartedness in their requests. Katerina and Eugenia found themselves the guardians of brooches, rings and pendants. They had nowhere safe to put such valuables themselves, but would sew them inside cushions where nobody would ever find them. Each one was embroidered with an elaborate cipher, formed of their owner's initials.

The following day, Saul and Roza visited their neighbours. Katerina was expecting them. In his arms, like a baby, Kyrios Moreno carried something that she recognised. It was the quilt within which the ancient *parochet* was concealed. She took it from him without saying anything and went upstairs to spread it over her bed. Kyria Moreno handed Eugenia the two embroidered 'samplers'.

'Would you mind putting them on your wall?' she asked.

'Of course not,' said Eugenia.

The other items they put in a trunk. Even if someone had been spying on Irini Street, nothing would have aroused their suspicions. The Morenos were moving house, and could not take everything with them. In fact, they had been obliged to leave many of their possessions behind. Several rugs, a bed, some chairs and a whole chest of linen were left inside number 7.

'We'll leave these for Elias,' said Roza to her husband. 'Perhaps he'll be back before we are.'

Over the next few days, the streets around them were jammed with the chaos of moving wagons. House contents were piled vertically: chests, chairs, pots and pans, and often a table, balanced on top of everything else like a dead animal in a state of rigor mortis.

Sadness and despair filled the streets. The cascades of rain did not help. Everyone was bent double under their possessions and even the young looked old, reduced to a uniform herd with their matching yellow stars.

Mothers held on tightly to the hands of small children. With tens of thousands on the streets they could easily lose sight of them, and the unstable towers of possessions made everyone vulnerable to falling objects.

Since the departure of the Muslims, Irini Street had been a mixture of Christian and Jew, and the Christians did everything they could to help their departing friends, just as had been done for the Muslims twenty years before. There were embraces and sincere promises to visit.

'I shall still see you tomorrow,' said Katerina to a tearful Kyria Moreno. 'Work carries on as normal, doesn't it?'

'Yes, my dear, I suppose it does,' she replied wearily. She seemed to have aged by a decade overnight.

As Katerina watched the retreating figures of the Moreno family, one thought went through her mind. How would Elias know where to find his family when he returned? She hoped she would be there to tell him. There was never more than a day when her thoughts did not take her to the mountains.

On the surface of it, the following day was strangely calm in the Moreno workshop. Everyone arrived as normal. There was not much work to do, so Kyrios Moreno set the task of making an inventory of everything that still remained, down to the last pin, button and scrap of lace. It kept everyone busy and resulted in meticulously clean and tidy premises. For several years they had all been much too busy to undertake such a task. Kyrios Moreno would almost have considered it an indulgence.

The day after, Katerina arrived at the workshop punctually as usual. It was strange walking there alone.

When she turned the corner, she knew immediately that something was wrong. All her colleagues were standing in the street. Although none of them could translate it, they were gathered around staring at a large notice, in German, which had been pinned to the door. A heavy padlock had been crudely screwed into the doorframe.

Katerina shared their utter dismay. The workshop had been seized by the Germans. Even without being able to read a word of the language, there was no mistaking what had happened.

For some of them there was a sense of great indignation, even of anger. Isaac was pulling at the padlock.

'How dare they?' he screamed. 'Let's just rip this thing off!'

'Calm yourself, Isaac,' said his father, gently touching his arm. 'I think we should go home.'

'Home!' he screamed.

The word rang out around the street. It was loaded with yearning and grief. For the first time in her life, Katerina saw a man break down in uncontrollable tears. It was a shocking sight.

Everyone began to disperse, back to the area that had been established for the Jews, their new ghetto.

'Come and see us soon, Katerina,' said Kyria Moreno, trying to sound normal. 'I think we should all leave here now.'

Katerina nodded, silently. She needed to be brave for her friends.

When they were first ghettoised, the Jews were obliged to return to their new accommodation before sunset. Within a short time, the rules changed. Wooden fences were erected around the entire area and the exits were guarded. They were no longer allowed to leave at all. Barbed wire over the fencing made sure of it.

The effect on Thessaloniki was immediate. Without the daytime circulation of fifty thousand of its inhabitants, whole areas had become ghost towns. Katerina was bereft.

One night at the beginning of March, Eugenia and Katerina were sitting close to the hearth eating dinner. It was about nine in the evening. They heard a quiet knock at the door. It was late for anyone to call and they looked at each other with trepidation.

The only people on the streets at this time tended to be soldiers or gendarmes. Eugenia shook her head and put a finger in front of her lips.

The knocking became more insistent. Whoever was outside was now banging hard on their door. They were not fooled by the silence within.

'Kyria Eugenia!'

It was a familiar voice.

'It's Isaac!' whispered Katerina, leaping up. 'Quickly! We have to let him in.'

She ran over to the door and opened it. Isaac slipped into the room.

'Isaac!'

His appearance was shocking. He had been thin when he went into the ghetto, but now his bones seemed about to break through his skin.

'Come in, come in,' said Eugenia.

He was shaking violently.

'Are you hungry?'

He nodded and she ladled out a bowl of lentils for him.

For a few minutes, Isaac did not speak. He put the bowl up close to his face and drank the lentil stew straight down, like soup. He had not eaten for days and his desperation for food did not leave time for manners.

'Give him some more,' said Eugenia to Katerina. 'Tell us what's happened . . .'

Isaac told them that their rabbi, Rabbi Koretz, had appeared in the ghetto and announced that they were all to be taken to a new life. Trains were already leaving.

'But where to?' cried Katerina with disbelief.

'Poland. Krakow.'

'But why there? It's so cold!' said Katerina.

'He says there's work for us there. My parents were even allowed out to go to the bank. We've been told to exchange all our drachma for zlotys. And we've been given instruction on what to take on the journey.'

Eugenia and Katerina sat quietly, their brows knitted in concentration and concern.

'Koretz is telling people it's no different from the last time.'

'What does he mean – "the last time"?' asked Katerina.

'He means that we were all moved in a huge mass once before, when our ancestors came here from Spain. And now it's time to move on again. So it's not really any different.'

'I suppose there might be some truth in that,' reflected Eugenia. She was mindful of her own enforced exile. She had made a new life, eventually.

'So some of us decided to break out,' said Isaac, defiantly. 'The men I was with are planning to join the resistance.'

'But won't they get caught first?' asked Eugenia. 'Won't your accents give you away?'

'And what about the gendarmes? They are always stopping people for identification,' added Katerina.

'There are people selling false papers,' answered Isaac.

It occurred to Eugenia why he had come. Fake identity was expensive and he would need his mother's jewellery to pay for it. It was concealed inside the pillow that lay upstairs on her bed.

'So do you need some money?'

'No, that's not what I've come for.'

Both women sat and looked at Isaac. He looked so frail and vulnerable. It was almost impossible to imagine how he had had the strength to climb the ghetto fence. Desperation must have urged him on.

'I've decided to go back. The moment I was over the fence and in the street, I realised I had to return. I can't let my parents go to Poland on their own. They'll need me to look after them.'

'I can imagine how worried your mother will be right at this moment,' Katerina said. 'She'll be so happy when you reappear.'

'I just hope they won't have left by the time I get back,' he said. 'People have started getting on the trains.'

'If you're going somewhere so cold, don't you want to take some extra blankets or clothes? Your parents left plenty behind in the house.'

'That's really why I came back here,' he said.

Eugenia and Katerina accompanied him into his family home. After only ten days, it had the air of somewhere already abandoned for a decade. Cobwebs that Kyria Moreno would have flicked away in a moment had appeared on the ceiling and there was an unmistakable smell of damp.

Isaac made straight for the wooden chest where he knew his parents had left some linen and bedclothes.

'I'm going to stay here tonight,' he said. 'I've worked out that it would be much harder to get back in while it's dark. One small noise and they'd have you. Once it's daytime, there are plenty of other distractions for the guards, with people moving around and queuing up for food and trains.'

'You can't sleep in here,' said Eugenia, with concern. 'So why don't you come and spend the night in our house?'

Isaac did not protest and within a moment they were back next door.

Eugenia noticed Isaac looking at the saucepan.

'Please,' she said, 'help yourself. Finish it off. And then go and get some sleep.'

Like a man used to obeying orders, Isaac did as he was told and wearily climbed the narrow stairs.

Even while she had been watching Isaac lifting blankets out of the chest, Katerina's imagination had been at work and as soon as she heard the sound of the door closing upstairs, she started cutting. One of the soft woollen rugs would make an ideal coat, and she had even planned how she would trim it and what sort of buttons she would use. She had twelve hours, and even with Eugenia's help, time was of the essence.

When Isaac woke up, there was a coat on the end of his bed for his mother, a jacket for Esther and a warm padded waistcoat for his father. They were beautiful too. Both coats had quilted linings and were carefully edged. For the first time in months, something lifted his spirits. He could imagine the pleasure on their faces when they saw their names embroidered into the lining and the pomegranate motif that appeared on the collars. Their main worry in the past few days had been the climate they were going to encounter in their new home, and now they had the solution.

'Perhaps I'll be sending you orders from Poland!' said Isaac, smiling. 'Thank you, thank you . . .'

Eugenia wrapped the folded garments in brown paper and, clutching the package under his arm, Isaac sauntered off down the street, back to the ghetto.

The two women watched him. They were tired after their long night of sewing. Katerina could have a sleep now as she no longer had a job to go to, but Eugenia must leave for the rug factory.

That evening they both agreed to walk down to the railway station. There was even a chance that they might be able to say goodbye to their friends. When they arrived they could see immediately that this would not be possible. The Germans were keeping everyone well away. From behind the fencing they could hear crying, the grating sound of train carriages being coupled and expulsions of steam into the air.

They stood for a moment before turning and walking away. Eugenia crossed herself several times and on their way home they called in at the little church of Agios Nikolaos Orfanos.

'*Kalo taksidi* . . .' Katerina said quietly to the flames of the four candles she lit in front of the icon. 'Safe journey.'

As they approached their house, Eugenia reminisced about their arrival in Irini Street when they had possessed nothing but the clothes they stood up in.

'We were shown such generosity by that family,' she said quietly. 'I hope they'll find even a fraction of such kindness when they reach their new home.'

# Chapter Twenty-one

THE MORENOS WERE on one of the early transportations, and trains continued to trundle north to Poland throughout the summer.

Eugenia and Katerina received a postcard from their friends during June. It was a picture of Krakow and all it said was that they had arrived and that they missed their city. When the last train finally left in August, the ghettos were silent and the city had lost one fifth of its population.

Irini Street seemed dead now and for a while the houses that had belonged to the Moreno family and other Jewish neighbours remained empty. One terrible day, however, the peace and quiet was broken. Katerina and Eugenia were woken up in the early hours by the sound of banging and shouting. It was coming not only from the street but also through the walls from the house next door. At four in the morning, they found themselves looking out of the window and down onto a crowd that was brazenly dragging things out of the Moreno house. Among several other familiar possessions, they saw the trunk in which Kyria Moreno had kept her linen. It was sitting on top of a cart.

They had read of similar ransackings in areas where there had been a concentration of Jews, but they had not expected it to happen in their street.

'We have to stop them!' said Katerina.

'I'm not sure it's a good idea . . .' said Eugenia, watching the vicious way in which two men below them were hacking open a mattress with a machete. They slashed the fabric with sadistic delight and pieces of white fluff drifted upwards like rising snow. There had been rumours that the Jews had hidden their gold inside their bedding and people were determined to find it.

The two women had to watch helplessly as their neighbours' house was systematically looted. Katerina knew that Eugenia was right: there was nothing they could safely do. The only consolation was that some of the things that the Morenos had really treasured were under a different roof. Their own.

A few weeks later a representative of Konstantinos Komninos arrived in Irini Street with a message for Katerina, asking if she could continue to sew for some of his wealthy clients who still had access to the fine fabrics he could supply. They still wanted the best *modistra* that the city could offer, and even had the Jewish seamstresses still been in the city, Katerina would have held this title.

The following day a porter turned up at her door. He was struggling to carry a large carton.

'Miss Sarafoglu?'

'That's right,' she said.

'Got something for you,' he said.

Katerina invited him in and he manoeuvred the box onto the table.

'Want to open it?' he said. 'It's from Kyrios Komninos.'

'Oh,' she said, with surprise.

She had mixed feelings about Dimitri's father. She knew that

Dimitri did not get on with him and she had often wondered if Olga's fears were something to do with the way he treated her. Every time she had met him, he had been cold and unfriendly, so it intrigued her that he had sent her a gift. She opened the top of the box. Glinting in the darkness, she saw the shine of black metal and as she removed the tissue-paper that protected it, she recognised a familiar, ornate pattern of flowers and foliage. It was a Singer sewing machine.

'He said to give you this as well,' said the delivery man.

She opened the note and read it straight away. 'While you are working at home,' it said, 'you will need this.'

Between them, they lifted the machine onto the table. It was beautiful and her own, and she could see her face reflected in its gleaming, pristine curves. Katerina did not stop to question how Kyrios Komninos had come by such a thing in a time of war.

She was sorely tempted to ask about Dimitri. As one of Konstantinos Komninos' staff, the delivery man might have heard something, but she restrained herself as she knew it would appear inappropriate.

Within days, the same Komninos employee returned to Irini Street. He had another note and a package containing some fabric.

'Dear Katerina, I would like something made from the enclosed for Kyria Komninos. Perhaps you could come as soon as possible to take some measurements.'

Katerina was flattered but nervous. She sent a message back with the man to confirm that she would be there at midday the following day.

She arrived punctually, excited to see Kyria Komninos. Pavlina let her in and showed her upstairs. After they had greeted one another and Katerina had fulsomely expressed her gratitude for the sewing machine, she got to work measuring Olga.

Almost immediately, Olga raised the subject of the Morenos, expressing her sadness that they had been obliged to leave the city.

'I hope they'll be all right in such a cold place.'

'Well, Thessaloniki can be very chilly sometimes, can't it?' said Katerina. 'And we are quite used to snow here, aren't we?'

'I think it's much colder than Thessaloniki,' said Olga.

Katerina told her about the warm clothes they had produced for the Morenos, and for a few moments neither woman spoke. The absence of the Jewish family had left a huge void in Katerina's life and Olga was well aware that the young woman had lost people who were her neighbours, her employers and her friends. The years Olga had spent in Irini Street had been the happiest of her life and she knew that the area must seem very empty now.

'Have you heard from Dimitri?' asked Katerina, seizing the moment.

'Just one letter,' Olga replied. 'A few months ago.'

'Is Elias still with him?'

'Well, he was when Dimitri wrote,' she answered. 'But now, I don't know.'

'Where did the letter come from?'

'I really don't know. It had no postmark.'

There was a finality about the way Olga answered that told Katerina she did not wish to pursue the subject. Either she had no information or she did not want to give it. Whichever was the case, the subject was closed.

They were in Olga's dressing room for the measuring. The doors of a vast wardrobe were open and Katerina saw a hundred dresses hanging on a rail. They were as numerous as the pages of a book. She noticed that one of them was the first dress she had embellished, and she remembered how the tiny amber beads around the hem had taken her a week to sew.

The new dress was going to be in a purple shot silk. The fabric was from Komninos' own silk factory and she doubted that Olga had ever even seen it. As Katerina carefully recorded her customer's measurements in a small notebook, she realised that the rich blue-mauve would look like a bruise against Kyria Komninos' pallid skin.

She sketched a design for the dress opposite the row of numbers.

'I thought this might be elegant,' she said. 'With three-quarter-length sleeves. Perhaps with lace cuffs? And the skirt will be cut on the cross.'

'I am sure it will be very nice,' said Olga, giving the drawing a cursory glance. She smiled at Katerina.

'Go into the kitchen to see Pavlina before you leave,' said Olga. 'She'll make you a cold drink.'

'Thank you, Kyria Komninos,' said Katerina politely.

The temperature had soared that day.

Down in the kitchen, Pavlina was busy chopping. She was bright red in the face.

'In my view it's much too hot for such events, but Kyrios Komninos is having one of his big dinners tomorrow night. And he wants everything "just so" as usual. Four courses, four wines, eight people, eight o'clock.'

'Poor Pavlina,' said Katerina. 'Can I do anything?'

'Of course not,' she said, smiling. 'Just help yourself to some lemonade from that jug and pour one for me as well, would you?'

Katerina took a seat at the big kitchen table and sipped her lemonade. She was fascinated by Pavlina's dexterity with a knife and watched her slice, dice and finely chop a series of vegetables and herbs as though she was a machine. To Katerina, it seemed that the ingredients for this meal would be enough to feed the entire population of the city, most of whom were still starving.

'Don't ask me how we get all this,' Pavlina said. 'It's more than my job is worth to know myself.'

She continued to chat as she worked. Nothing ever stopped her talking.

'So,' she said. 'It must be as quiet as a grave in Irini Street.'

Katerina nodded.

'It feels deserted,' she said. 'There are still plenty of families living there, but the Morenos were at the heart of everything somehow.'

'And what about Elias?'

'I suppose he must still be with Dimitri,' answered Katerina. 'His parents hadn't heard anything from him before they left for Poland. I thought Kyria Komninos might know where they were, but she didn't seem to. It must be awful not knowing where your son is . . .'

Pavlina was now peeling potatoes. Round and round went her knife as the skin unfurled in one unbroken ribbon and when she had completed a dozen in exactly the same way, she rhythmically sliced them into discs of precise and even thickness.

'His father wasn't best pleased when he found out that Dimitri had joined ELAS,' said Pavlina, her words almost buried by the sound of her slicing.

'Well, I can't say that surprises me,' replied Katerina. 'But maybe he'll be happier now that they're winning parts of the country back from the Germans.'

'Oh, Katerina, if only that were so.'

'You mean his father isn't proud of him?' said Katerina with incredulity.

Pavlina shook her head. 'I'm afraid precisely the opposite. He is furious. ELAS are Communist, you see.'

'Does it matter what party they are when they're doing something to get our country back?' queried Katerina.

'Shhhh!' whispered Pavlina, putting her forefinger to her lips. 'Just in case Kyrios Komninos comes back. He doesn't see it that way at all.'

Pavlina, who moved about the house like a shadow, had overheard a thousand conversations between Olga and Konstantinos over the years. She had always kept them to herself but she had been outraged at the way her employer now regarded his son. Some of the things she had heard him say to Olga were no less than spiteful.

'As far as Kyrios Komninos is concerned, his son is living in the mountains like a peasant,' said Pavlina.

Katerina was still slightly puzzled by such a reaction. It sounded to her as though Dimitri and Elias were part of a heroic effort.

'He sees it as a class struggle,' Pavlina explained. 'And his son is on the wrong side.'

Katerina was thoughtful for a few moments, watching Pavlina stirring.

'I listen to them all,' she continued, 'when they come to dinner. And it's as much as I can do to stop myself pouring the soup down their necks. I know Kyria Komninos feels the same. She sits there all . . . rigid.' Pavlina did an impression of her mistress's stiffness. 'I can see she hates most of the guests. Sometimes there'll be a wife who looks as if she might be feeling the same way. But mostly, she sits there looking uncomfortable and alone.'

'So who gets invited?'

'Industrialists, who complain that their warehouses get broken into by the resistance, and bankers, who moan about inflation. In fact, what they mostly do is complain about ELAS. One of them was saying last week that he'd had a demand from them for protection money.'

'Those people are happy that we're occupied then? They don't mind having the Germans here?'

'As far as I can tell, even though they do nothing but complain, some of them have never had it so good. They're certainly not short of money. And when there are German officers here, it seems they're not short of friends in high places either.'

'German officers! You don't mean it!'

'Keep your voice down a little, Katerina,' Pavlina whispered. 'And sometimes a senior gendarme, too.'

Katerina was shocked. 'But how can you cook for those people?'

'I don't really feel I have a choice,' she reflected. 'I do it for Olga. Even though she doesn't eat most of it, I think she needs me here.'

'Now I'm beginning to understand why Kyrios Komninos doesn't like what Dimitri is doing.'

Pavlina had even heard rumours that her employer was funding collaborationist troops, but she did not share this with Katerina. Nor did she describe to the *modistra* how scornfully some of the wives talked of the women in ELAS who were fighting as equals with men.

'Do you think they're safe, wherever they are?' asked Katerina. 'Dimitri and Elias, I mean.'

'My dear, I don't know,' answered Pavlina, pessimistically. 'A letter takes so long to reach its destination, so even if Dimitri wrote to say he was fine, by the time it got here, he might not be.'

Katerina drained her glass and got up. Olga's dress was needed at the end of the following week, so she had work to be getting on with. At least now she had the perfect excuse to come to Niki Street. Pavlina would be the first to tell her if there was any news of Dimitri.

She called back a few days later. The new gown was roughly tacked together and needed its first fitting.

Pavlina seemed happier than ever to gossip.

'They were awful, the lot who came on Saturday,' she said. 'It's not surprising women don't get the vote in this country. This bunch would be too stupid to spell their own names.'

Katerina laughed. She could work on the dress while she was sitting there, so she was in no hurry that day.

Pavlina suddenly looked more serious. 'Shall I tell you what they were talking about?' she said.

Katerina did not need to answer.

'Well, there was lots of talk about what the Communists are doing,' she began, 'especially how they are behaving up in the mountains. Apparently, even if they're not welcome, they are taking over the villages, taking all the food and setting up their own courts. That's what the dinner guests were saying, anyhow.'

'So they're reclaiming the country for Greece? Isn't that what we want to happen?'

'Well, you and I might, but most of the visitors to this house don't see it that way,' responded Pavlina.

Olga had come into the kitchen, where the two women were sitting at the big central table. Pavlina was polishing the silver cutlery, while Katerina meticulously finished a French seam, and both women automatically sprang to their feet when they saw her.

The door had been half open and what she said confirmed that she had overheard the last few words.

'Not everyone sees ELAS as the saviour of Greece,' she said. 'Some people are so anti-Communist that they take the Germans' side against them.'

Katerina and Pavlina glanced at each other and then at Olga.

'Could you bring some mint tea upstairs, Pavlina?'

'Of course,' responded Pavlina. 'The water has just this minute boiled.'

Katerina waited until Olga's footsteps had retreated up the stairs before speaking again.

'It must be so strange to listen to stories about the Communists,' she said. 'When you know your son is with them.'

'I think Kyrios Komninos has denied so completely to himself that his son is fighting with ELAS,' said Pavlina, 'that it's not in the least bit strange for him. And Olga is so quiet anyway. People don't really notice her discomfort.'

'Anything could have happened to them, up in the mountains,' Katerina reflected.

'Lord only knows,' answered Pavlina. 'I just pray that Dimitri is safe. That's all any of us can do.'

'Can you pray for Elias too?'

The months passed and Konstantinos Komninos continued to invite his fellow businessmen for regular dinners. They needed each other's support. Those who were doing well during the occupation were only doing so because of their collaboration with the occupying force, and now they began to give financial support to the Greek security battalions who helped prevent the resistance from coming into the towns.

Occasionally some gendarmes or policemen were killed in Thessaloniki, and efforts to hunt out Communist elements were stepped up. With a combined force of occupying troops, the security battalions and the gendarmes, they were usually successful.

The regularity of Konstantinos' orders for his wife's dresses during this period meant that Katerina was a frequent visitor, and Olga often invited the seamstress to sit with her in the drawing room. She enjoyed watching Katerina sew. Sometimes the *modistra* asked her how she would like a gown finished. Olga was so used to accepting whatever she was given that she had difficulty expressing a view.

'You always seem to know best,' she would say, smiling at Katerina.

Occasionally, Olga attempted some embroidery herself, but it was purely an exercise to kill time. She had no gift for it. Each stitch passed another second and took her a moment closer to her son's return. At least this was what she hoped.

On her way out, Katerina always went into the kitchen to see Pavlina.

'I actually don't think I can cook for these people any more,' said the elderly housekeeper one day. 'I am serving them and listening to their views and they disgust me. They seem to enjoy the fact that Greeks are beginning to fight Greeks.'

'You are exaggerating, aren't you?' questioned Katerina.

'No, I'm not. They're the kind of people who would go to a bear fight.'

'I'm not sure any of us have a choice, Pavlina. If we make a living it's usually because we're being paid with tainted money. My wages are coming from the rich. And at the moment, it doesn't seem as though you can be honest and rich. The option is to starve.'

Pavlina bustled about the kitchen, red in the face from the heat and irritation.

'I have to go home now,' said Katerina. 'I have to do some machine-stitching on this dress. Kyria Komninos has lost even more weight and she wants two of her gowns taken in before the weekend.'

The situation in Europe was beginning to change. That summer, Germany had begun to lose its grip on its occupied territories and in June the Allies had landed in Normandy. Paris was liberated in August and the Germans withdrew from France. With the Red

Army on the march and heading for Bulgaria, the Germans knew there was a danger of being cut off in Greece, and within days they made the decision to begin moving out.

What had seemed an impossibility in Greece was now happening. The Nazis were defeated and liberation was in sight.

One day, just before the Germans left Thessaloniki, Katerina was in Olga's dressing room, carefully pinning a hem. Fashions had changed during the war, which meant that most of Olga's clothes needed remodelling. She slipped off the gown that Katerina had pinned, put on a day dress and went back into her bedroom. Katerina stayed in the dressing room to fold the dress, ready to take home for sewing.

Almost immediately, she heard Olga scream.

She ran out into the bedroom and to her astonishment saw Olga being embraced by a man. If it had been her husband this would have been surprising enough. But it was not even him.

For a moment, Katerina was frozen to the spot. She did not know what to do and her indecision left her standing there, eyes wide, mouth gaping.

With their faces buried into one another's shoulder, the embrace shut out the world and their stillness and entanglement reminded her of the classical sculpture in the hallway below.

The obvious thing was to run back into the dressing room but, before she turned round to go, she saw the couple move apart. Katerina's embarrassment was all the greater now.

In the next one and a half seconds, she took in the incongruity of Olga's pale elegance and the man's grubbiness. Even from a distance of a few metres, she could smell the unfamiliar odour he had brought into the room. It was like an animal's.

Suddenly Olga remembered that Katerina was there and turned

round. She was smiling in a way that the *modistra* had never seen, her face almost transfigured with joy.

'Look!' she said, gripping the man's left hand, as if unable to let it go. 'He's come back!'

Katerina felt herself go crimson. She was obliged to look at the stranger whom she had caught embracing a married woman. He was bearded, dark-skinned and had cropped hair, and he was much younger than Kyria Komninos.

She realised then that she was looking into a pair of familiar brown eyes.

'Katerina!' he said.

It was a voice she knew. Dimitri's.

Katerina almost choked.

'*Panagia mou! Dimitri!*'

In a gesture of unconscious spontaneity, Katerina reached out and touched his face. She wanted reassurance that he was not an apparition.

His response was to take her hand and, for a moment, the three of them stood, hands joined.

Katerina's smile was broader even than his mother's. 'I can't believe you're here,' she said. 'It is so wonderful to see you.'

He smiled at her and looked into her glistening eyes. 'It's wonderful to see you too, Katerina. I have missed you so much.'

His gaze held hers.

'Dimitri,' said Olga, 'you know we have to be careful. Your father might come home . . .'

'And I know he wouldn't be happy to see me,' said Dimitri. 'How long have I got? Can I have something to eat before I go?'

'Let's go down to the kitchen,' Olga said, with more energy in her voice than Katerina had ever heard. 'Your father doesn't usually come in until late, but we should listen out. And does Pavlina know you are here?'

'Yes, she opened the door to me. You should have seen her face, Mother. She was more astonished even than you!'

They were all laughing together as they went downstairs to the kitchen. Dimitri was in the middle and Katerina was surprised to find that he still held her hand as they descended.

Katerina made her excuses to leave, but Olga was insistent that she should stay. She needed no persuasion.

While Dimitri made his way through plate after plate of meatballs, peppers, baked aubergines, stuffed vine leaves, potatoes and finally a whole dish of sweet pastries, the three women sat and gazed at him admiringly.

Then they began to ask questions.

Were he and Elias still together? Where had they been? What activities had they been involved in? What was expected to happen next?

'Elias and I are in different units, now,' Dimitri answered. 'So I haven't seen him for a long time. To be honest, I have no idea where he is.'

'You know that the Jews have all gone?'

'I heard,' said Dimitri regretfully. 'If he comes back here and realises they've left, he might go and join them, I suppose.'

'We often go into the house,' said Katerina. 'We tidied it up after it was looted and try to keep it dusted. Eugenia and I have left him a note, just in case he turns up and we aren't at home. It would be a bit of a shock to see it.'

'Are they planning to come back, do you think?'

'Hard to say,' said Katerina. 'Their business is still standing there empty. But it probably won't be like that for long.'

'What do you mean?'

'One of your father's business associates has got his eye on it,' said Olga. 'He was one of the people who came here for dinner the other night.'

'But supposing the Morenos decide to come back?' asked Katerina, slightly indignantly.

'Then they'd be compensated, I expect,' chipped in Pavlina.

'Anyway, this man has tailoring businesses here and in Veria and Larissa,' Olga continued. 'And he's looking to expand in Thessaloniki when the war ends. But tell us what you have been doing all this time, Dimitri—'

'I know one thing about your time in the mountains,' interrupted Pavlina gaily. 'There wasn't much to eat!'

She was overjoyed to have Dimitri sitting at her table and eating her cooking.

Dimitri smiled to please her, but soon his smile faded. 'To be truthful, it was really terrible up there,' he said. 'More awful than I can begin to tell you.'

All three women were silent. Pavlina had stopped bustling about for once and even she sat still and listened.

'At the beginning we were distributing supplies to people who had nothing, robbing the Germans of food that they had stolen from us in the first place and giving it out to people in need. We were all working together at that stage, ELAS with EDES and the British. All co-operating. We all had a common enemy. They spoke German. It seemed simple.'

They were all quiet while Dimitri gathered his thoughts.

'It was strange being loathed when we believed we were doing the right thing,' he said. 'And some people hated us even more than they hated the Germans because the Germans were using us as an excuse to brutalise people. They massacred whole villages if they suspected them of giving food or shelter to any *andarte*. There were even people up in the mountain with German weapons and they used them against us!'

'The world's gone mad!' said Pavlina, shaking her head.

'I have done everything I can to keep my hands clean,' he continued. 'But it wasn't always possible. There's blood up there; the rivers are running with it.'

'Try not to think about it now,' Olga said, gently stroking his arm.

'People like my father regard ELAS as a bunch of bandits, but I hope one day they'll understand our ideals.'

'I hope so too,' responded Olga.

He was exhausted. They could see it on his sunken face and hear it in his weary voice. At times there were tears in his eyes as he recalled some of the things he had witnessed.

'There's been an order to go to Athens so I'm on my way there now,' he said.

'What?' cried his mother. 'You can't go yet!'

'You need a good rest,' added Pavlina.

Katerina sat quietly. Pavlina was right.

'But there's something else to do now. Something just as important,' he said.

The three women listened to his explanation. ELAS's primary goal to rid their country of Axis troops had virtually been achieved. Now they had another task: to make sure that the Left was fairly represented in a new government.

'Why should people who collaborated with the Germans now rule the country?' he asked.

Olga shook her head. 'It's wrong, I can see that.'

'So I have to go. When the job is finished I'll come back home, I promise.'

He was looking at Katerina as he said this.

Dimitri left well before his father returned. Though the three of them were sad to see him go, they were greatly cheered by the thought that he might soon be back.

It may have been nothing more than a gesture of brotherly love, but Katerina endlessly replayed the memory of Dimitri holding her hand. The feeling of his rough fingers stroking her palm may have lasted only a few moments but she could not forget the sensation of his affection. It was the first time she had known such an experience. His touch had made her feel simultaneously both weak and strong, and though this puzzled her, there was something she was sure of: knowing he was alive made her heart soar.

# Chapter Twenty-two

THE MUCH-HOPED-FOR WITHDRAWAL of the Germans became a reality for Thessaloniki at the end of October. People on both the Left and Right were glad to see the back of them but liberation proved hard to celebrate. On their way out of Greece, the Germans had created havoc and, by the time they were over the border, few roads, bridges or railway lines remained useable.

In the three years of occupation, the entire country had been stripped of fuel, food, livestock, medical supplies and building materials. Greece was in a state of total destitution and its infrastructure destroyed. Only those who had meticulously protected their own interests or had devised ways of profiteering from the poverty of others had any hope for the future, but for everyone else, even the bare necessities were beyond reach. Hyperinflation had struck the economy that autumn and bread that had cost ten drachmas for a kilo just before the war now cost thirty-four million. The Germans had lost the war, but the Greeks had lost almost everything they had.

On a cool autumnal day, when the last German had left Thessaloniki, Eugenia and Katerina took themselves out for a *volta* around the streets.

'We may as well mark the moment of our freedom,' said Eugenia. 'It's a long time since we've been for a stroll.'

From Irini Street they walked down to the seafront. The prows of half-sunken ships stuck out of the water like shark fins. Many of them had been there for nearly two years now and were rapidly rusting, the sad corpses of a once-strong merchant navy. There was no activity at the port and the vast expanse of dockyard, once so alive with movement and noise, was eerily silent.

'I don't suppose you remember . . .'

They were standing in the open space next to the customs house and the building stirred a distant memory for Katerina. It had not been whitewashed in decades, and the same huge clock on the outside miraculously still told the time.

'I think I do remember something. Were we standing for ages over by that building . . . and queuing for something?'

'Yes, we were,' Eugenia smiled.

'And there were lots and lots of people. That's what really sticks in my mind. And a woman wearing white.'

The emptiness of the space now contrasted so completely with that first memory that they both turned away. Eugenia shuddered. A breeze was blowing in across the sea and over the empty cobbled space. A few pieces of litter danced.

'You're thinking of the woman from the Refugee Commission,' said Eugenia. 'She found us our home.'

'We were all so dirty, and she was so clean! I remember that so clearly. I thought she must be a fairy.'

They continued walking, unrelaxed, finding it hard to forget the constant fear of a sudden tap on the shoulder and the demand for identity papers. Even though the Germans were no longer there, nervousness and a sense of ill ease remained.

They took a circuitous route around the town, walking eastwards towards the White Tower. A glimpse of the Arch of Galerius and the ancient Rotunda reminded them that the historic monuments of the city were intact, as though they had enjoyed the Germans' special respect. The more workaday places, on the other hand, had been badly bruised by the occupation. The little streets of boarded-up shops, gutted buildings and vandalised synagogues were all its victims. Although some areas still bore the scars of the 1917 fire, more of the city than ever was in a state of dereliction. In some neighbourhoods, there was a sense of ghostly vacancy and their footsteps echoed eerily back at them.

Even in the still inhabited areas, people had got into the habit of staying inside their homes, and the coolness of autumn did not encourage the old habit of bringing a chair onto the doorstep.

They kept walking and talking, occasionally seeing a kafenion where men sat drinking and playing *tavli*, just as they had done in the days before the war, and such glimpses of normality reassured them.

Eventually, they reached a street that was as familiar to Katerina as Irini Street: Filipou Street, where Moreno & Sons was situated.

Eugenia felt Katerina's grip on her arm tighten. The hoarding that had been placed over the doors and windows had been taken down and all the graffiti and crudely scrawled Stars of David that had been daubed over the walls had been scrubbed off. There were men walking in and out carrying boxes, and sounds of activity came from inside.

Katerina had noticed something else as well. There was no longer a sign over the premises and the door had been repainted. The emerald green that Kyrios Moreno had always favoured (to match the delivery van of which he had been so proud) had been replaced by a deep ox-blood red.

They stood and watched for a few minutes.

'It's going to be reopened,' said Katerina with a note of dismay.

It was unbearable to see it and they hastened back to Irini Street in silence.

The following day, the entire population of the city descended on Aristotelous Square for the official celebration of the liberation from the Germans. The cafés where enemy soldiers had lounged in the sun for four whole summers were once again full of Greeks.

There was one thing the city's residents had not lost during the occupation and that was their resilience. Their magnificent city, so multilayered and rich in history, had suffered a multitude of tribulations in the past decades but once again, they were faced with the challenge of making it better than before.

A month before the Germans departed, an agreement had been signed between the various factions and opposing interests on both right and left. In the Caserta Agreement, as it was known, the resistance leaders pledged to forbid any of their units to take the law into their own hands once the Germans had gone. The Government of National Unity was installed and, just as the agreement had specified, there was no attempt by the Communists to seize power.

The head of the right-wing army, EDES, even went to London to assure the British that he would work together with the Communists and with the new government to ensure the country's democratic development. Peaceful transition was looking hopeful.

Late one afternoon, Katerina called in to the Komninos house to deliver a coat she had repaired for Pavlina. In the hallway, she saw Kyria Komninos.

'I haven't heard from him, I'm afraid,' Olga said without prompting. 'It's hard for him to get in touch.'

Only a few weeks had passed since they had all been sitting

around him in the kitchen, but Katerina had found Dimitri constantly occupying her thoughts.

'I'm sure he'll be back soon,' she said, trying to conceal her own concern.

'I think there might have been some kind of truce between him and his father if he had returned when the Germans left,' she said regretfully, 'but I think his father realises now how committed he is.'

'Well, he is, isn't he?' Katerina responded.

'Yes, Katerina. But I'm so afraid,' Olga admitted. 'We thought the war was over but some people are saying that there might be more fighting. Kyrios Komninos is saying that the Left are making demands and the government shouldn't give in to them.'

Olga's voice betrayed the disappointment that many people were sharing. Winter was rapidly approaching and, with the lengthening nights, a pall of pessimism was descending.

Olga disappeared upstairs and Katerina went into the kitchen.

'Here you are, Pavlina,' she said. 'I hope you like it.'

She held out a green coat. It looked almost new. Using scraps of fabric from a box that still sat in the Morenos' house, she had covered the old buttons with deep red velvet and given the collar and cuffs a fine edging with a piece of the same material. Additionally, she had relined the coat with the fabric from an old floral dress.

Pavlina, who had been washing dishes, immediately dried her hands and took the garment from Katerina. She put the coat on and did a slow twirl to show it off. Pavlina's access to good food meant that she had remained quite plump even during the years of hardship.

'It's just like new,' she cried. 'But better! You're such a clever girl! Thank you so much. I can look forward to the winter now!'

Katerina then remembered something. She needed Pavlina's advice.

'I had a letter today. Will you tell me what you think?'

Producing an envelope from her pocket, she handed it to Pavlina.

Pavlina read it aloud. '"Dear Kyria Sarafoglou, I hear on good authority that you are an excellent *modistra*. I have several vacancies in my new business in Thessaloniki and would like you to come for interview on Friday morning at ten o'clock."'

'That sounds good. You need to be back in a workshop now.' She handed the letter back and teasingly added: 'You'll never meet anyone working on your own at home . . .'

With so many young men away fighting, there were thousands of girls who, under normal circumstances, should have been married. Now that many men were coming back, she felt it was high time that Katerina had what she called 'a nice young man'.

'But don't you recognise the address?' Katerina said with a note of exasperation. 'It's the Morenos' workshop!'

She handed the letter back to Pavlina, who scrutinised it.

'I went past with Eugenia and there were lots of people there, repainting it and getting it ready.'

'And that name . . . I recognise that too. Grigoris Gourgouris has been here lots of times in the past few years. He and Kyrios Komninos obviously do lots of business together.'

'But when the Morenos come back . . . ?'

'They'll be given some compensation, Katerina,' said Pavlina. 'Don't worry. The authorities can't just leave all those businesses empty! We've got to get this city going again!'

Katerina looked thoughtfully at the letter.

'And if they return and get the workshop back, then they'll be pleased to see that you are already working there!' Pavlina added.

Katerina could appreciate Pavlina's neat and tidy logic.

'I suppose I have to earn a living,' she said. 'Kyrios Moreno would definitely understand that.'

Later that week, Katerina attended her interview. There was a room with fifty other women waiting to be seen, and while they were waiting they were each given a piece of linen on which they had to demonstrate five embroidery stitches, five edging techniques and a rouleau buttonhole.

One by one, they were summoned to the interview room. By the time she was called, Katerina had been kept waiting for two hours.

The man at the desk was three times the size of the diminutive previous owner. Katerina handed over her sampler and noticed big hands with soft pudgy fingers.

'Mmm, good, good,' he said, inspecting it closely. 'I see your reputation is justified, Miss Sarafoglou.'

She stayed silent.

'I have seen your work,' he said, looking up for the first time. 'You make gowns for Konstantinos Komninos' wife, don't you? She is an excellent mannequin!'

As he spoke, she noticed yellowing teeth beneath a silvery moustache and eyes in a full-moon face that almost disappeared when he grinned, just as he did at this moment.

'I know children who can sew better than some of those women out there,' he said wearily. 'But this is good. This is what I was hoping to see.'

Katerina attempted a smile. She thought it was the expected response to what was supposed to be a compliment.

'I expect a lot of my *modistras*, so don't expect to be sitting about chatting all day. In my workshops, it's a twelve-hour day, half an hour for lunch. Half-day on Saturday. Sundays off. And if there is something that needs finishing for a customer, then it has to be finished. This is how I have made my reputation in Veria and Larissa, and soon it will be the same here. It's why I am known as the "Top Tailor in Town". You'll see it on the side of my vans: "We make the date! We're never late!"'

He coughed once, as if giving his speech a full stop. He had made it a thousand times and his flowing truisms and mottos tripped fluently off his tongue, inviting no response. Katerina knew she had got a job.

'Monday next. Eight o'clock. Good morning, Miss Sarafoglou.' He smiled at her and she knew this was the sign for her to go.

As she left, she saw a queue of applicants that tailed down to the end of the street. There must have been two hundred women still waiting to be seen and she realised she was one of the lucky ones.

The gleaming sign above the door, 'GRIGORIS GOURGOURIS', made her feel uneasy but at this moment, with hunger nagging at her insides, there seemed no choice.

The company officially opened for business the following week. The *modistras* had been locally recruited, except for one, who had been brought by Grigoris Gourgouris from Athens. She was put in charge of the finishing room and oversaw the younger women with distinctly undermining condescension.

Gourgouris had brought a handful of his tailors from Veria and Larissa but most of the new recruits lacked the experience that he would have liked. Many of the best tailors in the city had been Jewish, and their absence had left a huge gap of skilled labour. It would be a long while before the Gourgouris label carried the same cachet as the Moreno name.

Grigoris Gourgouris came himself to inspect the women's work several times a day, even though they felt his interest was over-zealous. As far as they could tell, their boss did not even know how to run a straight line of stitches to join two pieces of fabric. As soon as he left the room, the girls gossiped about him, speculating on why he spent so long leaning over particular members of his staff. After several weeks, Katerina became the object of much teasing.

'It's Katerina this and Katerina that,' they chanted. 'Look at her satin stitch! Look at her ruching! Look at her edging!'

They were right. It had become obvious that the person in whom Gourgouris took the greatest interest was herself. She became familiar with the strong waft of garlic that usually forewarned her that the boss was on his way, ambling slowly down the row of workers to see what they were doing, before stopping and leaning slightly too close to hear about the assignment she was working on.

Katerina always answered his questions precisely and politely, holding her breath in between answers to reduce the effect of his vaporous breath. He was sincerely lavish in his praise of her work and when she was sent round to see Olga Komninos for a fitting, she discovered that he had broadcast his high opinion of her at the Komninos dinner table too.

'He is very impressed by you,' said Olga to Katerina's reflection, as the latter fastened a dress for her in front of a large mirror. 'He was here on Saturday and he kept saying how thrilled he was with your work. Apparently you are in a different class from anyone else.'

Katerina said nothing. She found it awkward that he paid her so much attention. It was uncomfortable to be singled out and she often found herself touching the *mati* that she had on a chain around her neck, the 'evil eye' that was meant to protect the wearer from jealousy.

\* \* \*

While Thessaloniki was beginning to regain some kind of normality, events were moving on apace in Athens. As the citizens of Thessaloniki read their newspapers, they knew that whatever happened in their capital, the consequences would have a profound effect on them.

The Prime Minister, Georgios Papandreou, was showing little interest in pursuing and punishing those who had collaborated with the Germans, but instead seemed more interested in total demobilisation of the left-wing forces. The Left were unhappy and suspicious, and called for a demonstration to take place on 3 December. Thousands gathered in Syntagma, Athens' central square, and without apparent provocation, a policeman fired into the crowd. In the ensuing chaos, sixteen demonstrators were killed and open fighting broke out in the streets between the police, British troops and ELAS fighters. In the next few days, the Left began to hunt down those who were known collaborators.

ELAS captured police stations and a prison but overall had underestimated the strength of their opponents, who were often well disciplined and armed. Massive reinforcements arrived a week or so later and ELAS then found themselves engaged in a running battle with the British.

By early January, most of ELAS had abandoned the capital in disarray, having lost up to three thousand of their forces. Seven and a half thousand others had been taken prisoner. The right-wing forces had lost over three thousand too and many were captured. During those weeks, Athens had become a battleground.

'So this is what your son wanted?' screamed Konstantinos to his wife. 'And what has he gained?'

'It wasn't just him,' said Olga reasonably. 'Why do you always make it sound as though the entire situation is his fault? I don't think he is the only one.'

'Well he's the only Communist I know!'

As usual, Olga had to bite her lip. She refused to think of her son as a Communist, but instead regarded him as someone who wanted democracy and justice. She never argued with her husband. One civil war seemed enough.

In Thessaloniki itself, hunger was already increasing. Shoes, clothes and medical supplies were also vanishing again. Many were attributing this to the activities of ELAS and were blaming them for new levels of starvation. Komninos was one of thousands who were against ELAS. With pictures of their victims circulating in the right-wing press and stories of mass graves and brutal vendetta killings, there were many others who did not feel they could side with people who executed enemies for personal revenge.

ELAS now took thousands of civilian hostages in Athens and in Thessaloniki. Most of them were members of the bourgeoisie, such as civil servants, army officers and police, and they were forced to march long distances in bitterly cold weather, without adequate clothing or shoes. Many died from exposure. Brutality and the cruelty of the executions that had been perpetrated began to fill the newspapers.

'He seems so sure that his son is capable of such things,' lamented Olga to Pavlina. 'How can a father imagine the worst of his son? He thinks that being a Communist automatically makes you a murderer.'

'And it's not as if the other side are whiter than white, is it?' responded Pavlina. 'I've heard plenty of stories about things they've been up to and they're not all so nice.'

Pavlina was right. There was extreme brutality on both sides but the Left was losing support, even in the areas that they had liberated from the Germans. Most people were sick of war and hungry for peace, and the Left seemed to be getting in the way of it.

In February 1945, it seemed as if their wish was going to be fulfilled. In the Varkiza Agreement, ELAS undertook to hand over their weapons in exchange for an amnesty on political crimes and a plebiscite on the constitution. For a brief time, both Olga and Katerina fondly imagined the return of Dimitri and a reconciliation with his father.

However, the Agreement soon turned out to be worthless. Right-wing death squads and paramilitary groups went on the rampage to hunt out Communists, and a reign of terror began against all of those who fought for the Left.

These developments were, of course, the main topic of conversation at Konstantinos Komninos' dinner table, when he next entertained. The merchants and businessmen of Thessaloniki wanted nothing more than for business to return to normal, and the messiness of politics stood in the way of their profits.

Pavlina bustled about in the kitchen, waiting to go into the dining room to clear up after the main course. As soon as the conversation could be heard above the clatter of knives and forks, she knew that people had finished eating and were ready for the next course.

She hummed as she worked and stood back to admire her efforts. She was proud of her individual strawberry tarts: pert preserved fruit under a glaze of syrup with a chocolate crème patissière waiting invisibly beneath. She knew the latter would surprise the diners when they stuck in their forks and discovered that there was something else beneath the soft red flesh. She gave them a light dusting of icing sugar and moved them to the trolley, ready to take in.

At precisely that moment, she heard the doorbell ring. None of the guests was late, and ten thirty in the evening was a strange time for anyone to call. She put down her sifter and went to the door. She knew that if Olga had heard the sound, she would be thinking the same. Was it Dimitri? Each moment they hoped for his return, but their desire was always mixed with fear for the consequences.

She opened the door cautiously and peered out into the dimly lit street.

'Pavlina!' whispered a voice from the shadows. 'It's me.'

# Chapter Twenty-three

Pavlina went out onto the doorstep.

'Who is it?' she hissed into the darkness. She knew it was not Dimitri. This voice had an accent.

'It's me. Elias.'

After a moment of hesitation, Pavlina reached into the shadows and pulled him gently into the light.

'Come into the house!' she whispered. 'You must come into the house!'

The small figure shuffled in behind her and followed her to the kitchen.

'Sit down there a moment,' she said, taking in his pale and emaciated appearance. '*Panagia mou*, you look terrible. Even worse than Dimitri did when we last saw him.'

Elias looked up at Pavlina with his dark, hollow eyes. Every feature was exaggerated on his shrunken face. He seemed hardly human.

'You look like you need feeding,' she said, continuing to bustle and fuss. 'Just give me a moment to go and clear the plates and serve the dessert.'

Within minutes, Pavlina was back in the kitchen. A pale, ethereal figure followed silently behind her and shut the door carefully.

'Hello, Kyria Komninos,' Elias said politely, standing up.

'Elias! It's been such a long time . . .'

She went to grasp his hands but he instinctively backed away, all too aware of how long it was since they had been washed.

They sat around the kitchen table. Elias' filthy, sweat-stained shirt and the creamy perfection of Olga's dress were the uniforms of different worlds.

There were a thousand things the women wanted to ask, but they knew Elias would have questions too. That must be why he was there. The women would wait their turn.

'I've been to Irini Street and to Filipou Street,' Elias began. 'Our house is locked up, and someone else has taken over our business. Where are . . . ?'

There was no point in deceiving him. He would find out the truth soon enough.

'Your family went to Poland,' said Pavlina. 'Nearly two years ago. Katerina and Eugenia had a postcard a long while back, but nothing since.'

He had heard of some transportations to Poland.

'But the workshop?'

'The authorities think that some people may not come back, so they are selling them off.'

'But it belongs to us!'

'We must keep our voices down,' warned Pavlina, putting her finger to her lips.

'I think they want to get businesses going again,' explained Olga. 'But if your parents came back, I am sure they would be compensated.'

Elias choked back tears of anger. 'But why wouldn't they come back? The war is over in Greece, isn't it?'

Olga and Pavlina exchanged uneasy glances. There had been rumours about the fate of some of the Jews, but as yet no first-hand information.

'And what about our house?'

Half a decade of guerrilla warfare had toughened Elias almost to the point of brutality, but he was on the edge of breaking down. The plate of food that Pavlina had brought him lay untouched. It was hard to recognise him as the gentle young man who had been Dimitri's closest friend.

'What's happened to our house?' he demanded, almost aggressively, as though the two women were responsible. 'Why are the windows all boarded up?'

'I don't know, Elias,' said Pavlina, 'but I think it might be to keep it safe.'

She talked to him slowly and gently as though he were a simple child, and he responded with appropriate petulance.

'I want to get in!'

'Eugenia has a key. Wasn't she there when you went?'

'No. Her house was dark.'

'She was probably asleep,' said Pavlina gently. 'She and Katerina tend to go to bed very early. Let's go together first thing tomorrow.'

'I have to get back to the dining room,' said Olga. 'But before I go, can I ask you something. Have you seen Dimitri?'

'Not for a couple of years,' he replied. 'He was moved to a different unit. I thought he might be back here, with you.'

Olga watched Elias. He was now devouring the food in front of him and she recalled how Dimitri had sat in the same chair the last time she had seen him, eating in the same ravenous way. She observed the movements of his jaw, the bone so close to the surface of the skin that she could see every muscle in his face moving up and down, side to side.

Between mouthfuls, Elias told them more about the situation for the Left.

'With everything that's been going on, lots of the units have moved into the mountains. So it's quite likely he's up there.'

The women watched him use a piece of bread to wipe every last trace of sauce from the plate. Pavlina had already ladled him a second helping, but still he needed more. Then, as if to shock them, he looked up and made a gesture suggestive of throat-slitting.

'They're hunting us, Kyria Komninos,' he said. 'Like *animals*.'

The emotion that he had shown a few moments earlier had vanished. In its place was something steel hard. He put down his fork and looked Olga straight in the eye.

'I've heard stories, Kyria Komninos. I've heard that the Russians have found evidence that the Germans have killed thousands of Jews. Have you heard that?'

Olga looked down at her feet before answering. 'Yes, Elias, but we don't know if it's true. We hope it isn't,' she said. 'Look, you should stay here tonight. But you will have to be careful. It will be difficult if Kyrios Komninos finds out that you are here.'

Elias nodded and Olga left the room.

'You can sleep on my sofa. It will seem like a feather bed after what you've been sleeping on!' said Pavlina. 'Kyrios Komninos leaves very early, so we'll be safe to go after that.'

'To my house?'

'Yes,' said Pavlina. 'As I said, we'll go first thing in the morning.'

Elias slept fitfully, in spite of the relative comfort of Pavlina's sofa. There was no depth to his slumber and his mind was active the entire night with images and visions without sequence or logic. The faces of his parents and brother appeared in bright flashes, laughing or screaming – he was not certain which – but the ill ease with which he awoke the following morning suggested that it had been the latter. These were nightmares, not dreams.

As usual, Konstantinos Komninos left the house at six thirty. Elias heard the door slam and sprang out of bed. He had been awake for two hours. He shook Pavlina to wake her and within fifteen minutes they were on their way to Irini Street.

It was a cold day so, before they left, Pavlina had run up to Dimitri's room to find Elias a coat.

'Two of you could fit into it,' said Pavlina, 'but at least it will keep you warm.'

He looked ridiculous in the heavy cashmere coat with its big collar. Konstantinos Komninos had had it made for Dimitri at Moreno's just before he began at university. He had hardly worn it, so it had the distinctive stiffness of an expensive but unworn garment.

Katerina was leaving her house to take the brisk fifteen-minute walk to work when she saw Pavlina coming towards her, accompanied by a man. He looked strange, drowning inside a huge dark coat, but it took her only a second to recognise his features.

'Elias! It's me, Katerina.'

'Hello, Katerina.'

It was a strange encounter. Knowing where she was going, Katerina reddened with shame.

'Pavlina says that Kyria Karayanidis might have a key to our house.'

Katerina, who normally worried that she was going to be late, turned back into their house and called out for Eugenia.

Eugenia was overjoyed to see Elias. With all the rumours that were circulating, she had resigned herself to the idea of never seeing any of the Morenos again.

He was aware of being treated as though he had come back from the dead, but he did not dwell on it. He was impatient to see inside the house.

'I've kept it as clean as I can,' Eugenia explained. She was holding an oil lamp in an attempt to illuminate the almost empty room. The house no longer had electricity.

Elias threw open the shutters but the dim dawn had brought little light.

'But where is everything? Didn't there used to be a big chair here? And where's my mother's linen trunk?'

Eugenia remained silent. Elias did not seem to expect answers. He went upstairs and Eugenia remained below, listening to the sound of crisp, agitated footsteps marching from room to room. The bare floorboards magnified every sound.

Soon he came running down again and his breath came out in a cloud of vapour in the chill of the room. Even in Dimitri's coat, he shivered.

'They've taken everything with them!' he said indignantly. 'Even my bed. Even the picture I had on my wall.'

Eugenia was not going to disillusion him. It was better, in her view, that he should have an image of his parents carefully packing up their home to move to another country, rather than to know the truth: that the house had been pulled apart by looters when the Morenos had already left, almost empty-handed, for Poland.

So she nodded. Katerina stood by her side, scarcely daring to breathe. Sooner or later, she knew, he would ask about the workshop.

'Why don't you come next door and I'll make us some coffee?' Eugenia said kindly.

'Well, as far as I can see there's nothing in here to make it with,' he said sardonically.

Eugenia remembered so clearly sweeping up the remnants of smashed cups on the morning after the house was broken into. Not even a fragment of Kyria Moreno's china had survived.

They followed her out and into the house next door. A wave of warmth from the stove enveloped them and soon the pan was boiling.

'What are you planning to do, Elias?'

'I may as well head north to find my parents,' he said. 'What else can I do? I've had it with fighting. I've really had it. I don't like the people I am fighting for any more than the people I am fighting against.'

His tone was of total disillusion.

'Will you stay with us tonight?' asked Eugenia, as she poured out the coffee. 'Katerina and I can share a bed.'

Elias was staring into his coffee grounds. He had almost forgotten Katerina was there.

'I must be off now,' she said. She almost confessed where she was going, but lost courage and slunk out of the house, sickened by guilt.

For a few days and nights, Elias stayed in the house, eating, sleeping and sitting quietly by the stove. He had no desire to venture outside away from the warmth and security of the hearth. During those long hours he made the decision to go to Poland. He must find his family. All he required was stamina and money, and Eugenia provided both. She fed him several times a day, as though he were a baby, and gave him the two gold brooches of Roza's with which she had been entrusted. Elias would be able to sell them for his journey.

He left the house for the first time in five days and walked with trepidation into the centre of the city, avoiding the empty Jewish areas and making sure that he did not pass the workshop.

Katerina had confessed to him that she was working for the new 'owner' and he told her that he understood and accepted that life had to continue. If he said the words, he reasoned with himself, perhaps he would begin to believe them. He tried not to feel angry about what his parents had been obliged to leave behind. Bitterness was not a trait of either his father or mother, and he had a vision of them setting up a new tailoring business in Poland rather than dwelling on the injustice of their loss. They would be much too restless for retirement.

Pavlina had smuggled some of Dimitri's old clothes from Niki Street, and over a couple of evenings Katerina had adapted them to fit. By the time she had finished Elias looked quite respectable.

As he strolled along, he felt strangely light-headed – invisible, even. He was almost entirely certain that he would not see anyone he knew and found great pleasure in blending into the crowd. It was a long time since he had walked a street without feeling the need to look over his shoulder.

In one of the city's thriving pawn shops, he waited patiently in a queue before exchanging the brooches for a pitiful sum, a tenth of what he knew they were worth. There was no point in arguing. The pawnbroker could sense how desperate he was for the money and might even lower his offer if the customer haggled. So many people used these shops as a conduit for stolen goods that their owners could generally get away with agreeing risibly small prices.

Elias then went to make enquiries about his train journey and, strolling back towards Irini Street, he realised he was close to the kafenion he used to frequent with Dimitri. The comforting jangle of loose change in his trouser pocket spurred him to go in for a drink.

Just for a moment, he felt his senses awaken to all the casual, taken-for-granted ingredients of normal life: the hiss of steam, the smell of a cigarette, the squeak and pop of a cork extracted from a cognac bottle, conversation, the scrape of a chair on the tiled floor. All these almost forgotten elements mingled together. He closed his eyes, this momentary reconnection with the past giving him hope for the future.

It might be the last day he ever spent in Thessaloniki, but tomorrow he would be setting off for a new life. He sipped his cool beer. It was the best he had ever tasted.

Elias had not noticed another man joining him at his table. The kafenion was crowded.

'Jew?' said the uniformed stranger.

Memories of anti-Semitism stained Elias' childhood memories and the man's tone of voice brought back to him the hatred that he knew had always lurked beneath the civilised veneer of the city. His parents had done everything they could to protect him and Isaac, but on their way home from school they had often felt a vicious stare or occasionally the stinging blow of a well-directed stone.

He was not going to deny his race now, though. Tomorrow he would be leaving Thessaloniki and he hoped this was the last time he would ever have to face such open dislike.

'Yes, I'm Jewish,' he answered defiantly.

'S'pose you know all about it then?'

Elias realised that he had misinterpreted the man's tone. It had softened now.

'All about what?'

The gendarme scratched his head, slightly less sure of himself now. 'You obviously don't, then.'

Elias shrugged, bemused but curious.

'Well, you're going to find out, so I might as well tell you.' He leaned forward, conspiratorially. 'Don't know how you survived,' he said, 'because thousands didn't.'

'What are you talking about?'

Elias could feel a slow wave of rising panic. It turned his stomach over before pausing at his chest, tightening it so that he could scarcely breathe.

The man looked at him with alarm, realising the terrible obligation to continue.

'I can't believe you don't know this,' he began. 'There was this bloke in here last night – it's even been in the newspaper today.'

Elias sat immobile, staring at the other man, who took a sip of his beer before continuing.

'They gassed them. They took them on the trains and then when they got there they gassed them.'

It was impossible for Elias to take this in. The words seemed to make no sense. He wanted them to change or to mean something else.

'What do you mean? What do you mean?'

'That's what he said. This bloke who escaped. He says they gassed them and then they cremated them. In Poland.'

The gendarme saw the young man, this frail young Jew, begin to rock back and forth, back and forth, back and forth, silently, his head buried in his hands.

After what seemed an age, the rocking stopped and the gendarme put his arm around the stranger. He was as cold as the dead and, beneath his hand, he could feel the sharp edges of his shoulder blades. For thirty minutes they sat like this. People came and went and gave them curious stares of which they were unaware. The gendarme always came in for coffee at the end of his shift and people were vaguely curious about the young man whom he had befriended.

Eventually, he felt Elias stir.

'I'm going to take you home,' said the man.

The word was weighted with meaning. In this moment, Elias did not know who he was, where he was and, least of all, where his home was. It was as though he knew nothing at all. His rocking had taken him into a trance and he was numb in every cell and every sinew.

'Let me take you home,' urged the man.

That word again. *Home.* What did it mean? How would he ever find it again?

The name of the street where he had been born, whenever that was, wherever it was, he could not locate it. He knew there had been a room where he had slept with his brother, but beyond that there was no recall. The years of sleeping rough, mostly in the mountains, mostly feeling cold, those were still clear in his mind, but beyond that there was a black hole of amnesia.

He tried to stand up but even his legs seemed unable to remember their function.

'Look,' said the man, 'I'll help you outside. I think you might need some fresh air.'

Once outside, Elias' head became clearer. He could see the sea and knew that he lived up the hill away from it.

'I think it's this way,' he said, leaning heavily on the other man. As they walked he read the street signs, hoping that something might trigger a memory.

Egnatia Street, Sofokleos Street, Ioulianou Street. He took in the signs.

'Irini,' he said dreamily. 'Peace. That's the name. Irini Street. Peace Street.'

'I know it,' said the man. 'I'll take you there. Don't want you getting lost, do we?'

When they got to Irini Street, the man asked which house was his.

'That one,' Elias muttered, pointing to number 7. 'But I'm going to that one.'

Still feeling that his mission was not yet accomplished, the stranger waited while Elias knocked on the door of Eugenia's house.

Within a second, both Eugenia and Katerina were standing at the open door. Having heard the reports about the fate of the Jews themselves, they had been anxiously awaiting Elias' return. The news had spread fast and even though it was based on the evidence of a single person, no one doubted its veracity.

Their ashen faces, frozen into an expression of pity, greeted him. It was almost more than he could stand and he pushed past them, almost rudely, into the house.

Eugenia wanted to thank the man but he had already turned away by the time she called out. She looked at his retreating back and noticed his gendarme's uniform. These were strange times, she reflected. Only a few months before and the same man might have arrested Elias, but she could see from the brief glimpse she had got of his face that he had been moved by Elias' plight.

For a few weeks, more news began to drift back from Poland, verifying that the Jews had been exterminated on a massive scale. The handful of survivors who returned with first-hand information, the tell-tale tattooed number on their arms and horror stories of the fate of their fellow Jews, all reached the same conclusion: the city was not glad to have them back. Like Elias they returned to find their homes and businesses were no longer theirs and whether, like Elias, they had been fighting as *andartes* during the occupation, or had been among the handful who survived the camps, Thessaloniki seemed to have no place for them.

Katerina and Eugenia came and went to work. They crept about the house each evening, as though by being silent they could deny their existence. Elias was always asleep when they returned and the food that they had left for him in the morning was gone and the dishes he had used were washed and tidied away.

For weeks, he had no desire to speak to his hosts. He knew that some Jews had been hidden throughout the occupation by Christian families. Elias felt betrayed by the world, but most of all let down by the neighbours who should have protected them.

Eugenia and Katerina suspected that this was how he must feel and hoped that one day they might be able to explain. Their chance came one evening when they returned to find him sitting at the table, obviously waiting for them. He was clean-shaven and had a bag at his side.

'I wanted to say goodbye,' he said. 'I'm leaving tonight.'

'I'm sorry you're going, Elias,' said Eugenia.

'You know you're welcome to stay with us,' said Katerina, 'for as long as you like.'

'There's nothing to keep me here, Katerina. Only memories,' he said, 'and even the sweet ones have turned sour.' His tone was accusatory.

'Whatever you think,' said Katerina, pleadingly, 'your family went willingly. If they had asked us for help, we would have given it to them. I promise.'

'The rabbi encouraged them, Elias. None of us had any idea what was going to happen.' Eugenia was in tears.

'So, where will you go?' asked Katerina softly.

'There are a few of us going together. We've been planning it for some days now. Palestine.'

'You're going to settle there?' asked Eugenia.

'Yes,' he said. 'We have no plans to come back.' The bitterness in his voice was unmistakable.

'Look,' said Eugenia, 'if you are leaving, there are some things you should take with you. Your parents left some valuables with us to look after. They belonged to the synagogue.'

She got up. 'Katerina, will you go and get the quilt?'

As Katerina disappeared up the stairs, Eugenia crossed the room and took down the framed samplers. With a knife she began to cut around the backing of the frames to remove the embroidered panels. Elias leaned forwards, his curiosity aroused.

'There is a fragment of Torah scroll under here and some manuscript behind the other one,' she said.

'And here's the quilt,' said Katerina, holding up the embroidered masterpiece.

Elias gasped at its beauty. Eugenia had got out some scissors and was about to start unpicking the stitches.

'Don't do that!' cried Elias. 'It's a work of art!'

'But it has the *parochet* underneath . . .'

'Why don't I take it as it is?' he enquired. 'It will keep it even safer!'

'Elias is right, Eugenia. Let's roll it up. You can even use it as a pillow on your journey!'

'And there's the tallit too.'

'I think you should keep that safe here. Perhaps I will visit one day and retrieve it. I must go now,' he said. 'The boat is leaving at ten tonight and we arranged to meet at nine. I don't want them to leave me behind.'

He stepped away as if to avoid their embrace, then picked up his bag and the rolled-up quilt.

'Thank you,' he said, 'for everything.'

With that, he was gone.

The women held each other tight. Only once Elias was out of the house did they allow themselves to give in to their grief for the loss of the Morenos. Each day, more evidence of the scale of the crime that had been perpetrated against the Jews was being discovered. They had seen the synagogues wantonly destroyed and the ancient cemetery torn up, but the physical annihilation of millions of men, women and children was beyond the reach of any human understanding. The evidence of what had happened to their friends was now irrefutable and yet would always be beyond belief.

Somewhere in northern Europe, the physical remains of Roza, Saul, Isaac and Esther had ceased to exist except as particles of scattered ash, but Katerina and Eugenia would never forget them. With every candle they lit in the little church of Agios Nikolaos Orfanos, memories of them were rekindled, burning for ever, bright and true.

# Chapter Twenty-four

B Y APRIL, MUCH of the country had plunged once again into crisis. Konstantinos Komninos was obliged to close one of his warehouses and it infuriated him that the empire he had built up was being eroded by the effects of a civil war. His profits during the occupation had been more than satisfactory. He had always managed to continue his imports so that he could meet the demand that still existed among the wealthy clientele and the Germans, but now, as he saw it, a minority of Greeks were strangling the recovery of their own country.

Even at the age of seventy-three, Komninos still maintained the same habits, getting up at dawn and staying in the office until late at night, except on Saturdays, when he would entertain. The image of progress and success was one that he was eager to sustain, and he continued to ensure that his inventory was superior to any other fabric merchant in the city. Olga was still obliged to dress on those occasions in made-to-measure haute couture, and Katerina visited her several times a month to fit or deliver something new.

It was during one of these visits that she told Olga of Elias' departure. Pavlina was in the drawing room too, cleaning some *objets d'art*, whose only purpose seemed to be to gather dust.

'Well at least he's gone with some decent clothes on his back,' Pavlina said. 'It was such a waste having them hanging up in Dimitri's cupboard when he isn't around to wear them.'

Katerina winced. Pavlina's lack of tact not only hurt Olga, but her as well.

'Poor Elias. Poor man . . .' said Olga quickly. 'What *must* he be feeling?'

It was a question that did not ask for an answer.

There was silence for a few minutes as Katerina pinned Olga's hem.

'You will let me know if you hear from him, won't you?' urged Olga after a while.

'Of course I will,' affirmed Katerina.

'I'm afraid there's still no news of Dimitri,' Olga said.

'I thought the amnesty they were talking about might make a difference,' replied Katerina.

'Well, it didn't last, did it . . .' said Olga glumly. 'He's not likely to come now, with the way things are going.'

'It wouldn't exactly be safe if he did, would it?' interjected Pavlina, her duster in mid-air. After a moment's pause, she added: 'I don't think I'll be laying another place at the table just yet.'

Olga's hopes that one day Dimitri might walk through the door had faded when the far Right began to take revenge against the Left for crimes they had committed during the occupation. There was fighting between ELAS and the anti-Communists and collaborators who had worked alongside Germans, and thousands of leftists were rounded up and imprisoned. After a brief pause, Thessaloniki once again lived in fear. Its prisons were full of people whose only crime was to disagree with the government.

Whatever happened, Olga had always hoped that her husband would put aside his disapproval of his son's actions in the war but it seemed to her that Konstantinos Komninos happily nurtured the rage he felt towards his son.

In order to carry out this 'white terror' against the Left, the police and gendarmerie had been hugely expanded. Their brief was to destroy the Communist organisation using any means they could. They collected biographical information to compile evidence against their suspects. Giving support to anyone who had fought for ELAS was enough to warrant arrest.

Much to her own surprise, Olga found herself praying that Dimitri would stay away. She knew how vulnerable he would be and she feared for him. Thessaloniki was a dangerous enough place, but when there was someone inside your own home who might betray you, the perils were multiplied.

Olga need not have feared. Dimitri was four hundred kilometres away. Along with many others, his unit was now in a mountainous area of Central Greece where the toughness of the landscape had been its own defence against the Germans. Labyrinthine pathways, hidden valleys and villages that were only accessible by foot had allowed it to become an almost self-governing state during the time of the occupation. It was an ideal place of refuge for ELAS members.

When people in the villages heard that there was a medical worker among the soldiers they came for help. With little more than a few torn-up rags and a bottle of *raki* for antiseptic, Dimitri found himself dressing ulcers, helping women during childbirth, extracting rotten teeth and diagnosing diseases he could not cure. He never enquired about a patient's politics before helping them but sometimes he had to ignore a large picture of King George, who had been forced to remain in exile even when the occupation had come to an end and the government had returned. Of one thing he was certain: the vast majority of these people did not willingly support the Communists. The village folk that they were living amongst were being coerced into supplying food that they could ill afford, and they and their children were going hungry.

Dimitri could not pretend to himself that the side he fought on was without fault. Like most of his compatriots in this unit, he had joined the resistance in order to fight against the Germans, but once they had gone, he was pulled into a vicious fight between Communists and the government. Like many he was not a hard-line Communist, but there was one thing he believed: they offered something closer to democracy than the government.

Over the years, he had learned that no one had clean hands in this war. His own were covered in blood: Communist blood, Fascist blood, German blood, Greek blood. Sometimes it was innocent blood, sometimes the blood of someone he was glad to see die. It ran the same in everybody: thick, red and often shockingly copious.

Most of the time he was trying to save lives rather than end them, but treating any of the Communist guerrillas with whom he fought would mean that they could kill again. There seemed no end to the barbarity in which this country was caught up, and the twists and turns of politics were becoming increasingly lethal.

He was still in his twenties, but he sometimes caught sight of his gnarled old fingers with their skin as crinkled as the bark of a tree. They looked as if they belonged to an old man

In spite of a sometimes overwhelmingly strong desire to visit his city, something apart from fear of arrest kept Dimitri away. He would die rather than go home. It would seem like an admission of defeat. Such a loss of pride in front of his father, someone he despised with his whole body and soul, was unthinkable.

★　★　★

Olga managed to avoid confrontation with her husband but she could not avoid listening to the discussions over her dinner table. Everybody Konstantinos invited shared his own political views and they were all in favour of the war against those who had resisted the Germans.

'How can the government justify what's happening?' she asked Pavlina. 'They're letting these bullies persecute innocent people.'

'*They* don't believe they're innocent. It's as simple as that.'

At social events, Konstantinos Komninos always steered skilfully around the enquiries about his son. It was assumed by their guests that he was in the government army.

The talk was mostly of the rise of communism in the surrounding Balkan countries and there was obvious paranoia that Greece would go the same way. Dinner party guests avoided mention of the atrocities currently being carried out by the government army, but spoke warmly of the help the British were giving them to hold back the Communist advance. In their terminology, it was an *andartiko* that was being fought, a 'bandit war'. Olga thought of it as *emfilios polemos*, a war between brothers.

It was turning into a hot summer with temperatures soaring, but the mention of the 'red menace' caused them to rise even further. The wives fanned their faces with anxiety whenever it was mentioned. That season and for several following it, red, and even shades of pink, became distinctly unfashionable.

Outside the walls of the grand mansions, living conditions deteriorated further. Agriculture and industrial production were under half pre-war level and there were no ships to bring goods in or out. Roads, railways, harbours and bridges continued to be in the same state of post-occupation dereliction.

As if things were not bad enough, a severe drought wrecked the harvest that summer. While people fought against members of their own family, nature seemed to be turning against itself. The sight of children begging and going through bins to find food once again became commonplace. Foreign aid was sent but, even then, half of the population still lacked essentials, owing to the corruption among some of those government officials responsible for distribution.

Somewhere up in the mountains, Dimitri, who had not seen a newspaper for many weeks, learned that there was to be an election, with a plebiscite on whether the King should return.

'How can they promise a fair election, with this country in such upheaval?'

This was the general opinion. The disorder prevalent in the country did not seem conducive to such a democratic process.

The election went ahead, but the Left abstained to demonstrate their disapproval. International observers verified that it had been free and fair, but there was an inevitable victory for the Right. In September, the plebiscite over the monarchy then took place and was won by the monarchists with an overwhelming sixty-eight per cent of the vote.

Konstantinos Komninos was doubly jubilant.

'So, people have shown us what they want. Twice. There's one thing we definitely know now – people would rather have a king than a Communist leading the country!' he said, scarcely able to keep the joy out of his voice. 'Perhaps we can get this country on its feet again.'

'The people have chosen!' said the pompous Grigoris Gourgouris, who was at dinner in Niki Street that evening.

The men have chosen, thought Olga, wondering if the outcome would have been different if women had the vote.

She looked around at the faces of the wives at the table and asked herself if they had the same thoughts as she did. Mostly they wore a uniform mask of mild interest. Like her they had learned when to nod and when to make the kind of noises that would suggest both understanding and acquiescence. They came in perfectly in unison, like second violins in an orchestra. She and all the women here had a triple role. As wives, mothers and elegant shadows.

The conversation continued around her.

'So we should be able to make some progress now,' said Gourgouris. 'I reckon the country's had enough fighting. And not enough fancy clothes!'

A wave of laughter rippled around the room, but the person who laughed until the tears ran down between the folds of fat in his face was Grigoris himself.

The results of the election and the plebiscite finally pushed the Communist Party towards the decision that organised, armed struggle was the only path they could take and, in October 1946, they announced the formation of the Democratic Army.

'You see?' Konstantinos said furiously to Olga. 'The Communists will stop at nothing until they take over this country. Do you want to be ruled over from Moscow? What do you think will happen to businesses like mine? They'll be state-run. We will lose everything. Absolutely everything.'

'There might just be people who don't want to see the King back,' Olga said, knowing that her husband would not listen.

'There is no doubting who these people are now!' he screamed. 'You can't pretend they're the liberal left any longer, Olga! They are Soviet-backed Communists! Are you too blind to see that?'

He was screaming at Olga, but all she noticed was the fear in his eyes. She was so used to being abused for her stupidity that his invectives no longer bothered her.

Unofficial reports that week created further alarm by revealing that the Democratic Army leadership was intending to co-ordinate all the existing guerrilla bands and would be carrying out a concerted recruitment campaign to expand its numbers.

Something was beyond doubt for Komninos now. As far he was concerned, everyone fighting against the government was doing so under the red flag. His son was now carrying out the orders of a Communist general.

Wherever he went, the same taunts seemed to follow him: 'Komninos . . . Komninist . . . Ko-mmu-nist . . .' On and on they went, hissing and whispering inside his head: 'Comminos . . . Communos . . . Komnunist . . .'

People looked at him differently, talked of him behind his back and, when he came back late at night, he heard the prostitutes muttering in their doorways: 'There he goes again, that Konstantinos Kommunistos!'

These hallucinations pursued him to his bed and hounded him in his sleep. Night after night he woke soaked with sweat, panting like a hunted animal.

Once or twice from her adjacent room, Olga heard her husband scream out in his sleep. His mingled fear and anger over his son possessed him like a demon.

Customers did not look him in the eye, or so he thought, and he was sure he had received pitying glances from his staff. 'Fancy,' he imagined them saying, 'a Communist!' He felt himself branded, despised and an object of scorn.

If he was ever to sleep quietly again, something had to be done.

In the past few years, he had had neither desire nor means to find Dimitri. Now he had both. The organisational changes that the Communists had implemented for their army would work to his advantage, enabling him to locate his son with some ease. Back in his office, at his desk in the middle of the city, he sat down to write two letters. The first one was to his son.

The opening paragraphs were sorrowful and restrained, with repeated mention of his disappointment.

Dear Dimitri

As you know, the decisions you have taken in your short life have been a catalogue of disappointments to me. I was bitterly disappointed by your choice of careers and with your political leanings while you were at university. Most of all I was disappointed by your decision to fight for the resistance during the occupation.

In the past decade, every step you have taken has been a source of deep dismay and embarrassment.

All of those mistakes could have been put aside if you had seen some sense once the country was restored to our government and now to our King. But I know that you are now fighting for the Communists. You are siding with a movement that seeks to destroy all the individual freedoms that the Komninos family has always stood for.

The tone in the second half changed to one of vitriol and abuse. They were the slightly insane ravings of a man hearing voices, and yet while he was writing, his heart was as cold as ice and his intentions as measured as would be expected from a man who had made money from calculating to the last millimetre the profit on a bolt of silk.

The stigma and shame that you will bring to our name can no longer be tolerated. I hope every day to hear news of your death, but each one brings more disappointment. Even now you are letting me down. I assume that you are a coward and not even willing to risk your life for what you believe. I have done all I can to conceal the crime of your political affiliation from everyone we know, but it is slipping out of my control.

As far as I am concerned you are dead to this family. Your mother will be informed within the next few days that you have been killed. In due course you will be thoroughly defeated, I am sure of that, but meanwhile, I would advise you to leave for Albania or Yugoslavia, where your fellow Communists will make you welcome. This is the best thing for the honour of the family name. Never – and I repeat, never – return to Thessaloniki.

He would pay someone to make discreet enquiries, track his son down and then deliver the letter. He estimated it would take no more than a fortnight. Almost before the ink had dried, he had found his man and the letter was on its way.

The second letter he wrote was a draft. He would need someone to copy and make it authentic in every detail, from the addressee to the postmark. There was no shortage of people to help. Counterfeiters had done good business in the early 1940s, charging astronomical sums for fake identity cards. Jews trying to avoid the ghettos would give almost everything they owned for a good one. The canny counterfeiters had accepted payment only in gold, and when the rest of the country had been bankrupted by hyperinflation, many of them had more money than they could spend.

As everyone else saw their savings disappear, the counterfeiters seized their next opportunity. Banknotes became so quickly replaced by those of ever higher denominations that no one ever became familiar with the new notes before they were replaced with fresh ones, meaning that it was easy to pass off a good fake. These men were artists and some of them were now even richer than Komninos himself. He went to the best of them.

Komninos had allowed a few days to pass before having the second of his letters delivered. He left the house in the morning knowing that, when he returned in the evening, Olga would be in mourning.

Olga was in the drawing room when Pavlina brought the letter up on a small silver tray. It was eleven o'clock. 'Nothing good ever happens on a Tuesday,' she wept later. It had been considered an inauspicious day ever since the Turks had seized Constantinople on a Tuesday nearly five hundred years before.

Olga picked the letter off the tray and stared at it. It was an official letter with a seal on the reverse of the envelope. Correspondence of this style never contained good news. For a moment she wondered whether she should wait for her husband to return, but dismissed the thought within an instant. This letter concerned her son. Her son. Her beloved Dimitri.

Pavlina watched her mistress with trepidation. She had already held it up to the light in the hallway, but its thickness had guarded the secret of its contents. She held her breath as she watched Olga slide her finger under the seal, remove the single sheet from its envelope and read the few lines.

She looked up at Pavlina. Her eyes full of unfathomable sorrow. 'He's dead,' she said.

Her body was now racked with sobs.

Pavlina sat beside her and wept for the boy that she had seen come into the world. Though the possibility had always been there, it still came as a terrible shock to them. Pavlina had never imagined that her prayers for Dimitri's protection would be so disregarded.

★    ★    ★

Meanwhile, Dimitri was up in the mountain area, awaiting orders for action. He recognised his father's handwriting immediately and felt the rekindling of an old hatred. The contents chilled him. Judging by the date the letter had been written, he calculated that his mother would know of his 'death' by now, and the thought of what his father had subjected her to sickened him beyond belief.

Olga withdrew to her darkened room and Pavlina took the letter to the showroom. She left her employer alone to read it and then they walked back together to the house. Komninos asked her how his wife had taken the news. He did a reasonable job of feigning grief, knowing how important it was to get his performance right. Both his wife and their housekeeper were fully aware of how angry he was with their son, so his sorrow was restrained and his manner dignified.

Konstantinos Komninos went into his wife's room and stood at the door.

'Olga . . .' he said.

His wife was lying fully clothed on the bed and did not stir.

'Olga . . .' he repeated, approaching the bed.

As he got closer, he saw that her eyes were open.

'Go away,' she said quietly. 'Please go away.'

She could not bear to have him near and he willingly left.

For many days, Pavlina came and went with trays of food but failed to make Olga eat. She had her own sorrow, but the need to look after her mistress kept her occupied.

The day before anyone else had heard the news, Komninos sent a message to Gourgouris.

Katerina was working round the clock to finish a wedding dress. With its embroidered hem and beaded train, the dress still required another week of intensive work, but her employer told her to put it to one side to visit Kyria Komninos. Her protests were in vain.

'You have to go immediately,' snapped Gourgouris. 'Someone else can finish the wedding dress for you. If an important customer like Kyrios Komninos needs some new outfits for his wife, we don't tell him he has to wait.'

Katerina was in no position to argue, but she knew how anxious the bride would be that her dress was not yet finished and knew that it was impossible for a second seamstress to match the panel of stitching she had already completed. It would be asymmetrical. Usually she would be allowed to finish one project before being put onto the next but Katerina could tell she had no choice. She resolved to return to the workshop after hours and would sew all night to finish the bridal gown if necessary.

For a moment, the seamstress stood there, unsure if she was meant to leave the room. She felt uncomfortable under Gourgouris' beady stare and realised that he had something else to say.

'I've picked out these samples for her to choose from. Perhaps you can ask her to make her selection from these.'

He held out six fabric swatches. They were of varying densities, ranging from wool and velvet through to crêpe and fine silk. All of them were black.

He noticed the expression on Katerina's face changing.

'Ah. I see this is news to you. They've lost their son.'

Katerina bit her lower lip to stop it trembling and took the pieces of fabric, which were being held out to her.

'I'll go straight away,' she whispered, almost inaudibly.

Although her legs felt as if they might cave in beneath her, Katerina managed to get out into the street before her sobs came and tore her in two. Leaning against the wall of the building, she cried without shame, and people scurried past as though she were invisible.

Dimitri was dead. She gasped, trying to catch her breath between her sobs. After ten or perhaps twenty minutes, she managed to compose herself. She had a job to do. She would go to see the two people in the world who would feel the impact of this loss as much as her, and slowly she began walking towards the sea.

Pavlina answered the door quickly. The maid looked as though she had been punched in both eyes. They were so swollen with crying that she could scarcely see.

Katerina stepped inside.

'How is Kyria Komninos?'

Pavlina shook her head. 'Terrible. Absolutely terrible.'

The two women went into the kitchen and talked for a while. First one of them cried and then the other, their sorrow still fresh and hungry. Waves of sadness would overwhelm each of them in turn without warning.

'Kyria Komninos hasn't eaten for two days,' said Pavlina, getting up to prepare a tray for her mistress. 'Why don't you come up with me? Perhaps you can persuade her.'

The two women ascended the stairs together, the rhythmic tick of the huge ormolu clock keeping time with their steps.

'Wait out here a moment,' Pavlina instructed.

Inside the bedroom, she drew the curtains back a few millimetres to let in some daylight. Olga was lying on top of the bed, fully clothed, still and composed, like a body laid out for burial.

'Katerina is here, can I bring her in?' she asked, putting the tray down. 'Kyrios Komninos has asked her to come.'

Olga sat up. 'Why?' she asked.

'To discuss mourning clothes,' Pavlina answered.

'Oh, yes,' Olga said, as though she had forgotten the events of the past few days. 'Mourning.'

Katerina came in. She managed to mumble a single word:

'Commiserations' and over the course of the next hour, quietly made notes of measurements and drew designs in her notebook for Olga's approval. There was no conversation that could possibly have been appropriate.

It was soon common knowledge that Komninos' son had died fighting the Communists in the mountains. Several of Konstantinos' acquaintances had also lost sons in a similar way, and many people sent their sincerest condolences, imagining the wealthy businessman overcome by grief, rather than relief. Soon he was going about his business as usual, earning himself a reputation for courage and resilience.

Katerina came and went several times in the following few weeks to fit the new gowns. Black added at least a decade to Olga's appearance, and when she looked in the mirror now, a sad, elderly woman looked back.

As Katerina was leaving one afternoon, Pavlina thrust something into her hand. It was a small photograph.

'They won't notice it's gone,' she said. 'I found it in a box with several others exactly the same.'

Katerina found herself looking at a picture of Dimitri. It had been taken on his first day at university. It made Katerina both happy and sad in equal measure.

'Thank you, Pavlina,' she said. 'Thank you so much. I'll treasure it.'

As she emerged from the dark cavern of her grief, Olga began to notice that Katerina no longer wore the sunny smile that had once been such a distinctive characteristic of the seamstress. It had been like a light that she had carried around with her. Nowadays she had dark shadows beneath her eyes. Olga began to realise that the young woman carried her own deep sorrow.

# Chapter Twenty-five

For the next few months, Katerina was like a sleepwalker. She only functioned by doing the same things, in the same way, each day and was immersed in her grief.

Eugenia did all she could to help her survive these difficult months but knew that only time would really lighten the darkness.

The other girls in the workshop noticed how withdrawn she was and gave up trying to draw her out of this strange mood. Katerina was almost mute, finding conversation of any kind beyond her. The only thing that did not change was the brilliance and quality of her work. It was as fast and perfect as ever, and the only activity that absorbed her enough to take her mind away from the preoccupying obsession of her loss.

Gourgouris continued to single her out. One day she was not working fast enough. Another day she needed to be more original. On another he wanted her work to be less like a machine's.

Every comment he made was unjustified and somehow ridiculous, but the other women had no objection to hearing that the boss was often critical of Katerina's work. It made a change from having their own work criticised.

Life continued like this with regular summonses into his office. Even if she was tempted on every occasion, Katerina knew she must not answer back. Such behaviour could lead to immediate dismissal.

'I'll try and correct that, Kyrios Gourgouris,' she would say, or 'I'll see if I can improve on that.'

At the end of one afternoon, she was summoned to see Gourgouris by his clerk. He was sitting behind his desk, enveloped in a cloud of smoke, but stubbed out his cigarette as she entered his office.

'Sit down,' he said, smiling at her, his currant-like eyes disappearing into his face.

One of the girls had been given her notice the previous week and, with the economic climate once again far from stable, there was always a good chance that some more girls might lose their jobs.

'I've been thinking . . .' he said.

Katerina steeled herself for what he would say next. She was certain that it was going to be dismissal and sat there planning where she would go to look for work.

'. . . I would like you to be my wife.'

Katerina's mouth opened and closed a few times but nothing emerged, a reaction that Gourgouris mistook for pleasure rather than shock.

'I think I know your answer,' he said, grinning to reveal his stained teeth.

There was a moment of paralysis, followed by a desire to flee. Without apology or explanation, Katerina got up.

'I'll see you tomorrow morning, my dear,' said Gourgouris with a self-satisfied smile. 'You won't be so overwhelmed by then.'

With those words ringing in her ears, she left the room and ran home.

Eugenia's reaction was a surprise. Having been without a husband for decades herself, she saw this as a huge opportunity.

'You're not a girl any more, Katerina! You can't turn such a proposal down! If you don't marry now, you could be a spinster for ever,' she pleaded. 'And he's wealthy!'

Even though she would miss Katerina terribly, Eugenia felt it was an offer she should not refuse. The ratio of men to women in Thessaloniki was still heavily imbalanced. There were more widows and unmarried women than ever before, and she was almost beside herself at the thought that Katerina might squander the chance for such security. Her two daughters, though married and with children, had been obliged to return to the tobacco factory to make ends meet. It was tough and unrewarding labour, and if they had been lucky enough to have Katerina's good fortune their lives would have been so different.

'You'll be comfortable for the rest of your life!' Eugenia exclaimed.

Katerina sat quietly, waiting for her to calm down.

'But I have a comfortable life now,' she said.

'Well, if you turn him down, even your job will be gone,' she said bluntly. 'He won't be happy if you say no, mark my words.'

'But I don't love him,' Katerina said, and after a pause added: 'I loved Dimitri.'

With this inadvertent admission, she broke down in tears.

'It's hopeless. I can't stop thinking about him. What am I going to do?'

Eugenia had no answer to this, but later that evening they talked again.

'There have been plenty of arranged marriages in the past,' Eugenia explained. 'There used to be lots in our village, one family wanting a connection with another. Perhaps in time, you will grow to love Kyrios Gourgouris.'

'But supposing I don't?'

According to Eugenia, the absence of love was no obstacle. Marriages in the villages had often worked quite well without.

They talked well into the night but at midnight, when she went to bed, Katerina knew that she would not be able to give her employer an answer.

First thing the following morning, she knocked boldly on his office door. By then she had prepared exactly what she was going to say.

'Thank you very much for your proposal, Kyrios Gourgouris. I am very flattered but I need a little more time to think. I have to take into consideration whether I am the right person to be your wife. I hope you will allow me the space of one more week in order to consider.'

She almost curtsied before leaving the room and Gourgouris smiled back, as if charmed by her little speech.

When she entered the workshop, Katerina found the other women whispering. It seemed that word of their employer's proposal to Katerina had somehow leaked out. None of the women asked her directly, but she could tell from their glances that she was the subject of their gossip and felt her face go crimson with embarrassment.

The next day, Gourgouris commenced his campaign to win Katerina over. Each evening, she found a little gift tucked into her bag or pocket: a small piece of silk, some lace, once, even, some ready-to-wear lingerie. There was often a note: 'Just a glimpse of your trousseau.' In his view, no woman would ever be able to resist such a seduction technique.

The softness of silk, the coolness of crêpe, the lusciousness of lace, he thought to himself, as he furtively dropped the little packages into Katerina's bag or slipped them into the pocket of her coat, which hung in the cloakroom. 'I must use that line in my new advertisement.'

The sessions where he would call her to his office to vilify her work immediately ceased, which was a relief to her, but the gifts made her feel uncomfortable. Time was passing and there were only five days now until she had promised to give her answer. She knew Eugenia's opinion and it had not been the one she had wanted to hear.

The following day she was due to deliver the final mourning dress to Kyria Komninos. The seasons had changed, and the fine cotton one she needed was now ready.

When she opened the door, Pavlina could see straight away that something had happened to Katerina. She had hoped that the young woman might be getting over Dimitri's death . . .

'What's wrong?' she exclaimed. 'You've got bigger shadows than ever!'

Katerina had not slept for two nights and the skin under her eyes looked bruised.

'Come in! Come in!' urged Pavlina. 'Come and tell me all about it.'

Over the kitchen table, Katerina told Pavlina about the proposal.

'But what shall I do?' she asked.

'Well, I'm not the one to ask,' Pavlina said bluntly. 'I loved the man I married from the moment I set eyes on him. And it lasted until the day he died. In fact, it lasted well beyond that.'

'So how can I even think of marrying, when I love someone else?' she asked, her eyes filled with tears. 'Even if he is just a memory.'

'It's different, Katerina,' said Pavlina. 'I was in my forties when Giorgos died. We met when I was fifteen and we had twenty-five years together. I was lucky, but you must think of the future.'

They were meant to be kind, but the words sounded harsh. *The future*. It was a landscape without love.

'And it won't be long until you're thirty . . .'

'I think I know what I should do,' said Katerina after a few moments' reflection, 'but it's a question of whether I can bring myself to.'

It seemed wrong that her cotton handkerchief was soaked with tears of misery rather than joy. A marriage proposal was meant to be every woman's goal.

Katerina was shown upstairs to see Olga and together they went into her dressing room where she would try on the dress. Usually, they made small talk about the details that Katerina had sewn onto the garment, and Olga always enquired after Eugenia, but today the young woman was taken by surprise.

'Katerina, can I ask you something?' said Olga.

The seamstress looked up. She was kneeling on the ground, pinning the hem.

'Of course,' she replied.

'My husband mentioned something this morning. He said that you were marrying Kyrios Gourgouris. Is it true?'

Katerina was aghast. It was a moment as extraordinary and shocking as when Gourgouris had made his proposal.

'I . . . I . . . It's . . .'

'I'm so sorry,' said Olga, quickly. 'I was probably jumping to conclusions. It's just that Kyrios Komninos told me that Grigoris Gourgouris is marrying his best seamstress. At least that's what he had heard. I just assumed that he must be talking about you.'

Katerina concentrated hard on her task. She now held the tip of a pin in her mouth, which gave her an excuse not to speak. There had been so many times when Katerina had wanted to confess her feelings to Olga about her son, but it had never seemed right. Now it seemed less appropriate than ever.

Pavlina had come in with tea for them both. Katerina always sewed the hem *in situ* and always gave the dress a final press before she left, the whole process taking an hour or two.

'I feel so embarrassed,' Olga explained to Pavlina. 'I had heard that Grigoris Gourgouris was to marry his best seamstress, so I assumed it must be Katerina!' The unfamiliar sound of Olga's laughter rang out like a bell.

Pavlina and Katerina exchanged glances and then the latter burst into tears.

Olga was confused. Pavlina explained to her that Katerina had indeed received a marriage proposal but she had not yet accepted.

'And are you going to?' Olga asked her directly. 'It doesn't seem to fill you with joy, my dear.'

'I don't love him,' said Katerina.

'But I've told her that even if she feels that way now, things could change once she's married. Lots of people start their marriages with a bit of uncertainty.'

'She might be right,' said Olga, looking kindly at Katerina.

Katerina knew that Olga did not love her husband. Perhaps hers had been the opposite to Pavlina's marriage. She wondered if Olga had been in love with Konstantinos Komninos to start with and had then fallen out of love. Perhaps the third, ideal way, of being in love and then continuing to be in love did not exist. How could she tell Olga that she was still in love with a dead man? And that the dead man was her son?

'But what do you think I should do?' Katerina appealed to her, with desperation. Olga would have the final word.

'You could wait for love,' Olga answered sadly, 'but there is always the risk that it might never come.'

The collective wisdom of the three women who cared for her most in the world pushed her towards the inevitable.

A small wedding was held a month later. Grigoris Gourgouris appeared to have no relatives apart from a nephew, and the only other guests were Eugenia, Sofia, Maria, Pavlina, two of the girls from the finishing room, the manager of the business in Veria and Konstantinos Komninos. Katerina had written to her mother, inviting her to the wedding. Zenia replied offering her congratulations but she had been ill recently and would not be strong enough to come.

Everyone admired the bride's simple, pin-tucked wedding gown but she knew she had put less love and effort into it than the hundreds of others she had sewn. The current fashion for straight styles helped to conceal her lack of curves, and with the circle of fresh rosebuds in her dark, bobbed hair she might have passed for a fifteen-year-old.

After the ceremony, a dinner was held in a private room in the Hermes Palace Hotel, a place where the groom and Konstantinos Komninos seemed at home, but the rest of the guests felt out of place. The Komninos house was the most luxurious place that Katerina had ever visited, but the hotel took the use of marble, gilt and stucco to new levels. Everything about it was excessive, from the quantity of silver cutlery on the table to the flower arrangement that was so enormous it blocked Katerina's view of most of the guests. Fronds of jasmine and wisteria overflowed from a giant central urn that would have been big enough to fill the entire back yard of her home.

In front of each place was a row of glasses lined up like organ pipes, most of them full to the brim. Though she had only taken a sip from each one, the alcohol had gone to her head and when they had said farewell to all the guests, it was with some unsteadiness that Katerina climbed the sweeping staircase. She and her new husband were to stay there that night.

Their first kiss on the night of the marriage almost made her swoon with revulsion. Grigoris' breath reeked of stale nicotine, and on the lips of someone who had never smoked a single cigarette, the bitter-sour taste of his tobacco-steeped tongue almost made her gag. After the kiss, there was another ordeal to face. Katerina had seen Gourgouris' legs before when she had once been summoned in to his office to hem new trousers, so the hairiness of his body was no surprise, but the sheer volume of the man when he was not contained inside clothing was more shocking than she could ever have imagined.

As he unbuttoned his shirt, flesh poured out. For a moment it flowed towards his thighs before it was left hanging there, swinging like an independent being. The surface of this voluminous stomach was criss-crossed with varicose veins, like a river delta, and she now saw that his pendulous breasts were twice as large as her own.

Meanwhile, Katerina had undressed too and realised that her new husband was scrutinising her. He reached out to touch her scar and quickly withdrew his hand with obvious distaste. Her habit of wearing long sleeves winter and summer meant that her disfigured arm had come as a complete surprise.

The alcohol had dulled her fear of what was to happen next, but even so she was certain that she was going to die of suffocation, as his enormous bulk rolled on top of her. What he wanted was quickly achieved, and soon, without further conversation, they were on opposite sides of the vast bed. Katerina lay there contemplating the unfamiliar silhouettes of lamps and furniture and before long slipped into a deep sleep. With its smooth linen sheets and plump feather pillows, the four-poster was the ultimate in comfort.

The following day brought the real introduction to her new

life. She had already packed her belongings up in Irini Street and a van was sent round to collect them and to take them to Gourgouris' home in the west of the city. It was a new and rather characterless house in Sokratous Street, that he had bought two years earlier at the same time that he took over the Moreno business. The house was north-facing with small windows and heavy drapings, but none of these were the reason that it was in a state of semidarkness for most of the day. She discovered that her husband obsessionally kept the light away from his furniture.

'Much better for the upholstery,' he crowed. 'Don't let your furniture fade so fast, Gourgouris likes to make it last.' It was one of his catchphrases, to which she would have to become accustomed.

Over the next few months, Katerina would realise that there was nothing he liked more than a glib little rhyme. If he found a sentence with rhyme or rhythm then he would endlessly reuse it, usually accompanied with a cheery smile and the expectation of applause. Each week he took out advertisements on the front page of the newspapers and spent most evenings devising his own straplines.

'Go on! Be glamorous in a Gourgouris gown!'

On the first day as mistress of the house, Katerina realised that Gourgouris intended for her to stay at home.

'I think you should spend a few days acclimatising yourself here,' he said. 'And then we'll think about whether you need to come back to the workshop. Perhaps just part time?'

It had not occurred to her that she would stop working. She was dismayed. Even though the other women in the workshop had started to treat her differently when they knew she was to marry Gourgouris, she longed to get back to her seat in the finishing room.

That morning, she explored her new environment. There were two large rooms on the ground floor, in addition to the kitchen and dining room. One of them was a drawing room, and the other a study. It was monopolised by a desk and a bookcase that housed a row of alphabetically ordered works of the ancient philosophers. She carefully slid one off the shelf and, when she opened it, the stiffness of the cover betrayed that it had never been read. There was a book standing on its own, with a title she recognised as German: *Also Sprach Zarathustra.*

She could not resist opening it. She knew her husband spoke a little German but probably not enough to read fluently. On the title page, there was a dedication: '*Für Grigoris Gourgouris. Vielen Dank, Hans Schmidt. 14/6/43.'*

She snapped the book shut. It was enough to tell her that Gourgouris had counted a German among his friends. She put it back on the shelf with distaste, resolving to forget that she had ever seen it.

Every room had the same dark beige linoleum floor, cream Anaglypta on the walls, and the doors, skirting boards, picture rails, and the windowframes and shutters (permanently closed) were all painted a standard solid brown.

There were a few rugs on the floor and one or two landscape paintings in each room. The furniture was mostly new and some of it looked as if it had never been sat on. A long dining table with eight chairs around it and a candelabra in the centre did not have the slightest scratch, and the matching, glass-fronted sideboard was empty. On top of it was a huge cutglass rose bowl, bereft of flowers.

Katerina began to unpack her few things, placing an icon, which Eugenia had given her as a wedding gift, on an empty shelf in the drawing room. It looked lonely and out of place in this character-less house. She decided not to put the photograph of Eugenia on the sideboard. Along with the treasured picture of Dimitri, she would keep it in a small box, tucked away in the bottom of her wardrobe.

The kitchen was well equipped with a new-style cooker, and when she looked in the cupboards she saw nests of aluminium pots and pans. It was very different from Irini Street.

With impeccable efficiency the shutters had kept the light out, but they had also kept the air in and in each of these gloomy interiors, there was the same suffocating smell of dust and must.

Katerina wanted to throw open every window and door, and fill vases with fresh flowers, but she assumed that the house must be like this because her husband wanted it this way.

The space should have been a luxury, but it seemed a waste for two people, and the clutter of colourful rugs, blankets and embroidered cushions that filled her old home felt a world away.

Up in the master bedroom, there was an enormous empty wardrobe where she hung a few dresses. Considering her occupation, she did not have many clothes, and her husband had already told her that he wanted her to spend the next few months making some outfits for herself.

'My little lass must look lovely!' he had said that morning, patting her bottom. 'So you must get to work on making a few things for yourself. You have your sewing machine now, don't you?'

The Singer that Konstantinos Komninos had given her a few years earlier had arrived from Irini Street the previous day and was sitting on the floor of the dining room.

That evening, Gourgouris brought home some lengths of fabric: pale pink gingham, yellow with sprigs of red roses, mint-green stripes. They were not to her taste, but she surmised this was part of the new 'job': to dress as her husband wished.

The maid, it seemed, no longer had a brief to cook. She still came in once a day to sweep and polish the already shiny surfaces, but Gourgouris wanted his wife to cook for him. With trepidation, Katerina began to use the cookery book that Eugenia had bought her for her wedding. In the past she had only ever used recipes handed down by word of mouth, modified according to taste by adjusting the amounts of herbs and spices, so it was strange trying to follow a written recipe.

She went out for a walk each afternoon, often visiting Eugenia, who had been weaving at home since the end of the war. Occasionally, Eugenia came to Sokratous Street, though she did once tactlessly admit that the big gloomy house gave her the shivers.

'It does me, as well,' sighed Katerina, 'but I have to live here . . .'

They were sitting in Katerina's kitchen at the enamel-topped table, and the ingredients for dinner were piled up at one end.

'It's nice and spacious, at least,' said Eugenia hastily.

Katerina began to clear their cups. Her husband liked to have three courses each night and she needed to start the preparation.

'How is married life?' Eugenia asked teasingly.

'I'm managing,' came the answer, almost too quickly.

That was the truth of it. She was managing this new life as though it were a business. Tasks had to be performed each day in order to fulfil her role as a wife, cook and housekeeper.

Gourgouris had decided she should be at home full time. If there was something of particular importance or difficulty he would bring it to the house for her to finish, but he did not want her in the workshop.

Months passed quietly. Katerina began to make quilts for the bedrooms and began to add the feminine touches that the house seemed to lack. She learned to keep her mind away from past and future, and sewing, as ever, proved to be the way. Every stitch was done in the present, the here and now, and this was how she learned to survive. The past led her back to Dimitri, and the future took her forward to the daily dread of her husband's return.

With visits to the Modiano market, cooking, sewing and visiting Eugenia, Katerina kept herself busy, but she was soon to take on another task. Six months after losing her supplementary role as cook, the cleaner had become dissatisfied and handed in her notice.

'I shall place an advertisement in the newspaper tomorrow,' Gourgouris said, and with every 's' and 'p' and 't' he sprayed her with more of the soup that she had made that afternoon. It was a *bisque de homard* and the russet-brown spots stood out on the pale pink of her dress.

Katerina nodded. With the huge numbers of people unemployed it should not be too long before someone applied, even if there were plenty of women who would rather beg than clean someone else's home.

As she went round with a duster the following day, Katerina discovered that during all these months the cleaner had actually been very slapdash in her work. The surfaces had a superficial shine, but she had never gone underneath cupboards or round the back of furniture. Katerina happily threw open the shutters and began to spring clean. It was a satisfying enough job and the house looked much less forbidding with daylight streaming through the windows.

She began with the hallway and drawing room and then went into Gourgouris' study. There were dozens of books but the spines were all unbroken. They were just for show.

All these will ever do, she thought to herself, regarding the books, is gather dust.

She did not touch the volume of Nietzsche.

She moved some papers to one side in order to polish the desk to a shine and then started work on its tarnished brass drawer handles. One of the drawers was half open and something caught her eye. There was a file with two names written in large, neat letters on the cover: 'MORENO – GOURGOURIS'.

The sight of her new name and the name of her old friends juxtaposed gave her a jolt. She thought of the Morenos often and, whenever she was with Eugenia, they remembered them with anger and sadness. They still wondered what had happened to Elias; they had not even heard if he had reached Palestine.

Katerina felt a momentary pang of guilt, knowing that she should not look through her husband's papers, but nevertheless she found herself opening the drawer and removing the file. For a minute or so she sat at the desk looking at it. It was not too late to put it back but, like a demon, curiosity possessed her and a moment later she had opened it.

The first item was a single piece of paper with some figures, rather like an invoice, then there was a legal document with several stamps from the Municipality of Thessaloniki and, on thick parchment, the 'Title Deeds' of the property in Filipou Street. From what she could tell, the business had been sold to her husband for a very small sum, a fraction of the price that people would pay even for a house in Irini Street, and he had paid it in a single, lump sum. The business had virtually been given to him.

Then there was a sheaf of correspondence, all of it predating the sale, and she read the series of letters with increasing shock and disbelief.

Straight away, she recognised the signature on the first letter. It was the same name as the one that appeared inside the Nietzsche book. A few words of German had become familiar to her during those years of occupation when the officers had been frequent visitors to the workshop. Among them were '*Guten Tag*', '*Bitte*' and

'*Danke schön*'. It was those words that she saw repeated at the bottom of the letter: '*Danke schön*' – 'Thank you'.

Next there were several carbon copies of letters from her husband to 'The Service for the Disposal of Jewish Property' and their replies. She put them in date order and began to read. Her hands were trembling violently.

The first letter, from Gourgouris, was dated 21 February 1943 and was written from Larissa. Katerina calculated that this was even before the Morenos had left Thessaloniki. In the letter her husband outlined his request to take over the 'lucrative and thriving business of Moreno & Sons'. He described his already well-established businesses in Veria and Larissa and his desire to expand into larger premises in Thessaloniki. The response to this application asked for evidence of his support for the government. Several letters followed and she felt increasingly nauseous as she read them. There were mentions of several donations of money to the government but in the final one, written in July 1943, there was a list of names. She found herself reading them aloud:

'Matheos Keropoulos, *andarte*
Giannis Alahouzos, *andarte*
Anastasios Makrakis, *andarte*
Gabriel Perez, in hiding with false identity
Daniel Perez, in hiding with false identity
Jacob Soustiel, in hiding with Christian family and in
    possession of false identity
Solomon Mizrahi, in hiding with Christian family and in
    possession of false identity'

It was clear that through Gourgouris' tip-offs, all the men he had listed had been arrested. The first three might just have been imprisoned, but the others, Katerina knew without doubt, would then have been sent to Poland, or even murdered on the spot.

Now she knew. The gratitude her husband had been shown by the German officer was for these acts of betrayal and collaboration.

She closed the file, and for half an hour or more sat at the desk with her head in her hands, paralysed with shock and indecision. She could not reveal what she had found, and yet how could she live with the knowledge? How could she continue to live with this man?

Replacing the file in the drawer, she got up and left the room. The terrible mistake she had made weighed heavily on her. No one had forced her to marry Grigoris Gourgouris and she would have to suffer the consequences of her own stupidity. There was no one else to blame.

She went into the kitchen, closed all the windows and shutters and turned on the dim table lamp. As she mechanically began to prepare the evening meal, tears of anger and frustration poured down her face and she could scarcely see what she was doing.

*Thump-thump-thump-thump* . . .

The knife crashed down again and again onto the chopping board.

*Thump-thump-thump-thump* . . .

Through the mist of her tears all she could see was the flash of metal. For a mere fraction of a second, she pictured herself plunging the sharp blade into her chest. It seemed to her that it would provide instant relief from the self-loathing with which she had been seized. Never before had she felt this strange urge to punish herself. It lasted only a few seconds but she was amazed by how it had nearly seduced her. No, she told herself, you must face the consequences of what you have done.

She continued to dice the vegetables, but inevitably, the combination of anger, lack of concentration and a sharp knife was a dangerous one. With some inevitability, she sliced through her finger.

She dropped the knife and gripped her hand tightly, hoping to stem the copious bleeding. She had no idea there was so much blood in a finger. The pure white mound of chopped onions was now spotted with crimson.

The pain and the shock of the cut triggered uncontrollable sobs and she did not hear the opening and closing of the front door. When Gourgouris walked in she was vainly attempting to bandage her finger in a cloth.

'Ah, my dear. What on earth is wrong?' he said, approaching with open arms in order to embrace her.

Katerina ducked to avoid him. His vast bulk repelled her more than ever. Her crying stopped. She was determined to keep her dignity in front of this man.

'I've cut myself,' she said, concealing the wound. 'That's all. It's nothing.'

'Well, I can see you won't be able to make the dinner now,' he said with mild disgust, seeing that blood was already soaking through the cloth. 'Would you mind if I went straight out to eat? Grigoris is absolutely famished.'

As he spoke, Gourgouris was rubbing his stomach. Referring to himself in the third person was one of his many annoying habits. He was like a vast, jovial child and yet, beneath this exterior, she now knew there was someone very different.

'No,' she said. 'I'm feeling faint. I think I had better go upstairs.'

She could not even look at Gourgouris and was relieved that he was leaving the house again. His absence would give her more time to think.

When he returned late that night, Katerina lay still and feigned sleep until she heard the sound of his snoring. A gut full of rich food and brandy was guaranteed to keep him asleep until morning.

The horrifying discovery of the afternoon went round and round again in her mind, as did the question of how she should respond. Did everyone at the workshop know that Gourgouris' 'acquisition' was a reward for collaborating with the Nazis? Who could she tell and was there any point in revealing what she knew? She remembered that a few collaborators had been tried and almost immediately pardoned, or given perfunctory sentences. The crime of being a Communist was still considered a much more serious one than being a collaborator.

The following morning she kept her eyes shut until Gourgouris had gone and then swiftly dressed and left for Irini Street. There was one person with whom she must share this terrible burden.

'I am so sorry. I am so, so sorry,' Eugenia kept repeating over and over again, shaking her head in dismay and full of pity for Katerina. 'If I'd had any idea, I would have stopped you marrying him.'

'It's not your fault,' said Katerina. 'It's nobody's fault except mine. I made the decision and I've got to live with it.'

'There must be something we can do,' said Eugenia. 'You could come and stay here for a while.'

'He would find me,' said Katerina. 'And I would have to explain. I should never have opened the drawer.'

'Well, you can't turn back the clock,' said Eugenia.

'I know . . .'

'You discovered something you would rather not have known,' she said. 'But that something was true. And perhaps it's better that you know?'

'I found him repulsive enough before. But now . . .' Katerina's elbows were on the table and her head rested in her hands as she cried. Her hand was still crudely bandaged. '. . . now I know he's a murderer.'

'You must try not to think of him like that. There are collaborators all around us in this city.'

'But I am actually married to one!'

'Well, I don't think you should do anything rash,' advised Eugenia. 'Unless you are going to leave him, which you can't.'

Katerina was now very sure of one thing. Anyone who had told her that there was a possibility of love developing for Gourgouris had been wrong. In its place, hatred had grown instead.

'Let me look at your finger. Come on, take off that bandage.'

The wound was still raw and open, and Katerina winced as Eugenia bathed it.

'Are you sure you shouldn't have this seen to by a doctor?' she asked.

'No, I am sure it will heal up. And as soon as it does, I am going to tell Gourgouris that I want to go back to the workshop. At least for a few hours every afternoon. It will drive me mad being in that house all day. Locked up in there, with all those thoughts.'

Katerina left Irini Street, determined to ask her husband that evening about returning to work.

'Well, you can come in for a few hours a day as long as you can manage the house properly,' he said, with some reluctance. 'That's your priority, and looking after your Kyrios Gourgouris.'

'Yes,' she said.

'We've had plenty of applications for the maid's position, so that will be one worry out of the way,' he said.

'Good,' Katerina replied.

She kept her conversations with this despicable man as brief as possible and when he asked her what was wrong, she told him that her hand was bothering her.

'Oh yes,' said Gourgouris. 'You'd better not come back to the workshop until it's healed. It's not really the right time to start a fashion for red bridal gowns.'

He followed this with a toothy grin, amused by his joke, and did not seem to notice that she did not smile back.

# Chapter Twenty-six

MANY KILOMETRES AWAY, in the mountains outside Ioannina, Dimitri was now in charge of a constantly overstretched medical team. He had heard that Thessaloniki was being shelled by the Democratic Army and though he yearned to be there, for once he was glad to be far away. He would find it hard to attack his own city, the place inhabited by the people he loved most in the world.

Within the city itself, these attacks were not disrupting life unduly, and the workshop was carrying on as normal. Katerina began her morning shifts at the workshop and the women in the finishing room seemed pleased by her return. For a few days, she wondered if any of them knew the circumstances of Gourgouris' purchase of the business, but she did not ask.

Each day, at eight o'clock sharp, she began work in the finishing room and left at midday so that she would have plenty of time to make dinner. Gourgouris' interest in food bordered on addiction and it was the main task he expected her to fulfil.

A few weeks after her return to work she was asked to visit Kyria Komninos. Olga still wore black, but she had regained a little weight since Katerina had last seen her and, as a consequence, required some new outfits.

The two women had not seen each other since Katerina had got married and Olga was full of questions.

'Pavlina told me you had a lovely dress, Katerina. And did you enjoy your wedding day?'

Katerina tried not to think about the ceremony and the words she had spoken before God that committed her, for life, to Gourgouris.

'It was fine,' she said, noncommittally.

'And tell me about your house, Katerina. It's one of the villas in Sokratous Street, Pavlina tells me. Have you learned to cook?'

'I have,' replied Katerina. 'The kitchen has all modern conveniences, even one of those new electric cookers.'

'But it doesn't do the cooking for you, does it? You still have to do all the hard work, I suspect.'

'Yes, I do. And Kyrios Gourgouris is quite keen on his food.'

'I can imagine,' said Olga. She smiled at Katerina but noticed that not even a flicker of a smile came back.

She mentioned her observations to Pavlina later that day.

'She wasn't quite how I would expect a newlywed to be,' she commented.

'I agree. She seemed glum,' said Pavlina. 'But she wasn't madly in love to start with, was she?'

'No, but I hoped she would grow to like Kyrios Gourgouris a little more as time went on,' replied Olga.

'Well, it's still early days,' said Pavlina.

'I suppose she might not be feeling well,' ventured Olga.

'You mean, she could be having a baby? That would be quick!'

'It's not impossible, is it?'

'No, but I think she would have mentioned it to me, that's all,' replied Pavlina, with a slightly proprietorial tone.

'Well, I have asked her to come back again next week, so let's hope she seems a bit better then.'

When Katerina returned, Pavlina noticed that she looked even more lacklustre than on the previous visit. Pavlina looked for obvious signs of pregnancy but there were none to be seen. The spark had simply gone out of the seamstress. She recalled so clearly seeing Katerina for the first time. It was the day when Eugenia and the girls arrived in Irini Street and even then the six-year-old child, with her open, innocent face, had seemed luminescent. When everyone around her was fearful or suspicious, the girl in the pale, smocked dress somehow shone. All these years later a light had been turned out. The child who had always skipped rather than walked had turned into a woman who seemed to drag her feet. The sparkle in her eye and the readiness of her smile had vanished, as if all the energy had been sapped out of her.

It was mid-August and the hottest day yet that summer. The sea was flat and silvery, reflecting a colourless hazy sky. Having welcomed Katerina in, Pavlina offered her a cold drink at the kitchen table.

'Are you all right, Katerina? You seem quiet.'

'I'm fine, Pavlina. It's just so humid today.'

'Are you sure that's all it is? I thought there might be something wrong. Is everything all right with Kyrios Gourgouris?'

'Yes,' Katerina answered abruptly. She did not want to break the promise she had made to herself: to endure without complaint. 'Everything is fine.'

Katerina got up, wanting to escape from Pavlina's interrogation.

'Can I go and see Kyria Komninos?'

She went upstairs with the two dresses over her arm and met Olga on the landing.

'Hello, Kyria Komninos,' she said, consciously trying to inject some enthusiasm into her greeting.

'Good morning, Katerina. Shall we go into my dressing room?'

Katerina followed her and soon was pinning the darts and measuring for the length of sleeves and hem. Normally they would have chatted during these sessions, but Katerina's furrowed brow deterred Olga from striking up conversation.

Olga did not want to pry, but it was obvious that something was wrong. It did not need to be articulated: Katerina was unhappy and she knew instinctively that it was something to do with Grigoris Gourgouris. The smug, self-satisfied man who had sat at her dining table on several occasions laughing at his own dreadful jokes must have something to do with this sadness that hovered over her like a cloud. Olga knew about unhappy marriage and recognised the air of muted resignation. Silently, she felt a bond with the young woman. Both of them had made the same mistake and now had to live out their life sentences.

Katerina looked up from her work and noticed a framed photograph of Dimitri on the chest of drawers. It was the same as the one that Pavlina had given her and was the only one of him in the Niki Street mansion.

Olga saw Katerina looking at it.

'He was so handsome, wasn't he?'

'Yes,' agreed Katerina tentatively. 'Very. And brave too.'

There were tears in her eyes as she spoke. She was looking at the face of someone who had courageously fought to get the Germans out of Greece, and that night she would be sharing a bed with someone who would happily have had them stay. A collaborator. She was almost choked with shame.

Katerina came and went from the Komninos house a few times over the following few weeks. Pavlina always tried to give her a chance to tell her why she was unhappy, but the *modistra* did not want to confide.

It was over two years now since Dimitri's death and Olga was coming out of mourning. Katerina was there one day pressing a new skirt in pale blue with white polka dots.

'Won't it be nice to wear some colour?' asked Katerina.

'I'm not so sure,' Olga replied. 'It's going to feel strange.'

Pavlina appeared at the door of the bedroom, flushed. She had run up the stairs and was breathless, with emotion as well as exertion.

'Kyria Komninos . . . I have to speak to you. Something has happened.'

'Pavlina! What? What's wrong?'

'There's nothing wrong. But it's such a shock. It's such a shock.'

'Pavlina, tell me what's the matter!' There was a note of rising irritation in her mistress's voice.

Katerina stood, slightly awkwardly, holding the skirt. Pavlina was standing in the doorway, so she could not just slip out.

'I don't know how to tell you this . . . b-but . . .'

'Pavlina, what is it?' Olga was running out of patience.

The housekeeper was behaving very strangely indeed, and was now crying uncontrollably. It was hard to tell whether they were tears of joy or grief.

'I know he's dead. But . . .'

Katerina saw there was someone now standing behind Pavlina. A man.

Olga fainted. It was Katerina who spoke his name.

'Dimitri?' she whispered.

'Yes, it's me.'

When Olga came to, her son was sitting beside her on the bed.

'I'm sorry it was such a surprise,' he said. 'I was going to write first but that seemed too dangerous. So, I just came . . .'

Mother and son held each other in a long embrace. Then he turned and took Katerina's hands to his lips and kissed them.

'*Katerina mou*,' he said. 'My Katerina.'

'You gave us all such a shock,' she said. 'But I'm so happy to see you.'

Pavlina had gone downstairs to bring water for Olga and now returned with four glasses.

Olga lay propped up on pillows and the others sat on low upholstered chairs around the bed.

'But we had a letter . . . from the Communist headquarters,' Olga said. 'How could they make such a mistake?'

'Perhaps they didn't, Mother,' he said cautiously.

After a moment's pause he asked when his father would be home.

'He is away. There is a silk factory in Turkey he is trying to buy,' answered Olga.

Over the course of the next few hours, he broke the other side of the story to his mother. Though she was fragile he could not protect her from this truth.

He revealed where he had been since the Democratic Army had been formed and told them things that the newspapers did not report about the continually raging civil war. There was much that he was selective about revealing but he did admit that there had been unnecessary brutality and that he often found himself trying to patch up the victims, whichever side they were on. When someone was sick or dying he tried not to differentiate. Pain was pain, whoever was suffering it.

'I don't know what's going to happen,' he said. 'Things are going well for us at the moment. I just do my best out there. There are people dying on both sides and it's hateful and pointless – but I can't walk away from it now. I still believe that those on the Right should be sharing power with the Left.'

'And what about the children we have read about – the ones who are being taken from their parents and sent to Communist countries?' asked Pavlina. 'Is it true?'

'Some of that is propaganda, but there is some truth in it,' replied Dimitri. 'It's meant to keep children safe, not to indoctrinate them.'

'Your father was convinced that you were a Communist,' said Olga. 'And for him, communism is the great evil that wants to take over this country.'

'There are plenty who are committed Communists, but I'm not one of them, Mother,' he said gently. 'And I have no intention of going to live in a Communist country. Greece is my *patrida* and it's for Greece that I have been fighting all this time.'

The afternoon wore on and the four of them stayed in the bedroom. Pavlina came and went with plates of food and nothing could have seemed more natural than for Katerina to be there with them. Olga could not help noticing that the *modistra* had regained her lost smile. When she looked at Dimitri her eyes shone.

The chimes of the clock had been drowned out by their conversation, but then Pavlina had gone downstairs and left the door open. Katerina counted the hour.

'I have to go,' she gasped.

'Why so suddenly?' asked Dimitri. 'I will be going soon too.'

'Because I have to get home and make dinner,' she said. 'And I haven't even been to buy the meat.'

'Eugenia won't mind, will she?'

'It's not Eugenia,' Katerina said, almost inaudibly. 'I'm married now.'

'Married!' he exclaimed, and the word hung there for a moment. There was an unmistakable note of dismay in his voice.

Katerina noticed Dimitri glance down at her hands, where her wedding ring glinted on the third finger of her right hand, as if to check that she was telling the truth. If she could have torn it from her hand and hurled it through the open window, she would have done so. There was no point now.

'So,' she said abruptly, 'I had better be going. I hope you'll be able to come back soon.'

She left the house quietly and almost ran home, stopping briefly at the butcher. Her emotions were now at war within her.

Gourgouris was there when she arrived.

'So, my sweet,' he said, with quiet sarcasm, 'Kyria Komninos needed you to sew some curtains as well, did she?'

'I'm sorry,' said Katerina. 'We were talking. And suddenly it was late.'

'And dinner? Did you think of dinner?' he shouted. 'I come home after a long day to an empty house. And no dinner!'

'I did say I was sorry,' Katerina said meekly.

'I hope your talking was worthwhile,' he spat, 'because Grigoris doesn't really enjoy peeling and slicing.'

Gourgouris was panting from the exertion of being angry. He did not have the lung capacity to sustain his tirade and was running out of breath.

'I'm not feeling well,' she said over her shoulder, dropping the parcel of meat on a side-table as she ran from the room and up to the bathroom. She knew that he would not be able to pursue her up the stairs. He was simply too fat.

Soon afterwards, she heard the bang of the front door as her husband left the house. He would go to one of the city's many restaurants, work his way through enough food for a family and then return. By then she would be asleep.

The reality of the situation hit her. She was married to a man she hated and the man she loved had come back from the dead. The combination of these catastrophes was only half the punishment. The real torture was to behave as though nothing had happened. It was the only way to survive.

'Did it really happen?' Olga asked Pavlina that evening. 'Was he really here?'

Two days remained until Kyrios Komninos returned from his trip, so they were safe to talk of Dimitri's visit without fear of being overheard.

'Yes, it was truly him. I'm surprised we didn't all die of the shock. What was he thinking of, turning up like that, knowing we thought he was dead?'

'I think I did die of shock, for a second at least,' smiled Olga. 'I'm sure my heart stopped.'

'Well, you were out cold for more than fifteen minutes. If I'd had to get the doctor I'm not sure how I would have explained it.'

'Did you notice how happy Katerina seemed?' asked Olga. 'She was really overwhelmed.'

'Well, she did grow up in the same street,' Pavlina suggested. 'He's like a brother.'

'She loves Dimitri, Pavlina,' Olga said. 'I only realised that today.'

Unusually for her, Pavlina said nothing. There was no need.

As far as Gourgouris was concerned, Katerina's lack of punctuality that day had shown that she was not capable of working in the workshop as well as managing a house.

'It was never a good idea for you to start sewing again,' he announced to her the following evening. 'At least not outside the home. There's quite enough to do here.'

Katerina nodded. It was pointless to disagree. She ladled a helping of soup into her husband's bowl and stirred in a spoonful of cream. As long as he was eating, he did not seem to notice that she scarcely spoke and, between courses, spent increasing amounts of time in the kitchen.

Each day, when she was not shopping and preparing for the enormous meals that her husband demanded, she plunged herself into the oblivion of her embroidery.

Occasionally she went to visit Eugenia, though she had to make very sure to be back in good time to cook the evening meal. On her way home, she would call in at the church of Agios Nikolaos Orfanos to light candles for the Morenos.

She found praying impossible. Whenever she asked God to release her from her misery, a picture of a dead Gourgouris flashed into her mind. Images of what had been found in the death camps in Poland circulated in her mind whenever she closed her eyes, and knowing that her husband had been responsible for sending people there filled her with an urge for revenge.

Desiring someone's death seemed equal to murder, and knowing that she would wish it again the next time she was alone and on her knees made her feel as though she had committed a crime. To ask God for forgiveness at the very moment of transgression seemed a pointless exercise.

Deciding what was right and wrong to pray for was as difficult as deciding what was right and wrong in the continuing war. Stories circulated of atrocities, whether rumoured or witnessed, being committed by both sides. Katerina thought of Dimitri.

Very uncertain if God would listen, given the hatred that raged in her heart, Katerina prayed for all those who were in danger.

Then she hurried home and dutifully began to prepare the dinner. Each day, the meals she made became more elaborate, and all the artistry that she had once poured into her work was now diverted into her cooking. She would perform her duties faultlessly.

# Chapter Twenty-seven

KATERINA WAS NOT the only woman needing to put on an act in order to protect herself. Olga Komninos had to do the same. In the past decades she had had plenty of practice. From her early days as a mannequin, when she had been instructed to appear demure, or haughty, or bashful, or regal (depending on the style of the fashions she was modelling), she had been pretending to be someone else. When they had returned to Niki Street and her agoraphobia had set in, she then had to act another role, that of the perfect hostess.

If her husband found out that Dimitri had returned and told her about his letter of banishment, Konstantinos Komninos' anger would put both of them beyond safekeeping. She would not put it past Konstantinos to track Dimitri down, and she did not allow herself to imagine his wrath against her for welcoming him into the home. All of this gave Olga every incentive to behave as if nothing had happened.

A respectable period of mourning had now passed since the 'death' of their son, and Konstantinos Komninos decided that it was time to entertain again. Additionally, he wanted to show that things were carrying on as normal in spite of the upheaval taking place in the rest of the country. In the past few months, the government forces had been gaining ground over the Communists, so that in itself, thought Konstantinos, was grounds for celebration.

'I have invited Kyrios and Kyria Gourgouris,' he told Olga.

Poor Katerina, thought Olga. She must be dreading it.

She wondered if the young woman would find it strange to be a guest, when she had always come to the house as Olga's *modistra*. She recalled her own unease when she had made the transition from model to hostess. On the positive side, the guest list included a number of such strongly opinionated people that Katerina's shyness would pass unnoticed.

That Saturday evening, with ten people once again around the table, most of them politically like-minded, the conversation was dominated by the latest news of the civil war. It was now entering a new phase in the mountains of Grammos, which separated Epirus from Macedonia. The previous year, the Communists had successfully fortified the area but the government forces had now attacked. A battle had been raging for some days and the guests, who read the city's right-wing press, were gripped by their daily account of events. One aspect of the reporting that contained no bias, even if the rest did, was the detail of the massive American support that the government now enjoyed, giving them great superiority over the Communists with artillery, armoured vehicles and air power.

As Komninos, Gourgouris and the rest were wishing success for the Government Army and for the defeat of the Democratic Army, Katerina and Olga pictured Dimitri caught in crossfire, his life in danger.

Katerina was dressed in a new burnished orange gown. The colour did not suit her at all, but she had been instructed to make it by Gourgouris. She pushed her food around her plate to disguise her lack of appetite and from time to time mechanically lifted her glass to her lips without sipping. Her throat was so constricted with tension that she could neither speak nor swallow. Having Olga on the other side of the table, sharing her every thought and fear, was a great comfort, and when Pavlina came and went with new dishes of food she made sure to serve Katerina very little. She knew that the seamstress would be in no mood to eat.

At the end of dinner, the entire party went upstairs to the drawing room and onto the balcony. Clouds of smoke billowed into the night air and glasses of brandy chinked together in celebratory anticipation of the government's victory over the Communists. Olga and Katerina finally allowed their eyes to meet. None of the guests noticed this exchange of understanding and sympathy between the two women. They were too busy making toasts, refilling their glasses and leaning forward to light each other's cigarettes.

Beneath them, people strolled on the promenade, many of them arm in arm. They looked up when they heard the noise and excitement above them and saw this group of wealthy men and women of Thessaloniki *en fête*.

Overhead hung the thinnest arc of silvery light. On an ebony-dark night such as this, with a new moon and no clouds, the stars seemed infinite. Olga and Katerina stood close, able to exchange a few quiet words without being overheard.

'Can you see Orion?' Olga asked, gazing upwards. 'You know he's the Hunter, don't you? Dimitri used to love pointing him out.'

She gave Katerina's arm a reassuring squeeze and moved off to speak to one of the other women who was standing on her own.

* * *

Several hundred kilometres away on the mountains of Grammos, the intense darkness of this almost moonless sky was an advantage to Dimitri. With other members of his brigade he was attempting the impossible: to move out of the area before they were surrounded. Although the blackness of the night made it hard to see a route through the pathless landscape, it also made it easier for the soldiers to remain hidden.

Dimitri was exhausted. For five days he had worked night and day without sleep, tending to the wounded. Anyone who was not sufficiently mobile to make it out of this situation would find themselves trapped. It was a treacherous journey but there was every danger that they would be shot on sight if caught.

For the remaining days of August, both Olga and Katerina were in a state of high anxiety, reading the newspapers and listening to the radio, hoping and fearing in equal measure. There was a massive assault on Grammos, where twelve thousand members of the Democratic Army were still hiding out. The Government Army's ambition was the total annihilation of the opposition, and when it became clear that they faced defeat, the Communist leaders ordered their fighters to flee into Albania, through the one remaining route still open to them.

Four days after the final battle had begun, the newspapers announced that the Government Army was in full control of Greece. The civil war had come to an end and many people, Konstantinos Komninos included, celebrated. In October an official cease-fire was signed.

The three women who loved Dimitri met one day soon afterwards in the kitchen at Niki Street.

'We may never know what happened to him,' said Pavlina.

'But we'll always know he was fighting for something he believed in,' responded Katerina.

If Dimitri was in Albania they might hear from him one day. If he was not, then he would be hunted. If he was dead, they had to accept it. There was nothing they could do to find out.

They watched the city gradually returning to normal and life for the three of them continued as before, superficially at least.

Katerina stayed at home most of the time and, from her cookery books, devised increasingly rich and lavish menus for her husband. Ingredients were becoming less difficult to find and good meat and dairy products were available each day at the market.

In her spare time she was making a quilt for one of the guest bedrooms. They rarely had people to stay so it would probably never be seen by another soul, but the pleasure in doing the work was an end in itself.

The initials of Saul, Isaac, Elias, Roza and Esther Moreno, and a P for Poland and Palestine, formed a circle around a dove. It gave her great satisfaction to read the single word that she had spelled out in stitches: 'SIEMPRE'.

She had little knowledge of Ladino but she knew this meant 'Forever' and 'Always', and the stitching kept their memory alive.

With a pattern that mingled pomegranates and vines around the edge she used some of the most significant symbols of Judaism to create a private memorial for her friends. As she sat and sewed for an hour or so at the beginning of each afternoon, she would not have described her state as happy, but as hopeful. The radio gave her the company she needed and whenever she heard a song she liked, she tried to memorise the lyrics. Her current favourite was '*To Minore Tis Avgis*':

*Ksipna, mikro mou, ki akouse*
*Kapio minore tis avgis.*


Wake up, my little one, and hear
The minor key of dawning day.


The absolute sincerity and pathos of the music touched her right to the core.

One morning in December she paid one of her regular visits to see Eugenia in Irini Street. The postman had called the day before.

'There's a letter for you,' she said, smiling at Katerina. 'From someone who doesn't know you have got married. And can't spell your name!'

'That's not unusual,' said Katerina, taking the envelope. 'No one ever manages to spell Sarafoglou correctly!'

She looked at the words 'Kyria K Sarafolgaou'. Obviously it was not from her mother, who had long since ceased to write. There was something that had struck her about the name.

Katerina tore open the letter, bouncing with excitement and agitation.

'I thought so!' she said triumphantly, as she pulled the letter from the envelope. 'It's from Dimitri! He hid Olga's name in mine!'

She immediately stuffed it back into the envelope, almost dancing with joy, and kissed Eugenia.

'I must go,' she said. 'Olga must have this straight away.'

Katerina opened the door and took off down the street at a run. In all the months of overfeeding her husband, she had put on a few centimetres round the waist herself, and was scarlet with exertion when she arrived.

She hugged a bemused Pavlina but delivered her news in a

hoarse whisper. There was always a small chance that Konstantinos was in the house.

'Pavlina! He's alive. Dimitri's alive. Where's Olga? There's a letter!'

With watery eyes, Pavlina pointed up the stairs.

Olga was in her bedroom when Katerina burst in.

'Look!' she cried out. 'Open it!'

The two women sat on the bed together and Olga opened the letter, her hands trembling so violently that the paper visibly shook.

My dear Mother,

Unlike most of my fellow fighters, I have not crossed the border into Albania. I have not been fighting all this time in order to become an exile. I was fighting because I love my country. At this stage I have no idea what this will mean for my future but I wanted to let you know that I am alive. Hundreds of my brave comrades fell around me on that mountain. Like me, they all believed they were fighting for a just cause. I am one of the few lucky ones.

I am a wanted man so I will need to take great care about coming to see you, for your sake as well as mine. And next time I will let you know when I am coming. I don't want to put you in danger of having a heart attack like last time!

'He fears for my heart!' exclaimed Olga. 'I just feel it might burst with joy at this moment!'

'That could be just as dangerous!' said Katerina smiling.

The letter ended, 'Please give my love to our housekeeper and to the *modistra*. You are all so precious to me.'

There was no signature. Just the word *filia*, kisses, and the letter was only identifiable by her knowledge of his handwriting. No one was named, and no one could be incriminated.

Dimitri was as good as his word. Within a few weeks, another letter had arrived in Irini Street. It purported to be from a hospital and once again was addressed to: 'Kyria K Sarafolgaou'.

'The next doctor's appointment will be on Wednesday 25 January at ten o'clock.'

On the specified day, Olga, Pavlina and Katerina were sitting anxiously in the kitchen when there was a gentle ring at the doorbell. The clock on the landing was chiming the hour as Pavlina opened the door. Dimitri looked completely different from the last time they had seen him. He was equally slim, but this time he was clean shaven and wearing a coat and dark fedora.

Dimitri embraced first his mother and then Pavlina. Katerina stood back a little, her heart pounding.

'Katerina,' said Dimitri, taking both her hands in his. 'I've missed you.'

Her broad smile told him what he needed to know.

They followed Olga up to the drawing room where they sat and immediately began to talk, aware that Dimitri would probably not be staying long. Pavlina came and went with coffee and the *kourabies* biscuits she had just baked. They were Dimitri's favourites.

'You look so smart!' said Olga.

'It's just a disguise really,' said Dimitri. 'I have some fake identity which says that I am a lawyer, so I need to look like one!'

'Your father would like that!' said Pavlina facetiously.

'Yes, he would, wouldn't he!' Dimitri responded. 'Well, it's the closest I shall ever get to being one. How is he?'

Mention of Konstantinos Komninos brought an instant change of mood to the room, reminding them all that officially Dimitri did not exist.

'Just the same,' his mother replied simply.

There was an awkward silence.

'And, Katerina, tell me,' said Dimitri, wanting to change the subject, 'are you still making the women of Thessaloniki look like goddesses?'

'I'm afraid not,' she said, trying to sound cheerful. 'My husband prefers me to be at home.'

'Oh,' replied Dimitri. 'That seems a waste. My mother said you were the best in the city!'

'Yes,' said Olga. 'It's a huge pity. All Katerina's talent is now locked away.'

'When we were up in the mountains, the women fought along-side the men! As equals! I'm sure *they* won't be following their husbands' instructions any more . . .'

Katerina smiled at Dimitri. 'Well, I'm afraid most husbands still expect their wives to do what they're told.'

Dimitri turned to his mother. 'You know I can't stay in Thessaloniki. It's not safe at the moment and I think it's better for you if I don't tell you where I am going either,' he said.

'You know what's best, Dimitri. As long as we hear from you from time to time. I need to know you are safe,' Olga replied.

'I'd like to take a few of my things with me,' he continued. 'Some of my medical books. I want to begin studying again. There were so many things I wished I had known when I was up in the mountains. One day I'm going to qualify.'

He stood up. 'Katerina, come and talk to me while I pack,' he said.

She followed behind him.

Dimitri's bedroom was exactly as it had been almost a decade ago. All of his books were just as he had left them, in semi-disarray, some of them open on his desk, some of them propped against others. This was how Olga had instructed Pavlina to leave them.

Everything was dusted, but very carefully so that it was all in the same position. There was a medical dictionary, a human skull that he had been so proud to own – some scientific but strangely beautiful anatomical drawings on the wall and a pen lying across a sheet of notes. Incongruously there were still some childhood objects arranged on a nearby shelf – an abacus and a catapult – and, leaning against the wall, an old hoop.

Dimitri walked over to his desk and began to rummage while Katerina stood, feeling slightly awkward.

Suddenly he turned around, one of the toys in his hand.

'Do you remember playing in the street, all those years ago? You and me, Elias and Isaac, and the twins?'

He was staring into her eyes, his own ablaze with passion and fury.

'Of course I remember,' she replied.

'What changed everything, Katerina? What happened to those years? Those people?'

Time and cruelty were part of the answer, but she knew that one thing had not changed. She had loved Dimitri then and she still loved him now.

Holding her gently by her shoulders, he realised the same thing.

Dimitri had seen so much destruction and wasted life, so much brutality, fear and violence. He had experienced a father's hatred and had seen brother turning against brother. He had watched a whole country at war with itself and none of it made sense in the way that this embrace did.

Katerina too had experienced her own internal civil war. From the moment she had set eyes on the list of innocent names betrayed by Gourgouris, she had been in a state of turmoil. As she felt Dimitri's gentle touch on her scarred arm, she knew with certainty that she was loved. She found herself suffused with an unexpected sense of peace.

So it was also with Dimitri. He felt the kindness of her lips and all the bitterness of these past years seemed to lift.

Both of them had waited so long for such a moment and now, without the need for words, decided not to let it pass them by. What reason was there to resist such desire?

An hour went by and, two floors below in the kitchen, Pavlina was busy packing up some food for Dimitri.

Olga knew how Katerina felt about her son and was certain now she had seen them together that Dimitri felt the same. Knowing that he might not be able to return for the foreseeable future, she had wanted them to be alone.

'He looks thin,' said Pavlina. 'Wherever he's going to live, I hope he'll be fed properly!'

'I don't think he's eaten well for years, Pavlina,' said Olga. 'But it's the same for half of Greece, isn't it?'

She watched Pavlina filling a box to the brim with packets of cheese, *dolmadakia* – stuffed vine leaves – *tiropita* – cheese pies – and dried fruits.

'Are you sure he'll be able to carry all that?' Olga laughed.

Eventually Dimitri came downstairs, with Katerina following him. With his slight figure and an old school bag filled with books slung across his shoulder, he looked at least a decade younger than his thirty-two years. It was as if he was off for a day at the university.

'Dimitri!' Olga said with a catch in her throat. 'Are you going now?'

Saying goodbye never seemed to become any easier.

'Yes, I must. No one who fought with the Democratic Army

is safe, but I promise to keep in touch. Nobody wants to be back here in this city more than I do . . .'

'I don't know what we're going to do about your father,' said Olga.

'Nor me,' said Dimitri. 'Nor me.'

Both of them knew that Dimitri's real enemy was inside his own family, within his own home.

Pavlina and Katerina stood back as mother and son embraced. Dimitri picked up the brown box that Pavlina had neatly tied up with string, kissed each woman on the forehead and went into the hall. He could not delay his leaving any more.

Pavlina opened the door and looked out both ways.

'You're fine,' she reported. 'There's nobody about.'

With that, Dimitri left and did not look back. Two minutes later, Katerina set off in the other direction. It was time to start shopping for the evening meal.

Tonight she planned to make egg and lemon soup, roasted aubergines with feta cheese, lamb shanks with cannellini beans and walnut cake with syrup. There would be *loukoumi*, Greek delight, to follow, which had been made the previous day.

For many months now she had watched her husband's expanding girth. Apart from the embroidery she did privately whenever he was not at home, the only other sewing she undertook was the alteration of the waistbands on his trousers.

There was joy in her heart as she cooked. The meat was already marinading in its own fat and juices, just as Gourgouris liked it, and she set about the preparation of her dishes with enthusiasm. Eggs and fatty cheeses, sugar, oil and lard were innocent enough in small quantities, but in the proportions she used them, she was nurturing the perfect environment for coronary failure. At present the only apparent effect of these rich meals was to induce almost instant sleep but silently, by furring up the arteries, they worked towards another goal. Katerina told herself that she was only fulfilling her husband's wishes.

'I need to lie down before dinner,' he said brusquely. 'But have it on the table soon, will you, dear?'

Slowly he hauled himself up the dark staircase, one step at a time. An hour later, dinner was ready and he came down ready to eat. He paused between mouthfuls and even lifting a fork to his mouth seemed to leave him short of breath.

Katerina's inward happiness did not leave her. Even when she went to see Eugenia and there had been no letter from Dimitri, she did not mind. She could tolerate the passing of time when she knew that he would one day return, for it was beyond any doubt that he would.

Within a couple of months of Dimitri's visit, Katerina realised that, like her husband's, her waist was also expanding. Her breasts had increased in size too.

'You must be pregnant,' Eugenia said. 'I'm convinced of it.'

'But Grigoris will know it's not his,' exclaimed Katerina. 'We haven't made love for months and months! He always passes out even before I get into bed . . .'

'We'll think of a way,' said Eugenia, smiling. 'But if I were you, I wouldn't mention it to a soul. At least for a while.'

During the next few days, Katerina's own stomach for preparing meals decreased and nausea made her intolerant of everything but bread dipped in olive oil. In spite of that she continued cooking with increased determination. Spinach and filo pie, beef stuffed with haloumi and *bougatsa*, pastries filled with rich custard sauce, were all favourites of her husband, and she wanted to satisfy his appetite.

One night, Katerina made a meal that was lighter in cholesterol than the usual fare. She served fish as a main course and omitted the potatoes. Even the pudding was dainty: strawberries with a light dusting of sugar and a fine wafer.

'Have you put Grigoris on a diet?' her husband asked, waving the biscuit in the air. 'Do you think Kyrios Gourgouris is getting a little portly?'

He was rubbing his enormous belly as he said this, but Katerina just smiled sweetly and said: 'I just thought it would make a change.'

When he went to bed that night, Gourgouris did not fall asleep with his habitual speed and, as Katerina took off her clothes in the dressing room, she could not hear the sound of snoring. She put on the nightdress embroidered for her wedding night, came into the bedroom and, leaving the bedside light on so that he could still see the shimmer of pale fabric, climbed into bed next to him.

She felt his hand pushing the silk up her legs and then, without conversation, he rolled over on top of her. Seconds away from suffocation, she could not even cry out. She did not have the breath. Then, at the very moment of penetration, the crushing weight went still.

Realising that she was trapped by a huge lifeless body, whose dead weight made it all the heavier, she was seized with panic. A strong sense that she had everything to live for now empowered her with almost superhuman strength, enough to give Gourgouris one immense shove. She wriggled out from underneath.

Her first thought was for the safety of the baby. Her second was for how she would conceal her joy that Gourgouris was dead.

Once she had got dressed and composed herself, she went to a neighbouring house to get help. Within the hour, a doctor had arrived and confirmed Grigoris Gourgouris' death. The cause was massive coronary failure, quite common in a man of his age and with such an excess of weight. His heart had been a time bomb.

Katerina slept in the spare room for the rest of that night, underneath the beautiful quilt that she was embroidering in memory of her friends, and the following morning her late husband's body was collected.

Katerina did everything that she was expected to. She wore black from head to toe and received and replied to letters of condolence. There was a funeral attended by dozens of staff from the workshop, many of the customers and Konstantinos Komninos. Everyone commented on how stoical she was. It was a way of explaining to themselves why the widow did not cry.

A few days later, the will was read. Katerina learned that Gourgouris' nephew, who managed the workshop in Larissa, was to take over the Thessaloniki business. The will specified that the same nephew should also have the Sokratous Street house.

The solicitor looked over the top of his glasses to judge her reaction. It was not unusual for a man to leave his property to a male member of the family if there was no son and heir, but he thought it was a little harsh that this young woman was to be evicted from her home.

She seemed unperturbed, which he felt was very dignified.

'Ah,' he said. 'There is just one more thing here.'

He was smiling at her as though she was a child who needed cheering up.

'He's specifying that his nephew should pay you an annual stipend based on the wages of a part-time *modistra*.'

Katerina had an overwhelming desire to laugh at this display of meanness, but it was important to conceal her mood from this pompous man who was staring at her across his desk.

'Thank you,' she said. 'But I won't be needing that. How long am I permitted to stay in the house?'

'One month from your late husband's death,' he replied, glancing down at the document.

'That's fine,' she said. 'I shall be out before the end of the week.'

He was intrigued that this woman had been so shoddily treated, and yet she did not seem to care.

'I think I must have been a very unsatisfactory wife,' she said, sensing his curiosity. 'But he was a very unsatisfactory husband too.'

With that, she got up and left the room. By the end of the day, her suitcase was packed and the house in Sokratous Street was locked up. As well as a few dresses, she had taken the quilt and her Singer sewing machine. That was all she would need. With a lightness of step, she walked up to the main road and found a taxi to take her to Irini Street. Eugenia was there to welcome her.

Although her pregnancy was now beginning to show, her nausea had passed and she had never felt happier or more full of life.

'I wish I could put on something brighter to wear,' she said to Eugenia. Her widow's weeds felt rough and lifeless against her skin.

'I think you should wear black for a while longer,' advised Eugenia. 'It will seem hasty otherwise.'

Eugenia's advice was sound. In such a conservative city, it was important that Katerina was identified as a widow. In that way there would be no questions raised surrounding the paternity of her baby.

Katerina filled the final few months of her confinement sewing for her soon-to-be-born: bonnets, bibs, vests, gowns, jackets, blankets. Everything was sewn by hand and personalised.

When she was alone, she sang to her unborn child. Perhaps a thousand times the words of her favourite song drifted out across the air, given new meaning by her condition:

> 'Wake up, my little one, and hear
> The minor key of dawning day.
> For you this music has been made
> From someone's cry, from someone's soul.'

As soon as people noticed her changing shape, their sympathy and concern for her increased.

'What a tragedy,' they said, 'to be a pregnant widow.'

In the final few weeks of pregnancy, she spent many hours sitting on the doorstep with Eugenia, enjoying the gentle warmth of the early autumn in the quiet cobbled street. At their feet was a basket of different coloured cottons, packets of needles and some snippets of ribbon and lace. Both of them were intent on getting everything ready in time.

Eugenia had woven a blanket in pale colours and was now crocheting a decorative edge.

'All done,' she said. 'That should keep him snug. You know how damp these winters can be.'

The younger woman put down her embroidery, closed her eyes and turned her face to the sun.

In spite of her smooth, unlined skin, Katerina had shadows beneath her eyes that were as black as the widow's weeds that shrouded her from head to foot. She picked up the little gown that was resting on her lap and resumed her task. With a length of blue thread she added the final touch to the motif on the yoke. It was a tiny butterfly, and all that remained to be done were his antennae. Then he would be perfect.

'There,' she said, with a note of finality. 'I'm going in to have a rest now.'

She gave Eugenia a knowing smile, one that overflowed with joy and anticipation.

'Something tells me it won't be long,' she added.

The following day, 5 September 1950, her baby was born. She named him Theodoris – 'Gift from God'.

# Chapter Twenty-eight

K ATERINA REJOICED, KNOWING that this beautiful, silky-haired boy belonged to the man she loved. Pavlina gasped when she first saw him.

'He's the image of his father,' she said. 'Exactly what Dimitri looked like when he was born!'

During the statutory forty days she spent at home with her newborn, some of the *modistras* from the Gourgouris workshop called in to Irini Street to admire him and to bring gifts that they had sewn.

'It's such a shame,' they said, 'that his father isn't here to see him.'

'Yes,' said Katerina, with a smile as mysterious as the Mona Lisa's. Pavlina came too and brought gifts from Olga.

'Isn't even the birth of a grandson enough to bring her out of the house?' asked Eugenia.

'Sadly not,' replied Pavlina dourly. 'If you ask me, there will only ever be one reason for her to leave that house and it'll be in her own coffin. But she sends her love, along with these gifts. And I know she is hoping that you will call on her as soon as you can.'

Katerina enjoyed every moment of these days, when she had

little to do but attend to the needs of her newborn. Whole days passed by during which she did nothing but feed and hold him, and when he slept, she sewed for him, embroidering his name on every garment. Eugenia, who still wove on her loom at home, was always there to help and provide company.

They were together in Irini Street when Dimitri's letter came. It had been written some while back and, as before, was addressed to Katerina, but this time without any spelling error in the surname. When she saw the address at the top, her heart froze.

*Makronisos.*

This was the barren island off the coast of Attica used as a giant prison camp by the government for Communist captives. It had a fearsome reputation for cruelty, and stories surrounding the barbaric treatment suffered by its inmates had been circulating for some time.

Dear Katerina,

I am so sorry not to have written before to let you know where I am. As you will see from the address on this letter, I was arrested some months ago. I have nothing to tell you except that I love and miss you and the image I carry of you in my mind is all that sustains me.

Please can you break this news gently to my mother and give her and Pavlina kisses from me?

Dimitri

There was a tone of sad resignation in the letter. Everyone knew of Makronisos and the conditions that prevailed there. The government made no secret of how the island was used, because they wanted to make an example of the Communist 'traitors' who were sent there. They did not, however, publicise the lengths to which they went to extort confessions from its prisoners. Such details were only revealed by those who agreed to renounce their Communist beliefs and were therefore released.

When lovers and romantics went to watch the sunset at Sounion, the most inspiring and dramatic temple of their homeland, they found themselves looking across a stretch of water towards a grey and rocky island, where nothing appeared to live or stir. This was the island of Makronisos.

The landscape itself was almost enough to break the spirit of anyone sent there, many of them teachers, lawyers and journalists, who were unused to such conditions. Although the government claimed it was a correction camp for the misguided, it was a place synonymous with violence and torture. As well as hard labour, when the prisoners were made to undertake pointless and gruelling tasks such as building roads that would never be used, there was also systematised physical and psychological torture, from beating with iron bars and sleep deprivation to solitary confinement.

The goal for the government in all cases was the extraction of a *dilosei*, a renunciation of belief, and to get what they wanted, they would use any technique of brainwashing or torture. It was no secret that the island was one huge rehabilitation centre with up to ten thousand former soldiers detained there.

Sometimes people did not even last long enough to 'repent'. With thousands of them living in makeshift tents, hungry to the point of insanity and with insufficient water, disease and illness often wiped them out first.

The guarded tone of Dimitri's letter was enough to indicate that it had been censored, but it told Katerina enough.

'I must go and see Olga,' she said. It was time to take Theodoris for his first outing into the outside world, and who more appropriate to visit than his grandmother. 'Will you come with me,

Eugenia? I might need someone else there when I break the news.'

'Of course, my dear. Shall we go this afternoon?'

At three o'clock they called at Niki Street.

Pavlina was thrilled to have them there and cooed and fussed over the baby as though it was the first time she had seen him. The bulky perambulator was left in the hall and Theodoris was carried up the stairs with great ceremony to meet his grandmother.

Olga clasped her hands together with sheer joy and held the sleeping baby in her arms for an hour, gazing at him and exclaiming at the family likeness.

'Pavlina, fetch some pictures of Dimitri when he was a baby!'

Although they were studio pictures taken when he was at least one and sitting upright, there was a clear likeness between Dimitri and the infant who slept in her arms.

'He is so beautiful,' Olga said, smiling at Katerina. 'I wish we knew where Dimitri was. Wouldn't it be wonderful to tell him?'

Katerina exchanged glances with Eugenia, who was sitting opposite them slightly stiffly on an upright chair. She could procrastinate no longer.

'I've had a letter,' said Katerina, taking the envelope out of her pocket. 'I'm afraid he's been arrested.'

'Arrested!' exclaimed Olga. 'And where have they sent him?'

Katerina handed her the letter.

'You know what they do there, don't you?' said Olga faintly, as she read. 'They try to break them and make them renounce their beliefs.'

'I know,' said Katerina. 'But at least we know he is alive.'

'They'll never succeed in making Dimitri sign a *dilosei*,' Olga said firmly. 'Even if he is there for the rest of his life, he'll refuse.

He's the most stubborn person in the world. And he would see it as a victory for his father.'

'He must do what he thinks is right,' said Katerina.

Pavlina had come into the room to bring them some mint tea and had listened in horror to the conversation.

'There's one thing that could change his mind, though,' she suggested.

The three other women looked up at her and Pavlina looked down at the baby.

'No!' said Katerina. 'I don't want him to know about Theodoris.'

'I agree with you,' said Olga. 'Imagine the dilemma he would face. It would tear him in two.'

'And these men who come home having renounced what they believe – they're empty. The husband of a woman I used to know at the factory signed one and was released,' Eugenia said. 'But his wife says he's not the same man. And he can't get a job or anything, and sits around at home, angry at what he was made to do.'

'I can't bear to think of Dimitri like that,' commented Katerina.

'Who would Dimitri be if he was stripped of his beliefs? I'm not sure he would be able to live with himself,' mused Pavlina.

'You must write and tell him that Gourgouris has died,' said Olga. 'At least that will give him something to hope for.'

'Yes, I will do that straight away,' Katerina said.

Months later Dimitri received Katerina's letter and he wrote back freely declaring his love for her. The censors allowed such letters, believing that relationships outside the prison might hasten the writing of a *dilosei*.

He also described how he was working on the building of a miniature version of the Parthenon on Makronisos. 'It represents the spirit of joy and adoration for the *patrida* which we all feel so strongly here,' he wrote.

Katerina always shared his letters with Eugenia, and they both winced at his sarcasm. They had read that the inhabitants of Makronisos were obliged to work on such reproductions of classical monuments as part of their rehabilitation. They knew that such activity would only make Dimitri despise the authorities even more.

The exchange of letters was slow, but since neither of them could tell the truth they had little to say. A few months later, Dimitri's letters ceased to come from Makronisos.

We have been transferred to Giaros, a smaller island a few kilometres from Makronisos. There is little else to say. The conditions are the same as on the previous island. Prisoners and guards are the only inhabitants.

When Theodoris was nearly two, Katerina resumed her career as a *modistra*, visiting her customers for dress fittings in the afternoon while Eugenia cared for Theodoris. One small advertisement had been enough to bring her old customers flooding back to her and, once again, her reputation as the best seamstress in Thessaloniki soared.

'Why don't you use my old house as your workroom?' suggested Olga, whose home in Irini Street had been empty for some years. 'There isn't the space even for cutting fabric in yours.'

Olga was right. With Theodoris to take care of, and Eugenia's loom, the little house was very overcrowded. There was hardly enough room for Katerina's Singer sewing machine on the kitchen table.

On a warm, late summer's day in 1952, Pavlina arrived in Irini Street with the key to number 3. Together they cleaned and dusted the little house, and moved furniture around to prepare Katerina's workspace.

'How is Kyria Komninos?' Katerina asked as they worked.

'She's well, thank you,' responded Pavlina. 'But Kyrios Komninos is under the weather.'

Katerina could not feign concern. It seemed hypocritical.

'Kyria Komninos says it's ridiculous for someone of his age to be working like he is. I heard her telling him last week. He's eighty, you know, but he looks a hundred! "Well, it's not my fault there's nobody to take over, is it?" says Kyrios Komninos. And I wanted to say, "Yes, it is actually! It's your fault that Dimitri isn't here now." But anyway. I didn't. I kept quiet. But that man, he's overworking, running himself ragged. He looks awful too. Pale as pale, thin as a pin. You wouldn't even recognise him.'

Katerina said nothing.

# Chapter Twenty-nine

Two weeks later Konstantinos Komninos had a stroke at his desk and died instantly.

There was a huge funeral, for which instructions had been left in his will. Fifty *stefania*, huge wreaths of white carnations, stood propped against the outside of the church of Agios Dimitri with messages of condolence from the Mayor, the senior members of the City Council, Thessaloniki's chief business leaders and many other city grandees. After a service executed with much pomp and ceremony he was buried in the municipal cemetery between his father and brother.

'I thought Kyria Komninos would only ever leave the house to go to her own funeral, but you know what? There she was at her husband's. With everything that's gone on I always thought she would die first,' Pavlina rattled on to Katerina the following week, 'but something gave her the will to keep going, didn't it? And you know what I think it was?'

Katerina nodded. She understood the strength of Olga's love for her son and now for her little grandson too.

On Giaros, Dimitri received a letter from his mother telling him that his father had died. For a while he simply sat and stared at it.

Leaving this godforsaken island might be one kind of release, but at this moment he experienced an even greater one. His hatred of his father had been a great burden, but that was now lifted from him.

His decision to sign a *dilosei* was not taken lightly. He would always believe that the Democratic Army had fought for the right cause, but his urge to be reunited with the people he loved overcame any other issue now.

Although thousands had already signed, the guards were surprised when Dimitri volunteered to do so. His was an unexpected recantation and not done under duress.

He watched his hand pick up a pen to sign the declaration as though it belonged to someone else and his feeling of detachment grew as the nib moved across the page.

'I was misguided by the Communists and deceived. I renounce the organisation as the enemy of the fatherland, by whose side I stand.'

The one thing he feared was that his declaration would be published in the Thessaloniki newspapers. It was usual for the details of a *dilosei* to be published in the signatory's local press. Given that everyone imagined he was dead, he was anxious about the effect that this would have on his mother and the woman with whom he wanted to spend the rest of his life. As the ink was drying, he looked up and caught the officer's eye. Dimitri remembered that the officer had been ill during an outbreak of typhus on Makronisos, when he had volunteered his medical skills to look after the sick.

Although the officer had been delirious for many days, he still recalled Dimitri's face as he re-emerged from unconsciousness.

'So, you'll be off soon,' he said gruffly. 'It's about time you were using your medical training properly.'

'I won't be able to do anything if you publish my details, will I?'

'That's true. It does tend to ruin a career, doesn't it? Being a Communist.'

'Or even an ex-Communist,' suggested Dimitri.

He could see the officer softening.

'Where do you come from then?'

These details would provide the information which would allow the government to publicise the declaration locally.

'From Kalamata. Eighty-two Adrianou.' It was the first address that came into his head.

'That's not what it says here,' said the officer.

'My family moved,' replied Dimitri firmly.

The officer glanced up at him and winked. He crossed out the existing address, scrawled the 'new' one on his file and then signed a form, which he passed across to Dimitri.

As soon as he was back on the mainland, he sent letters to his mother and Katerina. He wanted them to have some warning of his return.

A few days later he was back in his own city. Since his last visit, there was a new sense of prosperity. The pastry shops were piled high with the triangular shaped pastries, *trigona*, and the pavement cafés were full of people sipping mint tea and coffee. The scent of baking bread from the *fournos* and flowers from the market had replaced the smell of fear.

He went straight to Niki Street and loudly rang the bell. There was no need for anxiety on this visit. Olga was overwhelmed with joy to see him. They talked for an hour and sat close on the sofa.

'Isn't it a problem,' he said, 'that my father told people I was dead?'

'Well, there was no death certificate. And if we need to, we can always prove that the letter I received was a fake.'

'I don't want people treating me like a ghost for the rest of my days!'

'We'll say it was a joyous mistake,' she said. 'I think Katerina might be waiting for you. You should go.'

Still weak from the poor nutrition on Giaros, he could not run to Irini Street as he wanted. All he could manage was a fast walk.

It was now spring, the month for almond blossom, and he plucked a sprig of blooms just before he arrived. The door was open when he got there and he could hear the sound of voices.

Stepping inside he was confronted with an unexpected sight: Katerina was sitting at the table next to a small, dark-haired boy whom she was intent on feeding.

As soon as she saw Dimitri, she dropped the fork and got up. The little boy turned round to see where she had gone.

'Hello, Katerina,' said Dimitri, handing her the flowers.

'Dimitri . . .'

They spoke as if Dimitri was returning after just a few days away and as they embraced, the little boy got down from the table and began pulling at Katerina's skirt.

'Mummy!'

'You didn't tell me you had a little one . . .' Dimitri said.

'This is Theodoris,' she said, smiling at him. 'Say hello, *agapi mou.*'

Dimitri was adjusting to the vision of Katerina as a mother. It was so strange of her not to have mentioned anything in a letter.

'He must have been so young when your husband died.'

'He hadn't even been born then.'

Katerina paused a moment and lifted the child up. Dimitri and he looked into each other's eyes and then the little one buried his face into his mother's shoulder, overcome with shyness.

'Theodoris is yours, Dimitri.'

'*Mine?*' said Dimitri with stupefaction.

'Yes,' said Katerina. 'This is your son.'

'But . . . ?'

'There is no doubt,' she said. 'He couldn't be anyone else's.'

Dimitri's bemusement turned to joy as he took in the news.

Back at the kitchen table, with Theodoris on Katerina's lap, Dimitri took her hand and they began to talk.

'But you said nothing in your letters. Nothing at all!'

'I was worried. I thought it might make you come back, before you were ready. So it seemed better not to,' said Katerina.

'Katerina *mou*. Thank you. I had to wait until my father died but if I had known about Theodoris it would have been much more difficult. You did the right thing.' He was almost overwhelmed by the intensity of the love he felt for this woman, a feeling that was made all the deeper when he reflected on her self-restraint.

Dimitri held Katerina's hands but could not take his eyes off his son, who now sat playing happily on the floor next to them. There was no denying that the likeness was a strong one.

'And I couldn't give him your father's name. Theodoris seemed right,' she said, smiling at Dimitri, who was smiling at his little boy.

'Gift from God,' Dimitri replied. 'It's a perfect name.'

For the next hour, they sat and talked of their future.

The stigma of having fought with the Communists would hang over Dimitri for a long while, and he was reluctant to brand Katerina and their son.

'Nothing you say will stop me wanting to marry you,' Katerina assured him.

'I won't get a probity certificate. You realise that, don't you?' he asked.

The Certificate of National Probity was necessary for state employment, and without it Dimitri would not be able to continue his medical training or work in a hospital. The right-wing government was not making it easy for anyone who had fought with the Communists to reintegrate back into society.

'We will manage,' said Katerina. 'And I know your mother will help us.'

'I can't accept any of my father's wealth,' said Dimitri. 'Not even one drachma.'

'Well, I will earn enough to keep us then,' said Katerina. 'And with the amount of work I have, we will be comfortable.'

Two months later, when Dimitri's identity papers were once again in order (the only occasion when he had to accept any money from his mother, so exorbitant was the amount required), the marriage took place.

For the second time, Eugenia and Pavlina were guests at Katerina's wedding but this time Olga came too. The *koumbaros* – best man – was Lefteris, Dimitri's friend since university. Invitations had been sent to Sofia and Maria but they had both given birth recently and were unable to get there, and Katerina also wrote a letter to Zenia in Athens asking if she would come, but it had never been answered.

Katerina had made herself an exquisite dress of *crêpe de Chine* and a veil edged with pearls, and a small white suit for Theodoris with a sailor collar. Dimitri could still get into the suit that had been made for him when he was eighteen, though Katerina had to tailor it to improve its fit. This small family unit made its way on foot to Agios Nikolaos Orfanos, where Katerina had prayed so many times. God had not answered every prayer, but standing in the church there that day she felt that a miracle had taken place.

The tall-hatted priest was surprised when the entire party of seven arrived together and he watched patiently as they each took a handful of candles and lit them.

The names of the Moreno family – Saul, Roza, Isaac and Esther

– were whispered over and over again, and they all prayed for Elias, hoping that somewhere in the world he at least was safe and carrying on the family name.

Katerina prayed too for the health of her mother and sister. One day, she would try to go to Athens to see them.

Five minutes of silence went by. They needed this time to reflect on all that had passed. When everyone was ready, the priest began to chant.

> 'Evlogitos o Theos imon, pantote
> Nin ke ai ke is tous eonas ton eonon.
> En irini tou Kyriou deithomen.'

For the first time in a decade the country was nominally at peace. Perhaps a million had died in the preceding ten years, during the occupation and civil war. Hundreds of villages had been burned down and thousands made homeless, but for Katerina and Dimitri this day marked a new beginning.

# Chapter Thirty

ANTI-COMMUNIST FEELINGS STILL lingered in the government, but at least Katerina, Dimitri and little Theodoris could lead something like a normal life. Mass production of clothing in factories was beginning to take off and so, although Katerina occasionally made a bridal gown, she was happy to leave fashion behind and do something new. Together she and Dimitri set up a new business and called it 'Soft Furnishings and Furniture for the Modern Age'. They took on a carpenter and made their own chairs and settees, which Katerina upholstered in some of the new, washable, synthetic fabrics.

In the following year, Katerina found herself pregnant again and when the baby was born they named her after Dimitri's mother. Six months later both the children were baptised. They were to grow up surrounded by people who adored them.

The death of her husband had released Olga. Many years after Dimitri's birth, a doctor had diagnosed that she had suffered from post-natal depression, and although her complete recovery from agoraphobia would take the rest of her life, at least she now occasionally visited Irini Street. She lavished even more attention on the children than most grandmothers. Theodoris and his sister both called in at Niki Street every day on their way home from school and were always spoiled with plates of Pavlina's freshly made cake and biscuits. The old housekeeper was too frail to come to Irini Street now, but she baked for them until the day she died at the age of ninety-five. Her funeral was the first time that Theodoris and little Olga had ever seen adults cry. Pavlina had been part of all their lives.

The two children were also close to their other *yiayia*, Eugenia, and it had never been appropriate to explain that she was not really their grandmother. With both parents working hard all day, the elderly lady kept the household running and shipshape. Sometimes she went to stay for a few weeks at a time with Sofia or Maria (who by now had nine children between them) but she was always glad to return to the relative tranquillity of Irini Street.

On Sundays the whole family, with both grandmothers, would sometimes go to their favourite café, Assos, on the seafront. The children would have ice creams, which they were only allowed once a week, and the women would all eat miniature *bougatsa*.

Dimitri and Katerina's business began to thrive. Apartment blocks were going up all over the city and thousands of families were moving to better homes. For the first time, many of them had bathrooms with running water and kitchens complete with modern appliances. This new lifestyle called for new kinds of interior furnishing and design, and they struggled to keep up with demand.

Just before Easter in 1962, Katerina received a letter from Athens. The handwriting was unfamiliar. It came from Artemis and announced the news of their mother's death. For Katerina, almost the worst thing was that she could not cry. Her memory of Zenia had faded to extinction and her sister was a total stranger. Naturally, she sent her condolences and said she would come to the memorial service to be held forty days after Zenia's death.

Sadly, she was unable to fulfil her promise. Only a fortnight later,

Eugenia developed a chest infection and within a week pneumonia had claimed her life. The whole family struggled to come to terms with their unexpected bereavement and Katerina found there was no limit to the depth of her grief. It was a far greater blow than the death of her real mother.

'But she was only sixty-nine,' wept young Olga, inconsolably. It was average for a woman at that time, but both children had assumed that she would live to be as old as Pavlina. The small house seemed empty without her presence and the loom, with a half-finished rug, stood idle in the corner. For many months Katerina and Dimitri could not bear to get rid of it, in spite of the fact that it took up half the room.

If there was ever going to be a right moment to move, perhaps this was it. The children were clamouring to leave Irini Street for somewhere more modern and with more space. It would have made their parents' lives much easier, if they could be in a brand-new building in a flat directly above their business, but their sentimental attachment to the old cobbled street was too strong. For both Katerina and Dimitri their ties to Irini Street were deeper than their children could begin to understand.

They now rented out a shop in a nearby area where they displayed their goods, and continued to live in number 5 and have their workshop in the house next door. They loved the fact that their children could still play in the street, just as they them-selves had done several decades before, without the danger of them being hit by a motorcar. These were now commonplace in the city, but it even infuriated Dimitri and Katerina when one of the young men in the street insisted on riding his motorised bike up and down.

The country had entered a period of economic boom. Greece was being reconstructed at last and businesses such as Katerina and

Dimitri's felt the benefit. 'Soft Furnishings and Furniture for the Modern Age' thrived.

In spite of this, the politics of the country remained uncertain. The right-wing government kept alive the notion that the Communists were still a serious threat, and early in 1967 they arrested a number of socialist leaders for supposed conspiracy to plot against the government. There was no evidence against them. Dimitri read of these developments each day with growing anxiety and he began to have recurring nightmares that he was on Makronisos once again. Katerina sometimes woke in the night, to find him sitting on the edge of the bed, shaking with fear.

'They're saying that there's danger of civil war all over again,' said Katerina, who had been listening to the radio all day long as she worked in the shop.

'It's a pack of lies,' responded Dimitri dismissively. 'Pure fabrication.'

Late that afternoon, Theodoris burst through the door. It was the year of his final school exams and he had stayed late for an extra class.

'Dad! Mum!' His voice was full of anxiety. 'Have you seen all the soldiers? There are hundreds of them, down in Egnatia Street. What's happening?'

On the pretext that they were saving the country from a Communist takeover, the army had staged a coup. The Colonels were now in charge.

This was not the first time in Katerina and Dimitri's lives that there had been a military coup and they knew of the terror that such a situation could instil into daily life.

Both their children were keen students and always achieved top grades. Encouraged by his teachers, who had rarely taught such a bright pupil, Theodoris dreamed of studying Law. It would suit his ability to write, to debate and to retain huge amounts of information. Dimitri kept his opinion on his son's choice of subject to himself. It was inevitable, he supposed, that there would be an occasional glimpse of his own father in the teenage boy.

In July, when exam results were posted up at school, Theodoris faced the biggest disappointment of his life. His grades were below even the average in his class. He rushed into the house and fled straight to his room.

From the backyard, where they had retreated to get some air, his parents could hear sobbing. They knew instinctively what had happened.

'He's such a clever boy and he worked so hard,' Katerina said with disbelief. 'How could they do that to him?'

'I'm afraid they can do what they like, now,' Dimitri replied. He was pale with sadness and rage.

Both of them knew that Theodoris' exam results had been tampered with because of his father's history. This was not uncommon. The stigma of Dimitri's days in the prison camps now hung over his children too. Dimitri knew that his association with the Left would always linger and had accepted, when he returned from Giaros, that he would never become a doctor. For a long while, this seemed the only enduring punishment.

'Do you think it will be the same for Olga?' asked Katerina fearfully.

Dimitri could not answer. He felt his anger against the men now in charge of his country rising up inside him.

Everyone knew that, under the new regime, exam results were often altered by the police before being made public, and children of 'undesirables' were given lower marks while those candidates with 'right-thinking' parents were boosted. Whilst he kept a very low profile, and had not attended one political meeting since returning from his island exile, Dimitri realised that his past was his crime, and that his children would continue to suffer from it. The same discrimination was being practised against university professors themselves and those known to be on the Left were sacked. The professors who were rising to the top of their departments were those who were prepared to give lectures on patriotism and the National Revolution.

'Even if he was given a place,' said Katerina, 'what kind of education would he get? They've sacked all the good Law professors for their views.'

Both of them knew there was a solution. Dimitri's mother wanted to pay for the children's university education, and could easily afford to send them overseas. The subject had been the source of endless discussion and had brought mother and son close to argument on many occasions.

'I understand why you don't want any of your father's money, Dimitri,' Olga said. 'But there is no reason why your children shouldn't benefit from it.'

Young Olga was now coming home from school with new textbooks that had been approved by the Junta.

'Look, Dad,' she said showing him the introduction. 'Listen to this: "On 21 April officers seized the initiative to save the country from a renewed attempt to destroy it by the Communists."'

'It's nonsense,' said Dimitri. 'Complete nonsense.'

That evening, when Dimitri and Katerina were alone, Katerina tackled the issue head-on.

'What's the point in their education if they are being fed all these lies, Dimitri?'

He knew where this conversation could go and it filled him with unease.

'You were never able to complete your own education, but there is no reason not to give our children the best that we can . . .'

Still he remained silent.

'And you know what happened to someone in Olga's class last week?'

One of her friends, Anthoula, had told a joke about the Colonels. It had been repeated by another girl to her father, who happened to be an officer, and the very next day, Anthoula had been expelled.

'Yes,' said Dimitri. 'It was outrageous.'

'We should give them a chance, even if it's painful for us . . .'

She noticed the sadness in his eyes. Like her, Dimitri loved his children with his whole being, but this only made Katerina's conviction that they should leave Thessaloniki all the stronger.

'I know you are right,' he said, looking up at her. 'But I'd do anything in the world to keep them here.'

A few days later the Prime Minister, Georgios Papadopoulos, came to the city and spoke at the university. Dimitri and Katerina had the radio on in the shop and stopped to listen to the broadcast:

'The university must become the church of the spiritual development of the nation. Teachers must guide the nation and the moral order must become once again the guiding thought, the framework of human life. We must return to the mentality which preceded the violation of the moral and social order.'

'I can't listen to that any more,' Dimitri shouted. 'It's intolerable, propagandist rubbish!'

'Ssh, Dimitri!'

Katerina reached up to the radio and turned the dial to find another frequency. She could never be sure of their customers' views and it was dangerous to be so outspoken against the regime. Some repetitive military music now blared tunelessly from the speaker.

'Can you turn it off completely, Katerina? I'd rather have silence than that.'

Occasionally memories of evenings with Elias listening to rebetika surged nostalgically over Dimitri. It grieved him that so much music had been banned. His children could not hear the singers they wanted to hear, or read the news they should be allowed to read. Plays, poetry and prose were all subject to censorship, and now, according to Papadopoulos, their thoughts were to be controlled. It was an oppressive regime.

When the shop closed at nine thirty, they returned to Irini Street in silence. Theodoris and Olga were in their bedrooms and Katerina went into the kitchen to prepare some food for them all. Dimitri followed her and sat down at the table. He watched her, deep in thought, slicing some bread.

'Katerina,' he said eventually. 'I know you are right. We can tolerate these restrictions on our freedom, but it's no future for our children. We must let them go.'

'Do you mean it, Dimitri?'

'Yes, I do. It's selfish of me. Mother has plenty of money, so there is no reason why they shouldn't go to university in another country. And she's right, my hatred of my father has nothing to do with them.'

When she looked up, he saw that big glassy tears were rolling down her face.

Within a year, Theodoris had gone to London to study and not long afterwards Olga passed an exam that would take her to Boston University.

Not once did Dimitri and Katerina regret their decision. The atmosphere of repression intensified, with the Military Junta sending thousands of dissenters into exile.

'I heard they're taking people to Makronisos again,' Katerina said, one day the following year. 'It can't be true, can it?'

'Sadly, I'm afraid it is,' he replied.

Extreme physical and psychological torture was now common-place once again but there seemed little anyone could do. There was no press freedom and demonstrations were now banned, so there was not even any means of effective protest.

Every Sunday evening, Dimitri and Katerina wrote a letter to each of the children. Sometimes, she would send something she had embroidered or sewn, a blouse or handkerchief for Olga and sometimes a shirt or a cushion cover for Theodoris. They kept the tone of their letters light, fearing that anything political or critical of the regime would result in them not getting through.

Katerina would love to have sent them food, but Dimitri re-assured her that there was probably enough for them to eat in Britain and America, and besides, the juices of her *dolmadakia* would be sure to escape from the box.

In November 1973, three days into a student strike, there was an uprising among students in Athens. Using an amateur radio, they broadcast their message to the people of Greece, urging them to fight for democracy. Students demonstrated in Thessaloniki to show their support, but were soon dispersed by the police and army.

'Do you think Theodoris would have been there, in the middle of it all?' pondered Katerina.

'Quite probably,' answered Dimitri.

In Athens mass demonstrations against the regime spread into the surrounding streets and three days after the beginning of the student strike, an army tank broke down the gates of the Athens Polytechnic, where the students had barricaded themselves in. During the struggle that followed a dozen people died and hundreds more were wounded.

It was the beginning of the end. As a consequence, Papadopoulos was overthrown, a year later the dictatorship came to an end and

democratic government returned. The Communist Party was legal-
ised for the first time since 1947 and invited to take part in the
elections that were held in mid-November. Dimitri was jubilant
when they won a handful of seats.

Theodoris and Olga came back for holidays that summer. They
were doing well at university and both had plans for post-graduate
degrees. There was no shortage of money to fund them. Theodoris
moved to Oxford for a D.Phil. and Olga remained in Boston.

Thessaloniki seemed to be thriving and, though they were very
proud that their children were doing well abroad, Dimitri and
Katerina harboured an unexpressed desire that they should come
back to Greece once their education was complete. Whenever they
came home, they showed them the new building work that was
helping transform the city and took them to see all the improvements that were being made to its infrastructure.

Theodoris was then offered a position by a large law firm in London
and Olga became a houseman in a hospital in a wealthy Boston suburb
and each step in their blossoming careers took them one further from
home. The summer of 1978 would be the first one when neither of
them would be able to visit. Perhaps this was fortuitous.

On the night of 20 June, a Tuesday, there was a full moon rising
in the sky and the promise of a perfect sunset behind Mount
Olympus. Above the Gulf there was a golden glow that would
soon darken to a fiery red. The sea glittered with both the silvery
light of the moon and the flames of the sun.

On this beautiful night, people strolled arm in arm along the
promenade, or sat at café tables gazing out towards the sea, intoxi-
cated by nature's spectacular light show. There was no need for
conversation or music, sun and moon provided all the spectacle
they could require.

At ten o'clock, the earth began to tremble. Thessaloniki was accustomed to the occasional small reminder of the earth's instability but this time it did not stop.

Dimitri and Katerina were working late in their Irini Street workshop and everything began to rattle. A pair of shears slid across the cutting table and landed with a clatter on the floor, and Katerina's sewing machine juddered across the floor on its stand. Windows rattled, chairs fell over and rolls of furniture fabric that had been leaning against the wall toppled like skittles. It was as if the ground beneath them was going to disappear.

'*Agapi mou*,' said Dimitri, grabbing Katerina's hand, 'this isn't normal. We have to get out of here.'

They ran into the street and turned into the wide main road that ran east to west. They felt a little safer once they were outside, but there were new dangers and they watched in horror as a building ahead of them swayed and then collapsed. Their eyes and throats filled up with dust.

The tremors had not lasted long, but the damage they had done was catastrophic. In the space of a few minutes, the foundations of every building in the city had been subject to a violent shaking and many of them were not designed to withstand it. For a short time there was silence and then began the continual sound of sirens.

As fast as they could, stepping over piles of debris and fallen masonry, Katerina and Dimitri made their way down the hill towards Aristotelous Square. The wide-open space seemed to offer a measure of safety and hundreds of people had gathered there. They stood about, some crying but others too shocked even for tears. There had been a premonitory quake the previous day, but no one had expected an earthquake of such magnitude.

Dimitri and Katerina did not stop there. There was something that concerned them much more than their own safety.

Turning left at the seafront, they hastened along Niki Street.

'She'll be so afraid in that house, all on her own,' fretted Katerina.

'I should have been more insistent about her having another live-in housekeeper,' said Dimitri, as they hurried along, keeping to the middle of the road to avoid any falling masonry. 'She wouldn't even hear of it. And you know how many times I suggested it to her . . .'

Since Pavlina's death fifteen years earlier, Olga had lived alone in the Niki Street mansion. She had less desire than ever to be parted from her unique view of the Gulf, which she sat and watched for hours on end. The vista of the constantly changing sea and mysterious Mount Olympus had never ceased to mesmerise her. Before they had gone away, her grandchildren had continued to call in to see her every other day and each had a 'bedroom' where they sometimes did their homework. The house in Irini Street had been very cramped for two growing children.

As Dimitri and Katerina hurried along the seafront, the light of the full moon illuminated the extent of the devastation. Some buildings had sustained considerable damage, others had survived almost unscathed. They held hands and quickened their pace.

Katerina had grabbed their key to Olga's house before they left Irini Street and her fingers grasped it nervously inside her pocket. When the house came into view, fifty metres away, they saw with relief that it appeared undamaged.

Only when they came closer did they realise that the façade was the only part of the house that remained standing. Behind it lay the wreckage of the entire building. Roof, floors and the three other outside walls of the house had all collapsed.

'Oh my God,' whispered Dimitri. 'My poor mother.'

There was not even the slightest possibility that anyone could have survived beneath such a weight of stone, brick, concrete and metal girder.

Katerina stood there, too numb with disbelief to speak. She held on to Dimitri's arm to steady herself and the useless key fell from her hand into the dust.

'Are you sure there is no point?' she eventually managed to say when her sobs had subsided.

'I'll go and see if I can find someone, but it's going to be so dangerous even going in there.'

The scale of the house meant that it would be a daunting task to search for a survivor, but Dimitri managed to find someone in charge of rescue efforts and was promised that a working party would be sent as soon as it was light.

Katerina and Dimitri kept vigil through the night. They needed to keep Olga company, whether she was dead or alive. At dawn, a group of men arrived with shovels and saws and ventured into the wreckage. Dimitri went in with them.

To Katerina it seemed an age before her husband returned. In fact it was less than thirty minutes. When he reappeared, his hair was white with dust and his face pale with sadness.

'We've found her . . .' he said.

Katerina held Dimitri in her arms as he wept, his body shuddering with great spasms of grief.

A beam had landed diagonally across Olga's pelvis and chest and trapped her. They were now waiting to put the machinery in place in order to lift it and free her.

'It looked as if she was lying on the chaise longue,' said Dimitri. 'I got a glimpse of the fabric. I know it sounds odd, and I couldn't see her face very clearly, but I think she looked quite peaceful, almost serene.'

Katerina managed a smile.

She was glad that Dimitri's image of his mother's beautiful face was untarnished.

Once they had watched Olga's body being carefully carried out, they stood there for a few minutes. Katerina was praying. Dimitri had been told to go to the municipal morgue the following day as he would need to formally identify his mother's body and they knew that, sooner or later, they must return to Irini Street.

Just as they were about to leave, one of the rescuers appeared. He was holding something out to Dimitri.

'We found these,' he said. 'They must have been lying on your mother's chest when the beam fell across her and were wedged underneath it. We thought you might like them. I'm not sure you'll be able to salvage much else in there. It's a terrible mess.'

The man's tactless words did not affect Dimitri and he took the package of letters with a nod of thanks and, after a cursory glance, put them in his pocket. It would have been impossible to convey to him how little he cared that his father's priceless collections of *objets d'art*, clocks, paintings and figurines had been pulverised.

As he and Katerina walked away, he took one last look back at the mansion's empty façade. It was all that now remained of Konstantinos Komninos' fortune.

Their normal way home was blocked by fallen masonry and many times they found the road was impassable. Eventually they came to the edge of the old town and, via a circuitous route, finally reached Irini Street.

When they turned the corner they were confronted with a scene of utter devastation.

Not one of the houses in the street had survived. Each one was reduced to its original elements of stone, wood and plaster. Irini Street may have withstood the fire of sixty years before, but nature's seismic power had finally brought it down.

Silently, the couple surveyed the scene. Dimitri had half expected what they saw. The damage done in the neighbouring streets had given him a sense of foreboding, and even as they had been leaving the workshop the night before he had noticed a floor-to-ceiling crack. There had seemed no purpose in pointing it out to Katerina at the time. The building had been flattened, as if carelessly trampled by a giant.

For a while neither of them spoke. The loss of Olga weighed heavily on their minds and they were still numb from the shock of it. Somewhere in the distance they heard the wail of an ambulance, which triggered precisely the same thought in each of their minds: 'Thank goodness our children are far away from here.'

Morning was just turning to afternoon, and the heat was rising. A slight breeze stirred the great volume of dust to which their house had been reduced.

Other residents of the street were poking about in the dereliction.

'It's futile,' said one of their neighbours. 'There's nothing salvageable in my place. Not even a knife and fork.'

People stood around. Most seemed to agree that it was pointless to venture into the spaces that had once been their homes. They valued their lives more than their possessions.

Katerina was agitated. She did not share the prevailing sense of resignation.

'Dimitri,' she said, 'we have to go into our house. There's something we need to rescue.'

'Something worth risking our lives for?' her husband replied.

'Perhaps,' she answered.

Without waiting for Katerina to answer, Dimitri had pushed open the front door of their house. It fell in with a crash and the doorframe went with it. With a gasp, Katerina ran forward.

She heard Dimitri calling out, 'Don't worry. I'm fine. I've got it, *agapi mou*.'

After several moments he reappeared, struggling over the threshold with a small trunk in his arms.

'Let me take one of the handles,' said Katerina, relieved to see him.

A few yards from the house, they put the box down on the cobbles. Its metal frame had protected it from the weight of the ceiling that had fallen in, and when Katerina lifted the lid she saw that the contents were safe.

The problem of where they were to sleep was easily solved. Old friends urged them to borrow the spare bedroom in their apartment, and for many weeks they were to camp there, with nothing but some borrowed clothes hanging on the back of the door and the trunk on the floor in the corner.

Their immediate priority was to arrange Olga's funeral. Her death was a devastating blow to the whole family but Dimitri felt it most keenly. He had never known such grief. In her quiet way, Olga had been his rock, and even in the years of his absence, the knowledge of her love and understanding for what he was fighting for had sustained him. She had no power to influence his father, but he had never faulted her for that.

During the interment, Dimitri was aware of nothing but the long, slim box going into the darkness and his tears created a misty world through which his wife patiently led him.

The priest sang the Kyrie Eleison as the four family members each dropped a flower onto the coffin before the marble lid was fitted into place. The stonemason had already done his work.

Olga Komninos<br>
Beloved Mother of Dimitri<br>
Cherished Friend of Katerina

Adored Grandmother of Theodoris and Olga
We will always remember you

There were a hundred graves in the cemetery, most of them well tended and constructed from the same pale, veined marble. The scale and design tended to reflect the status of the family, and the Komninos plot occupied a sizeable space where five generations of the family had been buried. Steps led down to a vault.

Something caught Katerina's eye that day. On Leonidas Komninos' tomb there was a photograph of him in his officer's uniform, complete with a row of medals. Even though it was a formal portrait in which he was obliged to look serious, his eyes smiled. It was not the picture that struck Katerina as strange, however, it was the spray of wilted roses next to it that puzzled her. On the adjacent tomb, that of Dimitri's father, there were none.

A week later, when Olga's will was read, the reason for the flowers became a little more apparent.

There was a generous bequest for each of the children and a few pieces of jewellery for Katerina that had been kept in the bank for some years. Olga was left a ruby necklace whose gems were so large that none of her friends in America believed they were real. Dimitri's request that he should not inherit even a drachma of his father's money had been respected. The business had already been sold to pay for the wing of a new hospital, helping to compensate for his thwarted ambition to become a doctor.

There was a codicil to the will. Instructions had been left for fresh flowers to be placed on Leonidas Komninos' grave every Friday morning. There was no explanation. Dimitri knew that his mother had admired her brother-in-law for his courage, and he had grown up with the knowledge that he was a man of honour and bravery, the opposite of his father in every way.

The will was read by the same lawyer Katerina had visited when Gourgouris had died, and the moment of mutual recognition was the only moment of levity in the whole encounter. The inevitability of his survival and ability to profit from disaster struck Katerina as almost absurd.

The ten days following the earthquake left the couple exhausted. They had already trekked around the city looking at potential homes and business premises, and on the night of the reading of the will they were retiring early. Katerina was sitting on the edge of their borrowed bed in a Crimplene nightgown lent by her friend. Dimitri was reading a newspaper.

'Dimitri,' she said, 'were your mother's feelings for your uncle common knowledge?'

'I doubt it,' replied Dimitri. 'I think everyone admired him, though. Except perhaps my father.'

'But do you remember him?'

'I have a few dim memories but I must have been very young,' said Dimitri. 'I just remember him being very tall and the sound of laughter when he was around.'

He suddenly remembered the packet of letters he had been handed after they had lifted his mother from the wreckage. He had tucked them into the trunk.

Katerina watched him lift the lid.

'You remember the letters my mother was reading the night of the earthquake? They were from my uncle. I saw his name on the outside.'

He handed her the packet.

'It doesn't seem quite right to read them,' she said gingerly.

'I think it's allowed when both the writer and the recipient are dead,' Dimitri reassured her.

Feeling like a spy, Katerina slid the first letter from beneath the ribbon and began to read. There were a dozen or more, all with different postmarks and written between 1915 and 1922. Without even a hint of impropriety there was nevertheless an obvious warmth and intimacy. Many of them ended with the words, 'Please send my regards to my brother.'

After an hour or so of reading Katerina opened the last letter. It had been written in Smyrna and was dated September 1922.

Dear Olga,

At this moment, I am ashamed to be Greek. Many of my men have behaved no better than the Turks and I have witnessed things from which my mind will never be cleansed. In all these past months, there was only one moment which made any sense. It's the only reason I knew there was still some humanity left inside me. I rescued a child. She was about to be trampled and I plucked her from the ground and held her up above the crowd. The skin on her arm was so badly burned it was falling away from the flesh, but I tore off my shirtsleeve, used it to wrap her wound and delivered her onto a boat. It felt like the only good thing I have ever achieved.

I feel sick at the thought of the other things I have done. God knows, I have asked for forgiveness but however often I am blessed by a priest, the memory is still there. I think of that child and wonder if she is still alive. I doubt it. But I did what I could.

Please give my kisses to little Dimitri. I hope he will never see the things I have seen. Tell him his uncle misses him and as soon as I am back, he can have my buttons to play with. They are stained with blood, Olga, and will need polishing.

You remain, as always, in my thoughts.

With warmest regards,

Leonidas

Dimitri was now undressing, obliviously chatting to his wife as he did so.

'It's a pity he isn't still around,' he said. 'It would have been nice if you'd met him too.'

Katerina reread the letter and then looked up at her husband. 'I think I did, Dimitri,' she whispered. 'I think I did.'

# Epilogue

MANY HOURS HAD passed since Mitsos had come back to his grandparents' apartment.

Katerina took her grandson's hand and stroked it affectionately.

'Every day, I wake up and feel so lucky that I arrived in this city, Mitsos. Life might have been very different – I could easily have died in Smyrna, or in Mytilini, or gone to Athens and starved. But I didn't. Call it what you will, but I would say that Fate brought me here.'

'I can see why you feel so connected here,' responded the young man. 'I really had no idea . . .'

'If Uncle Leonidas hadn't rescued me, then I would never have got to Thessaloniki at all, would I?' she smiled at him.

'The only really unhappy years of my life,' said Dimitri, 'were the ones when I was away from here. All that time I yearned for the horror to end so I could return to this city, to marry your grandmother.'

Mitsos sat quietly, listening with rapt attention as the two of them spoke with love and passion of their home.

'So you see, Mitsos, all our experiences are rooted here. We could go somewhere else and the memories would live on in our minds, but they are much more vivid here, in the place where everything happened.'

'We could easily light candles in London or Boston for those we have loved,' added his grandfather, 'but it wouldn't be the same.'

Each time Mitsos had visited his grandparents, he had been taken to the cemetery where he had watched his grandmother tending the family tomb. He knew that she went every week to sweep around the graves, to make sure the oil lamps still burned and to take fresh flowers. Watching over these activities was a statue of Olga. One year after her death, his grandparents had commissioned the best sculptor in the city and the seated figure was a breathtaking likeness, with its long, elegant limbs and patient expression.

Mitsos sat there thoughtfully, reminded of the words the blind man had spoken to him only that morning. The notion that all those people who had lived in Thessaloniki had left part of themselves behind suddenly seemed very real to him.

'There's something else, as well as the memories, that we keep here for our friends. They left some treasures behind too.'

In the corner of the living room, covered over with a white, lace-edged cloth, there was a wooden trunk. Katerina carefully removed the vase of artificial flowers and framed pictures of her children and grandchildren, took off the cloth and folded it. Then she lifted the lid.

'This is another reason we stay,' she said. 'These things don't belong to us, and even though their owners might never return, it seems wrong to take them away. We have merely been custodians.'

She lifted out the ornate red silk quilt inside which the ancient tallit had been sewn, several small cushions and two books. There was also the icon of Agios Andreas, which had been carried all the way from the Black Sea. When Eugenia had died, Katerina had wrapped it inside some silk and put it in the trunk for safekeeping.

'We're taking the quilt to the Jewish Museum in Agios Mina Street for their archive,' said Dimitri. 'They seemed very pleased when we went in to tell them what we had.'

'I want to keep the cushions, though,' said Katerina. 'In case the families return. Even Elias might come back one day. And there is the letter that the Muslim family left for us and the two books.'

'There's something else at the bottom,' said Mitsos, reaching in and lifting out a frayed piece of rather stained cotton. 'This doesn't look like "treasure" – unless this button is real silver!'

'Well, I think it might be,' said Katerina. 'But that's not why it's valuable to me. It's because I feel that piece of sleeve saved my life, and reminds me of the greatest kindness that's probably ever been shown to me.'

Almost unconsciously, she touched her arm. Most of the time, Mitsos forgot that his grandmother's arm was badly scarred as she usually wore a cardigan to cover it up, but tonight in the heat of the room, it was partly exposed.

'Most importantly, I promised to look after it in case I could ever return it to the soldier that saved me.'

They all smiled.

It was around 11.30 p.m. now, but still hot in the apartment. Mitsos' sweet grandmother poured him a glass of water and he looked at her, imagining her as a small girl setting off on her journey from Smyrna. His need to understand why they stayed here in this city was entirely fulfilled. But a question remained. He looked at the precious collection laid out on the table and then at his frail grandparents. Who would take care of these treasures when they were gone? What would happen if their owners returned?

'Shall we go for a stroll, Mitsos?' asked his grandfather. There was nothing he liked more than to take his grandson out for a late night beer in one of the bars on the waterfront, in the hope that some of his friends might be there so that he could show off this fine young man to them.

And Mitsos loved to go out at this time of night too. The streets were still buzzing. The air still balmy. He thought of the area in which he had grown up in Highgate, where homes were lined up like matches in a box behind their neatly trimmed privet hedges, and there was one pub that threw you out on the stroke of eleven.

They found a table outside on the harbour's edge and a waiter greeted them and brought them chilled beers. Pleasure boats took people on night cruises and their white lights moved about on the ebony sea. The blackness of the water seemed fathomless, the stars infinite. Every few moments, one of them fell.

There was a beauty in the stillness and the darkness that he had never seen before and it almost overcame him with its power. For the first time in his life, he had begun to understand what lay beneath these pavements and behind the façades of these buildings.

He looked over at his grandfather, whom he loved so deeply, and knew with aching certainty that he would not always be there.

What would it be like to make Thessaloniki his permanent home? It was a place where people thronged the streets from dawn till dawn, where every paving stone, ancient, modern, polished or broken, was dense with history, and where people greeted one another with such warmth. He suspected that the city would forever be challenged by adversity but there was something else he was sure of: it would continue to be rich and full, of music and stories.

Suddenly he knew he would stay. To listen and to feel.

# Thessaloniki

## by Victoria Hislop

THESSALONIKI IS MORE than a backdrop to *The Thread*. For me it is one of the most important characters in the novel, one that plays a main role in the story, suffering and surviving the various events and catastrophes thrown at it, just as Katerina, Dimitri and many others do.

I made my first trip there five years ago. For several decades, I had been island hopping, stayed in Athens a dozen times, travelled round the Peloponnese, and been more times than I can count to Crete. Until then, however, I had never been to the north of Greece.

As the plane made its final descent, I looked out of the window and saw acres of flat, agricultural land, organised, sub-divided and dark with ripening crops, very unlike the pale, often infertile landscape further south. I realised straightaway that in this cool, damp climate I would need an umbrella as much as I needed sun protection. It was only a twenty-minute journey from the airport to the city centre but I could see that I had arrived in a very different part of the country from those I had visited before.

Like most cities, Thessaloniki has sprawled in recent years but, unlike many, it has discernible boundaries: the sea on one side and a steep slope on another. I knew I could wander without getting lost but at least if I did lose my way, there would always be a glimpse of a sparkling bay to orient me.

A twenty-first-century view of Thessaloniki

On that first visit, both monuments and architecture began to tell me a story and to raise many questions too. Thessaloniki seemed to have a little of every period and every style. There are some magnificent third-century Roman remains including a massive triumphal arch on which are carved the achievements of the Emperor Galerius. There is also a perfect rotunda, reminiscent of the Pantheon in Rome, and I learned that it had had many different chapters in its history: originally it was a polytheistic temple, then a church, afterwards a mosque and was then reconsecrated as a church in 1912. A minaret still stands next to it as if to remind the passer-by of its three hundred years of use by Muslims.

The White Tower

There are plenty of the quickly built five- or six-storey 1970s concrete blocks which are ubiquitously erected throughout all Greek cities, but in addition there are magnificent neo-classical mansions, with pillars and double stairways leading to a grand front door, and many art deco buildings as well. By contrast there are narrow cobbled streets with gabled houses in a Turkish style.

A typical street in the upper town

As well as the richness of different building styles and its friendly atmosphere, two things made a particularly big impression on that first visit. The first was the Holocaust monument that I came across in one of the main squares. It is a striking piece of sculpture and from a distance looks like a small tree, but as I approached I made out a series of slim bodies interwoven with each other, many upside down. They seem to be both struggling and dancing. It recorded the fact that the entire Jewish population of the city (50,000 people) had been rounded up and taken to concentration camps in Poland in 1943. It was shocking. There is no other word. I knew for a fact that the Jewish population of Greece was almost non-existent. And now I knew why.

The Holocaust Memorial in Eleftheria Square

The second was equally unexpected. Right in the middle of the city, on one of the main streets, there is a large house, heavily fortified and guarded, with a sign in Turkish and English on the gate. On my first visit, parked right outside, there was a dark blue, armoured bus, the kind usually used for transporting riot police. I discovered that it was the birthplace of Mustafa Kemal, a.k.a. Kemal Ataturk, the founder of modern Turkey, and with my British passport (which I had to leave with an official at the door), I was frisked and then allowed in to look around.

I was alone in the mansion apart from the house's custodian, who followed me around in silence from room to room. I tried out my Greek on him to break the ice, but the response I got suggested either that my Greek was even worse than I thought,

461

or, as it turned out, he only spoke Turkish. On the walls were displayed black and white photographs of Mustafa Kemal at every stage of his life. In all the images a pair of pale, almost translucent eyes gazed out from a strong chiselled face. He was handsome, charismatic but chilling, just like the house itself.

I found myself asking what was behind these unexpected discoveries: a house in which local people seemed not to be allowed, but where I, a stranger, was welcomed. And a monument to tens of thousands of Jews in what is a relatively small city.

When I returned to the UK, I read Mark Mazower's *Salonica: City of Ghosts*, which is agreed by everyone, including the Greeks themselves, to be the best book ever written on Thessaloniki. He gives a detailed history of the city between 1430 and 1950, and explains how and why there are remnants of Muslim and Jewish culture in the city, even when there appear to be no Muslims or Jews now living there.

Mazower explains why the city's Muslim population was obliged to leave in the early 1920s. It was the end result of a long struggle between the Greeks and the Turks, and the eyes that had chilled me from the walls of the grand but gloomy house on Pavlou Street belonged to the person who had been pivotal in the destruction of the Greek army in the early 1920s. His first home, right in the middle of Greece's second city, is venerated by the Turks, but certainly not by the Greeks.

Mazower also describes the fate of the Jewish people who at one time formed the majority of the city's population. Thessaloniki had been home to a sizable Sephardic (meaning Spanish in Hebrew) Jewish community since the fifteenth century, when they first arrived from Spain. The Sephardic Jews' ghettoisation and subsequent departure for Poland in 1943 left a huge physical and cultural space in Thessaloniki's community.

Shops in a Thessaloniki street

Thessaloniki has seen many dramatic events and I wondered how people might have survived them. Out of this speculation grew the idea for *The Thread*. I made more interesting 'discoveries' in Thessaloniki by ambling without a map. As I had hoped, the topography of the city meant that I never got hopelessly lost (just a little disoriented, and only occasionally). The gradient of the land which takes you away from the sea tells you which way you are going and the relatively small scale of the city means that you can always find your way back to the centre. Most of the maps of the city seem only to have the large streets, but it wasn't really those that interested me. I wanted to stroll around the lanes and alleyways where my characters might have lived, and the residential areas with the big green bins overflowing with rubbish, and stray cats. I found those more exciting than the roads well-marked by tourist maps and these were the places where the ideas for the characters were formulated.

A fabric shop in Thessaloniki

One of the significant things I noticed was the plethora of dress shops. Narrow streets full of them. And to complement them, many places selling ribbons, buttons, lace and other haberdashery.

As most women would, I browsed in a few of these shops and fell in love. It was a midnight blue satin dress, short, with beading on a black ribbon beneath the bust. I tried it on but it was too big. A lady appeared with pins and quickly fitted it. Another woman stood back to give her view and I noticed there were several other women getting the same attention from the staff. How quickly would they be able to finish it? I asked, knowing I was flying home first thing the following day. 'Today,' they said. They were true to their word. The dress was ready later that afternoon. When I tried it on again, it had been moulded round my body like haute couture, a fully lined, satin, beaded cocktail dress. And all this for 80 euros. I had experienced first hand the talent for tailoring for which

Thessaloniki, I was to discover, has a reputation. These chatty ladies with their tape measures and shears were mistresses of a craft and I realised that I had found the idea for my main character. She was to be a seamstress, a *modistra*, a woman with enormous talent, someone who could take hold of her own destiny in a world where the fate of so many people was determined by the decisions of politicians and the random outcome of war.

A haberdasher in Thessaloniki

I wrote *The Thread* to explore for myself the strength and courage that the inhabitants of Thessaloniki must have had to survive the events of the twentieth century. I hope I have done them justice.

Victoria Hislop

# Pick up
# CARTES POSTALES FROM GREECE
## for HALF PRICE with this voucher.

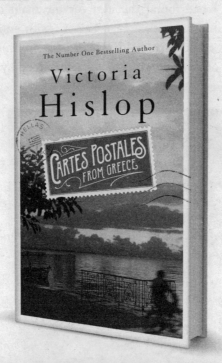